# The Factory Girl

# Maggie FORD

EBURY
PRESS

1 3 5 7 9 10 8 6 4 2

Ebury Press, an imprint of Ebury Publishing
20 Vauxhall Bridge Road,
London SW1V 2SA

Penguin
Random House
UK

Ebury Press is part of the Penguin Random House group of companies whose
addresses can be found at global.penguinrandomhouse.com

First published in 2002 as *From Bow to Bond Street* by Judy Piatkus
(Publishers) Ltd
This edition published in 2015 by Ebury Press

www.eburypublishing.co.uk

A CIP catalogue record for this book is available from the British Library

ISBN 9780091956684

Typeset by Palimpsest Book Production Ltd, Falkirk, Stirlingshire

Printed and bound by CPI Group (UK) Ltd, Croydon, CR0 4YY

Penguin Random House is committed to a sustainable future for our business,
our readers and our planet. This book is made from Forest Stewardship
Council® certified paper.

MIX
Paper from
responsible sources
FSC
www.fsc.org    FSC® C018179

Maggie Ford was born in the East End of London but at the age of six she moved to Essex, where she has lived ever since. After the death of her first husband, when she was only twenty-six, she went to work as a legal secretary until she remarried in 1968. She has a son and two daughters, all married; her second husband died in 1984.

She has been writing short stories since the early 1970s.

*Also by Maggie Ford:*

The Soldier's Bride
A Mother's Love
Call Nurse Jenny
A Woman's Place

For Gilda O'Neill, novelist and friend,
who suggested the title

# Chapter One

February, a raw Saturday afternoon – not a day to choose to go up to the West End, more one for huddling by a nice, warm fire, with her nose in the romance she was currently reading, *Drifting Petals*.

Today, though, Geraldine Glover had a purpose in mind. Time was running out, cold weather or no. In four weeks her older sister, Mavis, was getting married to Tom Calder. Three months had passed since the Armistice. Young men were still coming home, couples were making up for lost time and all a man wanted after maybe four years of hell in the trenches was to get married to the girl who had waited for him. Mavis and Tom wanted the same thing: to get married, settle down and forget the war.

It wasn't as easy as it sounded. Men coming home in droves to no jobs, and with little money to find the rent for somewhere to live, usually ended up living in one room in a parent's house. This was what Tom and Mavis were going to have to do. With no room at home with Mum and Dad, who had two sons and three daughters crammed in a shabby East End terraced two-up two-down in Burgoyne Road off Grove Road, they'd go to his parents' house.

It would be a frugal wedding with no frills or flounces. With food shortages the wedding breakfast would be made up of whatever the family could bring. At least Dad had work at the docks and there was the promise of a job there for Tom if Dad could pull strings, so Mavis would have her trousseau.

Even so, Geraldine envied her sister, wishing it was she who was getting married and leaving her cramped home where three girls had to share one bed, while her brothers, one older, one younger, shared a single bed in the back room where the family ate. It meant they couldn't go to bed until everyone else did or went off into the front room, normally kept for best.

Some families around here had even more kids and heaven knows how they coped. But all Geraldine ever dreamed of was one day having her own room to do what she liked in, as Mavis would four weeks from now. But as yet she didn't even have a regular boyfriend, let alone one to marry. There were plenty who fancied her and whom she'd been out with, but none she'd want to marry. The only one – Alan Presley from Medway Road – was married although going through a divorce and had no interest in other girls these days – a case of once bitten twice shy.

When she was fifteen and he was seventeen they'd gone around together in a group and he'd been sweet on her, but they'd lost touch when he went into the Army in 1917. Writing letters was a chore and later she heard that he'd found a girl from the next street to hers while

2

home on leave. The girl had got pregnant and on his next leave they had to marry, but a year later he'd come home from France to find her in bed with another bloke and that was it. Even so, you can't start making eyes at someone still married, if separated and waiting for a divorce. Wouldn't be appropriate. But he was a handsome-looking bloke and her heart still went pitter-pat for him.

Standing in the bus queue outside Mile End Station, Geraldine eyed the clock outside a watchmaker's opposite: ten to two. If a Number 25 didn't arrive soon she'd end up frozen stiff. Huddling deeper into her thick jacket with the wind pressing her heavy hobble skirt against her ankles, she sighed.

The queue was growing steadily as there had been no bus for nearly fifteen minutes. The first one along would no doubt be full by now, not even standing room, and would probably sail right by, though it might be followed by another after all this delay – buses seemed to love keeping each other company.

Geraldine turned her mind to signs of life from the London & General Omnibus Company. She was partially correct about buses keeping each other company as finally two 25s appeared, the first doing exactly as she'd expected, the driver looking smug as it trundled straight by.

Crinkling her pretty face into a wry grin as she took her turn boarding the second bus, she managed to find a seat on top where at least she could have a smoke. Lots of girls doing men's jobs during the war had learned to smoke and it had become accepted. She didn't smoke all that much herself, but the odd puff helped a girl of eighteen get through a humdrum week as a machinist on piecework in a clothing factory where utility dresses, blouses and skirts offered very little variety of design. Anyway, she was tired having worked like mad all Saturday morning and a cigarette helped to perk her up.

Today, however, she felt perky enough, eagerly looking forward to what she had in mind to do once she'd alighted on Oxford Street. She'd done it many times before but today was special for she needed to look good at her sister's wedding, and for someone on a meagre wage there was only one way to do it.

She found little in Oxford Street to tempt her even though London's West End had all the newest fashions. Moving on to Regent Street, there was nothing there either that really caught her eye. Disappointment growing, she found herself wandering down New Bond Street. If there was nothing here she'd be properly stuck. There was such a scarcity of fabrics even though the war was over, and unless you could afford to pay something like ten or twelve guineas, which for her represented nine to ten weeks' earnings, a really stunning dress was out of the question. But what she was looking for had to be extra special to make her stand out at this wedding, though she always aimed to stand out anywhere.

True, for most of the time she and her fifteen-year-old sister Evelyn would be wearing bridesmaid's dresses – skimpy things in cheap rose-pink cotton that would make them look like a pair of candlesticks following the bride up the aisle. Tom's six-year-old cousin Lily, in pale blue, to Geraldine's mind would just about put the kybosh on the whole ensemble. Though it was all Mavis could do on so little money, she'd never had any dress sense.

How they could have ever been sisters was beyond Geraldine.

'Let me make the dresses,' she'd implored. 'I'm a good dressmaker, as good as anyone.'

But Mavis had been adamant. 'I want ter buy them ready-made. That way I can be certain of 'em.'

'I could make them all at half the price.'

'I want proper ones.'

'And I don't know how to make proper dresses, I suppose!' she had stormed at Mavis, getting angry. 'Look at what I make for meself – everyone thinks they've been bought. And I save loads of money.'

'I don't care!' Mavis had stormed back. 'It's my day. And I decide what I want and 'ow I want it.'

'And end up makin' a pauper of yerself!'

'No I won't! Cos I've bin puttin' by fer ages for a decent weddin' dress.'

Mavis and Tom had been saving for this for two years but still hadn't much to show for it, with Tom away in the Army while she had got herself a job in a munitions factory, though now she worked in a local bread shop.

'All I want is a decent wedding,' she'd gone on. 'And I'm buyin' me own dresses.'

'Sewn tergether with cheap cotton what breaks as soon as you stretch a seam by accident, you wait and see. And, I'm sorry, Mave, but I think that rose pink you want us to wear is an 'ideous colour.'

Mavis had yelled at her again that she liked pink and it was her day and she'd do what she liked, walking off close to tears, leaving Geraldine to give up on her. Mavis was getting more uppity and highly strung the nearer her big day came and was best left alone. She would put up with the horrible colour as best she could and anyway, it would only be for a couple of hours.

Thinking of it, Geraldine wandered on down New Bond Street, gazing in the shop windows she passed. Moments later all other thoughts were swept from her mind at the sight of the most beautiful dress she had ever seen.

Mesmerised, she stared at it through the window. Draped tastefully on a graceful papier-mâché manikin was an ankle-length afternoon gown in pale-blue silk with separate dark-blue velvet panels. It had a square neckline and was cut in the latest barrel line, loose panels of velvet falling from the waist back and front with a square, tabard-like silk overbodice from shoulders to hips.

*Real silk!* It could be seen at a glance. She could never afford *real silk*. But artificial silk like Courtauld's Luvisca and a cheaper velvet would look every bit as good.

It took some courage to push open the boutique door. Usually she'd aim her sights lower. Big London stores held no fears for her, nor did most high-class shops. But this place – the opulence of it, the perfume wafting out of it crying, 'Nothing under fifteen guineas!' She was stepping on hallowed ground.

Clenching her teeth and trying to look as though fifteen guineas was nothing to her, although her beret decried all that, she approached another manikin draped in an identical dress to that in the window. So at least the outfit wasn't exclusive. Even so, she needed time to browse, to study the garment and make mental notes of every stitch, the cut, to see how the material fell. Real silk always fell beautifully. Would cheaper artificial silk do the same?

'May I be of assistance, madam?' The measured, almost sarcastic, cultured tone right behind her nearly made her leap out of her skin, as though she was already being accused of stealing.

Gathering her wits, she turned to the voice, immediately aware of the haughty, intimidating frigidness on the face of a woman neatly clad in a black dress with white collar and cuffs, her hair pulled back from her brow and not a trace of powder on her face. There was no warmth in her enquiry such as she might have used to a valued customer. The way it was couched practically screamed her opinion of a common working girl trespassing on her domain, riff-raff needing to be got out as quickly as possible and without fuss.

Steeling herself, Geraldine stood her ground, putting on her best high-class accent, which she could do when needed. 'I am browsing at the moment.'

She knew immediately that the sort of patron who entered here did not *browse* but would make straight towards an assistant to state what they had in mind and request to be conducted and advised.

The woman's face was vinegary. 'I should not imagine we have here anything that would suit madam.' In reality she was saying that would suit her pocket. 'Perhaps if madam tried one of the large stores.'

Geraldine ignored the broad hint. 'No, thank you,' she replied in her best West End voice, though even she was aware that to an ear accustomed to such there was no disguising a trace of flattened East End vowels.

'This caught my eye,' she went on, 'and I felt I needed to decide as to whether it would suit me or not.' She was overdoing the accent a bit.

The woman, thin, middle-aged and no doubt a spinster, was shorter than her, which gave Geraldine some feeling of advantage.

'I will let you know what I decide,' she dismissed her as haughtily as she could.

But still the woman hovered, saying nothing, her mien one that announced she would be keeping her eye on this intruder. It was humiliating but there was nothing Geraldine could do except turn back to the garment on the pretence of being deeply interested in buying it. All the time she could feel those eyes boring into the back of her neck lest she made off with something without paying for it. Suspicious old crow, trying to make her feel she was the lowest of the low.

There was no ticket on the gown – a place like this would never stoop to such practice. The type of customers who frequented here probably took it for granted that they'd be able to afford it whatever the price. Rude even to ask and she for one wasn't going to lower herself to ask either.

How exactly did they handle themselves, these people who frequented places like this? She could still feel those eyes burning into the back of her neck.

But there, it was done – every stitch, every fold and tuck, every line committed to memory. Turning back to the hovering assistant, she smiled.

'Thank you for your assistance, but I don't think this will suit me after all.'

How delightful, seeing the look on that prim face at being robbed of its triumph of catching her out for a tea leaf or turning her out as a common time-waster.

Even so, it was a relief to be away from those peering eyes. What she had selected was etched in her brain as clearly as though she still circled it – now to find the material as near a match to those lovely blues as possible.

A week perhaps to make it, meticulously copying the design now fixed in her mind, and then on the evening of the wedding, once out of that awful bridesmaid's gown, she'd have all eyes on her. And on her the next day too, compliments from all the family at Mum's – aunts and uncles, cousins and grandparents – as they gathered around the big table in the front room for Sunday dinner to round off the celebration, the newly-weds having gone off on honeymoon to Eastbourne.

In her fifteen-guinea outfit – it had to be at least that, though hers would cost not much more than fourteen shillings at the most, still a whole two weeks' pay – she'd be the talk of the family. She could hardly wait to seek out just the right stuff that would make her look like a lady of means.

It was in triumph, if very wearily, that she made her way back home, the parcel she clutched containing material from Selfridges in nearly identical colours to those she'd seen in New Bond Street, together with poppers and buttons that nearly matched, a spool of light-blue cotton and one of dark blue.

She'd need a nice row of beads to set it off, stones of rich sapphire blue – not the real gems of course. And she knew just where she could get something exactly like that, made and strung especially for her at nothing like what the real gems would cost.

Perhaps she would put in her order right now. Oddly, the thought of doing that, of going into the shop and speaking to its proprietor, made her heart step up a beat, and not just because of a mere necklace.

# Chapter Two

It was well dark by the time she reached home, walking through the streets from the bus stop. Ten to five. The jewellers near the corner of Grove Road and Burgoyne Road where she lived was already closed. She'd have to wait until Monday, calling in on her way home from work, which was a nuisance.

Geraldine itched to secure just the right sort of necklace for the gown she would make. On the other hand she ought not be too impatient – better to finish it properly before looking for jewellery. She'd know by then what she really wanted and it would only take three or four days to do. Best to wait until then. But it would have been nice to pop in there now, if only to tell the proprietor what she was looking for.

She'd been in there a couple of times for cheap Christmas presents for her mother and sisters. The goods being cheap were an attraction and she'd found him very polite and helpful; being young and nice-looking was an even greater attraction to someone her age. The name above the shop said Hanfords and she assumed he was the Hanford who ran it but she didn't know his first name and she longed so much to know, especially as just lately she'd been seeing him in her dreams.

He'd only set up in the shop a couple of weeks before Christmas. Before that the place had been a store for clothing until the small factory renting it had closed a year ago. Its windows gradually became begrimed from neglect and it had stood there all forlorn among other busy shops.

Then last December there had been signs of work being done on it. Some evenings as she cycled home from work, she'd seen the young man supervising the refurbishment, her mind already rushing ahead of her.

As soon as the shop had opened she had gone in on the pretext of looking for Christmas presents, but while busily inspecting affordable trinkets laid out on the counter and in glass cabinets, her eyes had been on him. He'd seemed more interested in selling than returning her gaze, which was a pity, but after her third foray – she making sure to buy only one present at a time – he appeared to recognise her and she was sure there had been apprasial in those dark-grey eyes. She hoped so. It hadn't progressed any further so probably she was wrong. Since Christmas, though, she'd not had cause to go in there. She was not so well off that she could go buying things willy-nilly, even to get a glimpse of the proprietor who'd had the ability of making her heart do a little flip when he'd looked at her.

She noticed that he always closed his shop a little earlier than most on Saturdays. Perhaps he could afford to. He did seem to take more satisfaction from making jewellery than selling it. Even coming up to Christmas, a busy time, he'd never been in the shop when she'd gone there, the tinkle of the doorbell bringing him hurrying from the back, dragging off a heat-soiled blue apron as he came. And he sold only jewellery made by himself. That wasn't any way to make a living unless he was well off. Perhaps he'd find out soon enough and close up and go away and she would never see him again. Geraldine's heart sank at the thought.

Not all that many people appeared to go into his shop despite what he sold being cheap. Not cheap and nasty – cheap and nice, attractive, different. The stones were only semi-precious – garnets, tiger eye, moonstones, that sort of thing – and the metal was silver rather than gold, but his workmanship was wonderful, delicate and unusual, attractive to those with little money to spend on expensive stuff. It was still early days of course. Surely in time he would make a real living and stay on. Life would be bleak if he were to pack up and go.

She spent as much time as she could gazing through the tiny window at rings, pendants and brooches, always hoping for a glimpse of him. Not earning enough to keep forking out on jewellery, she couldn't keep on going in on the pretext of buying, but next week she'd have a legitimate excuse to be there, wouldn't she?

The Glover family always used the back door of the house. The passage from the front door was an assault course, with bicycles, tools, household bits and pieces not immediately needed, and what her younger brother Fred called *his stuff* – old toys mostly, toys he'd grown out of as he was now thirteen and due to leave school soon, but was still loath to part with. So with no access by the front door everyone went round to the back to get in.

Every house in Bow, like everywhere in the East End, was identical to the next – row upon row of two-up two-downs in an unbroken terrace, back to back but for a small backyard; every street was the same, in a grid pattern without a tree or one touch of greenery, not even a bend in any of them to break the monotony.

The streets were playgrounds for the kids – cobbles, broken kerbs, bucked pavements, scuffed doorways and the peeling paintwork of windows bravely cleaned of East London's incessant smoke and grime were witness to every game a child could devise.

Of course there was always Victoria Park, that huge expanse of open space that was the nearest East London dwellers got to accessible countryside. But that was quite a traipse up Grove Road. It was easier playing in the street where a kid could be home in a second if hurt or upset, or wanting a wee or a skipping rope, or whatever. Victoria Park was for Sundays. Take sandwiches, a bottle of drink and spend a whole afternoon there feeling as though it was miles away from London.

Geraldine's house being an end terrace on the corner of Burgoyne Road and Conyer Street had an opening dividing it from the backyard of the end house in the adjoining street. But to come in by the back way had its unsavoury moments. As she came in, Geraldine wrinkled her nose in distaste at the smell of pee that wasn't coming from the outside lavatory. Each house had its outside lav. Mum kept hers scrupulously clean; some didn't. Brick-built, it was stuck on the back of the house, had a concrete floor and a wooden door, was dark, cold, uninviting and noisy when the chain was pulled, enough for all to know every time someone went, so that their next-door neighbours were starkly aware of Dad's weak bladder.

'Mum, it stinks out there!'

In the kitchen Mum was unwrapping newspaper containing fish and chips bought on the way home from the flicks. She, Dad and Fred went off regularly on Saturday afternoons no matter what films were being shown. Mum, not being much of a reader, had young Fred read the words out loud to her while the pianist gave it his all as drama or comedy unfolded.

Young Fred was hovering with his mouth watering but the walk from the fish shop on a cold evening had taken the heat out of the food and it needed to be rewarmed for a few minutes while Dad was upstairs taking off his suit and getting into something more comfortable.

'Mum, has Dad been peeing outside the door again?'

Her mother looked up from inserting plates into the warm gas oven, her face registering defence of her husband. 'Yer dad was busting and Fred was in the lav, taking 'is time as usual.'

'It weren't me,' protested Fred. 'It was 'im in there and me what was bustin'. I 'ad ter go.'

'Then you're a dirty little sod!' his mother rounded on him.

Young Fred looked belligerent. 'If 'e can do it, why can't I?'

'Because yer dad's got a weak bladder. He can't always wait, that's why.'

'But 'e does it in the night too, an' no one's in there.'

Ignoring the fact that as a mum she ought not let herself be drawn into argument with a thirteen-year-old, she said, 'I don't like yer dad usin' a po and it stinking the bedroom out all night. I'd sooner 'e goes downstairs. But sometimes 'e can't hold it and 'as ter go as soon as 'e gets out the back door.'

'It's only a couple of blooming yards away,' retorted Fred. 'It ain't the other end of London! It ain't the other end of Timbuctoo, is it?' he added, pleased with himself at the extent of his geographic knowledge.

Now she was cross. 'You mind your lip!' she shot at him. 'And wipe that grin off your face or I'll wipe it off for yer.'

'Don't matter who did it,' cut in Geraldine, 'it still stinks out there.'

Mum ignored her, her glare riveted on her son. 'What your dad does ain't nothink ter do with you, yer cheeky little bugger. He's excused if he can't make it to the lav in time with 'is waterworks. He's got an affliction – you ain't. An' I won't 'ave you piddling anywhere yer fancy. I don't care if you are leavin' school soon, I won't 'ave that sort of behaviour in me own house.'

Another slow grin spread across young Fred's face despite her earlier warning. 'I didn't do it in the '*ouse*,' he sniggered, the snigger sharply cut off by an aggrieved yelp as a clout caught him across the back of his head.

'Get up them stairs,' his mother exploded, and as he made his escape she yelled after him, 'Gettin' backchat from you – a bloody kid! And don't come down again till I say. I might even sling your fish and chips away.'

'Aw, Mum?' came the protest from the top of he stairs. 'I'm starvin'.'

'Then serves yer right fer being so cheeky,' she called up then, turning to Geraldine, now taking off her jacket in the warmth of the kitchen, added angrily, 'He's a little sod, that Fred. I won't 'ave him takin' after 'is dad. Yer dad's got trouble.' There was apology in her tone now. 'I'd sooner 'e do it out there than the chain going a dozen times a night and the neighbours 'earing it. He can't 'elp leaking, there's somethink wrong with 'im. He should see the doctor but that costs and we can't afford ter fork out just to 'ear he's got a weak bladder. Poor bugger, it's rotten fer 'im at work. Them dockers can be cruel and if they noticed it they'd be the first to take the piss out of him.'

Geraldine ignored the unwitting pun and went to hang her jacket in the passage, negotiating the four bicycles leaning one against the other to do so.

They all used bicycles – she to get to the clothing factory, Fred to get around with his mates, and a battered, second-hand old thing it was too, Dad to go to work at the docks, and Wally her older brother also to the docks, Dad being fortunate enough to have got him a job there after coming home from the war.

Reaching over them to get to the coat hooks on the wall, she heard Mum call to her, 'While you're there, Gel, call your dad down for 'is tea.'

She hated being called Gel. Her workmates called her Gerry, which wasn't too bad. But Gel! It was East End practice to shorten a long name. You couldn't do much with Fred, but Mavis was Mave and young Evelyn was Evie. Dad called Mum, Hild. But why give someone a decent name if it was going to be shortened to something horrible or ridiculous? Saying Hilda in full wouldn't take all that much more energy, but no, it was Hild. She called him Jack, because not even God Himself could shorten that name any more.

Dutifully she yelled up the stairs to Dad. 'Mum says your fish 'n chips is ready.' His okay floated down from behind the bedroom door.

Fred adding his plaintive voice to it called, 'Can I come down too?'

'I don't know. Better asked Mum.'

'M . . . u . . . m!'

'You stay where you are, you little bugger,' came the responding yell. 'I don't want no dirty little devil sittin' at my table.'

Mum, skilfully carrying cutlery, salt, vinegar, a jar of pickled onions and several large, white, somewhat chipped plates passed her on the way from the tiny kitchen where you couldn't swing a cat, let alone feed a family, to the back room. The flap-leaf of the table had been raised to accommodate them all, a cloth spread over it, a loaf waiting to be cut into slices and spread with dollops of margarine.

The back room was where the family ate, despite Fred and Wally's bed in one corner. With just two bedrooms it was the only place for them, the main one being Mum and Dad's, with the girls in the other one, it being unthinkable for them to sleep downstairs and their brothers accidentally seeing them in their nightdresses or worse, in their underclothes. Boys were different – sharing a bed downstairs, it didn't matter them being seen in their vests.

Even upstairs all three sisters shared one bed, it practically taking up the whole room with just enough space for the wardrobe, chest of drawers and a board they called a dressing table that housed a sewing machine belonging to Geraldine, but shared by all three. How families with even more children managed was a mystery to Geraldine, though friends had at times mentioned four or more to a bed. After evening meals, if not going out, everyone would end up in the front room, most of which were spent around the gramophone, allowing the boys to go to bed when they were ready.

'Mum, let Fred come down,' pleaded Geraldine, following her mother into the back room.

'It'll do 'im good ter stew up there for a bit,' said Mum, laying out plates. 'Teach 'im a lesson.' By this, she knew Mum would relent before the meal was finished.

Mum turned to her as Dad came creaking downstairs. Every stair creaked, as did the beds, chairs and cupboard doors. There were no secrets in this house.

'I didn't get you any fish 'n chips, Gel. Didn't know when you'd be 'ome. I could take a bit off each of ours if you like.'

'No, I'm fine, Mum. We 'ad a big dinner, remember. I'd much sooner 'ave a sandwich. Fish and chips make you fat.'

Her mother smiled, glancing at her daughter's slim figure, still in the best dress she'd put on for going up West, one she'd made herself in slate grey some while back. Geraldine had more dresses than most, being skilled on the sewing machine, artistic. She was proud of her.

'I got some in for Evie. She's at 'er friend's 'ouse down the street – should be 'ome any minute now. You could 'ave a bit of 'ers.'

18

'No thanks, Mum.'

'Well if yer don't want any there's some cheese in the larder. Yer could 'ave that. I weren't sure when you'd be 'ome, that's why I didn't get yer any.'

She eyed the parcel Geraldine had put down on a chair on coming in. 'Is that what yer went up the West End for? Spending yer 'ard-earned money on more stuff ter make. What yer goin' ter make now, as if you ain't got enough?'

This at least was a secret. No secret that she'd gone off up the West End – it was a rule of Mum's that her family always said where they were going in case they were needed urgently at home or had an accident out. Though how they'd have contacted each other if there had been any trouble had never been explained. The police coming round, she supposed, or some messenger from a hospital.

But the dress was a secret, at least until she had it all finished or the moment she started treadling away on the machine, the noise rumbling all over the house and Mum coming up to see what it was she was doing. She'd want to know all the ins and outs of what she was making, and in the end when it finally came out, she would inevitably say, 'Yer'll be wearing a bridesmaid dress, so why make somethink else? Yer'll upset Mavis thinking yer don't like what she got yer.' Though Mavis knew that already. She'd told her so, that she hated rose pink.

'Did yer go with a friend then?' Mum was asking.

Geraldine shrugged. 'No, on me own.'

Her mother moved past her to get the food from the oven as Dad went into the back room to seat himself at the table. ''Bout time you got yerself a boyfriend,' she said.

19

'I've got boyfriends.'

'I mean a real boyfriend, someone steady. You'll find yourself left on the shelf if you ain't careful.'

'Mum, I'm only eighteen. I've got time.'

Not bothering to reply to that, Mum hurried off into the back room, each hand now carrying a loaded plate, a tea towel protecting her skin from the oven's heat. 'Fred!' she called out as she went. 'Yours is on the table.'

As Fred came thumping down the stairs, all forgiven, the back door burst open to admit Evie. 'Blimey!' exploded the twelve-year-old. 'It don't 'alf stink out there!'

Her mother gave her a warning look as she returned to the kitchen to get two more plates from the oven. 'That's your sweet brother!' she said, her tone sharp. ''Cos he's leaving school this summer, he's feeling 'is feet and thinks he can get away with murder. I wish you lot wouldn't keep blaming yer dad for everything.'

'I never even mentioned Dad,' protested Evie hotly, dropping her coat on a kitchen chair and following her mother into the back room.

Left alone in the kitchen, Geraldine heard her mother call out one more request. 'You sure yer don't want some of ours divided up for yer?'

'No, Mum,' she called back. 'I'm getting meself a sandwich. I'm going out again in a little while.'

In fact she was seeing Eileen Moss, who she worked with. They were going to see the films her parents had seen this afternoon. They'd sit eating peanuts as fast as they could shell them and stare at the silent drama of Gloria Swanson's *Male and Female* and laugh at Charlie

Chaplin's slapstick comedy, *Sunnyside*, both of which Mum had said were very good.

Though it was nice going to the pictures, she'd have rather stayed at home this evening to start on her dress, itching to see how it would turn out, but she'd promised to go with Eileen, and anyway, there were too many at home tonight no doubt wanting to know what she was doing, what she was making, and what for.

Sunday was quieter. Dad was down the Working Men's Club with his mates this morning and Fred was off somewhere – God knows where – with mates his own age. Wally, mad keen on football, his team Tottenham Hotspur, was on the other side of the fence this morning coaching a local boys' club team. He'd got involved with them because having stepped in as a temporary coach a couple of months back when the previous one left, he'd noticed that the girl helping with refreshments was very attractive. He was now thinking seriously about asking her out and that meant staying on as coach until she accepted.

Evie was at her friend's house again down the road. Mavis was out somewhere with her Tom, probably enjoying getting all lovey-dovey. Mum was next door having a cup of tea, a biscuit and a chat with Louis Golding, a woman her own age, whose husband always seemed to be away somewhere.

Geraldine had the house to herself. By the time they all came trooping back she'd have had the pattern she'd retained in her head cut out of newspaper, the material shaped and pinned and much of it tacked together ready for stitching.

The garment needed lots of concentration. She started on the dress first. The panels would come later but she was skilled and quick and accurate – a girl on piecework needed to be – and the design was clear enough in her head. She reckoned on two hours for cutting out and tacking and just hoped Mum wouldn't come back to start putting her nose in before she'd got a good way through it.

The two hours slipped by so quickly she hardly noticed the time going; the sleeves fitted in wonderfully and hung well, the back and front panels draping just like the real silk creation in that boutique. She couldn't help smiling every time she recalled that woman's face, all prim and proper and stuck up and suspicious – she ought to know what was going on. She ought to know how that exclusive gown displayed in her shop was being copied in cheap material and looking every bit as expensive as the original. The only thing Geraldine had conceded was to reverse the shades, making the dress in dark blue and the panels in a lighter blue instead of the other way around as she had seen it on the manikin. If anything it was an improvement and she grinned again at the woman's mortification if only she could see it looking even better.

The seams were setting perfectly, pressed under a damp ironing cloth at various stages, being tried on frequently to see how it hung. The loose long sleeves had set into the cuffs a treat. Tomorrow she would start on the panels of the removable tabard-like overbodice and the front and back panels that would fall from the waist to finish off the fashionable barrel line.

Mum came in as she was draping the almost complete

gown on a hanger, hooking the hanger on the bedroom picture rail, pleased with the way it had gone together and how quickly it was shaping up.

Mum was in the room before she knew it. 'Sorry I was a bit delayed, leaving you 'ere all on yer own. Hope you weren't bored. Mrs Golding was telling me about . . .' She stopped, her eyes on the lovely garment hanging from the rail.

'What's that? Not something yer bought yesterday? Wasting yer money again.' It was then she noticed the machine and the offcuts and cotton littering the room. 'Oh, you're *making* it. It's a nice colour. Making it fer going out somewhere special?'

Geraldine suppressed a smile. Mum's idea of *somewhere special* was hopefully a date with a young man – a young man who one day might be *the* one! Mum waiting and hoping, concerned about a daughter coming up to nineteen and still without a regular boyfriend to introduce to the family.

'It's ter wear for Mavis and Tom's wedding.'

'But you'll be a bridesmaid.' Mum was engrossed inspecting the gown, turning it this way and that on its hanger and making faces of approval at the workmanship even though there was still a lot to do to it.

'I don't want ter be a bridesmaid the entire evening,' said Geraldine.

How could she tell her that she abhorred the thing – was going to feel a right idiot in shocking pink? All right for Evie who was looking forward to it all.

'I 'ope Mave and Tom won't be upset, you wearing something else in the evening.'

'They won't know. They'll be gone off on their

honeymoon by the time I put this on,' said Geraldine firmly and ushered her mother out of the bedroom so she could put everything away before Mavis came home for Sunday dinner and asked her share of questions, and put Geraldine in an awkward position in trying to answer them.

Monday morning – again! Apart from bank holidays, she said this to herself every Monday along with millions of others as she cycled off to work.

This Monday, however, wasn't followed by the word 'again'. This morning passed in a stir of anticipation and excitement, her eyes fixed on the fast-moving machine needle with its bursts of deep-throated whirring as she thought of where she'd be at lunchtime. Not much time; she'd have to cycle like fury to get to Hanfords and back and have time to look for her necklace. It was no use waiting until after work – he shut at six.

As soon as the buzzer went for the three-quarters of an hour lunch break, she was up and ready to leave, aware of her friend Eileen looking at her. She'd already said she had to go out instead of eating sandwiches at her bench as always.

'You ain't even said where you're going,' came the complaint. 'What's so secret?'

'Tell yer later,' said Geraldine and dashed off to gather up her coat and handbag from the cloakroom before any more questions could be fired at her.

He was serving some woman when she walked in. He looked up casually and smiled. 'Be with you in a tick.'

Was that smile not quite as formal as he might use for anyone else? Did he recognise her? She hoped so. It had been a couple of months since coming in here at Christmas, but she hoped so.

The woman, having chosen a bargain pendant, was having it wrapped and Geraldine noticed with a little thrill just how skilled his hands were at wrapping the purchase in bright fancy paper. The woman departed, leaving Geraldine to approach the counter displaying a shining array of beautiful things beneath its glass top.

'Right, can I help you?'

The voice was deep, smooth and brought a delicious shiver to her.

'Yes please,' she managed.

Quickly she explained what she was after, bringing out two offcuts of the material to show him. He came round the end of the counter to take a closer look at the shades. His head seemed very close to hers as she held the material out for his inspection and the fragrance of brilliantine wafted to her. His hair was dark, very luxuriant and wavy. She'd never been this close to him before. When she'd come into his shop those few times before Christmas he'd always been on the other side of the counter.

He looked up suddenly, catching her in the very act of gazing at his head. Almost as though divining her thoughts, he smiled.

'I've seen you in here before, haven't I?'

She stared at him. 'I love looking at jewellery,' was all she could think to say. It sounded so inane and she was sure her voice had trembled. She needed to say something else, but sound more confident.

'I'm really glad you've opened up here. I live round the corner. Well, a couple of streets away. It's so convenient coming here.' She was trying to put on the nice talk, but she was gabbling on. He didn't seem put off.

'I've noticed you several times looking in the window.' He spoke well and had a nice accent that put her efforts to shame.

'They fascinate me. I think it's ever so clever being able ter . . . to make lovely things like you do. Did you 'ave . . . have to learn how to do it at school or some-thing, or is it just a sort of talent?' Trying so hard to sound nice she was making a mess of it, but if he noticed he gave no indication.

'Thanks for calling it a talent. People usually come in here and never give a thought to the joy I get from making these things. No, I never went to school for it. I've read plenty of books on it, and when I came home from the war I started experimenting, as a sort of hobby.'

Geraldine was nodding to every word, her eyes trained on his face, taking in every movement, every small contour. She still had hold of the pieces of material and was conscious of the faint pull of his fingers also still clinging on to it. He was smiling, a crooked sort of smile that made the right corner of his lips tilt upwards a little.

'My father wanted me to continue practising law with him when I came home,' he went on, speaking as though he had known her for years. 'He's a solicitor with a good practice. I didn't wish to upset him but I find law boring. It didn't seem so when I started back in 1913 but since the war I just couldn't settle. I took up this as a kind of hobby, a healing process, I suppose, being that I was a bit . . . well, they called it shell shock. Not too bad but

I decided on this as a way of settling myself down and I became absorbed by it. My father wasn't too pleased when I told him what I really wanted to—'

He broke off abruptly, a look of apology in the dark-grey eyes that, so close up, were like velvet. 'I'm sorry, I didn't mean to go on so.'

Abruptly he let go of the piece of material, the release making her start. On an impulse she leapt at what threatened to be a lost opportunity.

'I'm Geraldine Glover,' she burst out, instantly feeling an idiot. People didn't normally introduce themselves to shopkeepers, but his response was far from discouraging.

'My name's Hanford. Anthony. Tony to my friends, but since leaving my parents' home in Berkshire I've lost touch with friends.'

He sounded suddenly very lonely. 'But you've got friends here?' she asked in an effort to comfort him.

'Not really. I've lived above the shop since opening up. Most evenings I keep occupied making this stuff.' He glanced around with a proud, somewhat loving glow in his eyes, then brought them back to her, the glow fading. 'To be truthful I make more than I can sell. It's become an obsession.'

'It must be very absorbing.' She felt pleased with the word absorbing, it sounded learned. She hoped he thought so too. Anthony – Tony – such an attractive name, for an attractive man, a young, unattached, attractive man. Having mentioned living with parents told her that much. And telling her all about himself was encouraging – he must like her. Thoughts were pounding in her head like an express train. 'You must have a real gift for it,' she said.

He shrugged briefly. 'None of it is expensive stuff.

I don't think I'd be clever or brave enough to use expensive materials. This way if I make errors I haven't wasted much. But I'm learning all the time and one day, who knows, I may hit the big time – a jewellers in the West End. That's what I'd like.'

Geraldine fixed her eyes on him. She wanted to hear more but time was rushing on. She suddenly hated her work, not just because it would take her from the conversation they were having but that what she did was humdrum and repetitive and demeaning compared to his, having studied law while she was just a machinist on piecework in a clothing factory.

'I've got to go soon,' she cut in, hating to. 'Do you do necklaces?' He became business-like, put in his place. She'd spoiled everything.

'Sorry, I've been taking up your time talking about everything but what you came in for,' he was saying formally. 'Now, let me see.' He looked again at the material she held. 'Something dark blue.'

She watched him retreat behind the counter to survey the rows of beads hanging on hooks behind him. She could see the time on the large clock over the door. Angry again, she knew she must cut this trip short and would now have to explain why to him, or otherwise look churlish. And that was the last thing she wanted, creating a bad impression.

'Perhaps if I come back,' she said feebly and had him turn to look at her. Did he detect the regret in her eyes? Perhaps he did for he gave her a bright, friendly smile.

'I tell you what, Miss . . .'

'Gerry,' she broke in, unable to curb the sudden impulse.

His smile seemed to light up the shop. 'Gerry. Tell you what. I'll spend this evening fashioning something for you. I'll have it ready by tomorrow – lunchtime? You don't have to have it, but I'm sure you'll like it. How about that? Would that suit you?'

'Oh, yes.' Despite all her efforts, the words gushed out of her in a sort of feeling of relief and ecstacy. 'I'll come in around twelve or just after.' It would only take her eight minutes if she cycled fast.

'I'll be open,' he called after her as she rushed out to reclaim her bicycle propped against the shop front, her heart pounding fit to bust.

# Chapter Three

Her mother, not in the best of moods at the moment, looked up from darning one of Dad's socks to glare at Geraldine wandering aimlessly about the room.

'Why don't you sit down and find somethink ter do? Honestly, you've bin moping around the 'ouse ever since you got 'ome from work. What is it, someone at work upset yer or ain't yer got nowhere ter go tonight?'

'No one's upset me,' returned Geraldine. 'And I've me dress ter make.' Somehow interest in finishing it had waned, unable to get her mind off Anthony Hanford and the way she had interrupted their conversation. It had probably squashed her chances for all he had been so nice about it, apologising and all that. But it had clutched at her heart, him apologising.

'Then go up and get on wiv it,' continued Mum. 'I don't want you 'anging around us all night with that face long as a kite. Life's miserable enough without you adding to it. Weather's making us all more fed up than we already are, blooming freezing draught coming through all the blooming cracks, and now yer dad laid off work again.'

Mum, leading off, looked older than her years in a wide, brown skirt to her ankles dating back to an earlier decade, her once flaming auburn hair, now streaked grey, scraped back into a bun. The brown, full-sleeved blouse too was dated, high collar fastened by a jet brooch that had been her mother's and which she wore day in day out, enough to make Geraldine swear it must be fastened to her flesh as well. Her hands were red from her usual Monday washday. In fact the whole house smelled of washday.

She had once been exceedingly pretty, judging by photos of her. She still retained traces of that prettiness and spruced up in something a bit more fashionable, her hair bobbed in the current style and with a dab of face powder on her cheeks, she'd look half her age. But money to spruce herself up was needed to feed a family and even if she could have afforded it she wouldn't have. Women like her abounded in the East End. Marrying meant the end of gaiety; raising a family was a responsibility, it made them old before their time, and that was that.

As she spoke Mum glanced at her husband sitting staring into the fire but he didn't respond to her words, his mind no doubt on tomorrow, 'on the stones' as waiting to be called for dock work was termed. At present he had no gang. A gang would always be selected above men on their own and it was every docker's quest to be in one, the ganger being an expert at keeping his nose to the ground to sniff out anything going before others did. A man in a gang got good work and food in his family's stomachs even if ships coming into dock were a bit thin on the water since the end of the war. Every nation had been pulled down by it, every nation struggling to recover, the working man along with them.

Being without work since last week was Dad's fault this time. He'd had a shouting match in the pub where dockers would gather for breakfast and a pint while waiting to find out any news of a ship coming in. A mate had chuckled at the times Dad had gone off to the carsie. Sensitive about his affliction, Dad had almost come to blows and when his ganger had tried to reason with him he'd told him he could stuff his bloody gang. So now he was on his own until the wounds healed, but meanwhile he had come home seething and full of complaint. He'd been going on about it since teatime until a few minutes earlier when Mum snapped that she too wasn't in the best frame of mind with no money coming in.

Her darning needle had fairly flown across the hole in the heel of his sock. 'I ain't runnin' an 'ome fer moanin' minnies, y'know. What with Evie moaning about 'ow much she hates that new job she's got. She's lucky to 'ave one, gettin' it straight after leavin' school. But now she wants ter find somethink else!' Mum waggled her head in sarcasm. 'Fred's gone off in a temper 'cos 'is mates ain't knocked for 'im, and Mavis is upstairs staring all moony-eyed at her Tom's picture 'cos he don't see 'er on Monday nights. That just leaves Wally. He ain't 'ome yet, but there's still time.'

She continued to hold Geraldine in her glare. 'So what's up with you?'

How could she tell Mum what was up with her? She was sure Mum's eyes wouldn't light up all that much at the mention of her falling head over heels for some shop owner, someone right out of their class. She knew exactly what Mum would say: 'Aiming a bit 'igh, ain't yer, yer silly bitch, making eyes at a bloke what ain't going ter give yer the time of day? Why don't yer find a proper bloke what's got 'is feet on the ground?'

No, she wouldn't tell anyone about him, not even her best friend. Not until he responded. Even then she'd have to give it some thought because they'd still poke fun, calling her a jumped-up snob, thinking herself above everyone else.

'Nothink's got into me,' she told her waspishly and more in defiance than anger took herself off to her bedroom to finish the rest of her dress. It would at least help take away this wistful feeling.

Mavis was sitting on the edge of their bed. In her hand was the framed photo of her husband-to-be. She was all dewy-eyed as she gazed at it. But now, with her self-imposed solitude shattered – she had plenty of friends she could have gone to see but of course she preferred her little drama – by her sister bursting in on her, she turned on Geraldine in anger.

'Can't any of you leave me alone? What d'yer want?'

'I want to finish me dress,' Geraldine snapped back. 'It's my bedroom as well. You ain't got first claim on it.'

For an answer, Mavis threw Tom's picture onto the eiderdown and leapt up as though the bedsprings had broken through under her bottom and made for the door. 'There ain't never no peace in this rotten 'ouse! I'm going round ter see my Tom's mum and dad. I might find some peace there!'

'I thought you don't see each other on Monday nights.'

'Well, tonight's different, ain't it?' came the parting shot.

Left to her own devices, Geraldine began clearing the clutter from the top of the sewing machine stand, that when not in use served as a dressing table, lifted off the mirror and opened the top flap to ease the heavy machine into its position. With the bed as a seat, she sat down to refill the shuttle with blue cotton and threaded the needle.

All else forgotten, she worked steadily for the rest of the evening with no interruptions, thank goodness. By the time Mavis came home looking a little more disposed and eager to get to bed and dream of her Tom, the dress was more or less finished. All that was needed was a final pressing but, with no chance of going downstairs to press it on the kitchen table with everyone about to go to bed, it would have to wait until tomorrow.

Tomorrow gripped her with excitement the second she opened her eyes to realise it was today. For once she actually looked forward to going to work, but especially to lunchtime.

The moment the buzzer went she was up from her bench, rushing to the grubby, smelly little cloakroom for her coat and handbag. It was always a jumble of coats, bags, wet boots if the weather was bad and a variety of shopping bags holding food for lunch. It was a scramble to find her own things from among it all, with other girls coming in to get theirs, having first rushed into the single, somewhat mucky lavatory before anyone else could to empty out before leaving. Needing to go would spoil even the briefest chat with Anthony Hanford and she would have rather died than ask to use his toilet.

'You ain't off out again!' admonished Eileen who had followed her in to pick up her flask and sandwiches. 'Yesterday, now today – where d'yer go?'

Geraldine gave her a grin. 'Tell you later, but not now, I'm in a hurry.' Already she was guarding her diction, preparing for her conversation with Anthony Hanford.

Eileen began to grin too. 'Secret, eh? Seein' a boyfriend?'

'Tell you later,' Geraldine shouted over the babble of voices around them and hurried away before any more questions could be asked.

'Don't be late back,' Eileen called after her as Geraldine squeezed herself out of the door between several other girls coming in. 'Greenaway'll 'ave your guts for garters if you are!' Mrs Greenaway was their forelady, those beady eyes behind her pince-nez never missing a trick.

All morning Geraldine had itched to tell Eileen Shaw of the man whom she was – she had to admit it – chasing after. Eileen would have burst out laughing, saying, 'Who d'yer think you are? Lady Jane? A bloke what's got a shop ain't even goin' ter look at you.'

But he had looked at her, and his eyes had surely glistened.

They glistened now, she was certain, as he came from the back room on her entering the shop. And so they ought. She'd done herself up for this occasion – under the wrap-around apron she used for work she'd worn her best skirt and blouse. The apron now stowed under

35

her bench back at work, the skirt and blouse were having their moment of glory. Not that he'd see much of them with February necessitating a winter coat, but it made her feel better dressed and that must surely show on her face. Having added a touch of face powder, she knew she looked good without his eyes telling her as his smile widened in welcome.

'Hullo, I did wonder if I'd see you this lunchtime.'

'It's the only time I get off during the day.' She wasn't yet prepared to tell him what she worked at though he would know sooner or later if things got more serious.

'Do you work far from here?' he asked, obviously happy to make conversation.

'No, not far,' she obliged.

'What do you do?' Heartening that he should be interested, on the other hand alarming that she must now lie, or dare she tell the truth? She decided to prevaricate.

'I'm a . . . a high-class dress machinist,' she stammered. 'My work goes mostly to the West End.'

What a fib! Rubins' garments mostly went to shops in Petticoat Lane and Roman Road markets. She did intend one day to go in for better-quality work – she was up to it. Even at Rubins she was always given all the better garments to do. Leaving there to better herself would of course mean saying goodbye to her mates, especially Eileen. Eileen, not all that skilled – a moderately fast worker but happy to tick along and draw her pay packet on Friday – would never be accepted by people like court dressmakers such as she herself hoped to be employed by eventually.

'I mean to do even better,' she went on, hoping she didn't sound too boring, but he looked interested and she was encouraged. 'Have a business of my own one day – do what I've always enjoyed most.' Thoughts of it were beginning to make her speak better. 'Creating my own designs.'

'I understand what you mean,' he returned. 'There's something very satisfying about working with one's hands. I never really felt fulfilled by what I did prior to the war. I told you, my father is a solicitor. Wanted me to continue in the legal profession. But it never appealed to me. I hated to disappoint him and joining up helped me escape, so to speak. I suppose I've come back a different person though the process isn't quite what I would recommend.'

Geraldine devoured all that he was saying, seeing for the first time the haunted expression behind his eyes, wondering what sort of war he'd had, what might have happened to him, though like a lot of men back from France, if that was where he'd been, he'd never say even if it was there in his eyes. But there was no time to dwell on it. Time was flying by. She dare not be late back to work, yet dared not make the same mistake she had made yesterday.

'But you would recommend making beautiful things,' she prompted. It had the desired effect, bringing him back to the present.

His eyes lit up. 'Ah, yes, your necklace. Just a tick! I hope this is just what you had in mind.' Making for the back room, he reappeared moments later with an oblong velvet box.

'I spent last night on this,' he announced, unwrapping it as though it were as delicate as spider silk. 'I hope you like it.'

Geraldine gasped as the box was opened to reveal the most delicate thing she had ever seen – a string of small,

37

rounded, dark-blue stones, each one separated by a tiny seed pearl that glowed with such lustre that it seemed impossible they were merely artificial.

'They look so real,' she sighed. God knows what this was going to cost. Now she'd have to tell him it wasn't quite what she wanted, to save the humiliation of having to admit she couldn't afford such a thing.

He was smiling. 'The blue ones are meant to be lapis lazuli, not real.' She'd never heard of lapis lazuli. 'I'm afraid the pearls are also artificial.'

How could she tell? The tiny pearls in particular had such a soft delicate glow about them that they could easily have been real. There was a look in his eyes when she looked up at him suddenly that made her feel that he wasn't in fact telling the truth.

'How d'you make beads like this?' she burst out in admiration and again he smiled. It was such a lovely smile.

'Secrets of the trade.' He sounded teasing. 'I buy them and string them.' He pointed to the blue stones. 'Lapis lazuli has gold flecks in it, so a little gold colour dabbed on makes it look authentic. The pearls are glass and lined with the material that comes from the inside of oyster shells, called nacre.'

From the seemingly diffident young man he had now assumed a voice of authority that rather surprised and somewhat overawed her. All she could say was, 'It's lovely. And I do like the pretend silver clasp.'

'It's not pretend,' he said, 'It *is* silver.'

Geraldine stared at him in alarm. 'I didn't ask for real silver. I really can't . . .'

She was going to say she couldn't afford real silver

but stopped in time. Dare she ask the price? But he must know what she was about to say and, telling her the price, he would grin in amusement at her horrified expression. She'd put her foot in it yet again. What man who had a solicitor for a father, who had pots of money, or at least whose father had, and who could turn down a promising career to play at making cheap jewellery, wouldn't be turned off by a girl who earned a living slaving away at a sewing machine and couldn't afford anything more than half a crown at the most for a row of beads? She earned seven shillings and sixpence a week: two and six was a third of a week's wages.

Instead of grinning, he was surveying her in all seriousness. Gone was the efficiency that had awed her a moment ago, replaced by uncertainty that instantly melted her heart and took away all her earlier dismay.

'What would you say to two shillings? It's not as expensive as it looks.'

With an effort she regained control of her emotion and gazed down at the necklace. 'I can't believe it.' Was he merely being charitable? She didn't want him treating her as though she were unable to pay her way. 'I must give you more than that.'

'I wouldn't dream of it,' he replied quickly. 'It didn't take that long to make, nor did it take up much material. A bit of silver I had by – see, it's quite thin.' He turned the clasp over for her to see the hollowness on the inner side. 'The beads I already had in stock. As for the blue ones, a dab or two of colour cost me nothing.'

It seemed to Geraldine that he was using the term 'beads' deliberately. Most jewellers would automatically say stones. Was it in order to come down to her level, or minimise the real value of the necklace? She wanted to think it was the latter though either way made her uncomfortable. If it was the latter why didn't she believe him? He'd admitted that the clasp was real silver. Why silver if the stones were fake? Any old metal would have done for just 'beads'. It didn't make sense.

'You don't have to have it if you don't want,' he was saying.

'No!' she burst in, mortified that she could think bad things of him. 'It's lovely. I just thought . . . No, it's lovely.'

That seemed to satisfy him. 'You should have earrings as well,' he said, immediately alarming her. 'I took the liberty last night of making some. Of course, if you don't like them they can go in the window.'

The suggestion was almost apologetic and she found herself hastening to reassure him. 'I ain't . . . I've not had my ears pierced so I don't wear . . .' She let the explanation die. It was hard keeping up the nice accent, her mind in a whirl of mixed feelings, but he shouldn't have assumed she'd want them. It put her in an awkward situation, hating to admit that she couldn't afford earrings on top of a necklace, even though he'd said only two shillings. Two shillings! She still couldn't believe that, not for a necklace of this beauty and length.

He was still looking at her intently. 'I was wondering,' he said, 'if you'd accept them as a . . . as a gift.'

A twinge of wariness, alarm even, welled up because he was trying to get friendly with her in a way she hadn't expected. 'I don't . . .' she began then paused.

She'd been about to say she didn't want his gift but

it would have sounded hurtful. She should explain that a girl didn't accept presents from a man she hardly knew. Yet if she said that, he might take it as an insult and she'd never be able to bring herself to go into his shop again. Then she would never get to know him.

Muscles taut, one hand clutching the edge of the counter, the other clasping her handbag handle as if both hands were glued there, she began again.

'I mean, I don't know you well enough for you ter give me presents. It ain't right.' Head down, she let go of the counter to fish into her handbag for the required money. 'I'll just pay for the necklace, if you'd wrap it up. Then I must go. But thanks.'

It had to cost more than he'd asked but she was too confused to query it, handing the money over, knowing she'd made a proper mess of things.

She stood dumbly aside as the till rang and he wrapped the box in pretty paper; she took it from him not daring to lift her eyes to his, managing to mumble, 'Thank you,' and made for the door.

As the shop bell tinkled, she heard his voice. 'The earrings will be here if you want them.'

In a flurry of confusion she nodded vaguely and bolted, practically cannoning into a passer-by as she grabbed her bicycle. In no manner could she ever go back into that shop. She'd made a fool of herself. She'd insulted him, spurned his generous offer, or that's how it seemed.

All day it stayed with her. She couldn't even confide the event to Eileen for all her friend was burning up with curiosity. 'Tell you tomorrow,' was all she said as she bent her head to her work, machining away furiously under the formidable eye of Mrs Greenaway, having come back after lunch three minutes late.

It was Wednesday and still she couldn't bring herself to tell Eileen what had happened. Eileen would have probably called her a fool to run from the shop like that. Rather than scoff at her for ogling at a man like Hanford she'd have probably chided her for refusing the offering, embarrassing her even further. But there was no going back now. Cycling past the shop at six-thirty, she was relieved to find it closed for the evening although a light glowed in the room above. What was he doing up there? Would he be reading the paper or having his supper or doing some chore or other? She tried not to imagine what he'd be doing and cycled furiously on past in case he looked out of the window and saw her, glad to turn down the side street leading to her own home.

Next day, lunchtime was spent at her bench eating her sandwiches and trying to avoid Eileen's questions on where she'd gone that Monday and why she had been so secretive about it.

'I bet all the tea in China you're seein' some bloke,' Eileen said, 'and yer mum don't approve. That it?'

'No, that ain't it,' snapped Geraldine, managing to change the subject sufficiently to take Eileen's mind off it. But she knew Eileen would come back to it, if not now, then eventually.

Passing the shop on her way home on the Thursday evening, she wasn't sure whether to be pleased or disappointed to find the place again in darkness, the upstairs light gleaming through drawn curtains. Was he disappointed that she'd never come back to claim her earrings? She slowed, taking one foot off the pedal and onto the kerb to come to a stop. The curtains drawn, she didn't think he'd be peeping out. Again daydreaming as to what he might be doing, a voice behind her made her start.

'Is it you?'

Turning her head in panic towards the voice, imagining it to be the man she'd thought was up there above the darkened shop, she almost collapsed with relief seeing Alan Presley hurrying up to her.

'It is you,' he said, joining her. 'Geraldine Glover. I ain't seen you in ages. What yer standing 'ere for?'

'Just coming 'ome from work,' she excused, gathering up her wits. 'I stopped ter put me skirt right. It keeps getting' caught in the pedal.' It was as good an excuse as any and to make it look more plausible she got off the cycle and began to walk, pushing the thing while he fell into step beside her.

'Wanna be careful. Could 'ave you over. Use cycle clips meself.' He chuckled at his own joke. 'Yer need them guard things when yer got a skirt.'

'I know,' she said.

'What yer doing with yerself these days?' he went on.

'Oh, this an' that,' she replied warmly, pleased now to have him take her mind off other things.

'Got a bloke?'

'No, not at the moment. And how're you doing?'

Probably the wrong thing to ask, being estranged from his wayward wife, but he didn't seem too put out; instead, he gave a small despondent grunt.

'Chuggin' along. You know. Don't do much with meself lately.'

He'd thrust his hands deep into the pockets of his long, beige topcoat, the collar drawn up against the cold of this February evening. There was a slight drizzle in the air that had every promise of turning to snow later on.

'Yer can go round ter see yer folks,' he continued, 'but there's only so much yer want ter see of 'em. An' I ain't that keen on airing me business. Yer know what people are like, prying, askin' questions.'

Yes, didn't she know it with Eileen going on all day about where she'd been these two lunchtimes, who it was she'd seen and why all the secrecy?

Feeling for him, she kept away from enquiring about his divorce, but he seemed ready to talk.

'Don't know whether to go back ter me parents or stay in me flat. She's gorn, me ole woman. Orf with 'er fancy man. So I'm on me own. It's only a couple of rooms we 'ad. I don't know whether to 'ang on to it or not.'

'I'd hang on to it if I was you,' advised Geraldine as they turned down her road. 'Nothing like independence. You can always go round to see your people when you want. If you go back and live with them you mightn't find leaving so easy.'

'That's true,' he admitted. 'It's just that I don't go out much. I seem to've got out of the habit of asking girls out. It ain't much fun goin' ter the pictures or standin' in a pub all by yerself.'

'Ain't yer got no friends yer can go with?'

'They're all married. They go out with their wives, and I ain't no hanger on.' For a second his step faltered, then he came to an abrupt stop. She stopped too and found him looking at her.

'What?' she challenged.

'It's just, I was wonderin'.'

'What?' she asked again.

'If yer'd like ter go to the pictures with me, say this Saturday?'

It was her turn to hesitate. She'd always liked Alan, in fact had once had a crush on him. Nor could she put any faith in Anthony Hanford taking a serious interest in her. She'd been a fool to imagine he would.

Alan, with his regular features, rugged, handsome, his chin strong, his mouth firm, a resolute mouth – she'd kissed those lips years ago and had found the experience enjoyable. He was tall, a good six feet, lean, muscles strengthened by army training and his experiences in France – he'd been in the thick of it, she'd heard. Yet he'd always had such a nice and easy nature. Maybe why his wife had taken advantage of him, thinking he'd take her back after her fling. Giving his wife her marching orders proved an inner strength that brought admiration flooding into Geraldine's eyes as she looked at him in the gloom of a street lamp.

It was no good pining after what she couldn't have – a husband with money. Here was an offer staring her right in the face in the shape of a modest bricklayer, and she was getting slightly desperate for a boyfriend. Not that she couldn't get one but she'd always been too choosy. It was time she stopped looking for that perfect someone and before she could give it another thought she'd said yes – yes she wouldn't mind going to see the pictures.

# Chapter Four

She'd seen Alan Presley four Saturdays running, going with him to the local picture house and once to the People's Palace to see a show, insisting on paying for her own seat because he wasn't that well off – well, neither was she, and also she didn't want him thinking she was his girl, not yet anyway; not until she could put Anthony Hanford from her mind, which was still proving a problem.

She hadn't told Alan about him. It wasn't any of his business. And besides, she still felt more than a bit embarrassed by the whole thing. Looking back on it, how she could have walked into his shop thinking he'd fall head over heels for her, or even dream that he would give her a second glance, was enough to screw her insides up with shame. Yet he had seemed to be taken by her, or was that just his stock in trade?

She still didn't know what to think, in fact preferred not to think about it at all if that was possible, mortified as she was by her behaviour. She could imagine him smirking over it, if he still remembered it enough to smirk – accepting Alan's invitation for a date had taken some of the sting out of it and it had gone on from there. She'd always been keen on Alan but felt nervous of getting too serious for the moment. For one thing he might see her as a handy convenience after his unhappy marriage, and for another, was she ready to get involved, also being on the rebound, so to speak, now that her own silly hopes had been nipped in the bud?

'Where'd yer like to go next Saturday?' Alan had asked her as they said goodnight to each other the previous Saturday. She had let him kiss her on leaving him at the end of her street. A light sort of kiss – she wasn't allowing it to get too serious, even though it sent a tingle up her spine. She was in a dilemma of uncertainty, part of her still yearning for the more sophisticated Anthony Hanford even as she chided herself for her silliness.

'I don't really know,' she replied. 'But if we go to the pictures again I want to pay for meself. You can't keep spending out.'

He leaned back from her. 'What, d'yer think I can't afford ter pay for yer? I ain't poverty stricken, y'know.'

'I know you ain't. But I'd prefer to pay for meself, that's all.'

'At least I got a job. Thousands ain't. I can turn me 'and to anythink. I'm a bricklayer, decorator, carpenter, plumber, you name it, I can do it. Jack of all trades, me. And if I get any spare time I go up ter West London where the posh lot live and do a spot of decoratin' or a bit of carpentry fer them, an' they pay well, I can tell yer. So I do 'ave dosh in me pocket.'

47

Gabbling on, he sounded just a little offended and she was sorry she'd mentioned paying her way.

'If I was laid off termorrer,' he continued, 'I could still keep me 'and in doing odd jobs like that. One day I'm goin' ter 'ave me own business. But time ain't right yet, not with all this uncertainty since the Armistice – no one's going ter put their 'and in their pocket to finance me and I ain't got sufficient readies ter take chances settin' up in business. But it'll come in time when things settle down.'

Carried away by his own plans he gave a sardonic chuckle. 'She'll be the loser when she sees me getting on in the world and 'er stuck with that crummy bugger I caught 'er in bed with. She wants ter marry 'im, what ain't got two brass farthings ter rub tergether from what I 'ear. Well, it serves 'er right, the tart! I'll show 'er when I'm rollin' in dough with me own business.'

It was his wife he was referring to, and that was another thing – she didn't particularly relish hearing the man she was supposed to be going out with talking about the wife, even if he had slung her out and was going through a divorce. After all, he was still married to all intents and purposes. A divorce took years, and it gave her a funny feeling about being with him – another reason she was worried about the goodnight kisses getting too serious. But she did like him, very much. It was a pity so many things got in the way.

In her bridal gown but no headdress as yet, Mavis was getting herself in a two-and-eight.

'Look, can't everyone stop milling about all over the place? I can't think straight.'

'Yer best place is upstairs gettin' the rest of yerself ready,' Mum told her in no uncertain terms. 'The wedding is in 'alf an hour and you ain't 'alf way proper dressed yet.'

'Then come up and help me put me headdress on.'

''Ow can I wiv everyone comin' in? I'll come in a minute.'

She'd been up there with Mavis most of the morning listening to her moans and groans as she helped her get into her gown and combed out her hair, which had been in cloth rollers all night so as to allow the curls to set tighter; the process of sleeping in them had deprived Mavis of what little sleep the prospect of the big day allowed.

She'd been tossing and turning all night, keeping Geraldine awake, though Evie had slept like a log despite the bouncing bed. So Geraldine felt as tired as Mavis in the morning.

'I need 'elp now, Mum,' flounced Mavis, 'not *in a minute*!'

'I'll come up with yer,' said Geraldine. As chief brides-maid it was her place anyway. Mum had her hands full with the guests.

'I'd sooner Mum,' snapped Mavis. 'She knows just what ter do.'

'And I don't, I suppose!' Geraldine flared. 'I ain't daft, I know 'ow to put a veil and 'eaddress on someone. I could of made the entire thing, dress an' all, if you'd let—'

'Will you two pack up arguing. It's yer wedding, love – yer special day. Don't go spoiling it.'

'I ain't spoiling it. It's 'er.'

'Then let 'er sort yer wedding veil out. She knows what she's doin'.'

In a huff, Mavis dashed up the stairs as fast as her tight-skirted gown allowed, closely followed by Geraldine, equally irascible. Why was Mavis like this towards her? They'd never been what people would call close. Right from tiny tots Mavis had snapped at her, found fault and shunned any offer of friendship. 'Sometimes I wonder why she's my sister at all,' Geraldine would tell friends when she went on about her.

With Mavis plopping ungraciously down on an upright before the little dressing mirror to suffer her headdress and veil to be arranged by her sister, Geraldine bet that Tom and his brother Sydney, his best man, weren't arguing like this as they got ready for the church.

There was certainly no reason for Mavis to be so tetchy. Everything was going fine so far. The day was sunny and cloudy in turns and as moderately warm as March could ever be. True, the house was in turmoil, food still being laid out for the wedding breakfast and people milling about getting under each other's feet as they prepared to leave for the walk to the church. Mavis would lead on the arm of Dad, followed by her brides-maids. This was the old style of East End weddings. Few had the wherewithal for conveying a bride to the church and the Glover family was no exception. A girl just prayed for it not to rain. At least she had people all along the route coming to their doors to see her pass and to send their best wishes after her, though Mavis wasn't so happy about the usual troupe of urchins following at a distance, whistling and catcalling, but there was nothing anyone could do about that –

50

they'd follow anything, fire engines, water carts, brass bands, and of course anything resembling a procession. All Mavis could do was to grin and bear it. But Geraldine thought it did add to the general excitement of the day.

The whole day went off with no hitches and hardly any nasty moments at the wedding reception with drunken differences of opinion. The kitchen became jam-packed with regular journeys to the beer barrel – a wedding present clubbed together from Dad's mates, him back in his old gang again – on the stone copper, sorties to the sandwiches, jellies and cake on the board next to it, and later for a piece of wedding cake and a sobering cup of tea just before people began wending their way home, some straight, some slightly more uncertain.

Around six o'clock the newly-weds, who'd done little but gaze adoringly into each other's eyes all afternoon, were finally seen off on their honeymoon to catch their train to Eastbourne, a couple of the men helping them with their cases to the bus taking them to Victoria Station.

This was the moment Geraldine was waiting for. Dashing upstairs the moment the two had gone, she dragged off the horrid bridesmaid's dress and with great care got into her beautiful creation. The gasps as she glided down the stairs and into the back room where most of the remaining guests were gathered, apart from those back to boozing in the kitchen or stuffing what was left of the food, did Geraldine credit.

'My Gawd!' came the cry from her Aunt Violet, one of Dad's three sisters. 'What you got up as? You look like yer've just stepped out of society. What she want ter dress up like that for?'

'She didn't like'er bridesmaid's dress much,' excused Mum to her credit and Geraldine felt like hugging her as pride came into Mum's voice. 'Made that all 'erself, Vi.'

Aunt Vi's tone turned to admiration. 'She could make my Edna a dress like that.' Edna was the eldest of her three daughters, the other two already married, and three sons, all of whom were in the kitchen swigging the beer before it ran out.

At the suggestion, Geraldine bit her lip. She hadn't counted on admiration turning to hints of hiring her talents, and hurried away before she was required to reply that, yes, she'd be overjoyed to make Edna a dress like hers, and most likely for love.

Dad's other sisters, Lydia and Jessie, merely looked at her as though she'd dressed herself up like a dog's dinner and was not worthy of comment. Several of her male cousins did raise their eyebrows in avid appreciation and said she looked smashing, while her female ones looked aside in jealousy, pretending not to notice. She was soon wondering if this had not been such a good idea after all.

'That's ever so pretty, love.'

She turned with gratitude towards the voice of her mum's sister Lizzie, and glanced modestly down at herself. 'D'you think so?'

'Oh, yes.' Aunt Lizzie nibbled a piece of cake. 'Where d'yer buy it?'

The tone suggested it must have cost a fortune, ringing with both envy of her having so much money and censure that the money would have been better spent on something more suitable.

It was confirmed by her adding, 'But where're yer

going ter wear it, love?' indicating the uselessness of such a dress.

Geraldine was compelled to admit that she'd made it to lessen the sense of her being too well off or overlavish, at the same time putting herself in danger of another offer to have her make something similar for her two girls.

But all Aunt Lizzie said was, 'Well, I think you're very clever, love. But you shouldn't of made it look so 'igh class.'

Which in a way annoyed her that people like her should be expected to keep to their station in life. Silly, old-fashioned ideas, held before the war. Well, things were different now. The war had done away with a lot of the old class distinction and women had proved they could do anything having done men's jobs all through those four years and could go on doing them. Soon it would be the start of a new decade – 1920 – and already society women were wearing Bohemian clothes with impunity and shortening skirts. So why shouldn't she be fashionable? She thought again of Anthony Hanford. She could be as good as him any day, learn to speak nice, behave like a lady, dress like one, especially if she could make clothes like this one that had already drawn comments, good and bad but none against the dress itself and its workmanship. She was aware of the looks of appraisal that even her uncles were giving her, as were the young men here, Tom's brother and best man, for instance.

Apart from the odd reference to dogs' dinners and putting on airs, which she put down to sheer jealousy, it was a successful weekend. Tom's brother Sid asked her to go to the Troxy picture palace with him the following Saturday and she'd said yes, because she wasn't ready to be pinned down by any one boyfriend just yet despite envying her sister getting married.

Mavis would return from honeymoon and become a housewife in the tiny two-roomed flat they'd found. Dad had started Tom in the docks as a tea messenger, not being skilled, but he had to start somewhere and it brought in a wage, she as a married women, of course, no longer working. Geraldine's envy of her melted at the thought, knowing she was still free to do as she pleased.

It was a good job she didn't tell Alan about Sydney. That one date had been her last – completely boring, him going on about football, and not being in work like so many. Not his fault, but she'd paid for her own seat and he'd let her, not even putting up an argument. To pay for herself wasn't the trouble – being expected to was. She didn't think she'd be seeing him again and what Alan didn't know wouldn't hurt him. If Alan didn't ask her out again after she told him she'd not be seeing him that Saturday, there were still her friends from work to go out with.

Then there was that Anthony Hanford still never very far from her thoughts. She'd even dreamed of him at night: cycling past his shop and he leaping out to stand in her path and she with no way of avoiding crashing into him. That was her biggest concern, having to cycle past there every day. What if he saw her? She'd never gone back to claim those earrings, so how could she ever face him if he did come out? What could she say?

He must have seen her on occasion pedalling by furiously and wondered at her never coming in. Or maybe he'd forgotten her so that there was no point in worrying at all. Maybe he had only been friendly like a good shopkeeper. And her running away with the idea that she could have attracted a man like him. What a high opinion she'd had of herself. On the other hand a shopkeeper's friendliness didn't usually include offering a gift to a customer. Perhaps he had fancied her. Perhaps he'd been hurt by her refusal. Or heartbroken? No, that was being melodramatic. Of course he wasn't heartbroken. More likely he had shrugged and got on with his life. It was she who was getting melodramatic.

If she went in now, what would she say? If only she'd handled things differently. From time to time she'd taken out the necklace worn just that one weekend with her dress, and Mum saying what a waste of time and money spent on it. She studied the thing and the more she scrutinised it, the more came the suspicion that those beads were real stones.

Running her fingers over the blue ones – what had he called them, lapis lazuli? – they'd been smooth to the touch. Having looked them up in a book from the library, the gold flecks, it said, were a type of mineral. If he'd painted them on they'd have felt raised. If they were real gemstones, it would mean the pearls were real too and the necklace worth a darn sight more than two shillings. She'd seen in jewellers' windows up the West End what real pearls cost. Surely he hadn't been that silly to give her real stones, real pearls?

It made her feel a little sick to think of it and set a dilemma as to what she ought to do about it. What she did do was to cycle even faster past his shop, wishing there was another route home from work without having to pass it unless she was prepared to go miles out of her way. The days were growing longer which meant coming home in daylight. He'd see her even more easily so she cycled faster still. The irony of it was that she hadn't worn her lovely dress since the wedding – her Aunt Lizzie had been right, there'd been nowhere to wear it since. It hung in the cupboard alongside Evie's things, Mavis having taken her clothes away with her – a thorough waste of her time just to reap a glance or two of admiration and that somewhat mixed, leaving her with a feeling of having shown off. On top of that had been the humiliating necklace and earrings business.

Nearing Hanford's this April evening, with daylight still lingering, she wondered if he still had those earrings or whether he had now sold them. As she prepared herself to put on her usual spurt, she saw to her horror that he was standing at the door of his shop. She couldn't ignore him and automatically her face turned his way.

He waved. Her best bet would have been to wave back and cycle on, but she couldn't be that rude. Instead, she slowed, put one foot to the ground to steady her cycle to a stop, aware that he was already starting across the pavement towards her. Maybe he had been doing that as she made to pass, prompting the reaction of stopping.

'Hullo! Haven't see you for some time.' His voice, low and full-bodied, made her tingle, despite feeling flustered.

'No,' she managed. 'I've been working all the time.'

'I saw you pass here a few weeks ago.' So he had

seen her. She felt even more flustered. 'But you were going at a terrific rate of knots.' Had he made to hurry out but had missed her? 'So how are you?'

'I'm very well, thank you,' she replied, finding the pavement and kerb to have become very fascinating.

'Did the wedding go well?'

'Yes, very well, thank you.'

'And you wore your dress?' She nodded furiously, loathing this odd shyness. She was never a shy person normally. 'And the necklace? Did you like the necklace?'

Again she nodded. Now was the time to confront him as to their genuineness or not, but no words came out. She merely nodded, her head lowered. In fact her brake handles became a thing to study, whether they were fixed tight enough to her handlebars.

'I'm glad you did. I wanted you to. Very much.' There was a pause. Then, 'Those earrings I made for you. I'd have sent them to you but I don't know your address. They've been here waiting for you to come in again.'

Now she raised her head. 'You've still got them?' Lord, such dark-grey eyes he had. They sent silly, unexpected shivers of excitement through her.

'Yes, I do.'

'I thought you'd of sold them by now.'

'They were a present for you.'

She let her glance fall away in embarrassment. 'I didn't think you meant it. You didn't know me all that well and . . . and after all, shopkeepers – I mean . . . people what don't know you don't usually make presents of things like that. I mean they were real . . . I mean, my necklace was . . .'

She came to a halt, confused, feeling awkward.

What must he be thinking of her? She looked up quickly to see him smiling.

'Clever girl.' It sounded almost derisive, but his eyes were soft. 'You discovered my secret. Please forgive me if I embarrassed you but it seemed right for you to wear something worthy of you. Your colouring was just right for blue, and there's no blue as striking as lapis—'

'But they're real and all you charged me was two shillings.'

He was still smiling. 'I had to charge you something or you'd have walked out. As you did when I offered the earrings. And please don't worry, Geraldine –' he'd remembered her name! '– they're not exactly precious.'

'They still cost more than I could ever afford,' she shot at him, angry now at the way he was smiling at her patronisingly, it struck her, his tone steady, but most of all his assumption that he could be familiar enough with her to use her given name without a by-your-leave. He was, after all, a shopkeeper, whether he had money or not, and as such she was better than he!

'I'm sorry,' she said tersely, gazing ahead towards her destination. 'I've got to go. I'll be late 'ome for me tea.' She was trying to speak nicely but it wasn't working. It came to her that why should she be trying to? Who was he anyway? She was really angry now, mostly with herself, seeing the chance she'd longed for all this time slipping away, and also that he was seeing her as an ordinary East End girl yet had the cheek to chat her up.

'I'll bring the necklace back tomorrow. I can't pay just two bob for something as valuable as all that. Even though you tell me it's not that valuable, it's still valuable

58

enough. Anyway I don't suppose I'll use it again. I don't go to places what call for that sort of jewellery—'

'Would you like to go somewhere where you could wear it?' he cut through her gabble.

She looked sharply at him. 'Pardon?'

'I wondered if you'd like to go somewhere nice, where you could make use of it, and your dress as well.' As she continued to stare at him, he cocked his head on one side to gaze into her eyes, his own holding an enquiring glow. 'If only to wear it in a nice setting in good company, or, let's put it another way, so I could see how you look in your lovely dress and the necklace, and of course the earrings.' His hand appeared to be moving towards hers, resting on the bicycle handlebar.

'What I'm asking is would you let me take you out to dinner, or maybe to a theatre, or both?'

She withdrew her hand before he could touch it, fiddled instead with the neck of her jacket. She wore it with her thick working skirt, not trusting the April weather as yet. She began to feel conscious of the way she was dressed.

'What would you want going out with someone like me? I'm just an ordinary working girl.'

'And I'm an ordinary working man.'

'You ain't,' she shot at him. 'You've got a father what's a solicitor. You only chose to do this sort of thing to get back at him for somethink or other. You don't really need to work at somethink like this, but me, I 'ave to work for me living. So why ask someone like me out?'

'Because I . . .' He hesitated then thought better of whatever he was going to say. 'Because I like you very much and I'd like to get to know you even better. Please, would you let me take you out? Say you will.'

She remained silent, looking down at the handlebars. How she longed to say yes, but fear of the unknown was gripping at her. She felt she should shake her head, grab the handlebars and cycle away, but she couldn't move.

'Will you?' he was urging.

It was all piling in on top of her, giving no time to think, to reflect on what the result of her reply would be one way or the other.

'Please, will you say yes?' he asked yet again.

Geraldine took a deep breath, felt her lips part for words that she couldn't give voice to. Her lips were moving apparently of their own accord, almost forming the word 'yes' even though her brain was in danger of forcing her to shake her head. She tried to close her lips but they refused to be closed and moments later she followed their lead with a hardly detectable nod of her head. She was aware of him relaxing.

'This Saturday then?'

Now she found her voice. 'I can't make it this Saturday. I'll be out.'

'With a boyfriend?'

'Girlfriend!'

The lie burst out of her before she could stop it. She was going to the picture palace again with Alan. She'd have to tell Alan she wouldn't see him the following Saturday. He was beginning to feel too secure with her, she was sure, even though there had been nothing going on between them – he was just a friend. Anyway he couldn't really have a proper relationship with any girl while he was still officially married. Divorcing his wife for adultery, he could hardly leave himself wide open to a counter claim even though he was doing nothing wrong.

As far as she could see there was no future with him for a long time yet and in that time all sorts of things could happen. She was free to go out with whomever she pleased, but she couldn't hurt him by saying what she'd really be doing the following Saturday, and anyway, this date with Anthony Hanford might only be this once. He might see her as not being his sort after all – well, she knew she wasn't his sort – and not ask her out again. Then where would she be? But if she didn't try, she'd never know, would she?

She came to herself with a start, aware that Anthony was asking her how she felt about going to the theatre. She looked up at him with startled eyes. 'The what?'

He looked a little concerned. 'You do like going to the theatre?'

'Oh, yes.' Quickly she gathered her wits. 'I love going.' She was about to gush, 'I go all the time,' but stopped herself. The only time she ever went was to the Queens Theatre in Poplar where they had variety acts, and of course stage acts put on between films at the picture palaces. Occasionally she had gone up to the West End with a couple of friends to line up with those like herself for the cheapest gallery seats, having saved up money for weeks for it. He wouldn't take her up there in the top gallery of course. More likely the upper circle, where people with just a bit more to spend would go, and definitely more suitable when treating a girl.

'Good,' he said. 'Which one would you like to go to?'

Fighting confusion, she fought to think clearly and came out with the only name that came to mind. 'The Hippodrome.'

He grinned. 'You like revues then. Okay, the Hippodrome it is. I'll get tickets for the dress circle.'

Stunned, she heard him instruct her to meet him here at six-thirty the Saturday after next, and not to worry, he'd take care of everything, getting her there, everything.

# Chapter Five

'See you next Saturday then?'

Alan's parting reminder brought Geraldine up sharp. She'd mentioned nothing regarding next Saturday, hanging back in the hope that he himself might decide to let that go. Now he'd referred to it, she'd have to tell him that next Saturday was off – but what excuse to make? There had been so many of them jiggling around inside her head all through the film show that not only had she been unable to concentrate or enjoy what had been showing but she was now spoiled for which one to chose, always the bane of those about to tell lies. She settled on the first one to pop back into her head.

'We're going round to me sister's fer tea.'

'Oh.' He looked dismal for a second or two then brightened. 'What about Saturday after that?'

Geraldine took a deep breath. 'I don't know yet. It's a long way ter think ahead.'

He was looking at her keenly, as if trying to judge her thoughts. 'Are yer sayin' yer don't want ter see me any more?'

'No, Alan.' She didn't want to burn her bridges just yet and she did like him very much. 'If I can let yer know after next Saturday.'

''Cos if yer don't want ter see me again, I'd rather yer let me know now, save me 'anging around 'opeful like.'

She squirmed with guilt. 'Don't be silly, Alan!'

'It's not silly. I know we're only friends. Can't be anythink else the way I'm placed. But even friends ought ter be straight with each uvver. If there's some uvver bloke yer seeing, I'd sooner yer tell me.'

'It ain't anythink like that. It's just . . . Look, I'll drop you a note next week. I've got ter go, Alan. It's gettin' late, an' Dad'll be wondering where I am. I'll see yer soon. Not next Saturday, maybe the one after. Let's say goodnight, Alan. I must go now.'

Tilting her face for his usual goodnight peck, eyes half closed, she was surprised to find him walking swiftly away from her, his parting words, 'See yer around then,' coming back to her in a strangled sort of tone.

Her heart gave a thud of remorse. She was about to chase after him to tell him not to be so silly but instead she just stood there watching him, the circle of fitful yellow glow from a street gas lamp further along lighting up his tall, straight figure for a moment before shadows swallowed it up.


She was seeing Anthony outside his shop at six-thirty and her stomach was all collywobbles, first and foremost at the prospect of the meeting itself and also at the idea of being taken to the theatre, the dress circle no less!

She'd never been in the dress circle in her life, nor

anywhere else in a theatre but up in the gallery, the gods as it was termed by those who could afford nothing else. She and a couple of girlfriends, with what was left of their weekly pay packet after handing over half of it to their mums for their keep, would line up outside and while they queued would be entertained by buskers, some every bit as good as the performers inside except that many were missing a leg or an arm or were blinded by courtesy of the trenches in which they'd fought, and all of them just about scraping a subsistence by kerbside entertainment.

She and her friends would finally be admitted by a side door to mount endless flights of stone stairs between pockmarked walls to where the tatty, grubby balcony jutted out just below the theatre roof, its occupants required to sit on tiers of wooden steps each with the minimum of padding for a bottom to sit on, and certainly no backrests. The audience there would be in everyday clothes and any woman too overdressed would be seen as a tart or worse, and any finely dressed man would likewise be looked on as a pansy.

Up there, laughter and catcalls were the order of the day, the rustle of sweet paper and crackle of peanut shells incessant. An attendant in that area was more a warder than a helper, watching for anyone dropping orange peel, apple cores, sweet papers or peanut shells down on the heads of those below, or dissuading the more unruly from giving out boos or catcalls during serious drama and seeing that no fighting broke out. The persistently guilty were hauled off to the delight of everyone, to be marched down the shabby back stairs to the street and thrown out. Being up in the gods was entertainment in itself and Geraldine had always enjoyed the treat.

Now she was to be treated to the dress circle, not even the upper circle where she might have felt more comfortable. In the dress circle she'd have little idea how to deport herself. There was a feeling too that Anthony Hanford would have taken a girl of his own sort into the stalls with the fur-coated and bejewelled. Perhaps he was sparing her the embarrassment of rubbing shoulders with the extremely wealthy, but though that should have been a relief to her it annoyed her a little. Wasn't she good enough to be with them in the really posh seats? Perhaps he didn't see that by considering her feelings he was in fact embarrassing her already.

Dad glanced up from his *Evening Standard* as she entered the back room. 'Where you off to, all dressed up?'

Mum was in the kitchen washing up with Evie wiping. They hadn't gone to the pictures this Saturday being that Dad was short of money this week. Geraldine had hoped that was where they would have been so that she could have crept out in her best clothes without being seen. But no, it had to be Sod's Law, didn't it, that they'd be home on this particular evening of all evenings?

'I'm just going out, that's all,' she answered sharply.

'Must be somewhere posh. You ain't worn that thing since Mave's weddin'. Showing orf that time like you was rollin' around in dosh.'

She was churned up enough by this business without having to explain herself away to Dad. 'I'm just going to see a friend of mine.'

'Bloke? New bloke. Posh is 'e?'

'That's my business!'

'Well, you be sure of 'im bringin' yer 'ome by ten-thirty.'

'I'm going to see a show, Dad. It don't finish before then.'

'Eleven then. And straight 'ome, mind – no funny larkin' abart, understand?'

'I've never done anything like larkin' about.'

'There's always a first time. You just see this ain't it, oo-ever 'e is.' Geraldine didn't reply. Her main worry was passing Mum in the kitchen and having to deal with her comments and questions.

Her only answer to Mum's startled enquiry as she rushed for the back door and the strong smell of carbolic as she opened it to the yard, was, 'I'll be 'ome by eleven, Mum!'

It was a good job this late April Saturday had decided to be warm and she could dispense with her outdoor jacket, tatty thing that it was, and not spoil the look of her lovely dress. At least she had a nice neck-wrap, spending out three shillings and eleven pence from her hard-earned pay on a blue feather necklet to suffice for evening wear. It made her look more dressed.

Anthony met her outside his shop. She had felt a bit conspicuous walking through the streets to meet him, sure all eyes turned to her as she passed, their owners musing on what she was up to all dressed up like she was, maybe on the game. Uncomfortable though it felt, she couldn't have asked him to call for her. Not that he didn't know what this area was like – he worked in it, but a young man didn't come calling until he'd been out with a girl several times. Even more people would have wondered at the expensively dressed young man and his transport and put two and two together.

As she had guessed, he did have transport, a motor taxicab, already waiting, so certain he was of her being on time. For a second or two she felt rankled that he was so sure of her, but moments later felt quite special that he should think she would be, and felt even more so as he helped her into the taxicab.

It was the first time she'd ever been in a motor vehicle other than a tram or omnibus and it was grand sitting beside him watching the shops go by without other people sharing the same view as her.

He hadn't greeted her with a kiss as she had somewhat feared he would, but had taken her hand saying how nice she looked and his eyes reflected that comment. Now, as she watched the world speed by from the taxicab window she said in her nicest manner, 'I am wearing the right sort of clothes for the dress circle, aren't I?'

His hand moved to cover hers in a reassuring pressure. 'You look very nice, lovely, the bee's knees as they say.'

'I hope you like revues,' she said tentatively. She hadn't asked him.

'Fine,' he said. 'Though usually I see the occasional play. But with no one to accompany me, it isn't the same. Maybe I can take you another time?'

He was implying that he would want to see her again and Geraldine's heart did a little skip. Tonight she must make certain to conduct herself with decorum so that he wouldn't be disappointed in her. And who knows where this would all end. To think that only a few weeks ago she'd only dreamed of being on his arm going to the theatre.

Mum was scrutinising her. 'So where was it yer went Saturday night with this new bloke of yours?'

All through Sunday Mum had been aching to know more about her evening, full of hope that her next eldest daughter might soon find a young man and in a year or so follow her sister down the aisle, although so far Geraldine had been able to parry her questions. But she couldn't go on evading her forever. Mum was persistent if nothing else.

'The Hippodrome,' she finally conceded over her breakfast on Monday.

'The one in Poplar?'

'The one in the West End.'

'Oh-h-h – posh!' Mum's mouth described a downward curve in a mixture of gentle derision and approval. 'Got money ter take yer up West End theatres 'as 'e? Wondered why you was all togged up Saturday. What's 'is name, this bloke? Do we know 'im?'

Geraldine picked up the bit of toast Mum had done her for breakfast before leaving for work. 'No, but if all goes well, I'll bring 'im to meet you.'

'Do it look like it might go well then?'

'I don't know. We've only been out the once.'

'Yer must know if yer like 'im. It don't take all that long ter know.'

'He was nice, acted like a gentleman. It's still early days yet, Mum.'

She took a slurp of tea, her need for the toast dwindling. All she wanted was to be out of the house and away from her inquisition. At this stage it wouldn't do to tell Mum too much and by the look in her eyes, she was already seeing this one as hopeful – a young man able to afford to take her daughter to a West End theatre, on their first date as well. It was usually a

69

walk in the park and a bob spent on fish and chips to round it off.

'Yer must 'ave some idea,' she furthered. Geraldine stood up sharply.

'I've got ter go. I'll be late fer work.'

They'd all gone before her except Evie, Dad and Wally having left very early, both in the same gang now and hopeful of being called on, and young Fred now a messenger boy for a newspaper in Fleet Street, proving himself to be a bright lad, needing to be the first one there in case he was wanted for an errand.

Evie didn't have to get in to the local co-op where she worked until half past eight so she was always last to leave. She now came leisurely down to the kitchen as Geraldine was making ready to leave.

Picking up a slice of toast Mum had spread with margarine, she began putting a scrape of jam on top while Mum poured the cup of tea.

'Had a good time Saturday night, all dressed up?'

'I ain't got time now,' evaded Geraldine and hurried off out the back door to retrieve her bicycle she'd earlier propped against the back wall, stepping over the white puddles of carbolic Mum had poured to cover the smell of Dad's nightly mistake. Yet again he hadn't managed to make it to the lavatory in the early hours.

As she wheeled her bike down the side alley to the road, Geraldine was elated. Tony – he'd asked her to call him Tony – had asked if he could see her again next Saturday.

'I enjoyed this evening,' he'd told her as the taxi drew up halfway down her street. Had her parents seen her getting out of it they'd have had a fit, thinking she'd been up to no good, or been taken ill, or something.

She and Tony had sat for a moment or two in the back while the driver stared prudently ahead but no doubt with ears cocked to what fruity things might be said, though he'd been doomed to disappointment, Tony merely saying that he hoped she too had enjoyed her evening, to which she had gushed that she hadn't had such a lovely time for ages.

'I'd like to take you out to dinner next Saturday,' he'd added, 'if you'd care to.'

Fearing to appear too eager, she'd nodded her consent and he'd said to meet him outside his shop at seven-thirty. Then to her complete surprise he had taken her hand and kissed it in a really gentlemanly way, saying that she'd best be off so as not to get on the wrong side of her father's humour. In fact he'd brought her home to the very minute that she'd said her father had asked her to be home. That was the kind of gentleman he'd proved to be.

Geraldine mounted her cycle and pushed away. On Saturday she would wear her best dress again with her lovely necklace and the earrings she'd felt she had to accept being as he had taken her out. But her thoughts were now more on what she must tell Alan.

She had told him that she'd see him this coming Saturday. Now she must break it to him that she couldn't see him after all. It wasn't a pleasant prospect. He was so nice and so honest and had been through such a rotten time in his marriage that he didn't deserve her putting him down on top of it all. Perhaps if she said she'd see him Friday instead, it would make things a bit easier, but it felt wrong even though theirs was only friendship.

Alan's eyes were trained on the middle distance. This last Friday evening in April had luckily turned warm and it was light still as he and Geraldine sat in Victoria Park.

He'd offered to take her to the pictures but she hadn't wanted to go. She still insisted on paying for herself and at first he had suspected that she didn't have the money this week. He'd told her he could afford it, but she wouldn't have it. It often worried him, her refusal to let him pay out for her. It spoke of a wish to keep him at arm's length and not to let their friendship grow into anything more. Now of course he knew the reason why.

It had taken her a while to get around to it but at least she had been honest in the end. He shouldn't feel down about it, for she had made it plain from the start that they were only friends.

He too had preferred it to be that way. He'd been done down badly by one woman and it had left its mark on him. The one person he'd expected to be his lifelong partner when he'd married her had thrown her marriage vows in his face. Every day he relived that moment when he'd caught her with that other fellow.

He could see it now, joyfully dropping his kitbag onto the floor of the tiny two-roomed flat he'd rented just before they'd got married and he'd had to go back to France. Two days after the Armistice he'd been shipped back to England. No time to tell her he was coming home, he'd let himself into the flat still with six months of French soil grimed into his uniform. He knew Madge was home because a thin shaft of light beamed from under the bedroom door as he gently closed the front door. He had called out that he was home, expecting her to come throwing herself into his arms with joyous relief that he'd returned all in one piece where so many thousands hadn't.

Instead, the four or five strides taking him across the living room to the bedroom door which he'd flung open in triumph had brought him upon a scene that haunted him still – Madge, stark naked, having come upright in bed, her blue eyes startled and as round as those of a china doll, her fair hair all unkempt, and beside her, his eyes almost as round as hers in stark terror, a naked man about his own age, face turned towards him but still with his body spreadeagled across hers, his buttocks the most prominent part of him. Alan knew at that moment that the man's penis still lay taut inside his wife as she shrieked with the shock of seeing the husband she thought to be miles away standing not three feet from her staring at them both.

In the twinkling of an eye the man was off the bed, covering his nakedness with part of the bed sheet while Madge had rolled off to end up crouched between it and the corner, as though the act of hiding herself would make some difference to what was happening.

He could still hear her voice, half defensive, half accusing. 'It ain't what yer think, Al. 'E made me do it. 'E forced 'imself on me. Honest!'

Speechless with shock he'd simply stared at her, the pounding in his chest like he was inside his own heart rather than the other way around. He could hear the man making strange gurgling noises as he tried to gather up his pants, his trousers with the braces flapping like pale dead tentacles, his shirt and collar falling out of his grasp as fast as he gathered them up, and all the time, Madge crouched by the bed sobbing, 'I didn't expect yer 'ome, Al. Fergive me, I didn't mean ter do noffink wrong, Al, it just 'appened.'

It was then he'd come to with a roar, throwing himself across the room, his forage cap flying from his head as he launched himself at the man who'd been trying to wrestle himself into one trouser leg.

The blighter hadn't stood an earthly chance as he pounded into his face in blind, white-hot fury. What he actually did he couldn't recall now except that there had been the taste of blood, not his, in his mouth, the man putting up no fight but merely squealing with each blow while from the corner the woman had let out shriek after shriek for him to stop before he killed him.

He remembered the room being suddenly full of people dragging him off a now felled body, of that body clambering to its feet still half-clad and staggering to the door, of seeing a face that resembled a piece of freshly chopped butcher's meat. He couldn't recall much after that. He couldn't remember speaking to Madge, but that after a while he was alone. He hadn't seen her since. He thought she'd gone off with the man whose name he now knew was Bert Copeland. Other than that he knew nothing about him nor wanted to. He'd seen someone about divorce and Madge apparently wouldn't contest it. He thought she and this Copeland were living together somewhere in Hoxton, apparently like man and wife.

That he would be granted a divorce there was no question. He had witnesses enough to the adultery, those in the other flats who'd broken up the fight seeing with their own eyes his wife naked, the man partly so, the bed rumpled from what they'd been up to while he'd been fighting in France. It had been the talk of the neighbourhood, he given all their sympathy that served only to heighten his shame of being cuckolded. It was the legal costs of a divorce that was doing for him. The ten or fifteen pounds he'd been quoted, even for an undefended divorce suit, was beyond him and because he was earning he'd receive no aid at all from a Poor Person's Committee.

He was still trying to get the necessary cash together, but by the way costs of living had escalated since the Armistice, he was making no headway and it looked like he'd be saving for years even though he'd given up the flat and gone back to his parents.

In all this time he hadn't so much as looked at another woman, all interest knocked out of him, even fearful of being done down again and thinking that it would be a long time before he would ever trust another woman. Then along had come Geraldine Glover after having parted company those years ago when they'd been youngsters together. He had even dared to raise his hopes, but now it looked like they were being knocked down all over again.

It was true she hadn't led him up the garden path, had all along given him to understand theirs was just friendship, but as the weeks went by he'd come to hope something more might develop, had even believed it would.

Damn all women, came the thought as he stared across the park, his gaze unfocused. She had sat here telling him about a young man she'd gone out with. She didn't say when, just that it was one day in the week, but he was sure her tale about having tea with her sister last Saturday had been an excuse.

She was saying she hoped they would still be friends and still see each other from time to time and hoped he understood. And what was he saying in reply? Yes, he understood.

Damn understood! What he understood was that he was in love with Geraldine. He wasn't ready for love yet and it was tearing his guts to pieces.

There was relief in her voice. 'So we can carry on being friends, can't we?' she was confirming yet again and he was replying, 'Yes, of course,' as with his heart bleeding he looked up at the darkening sky and said it was time to go before the park gates closed, and that he'd see her home.

# Chapter Six

The Great War as it was now being called had been over for a year. The previous Tuesday at exactly eleven o'clock the whole country had stopped whatever it was doing to stand in silence for two minutes to contemplate the millions of men that had perished in that bitter four and a half years of conflict.

Geraldine's family had been so lucky, no one at all in her family lost to that war, not even to the devastating Spanish flu that had raged for months and months afterwards killing thousands in its wake. Mum was the one to point out how lucky this family had been to escape both onslaughts.

'Just that one old aunt of mine, an' she was in 'er seventies, and me cousin what I never see, and one of 'er daughters about your age, Gel. All in all we've come through without a scratch. I know we ain't got much money wiv yer dad and Wally always in an' out of work at the docks, but none of our family was killed in the war, thank Gawd. So we 'ave bin lucky I should say. And now you've got yerself a nice young man.'

Of all of them Geraldine thought herself the luckiest. She'd finally brought Tony to meet them in July and except for Mavis who had sniffed perhaps in jealousy and said on the quiet that she saw him as a bit of a snob really, he had made a great impression on them all.

Evie had been all over him, her young body aflame with desire to find a bloke so handsome and well off.

He had got on well with young Fred discussing the merits of one newspaper publisher against the merits of another, a subject lately dear to Fred's heart, proud of the modest part he played in the newspaper offices of the *News Chronicle* in Fleet Street.

He often had long and pleasant conversations with Dad and Wally, sympathising with the need for dockers to receive more money for the hard and dangerous job they did and that they had to resort to striking. The three would discuss politics until the cows came home, all the strikes the country had suffered since the war, that working men who were only fighting for their rights to a better life were looked upon by the Government as merely pulling the country further down than it already was. Dad thought him the finest man he'd ever met.

As for Mum, she was idolising him, glowing under his polite treatment of her and the little bouquet or the box of Cadbury's chocolates he would bring her when he came to the house. In turn, Mum couldn't do enough for him, seeing her daughter making a splendid marriage for herself, hopefully in the not too distant future.

'Don't you do anythink silly ter spoil it, will yer?' she warned as though fearing it all to be too good to last. 'Don't go getting' on yer 'igh 'orse an' showing off in case he gives yer up.'

'Of course not, Mum,' she promised.

'That's a love,' said her mother, reassured and visualising a bright future for her daughter.

She hadn't yet boasted to the neighbours about it all – never count your chickens was her motto, having all her life been put down one way or another though she'd always come up smiling. But when the time came and that engagement ring sparkled on her daughter's finger, then she would crow from the rooftops and see them all go green with envy.

'Your Tony must 'ave pots of money stashed away somewhere,' she remarked once. 'Never seems short, do 'e? He can't make it just from making cheap jewellery. I bet 'is father gives him a bit. Solicitor, ain't 'e? From what I 'ear, them solicitors make thousands of pounds.'

It amazed Geraldine too how well off Tony always seemed to be. Last month he had even bought a car, a Bean, and she'd been so excited when he took her out in it for the first time, taking her down to Hastings by the sea. The only other time she had seen the sea she'd been eleven years old in 1912, taken by charabanc on a Sunday School outing to Southend.

She'd gasped in awe at the sight of the glowing, dark-green body and all that shining chrome, stunned by what it must have cost; had asked how he could have afforded it on what he made from his shop but he'd grinned and tapped the side of his nose, indicating for her not to ask. She assumed it to be perhaps a gift from his father, though why he wouldn't say was beyond her. Maybe he'd been too proud to say that he had accepted a present from his father. He'd mentioned at odd times that he wished to be totally independent of his family and let them see that he could stand on his own two feet.

It was true, though, money did seem no object to him. In the six months they'd been going out together he had bought her a nice summer coat, a pretty summer dress, and a skirt and blouse, saying he wanted to be proud of her at his side. In September he bought her a winter coat, again saying that the one she had was too shabby to be seen in with him. She knew she should have been grateful but couldn't help feeling that he didn't consider her to be good enough for him as she was. But the feeling had soon been shrugged off when on her birthday in October he'd given her a lovely sapphire and diamond pendant, gallantly telling her that even its beauty was no match for hers.

She was becoming sure that whatever she might ask for he would give her except that she wasn't of a grasping nature. But it did mystify her at times where all this money was coming from. It seemed, shabby though his little shop appeared to be on the outside, the making of cheap jewellery was more lucrative then she'd imagined.

'It has its hidden profits,' he had said a little sharply and she had thought it better not to make him angry with her questioning his income. That was his business. Even her mother never queried what Dad earned.

At the light tap on the back door Tony turned from his workbench to answer it. It was dark. The shop had been shut for a couple of hours now but he'd hung on down there, finishing off a cheap ring while waiting for his caller.

'Okay to come in?' queried the small, thin man

standing there and without a word Tony moved back to allow him entry, glancing out to briefly check the tiny, cluttered backyard before closing the door.

The man was roughly dressed, a dirty old cloth cap, a threadbare jacket, a collarless striped shirt and trousers that sagged despite a thick, greasy black leather belt holding them up. This was a man Tony had met in the trenches, Herbert Dempster by name, who had been a sergeant while he'd been a second lieutenant. Until he had taken a lump of shrapnel in the thigh and got sent to Paris to convalesce, they'd whiled away the pauses between gunfire and fruitless advances talking of Blighty and what they'd do when they finally got back home if spared. Tony had told of his need to escape his father's future for him and mentioned how he'd like to set up in a jewellery shop, having been interested in a hobby of making trinkets before the war. Herbert had said that he had no ambitions except to get rich quick but had no job to go back to, being a bit lazy, he'd explained without embarrassment.

Herbert's way of getting rich quick had been to become a burglar, and being thin and wiry he had made a success of it judging by the bulging sack he now swung from his shoulder onto the floor of the workroom.

He had become a regular visitor. The last Tony had seen of him had been as they parted company after a riotous celebration as Armistice was declared, and they had gone their separate ways maybe never to meet again. But last January Herbert had appeared at his door, as unkempt-looking as he was this evening, but then with a starved look in his eye.

'Sorry to bother you, chum,' he'd begun. 'But I found

out you was operatin' here and I thought you might be just the bloke to help me out with something.'

Tony had thought he'd come to beg, but he went on to explain that through lack of work, he'd taken to roaming around the back streets of the somewhat better parts of London – 'Wouldn't dream of tea-leafing off me own sort,' he'd explained – and tried his hand at breaking in through windows carelessly left off the latch. 'Got some good stuff here,' he'd said. 'Thought you might like to take a butcher's at it, do yourself some good.'

Intrigued, he had taken a butcher's and had felt his eyes light up at a range of small silver *objets d'art*, a quantity of necklaces and pendants and had seen how he could make money to keep his shop ticking over, a shop that in that short while was proving to be a white elephant with all the signs of his having to crawl back to his father admitting defeat.

It wasn't the money but the humiliation. His father, a hale and hearty but overbearing man giving out that deep-throated guffaw that had always brought him down as a child trying to do his best and failing in his father's eyes, would bellow, 'I knew you'd fall by the wayside. Always have.'

Here had been an opportunity to make good, at least to keep going and show his father he was made of stronger stuff after all.

Herbert had asked if he could take the stuff off his hands, pay him what he thought it was worth. 'You're the first one I thought of,' he said. 'I've only just started this lark and am a bit chary of trusting anyone I don't know. You don't have to, of course, but we could work

together, you and me – I find the stuff and you get rid
of it. Do us both a bit of good,' he'd added meaningfully.

He knew of the problems his old pal had with his
father from those quiet confidences in the trenches when
each man thought the day might be his last.

'Will there be any risk?' he'd asked.

'Why should there be?' had come the reply. 'You ain't
got ter pass it on or anything and leave yourself wide
open. You *make* jewellery, don't you? Get yourself a
small smelter, melt down the precious metal, use the
stones to make other things, and the gold and silver to
mount 'em with. Easy.'

And so it had become a regular thing. This summer
he had branched out, begun selling to the trade, or at
least that part of the trade that asked no questions.

Slowly he'd found one outlet, then another, and on
the way had found others coming to his door after dark,
furtive figures trying to make a living out of thieving,
accepting what he said was the going rate. He had put
his ear to the ground and found out what was usually
offered to these people and they'd very often leave with
disappointed faces at the small reward for all their efforts,
but in this business it was a buyer's market every time.
They did probably deal with others, but anywhere they
went it would be much the same, take it or leave it! He
never told Herbert about them. As far as Herbert was
aware, he was his only client. Nor did he tell Geraldine.
As far as she was aware, he was making a success of
his business and that was all she needed to know.

It had been a lovely Christmas and New Year, the ghost
of the Great War being slowly laid to rest and the new

decade promising a more happy future to look forward to. A totally modern era stretched ahead of them – the horse-drawn vehicle fast disappearing, people who could afford them taking to cars, all travel done by motorised vehicles. Aeroplanes no longer made people gaze up at them in awe. Airships carried the wealthy across the Atlantic to America and back. The first plane ever to fly across the Atlantic had done so in three stages and Alcock and Brown had flown one non-stop across it. Young women had dispensed with corsets altogether and were wearing the new brassiers, dresses were looser with hems creeping up to calf length and sometimes a fraction shorter. People were beginning to enjoy the Jazz Age and indeed Tony had already taken her to a dance where jazz musicians had been playing.

Geraldine felt lucky to be young in this part of the twentieth century. The only fly in the ointment was an endless round of strikes for better pay, wages unable to keep up with rising prices so that for a time, announced the Government, rationing had to be imposed.

But for her the future looked rosy. Tony spent Christmas with her people, seeming to quite enjoy the sort of Christmas East End families indulged in, and had bought gifts, a turkey, a huge box of chocolates for Mum, a large tin of tobacco for Dad who rolled his own cigarettes – 'No taste in them shop things,' Dad always said. He'd bought Fred a pair of roller skates, 'To get you around your errands faster and soon you'll be given promotion, you'll see.' For Wally there was a leather cigarette case and for Evie a pair of gloves. He was totally at ease as though this was his family and Geraldine felt a little sad for him that he had no interest in going to visit his own. He did not speak about it and she wondered how deep the rift had been. One day maybe he would tell her.

He'd got nothing for Mavis, she living in her own home and hardly around when he called on Geraldine, so he didn't really know her. He said how awkward he felt but Mum told him not to be silly and anyway, when Mavis came for Christmas dinner she hardly acknowledged him, still seeing him as a jumped-up snob who'd have her sister in tears when he finally got fed up slumming it.

Geraldine couldn't help smiling, remembering when she had felt jealous of Mavis getting married and there seemed no likelihood of herself ever finding the man of her dreams. Now she'd found one and to prove it, on New Year's Eve he quietly asked Dad for her hand in marriage; that given, he proposed to her on the stroke of twelve, to everyone's delight going down on one knee for it.

'Fancy,' crowed Mum, while all the aunts applauded and came forward to hug her while the men came to shake Tony's hand, Evie giving him a huge, lingering kiss on the cheek, though Mavis for her part looked at the ceiling with a sour expression now that her doleful prediction of his going off into the blue seemed not to be coming true.

The following Saturday afternoon he had closed his shop and had taken her up the big jewellers in Bond Street to buy the ring.

She now flashed the half hoop of magnificent diamonds in front of Mavis, seeing envy reflected in those light-brown eyes. It would teach Mavis to snub her fiancé the way she had over Christmas and the New Year. Tony had done nothing to her, in fact had been polite and generous to all the family and could be excused for not having given her anything, the way she had treated him from the very start. If she was jealous, then let her really be jealous, Geraldine thought, trying hard not to be vindictive. The rest of them were well pleased, Mum especially.

'I'm so glad for yer,' she said. 'But once you two are married, yer won't look down yer nose at us, will yer?'

'Look down me nose?' echoed Geraldine in amazement. 'Why should I do that? We're hardly likely to be landed gentry, are we?'

'I just thought,' mused her mother. 'I mean, yer beginning ter talk posh, like yer was ashamed of bein' what you are.'

She hadn't really noticed. It had sort of crept up on her. Maybe it was Tony's influence. She remembered a time, only last year, when she'd made a conscious effort to improve her speech on first meeting him. Now it seemed to come naturally to her. Even friends at work sometimes pulled faces when she spoke so that she found herself making the same conscious effort to speak as she once had when with them. It wasn't difficult to revert, but just as easy to speak as she was now doing.

'Don't be silly, Mum,' she said, trying to modify her speech. 'I ain't trying ter be posh. I really ain't.'

'Well, so long as it don't go to yer 'ead, all this money yer marryin' into.'

'He ain't that well off,' she said.

With a grunt and a shiver from the freezing cold of the backyard, Jack Glover got gratefully back between the warm covers. It was three-thirty in the morning and he'd already been out to do a pee around one o'clock, his rest disturbed yet again. He'd gone to bed around ten-thirty, delaying his visit to the lav until the last minute and he would willingly bet his last farthing that he'd be woken up again around five by a bladder that felt it was bursting, to stumble downstairs and into the yard, hoping to make it in time to the lav itself, only to end up doing a dribble. It drove him mad. It spoiled his sleep and by the time he got up for work at seven he felt as if he'd hardly slept a wink all night.

Hilda came half awake, her rest broken by him getting back into bed.

'Sorry, love,' he whispered.

That brought her more awake and she turned restlessly towards him, protesting at being disturbed. ''Ow many times yer been?'

'A couple. An' its bloody freezin' out there.'

'If it goes on like this you'll 'ave ter start usin' the po.'

'Yer don't like me usin' one.'

'Well, I must admit it do stink the room out by mornin'. Ain't like it's little girl's water. But sooner that than you catchin' yer death of cold out there, you're going to 'ave ter use it. But I ain't 'appy about it.' She fidgeted with the bedclothes around her chin. 'It's gettin' worse, that bladder of yours. Worse than it was last winter. You'll 'ave ter try makin' it to the lav in time.'

'I managed it this time. But when I pulled the chain and come out, a light come on next door. They must of 'eard me pull the chain.'

'They know yer. They don't mind.'

'Well, I do.'

'I don't care if you do, Jack,' she groaned drowsily.

'Yer would if you was me,' he shot at her.

Hilda sighed. 'Time summer comes round yer'll 'ave to try an' make it to the lav, *and* pull the chain. I can't 'ave the smell all through next summer like last year – goin' out there dowsing it down with carbolic every mornin', people thinking we're dirty. But even carbolic's better than the smell you create sometimes. An' I won't 'ave yer not pulling the chain, don't matter what the neighbours think. That pan's stained as it is without you addin' to it with yer wee lying in it fer hours. I scrub that pan day in, day out, and it's still stained. You'll just 'ave ter learn ter pull it when yer go in the night.'

'I ain't 'aving every bloody neighbour knowing I've got an affliction.' He had sat up, his voice grown louder. Retaliating in no uncertain terms, Hilda sat up too, irritated by his sudden show of belligerence.

'Yer lettin' 'em all know now, though. Why don't yer shout out a bit louder, Jack? People across the road can't 'ear!'

He lowered his tone instantly, his voice adopting a note of pleading. 'I can't 'elp this, gel. Wish I could. 'Ow d'yer think I feel, dripping like a bloody tap, all me mates laughin' at me if I'm not careful. I'm ashamed, gel, I am.'

She too lowered her voice, immediately sympathetic. 'I know. But if it goes on much longer, you're goin' to 'ave to speak to the doctor. Yer've 'ad this trouble over a year now. You'll 'ave ter see a doctor about it.'

'I know what that'll mean. Me sent to orspital. I can't

afford time off work goin' to orspitals. What if they kept me in?'

'They won't keep you in,' sighed Hilda, snuggling down under the covers again. It was cold sitting up. 'More likely the doctor'll give yer some medicine to stop it. We can't go on like this. You're going to 'ave to see 'im.'

With that she turned over, away from him, obliging him to lie down and seek some sleep before it was time to get up and go to work. At the moment he was fortunate enough to be working, him and Wally together. At the moment they were bringing in money and perhaps if she put a little aside out of her housekeeping, she herself going without a few things, there'd be a bit of savings if Jack did go into hospital, though she didn't reckon it that serious to warrant it.

She lay on her side, eyes wide open as she thought about it. There was the Hospital Savings Club, contributions of just a few pence a week which sometimes she begrudged paying when Jack was out of work – that might help provide a little towards it if need be. National Insurance certainly wouldn't provide much. To her mind Lloyd George was quick to take from the working man but slow to hand out when it was needed and a few pence at that – an old Welsh thief was what she referred to their Prime Minister as being.

Her biggest worry was that if Jack had to be off work for any length of time it wouldn't be easy to get back. That's how it was in the docks, a hard life for sick people. You only had to look at the lines of ex-servicemen trudging along the gutters with their harmonicas, their off-key voices, their pleading eyes and their placards, forgotten heroes, living on pennies from passers-by.

She heard Jack begin to snore gently. Soon it would develop enough to raise the ceiling and she'd better find some sleep before it began keeping her awake for what was left of the night. She'd worry about it all tomorrow – not half as bad in broad daylight. Perhaps this trouble Jack had wasn't as serious as the nights made it seem. There was, though, one thing about his affliction for which she was thankful – he no longer claimed his marital rights for fear of disgracing himself. Humiliating for any man. But she was forty-seven and had just about had enough of that lark. Since young Fred was born, she'd had two miscarriages and one stillborn. Had she gone on like that she might not have seen many more years, that's how constant childbearing could drain a woman, but it wasn't easy to explain this to a man.

Fortunately, and she did feel fortunate if sorry for Jack, he being as he was avoided the unpleasantness of telling him she didn't want him pulling her about any longer, that she was past that sort of thing. Under normal circumstance he wouldn't be past it, certain he could go on enjoying it until they carried him out of the house feet first. She was sorry for his trouble but she could now put her hands together. Many women in their forties couldn't, still in the throes of adding to their families.

In his sleep Jack gave a loud snort, held his breath for a second then let it out in a throaty rumble that had Hilda closing her eyes in an effort to fall off to sleep.

# Chapter Seven

It was Monday evening and Hilda and her daughter sat alone in the back room. Jack had gone to bed early as he often did these days, having emptied out before retiring, needing to get as much sleep in as he could before being obliged to get up for another visit. Wally and Fred were out. Evie would be due home in half an hour from a friend's house down the road. It was an ideal time to unburden herself on to Geraldine.

She glanced at her daughter who had settled herself in her father's chair to read the *Evening Standard* he'd put aside to go to bed.

Geraldine was the only person handy whom she felt she could turn to. She'd kept her worries bottled up for so long she felt she might soon explode. There were people she could have confided in. There were her sisters, Lizzie and Daisy, but they might only pop in once a fortnight, maybe not even that often. They didn't live all that far away, Lizzie in Arbery Road and Daisy in Antill Road, but they had their own families. She could have gone round to them but she too had a family to look after.

It was nice when they met, but they weren't here this evening and Geraldine was.

Mavis came Thursday mornings, had a sandwich and left mid-afternoon to go home and cook Tom's tea for when he came home from work. She had no babies yet to take up her time, her first due sometime in June. She'd visit Mavis on Tuesdays, tomorrow in fact, but things had built up so much inside her that being as Geraldine wasn't out this Monday evening she felt she had to confide in her or go potty with worry about Jack. It had been building up all day since Jack had almost not gone to the docks, ashamed of his condition, and she couldn't keep it inside herself any longer.

Biting her lip, she let the stocking she was wearily darning after the usual Monday washday fall idle in her lap. The washing now hung on several lines strung across the kitchen, the weather being too damp for it to hang outside. On Wednesday it would be ready for ironing and then airing on a clothes horse around the old kitchen range, that in this weather was lit although they had the gas stove for cooking. By the time Mavis came on Thursday it would all be folded away out of sight and the house nice and tidy for her.

'I've been ever so worried about your dad lately, Gel,' she began and saw Geraldine look up at her as though in surprise. 'It's 'is waterworks,' she hurried on.

Geraldine gave a shrug and a smile. 'We're used to him.'

'I know, love. It's not that what worries me, it's that it's getting worse and I really am worried about 'im. I said 'e can't go on like this and should see the doctor but yer dad thinks they'll send 'im to 'ospital and he'll be kept in and lose time off work. We can't afford that, Gel, not if it went into weeks. I keep wondering what yer dad's got wrong with 'im. It's gone on so long, it can't be just a matter of being given a few tablets ter clear it up.'

Geraldine put the newspaper down, aware something was seriously wrong. 'You've got to get him to see the doctor.'

'You try makin' your dad do anythink 'e don't want to do.'

'Then you've got to put your foot down, Mum. If it's not getting any better there must be something badly wrong. You're going to have to, don't matter what he says.'

Her mother sighed and went back to her darning. It'd take some doing getting Dad to do what was needed, but Geraldine was right.

'I bloody told yer, didn't I?'

Jack burst into the kitchen, flinging his cap down onto a chair, following it with his jacket and checkered cloth choker.

'Bloody doctor! "I'm sending you to hospital, Mr Glover. Get them to 'ave a look at you. I think you might 'ave some trouble with your prostrate gland." That's what 'e told me, all bloody clever-like. "And that'll be two and sixpence!" So I've just 'anded 'im 'alf a crown what I've worked me bloody guts out for, just ter be told 'e's sendin' me to bloody orspital. What time've I got ter go ter bloody orspitals?'

Hilda looked up from her Wednesday ironing on the kitchen table, an old blanket and sheet yellowed from much use of the iron being spread across its surface.

'You are going?'

'I bloody ain't!'

He strode over to the mantleshelf above the kitchen range and picked up a taper. Lighting it from the fire that was helping to air what had already been ironed and generally keep the place warm against a cold, wet April, he held the taper to a hand-rolled cigarette he'd extracted from several in a tin box.

'I told 'im what ter do wiv 'is bloody orspitals. I asked 'im if he was ready ter pay fer me bein' out of work, and per'aps all fer nothink. He told me I could be very ill if I didn't take 'is bloody advice. Well, I'd sooner be ill than lose me work.'

Hilda put the iron back on its trivet in front of the range to warm up again, doing it with a sharp, angry thump. 'Yer will lose work if yer fall ill, won't yer? And yer might not be well enough ter go back ever if yer get seriously ill because yer wouldn't take the doctor's advice. Yer might even lose yer job. And all because yer won't see sense.'

He was unmoved. 'And where's the money comin' from ter pay the orspital fees then? Tell me that, Mrs bloody Know-All.'

She was really angry now. It had taken her all this time to get him even to go to the doctor, and now this.

'You're the only know-all round 'ere. I tell yer this, Jack, if you fall really ill because you ain't got the sense to at least 'ave yerself looked at proper, I ain't goin' ter struggle on nothink to try and feed this family. I'll go to one of me sisters, or me brother, and stay there and you can fend for yerself. What if yer died 'cos yer didn't take medical advice? What if yer've got somethink what could kill yer and you not knowing, but what could have been cured if yer took notice? I tell yer, Jack, you go and see an 'ospital or I won't be responsible for yer.'

With that she grabbed up the now heated iron, fingers protected from the handle by a thick wad of cloth, and began swishing the thing back and forth across the pillow-case she was smoothing, in her anger her elbow going like a piston rod.

Jack watched her for a moment, belligerence fading. When he spoke again his voice was dreary and defeated. 'Yer don't understand, ole girl. There's lots of unrest in the docks over pay. There's talk of goin' on strike. If that 'appens it could be weeks with no money comin' in. I can't afford ter be off from work just at the moment.'

The threat was enough to make her stop ironing and look at him as he continued, 'Things could get bad. Prices are risin' and pay ain't keepin' up with 'em. Everyone's struggling. This land they promised ter be fit fer heroes ain't what they said it'd be. There's unrest in the mines too. We're 'eading fer trouble all round and it ain't a time ter go worryin' about meself.'

It was another month before she could tell anyone about him, bottling it up inside her until it felt she might burst. Finally she told Geraldine, once again being the nearest person handy. Her daughter listened with concern but there was no advice she could offer, saying that what Dad said was true and he knew best about himself and his situation.

Now it was Geraldine's turn to fret and worry. Maybe Mum had thought of her as being unsympathetic but what could she do? She could hardly go to Dad and demand he do something about himself. Now she was the one bottling it up. It wasn't the sort of thing you talked about. 'Trouble with his waterworks' to people asking what was wrong if he did go to hospital would provoke an instant grin, striking the enquirer as funny. People would naturally want to know what was wrong with him. That meant lies and evasions. Better keep it to herself, but like her mother she'd become worried sick about him.

Finally she told Tony, it coming out by accident. That Saturday in May was wet and for something to do they'd gone to a lovely restaurant, going there in his car. The meal over, coffee and brandy having arrived, they were talking of the numbers out of work which promoted a comment from her on her own father's plight, how his sort of work was always so erratic and how if he did have to go into hospital her mother didn't know how they would manage. Immediately after it came out she wanted to bite her tongue off as he asked what was wrong with her father. She couldn't bring herself to lie to him and told the truth but he didn't laugh or even grin. He shook his head sadly, not lifting his eyes from the brandy glass he was toying with.

'It's unfair that a man must be afraid of losing his job because his health is in jeopardy. This country is so ungrateful. We were all led to believe we'd return to a better country after beating the Hun. Instead it seems the world has been turned topsy-turvy. I wish I could help your father.'

She tilted her head in silent agreement to the sad inevitability of what he'd been saying, and for a while they sat on without speaking, each taking sips of their brandy to help fill the hiatus.

He looked up suddenly. 'Geraldine, I do have the means to help your father over this difficult period so that if he is told he must go into hospital, he can do so without any worries.'

She looked at him aghast. What he was referring to was money. She hadn't meant for him to offer money and squirmed in embarrassment at having virtually brought the subject up. 'Tony, I was never asking you for—'

'I know that. This is my own idea. I'd like to help. After all, I intend to marry you. He'll be my father-in-law eventually. Who else better to help?'

She remained feeling awkward. They'd spoken of an autumn wedding and Tony had already taken it that he would pay for it all – a fact that had immediately annoyed her father when told. 'Who do 'e think 'e is? If I can't afford ter sort out me own daughter's weddin', what sort of man am I? I ain't 'aving us looked down on like we was paupers, someone else offerin' ter pay and slinging their money about like they was better'n us.'

Tony had gone very quiet when she told him her father's sentiments, though not in those exact words of course – she knew better than that. Even so, he was upset.

'I want my future wife to have the wedding she deserves, several wedding cars, a decent reception, plenty of high-class food, a big three-tiered bridal cake, a lovely bridal gown, all the trimmings. Why should you have to put up with second best to please your father, with him having to scrape the bottom of the barrel to pay for it when I can afford better for you? I don't want to be disrespectful to him but it is our wedding. You're going to be my wife. I ought to have a say in it.'

From then on there'd been friction between him and her family which struck her as very unfair being that all Tony had been trying to do was his best by her. Now having unintentionally let slip her father's present state of health, it seemed he'd seen a way to heal the wound, but offering to pay for Dad to stay in hospital if it came to that was only rubbing salt into it, or worse, opening the cut even more, knowing how Dad felt about being helped out by someone else. Being made to eat humble pie, as he'd see it.

'I don't think you should say anything to him,' she said hastily. 'For one thing he'll know I've been blabbing about him and it's something he'd rather people didn't know about. Understandable when you come to think of it – a sort of delicate subject. For another, it'll give his pride a knock having someone assume he's too hard up for money to take care of himself, and us. That's how he'll see it.'

After a while, Tony shrugged although rather reluctantly, and she was glad that he didn't return to the subject again. Had he done so it would have put her back up and maybe started an argument.

Whereas their engagement in January should have made her utterly certain of him, she was growing anxious of it all falling apart. He seemed to sense it and did all he could to avoid any cross words that might cause that to happen. She sometimes wondered if he wasn't as terrified as she of their breaking up – they being from different backgrounds, the slightest jolt might so easily cause it to happen. It made them both edgy and she could hardly wait for autumn when they would be husband and wife with no more need to fear such things.

Geraldine had no idea if their courting was the same

as other couples. She only had Mavis and even then felt embarrassed when asking her what she and Tom got up to in those days.

'What yer mean, *did anything*?'

'Well, you know, getting lovey-dovey. What did you do?'

'Kissed and cuddled, I suppose. What do you want ter know for?'

'It's just that, well, me and Tony kiss and cuddle, but we don't . . . Did you go any further?'

'That's none of your business.'

'I just . . . need to know. So I know what me and Tony do is what courting couples usually do.'

Mavis had eyed her with suspicious alarm. 'You two ain't been up ter tricks, 'ave yer? You ain't got yerself in trouble?'

'No, of course not!' She'd become angry. 'What d'you take me for?'

'Because if you 'ave—'

'I ain't! Because I've never 'ad the chance.' In anger and confusion she'd lapsed back into her old speech. 'We don't do enough fer that sort of thing to 'appen to me.'

For a second Mavis had looked pityingly at her. 'You mean he ain't never tried it on?' she said in a way that intimated Tony couldn't truly be in love with her. 'Don't he ever get all worked up an' trembly when he's wiv yer?'

He had tried it on, as Mavis put it, last summer a month or two after they'd started going out together. They'd been strolling in Hyde Park on a cool evening, having listened with a good audience to music being played by soldiers of a Guards regiment in the bandstand. They'd finally come away as the band finished and the audience dispersed and sought a more secluded place as all lovers do.

After the music all had been quiet. The soft shadows of that summer night had spread themselves across the park to enfold leafy copses in darkness. It was to one of these that Anthony had led her, the two of them sinking down onto a small, dry, grassy patch well hidden from any passer-by and filled with the warm dank breath of last year's undergrowth. He'd gently kissed her and as she returned his kisses, something inside her responded in a way she didn't understand and which frightened her a little. He began to tremble and it occurred to her that he might be taking ill, the evening not so cool as to make him shiver. Then his kiss hardened against her lips as he began to ease her back until she was lying beneath him. Thinking about the damp from the grass penetrating her blouse, she became aware that his hand was cupping her breast, the other easing her skirt up above her knees.

Alarm had driven away the strange sensation inside her and she tried to push him away but his body had been so heavy on hers that it refused to move at first. Her hands on his shoulders, she had beat at him in mounting panic, consumed with suspicion that all he'd wanted her for was for *that sort of thing*. She'd been enraged too, seeing herself taken for a girl of easy virtue and it had made her feel sick knowing how she had so fallen in love with him, had felt so happy being chosen by him.

Disappointment in him had churned even though he lifted himself off her, his hand leaving her breast as though it had become searing hot to the touch, he rolling away from her as she burst into tears of humiliation.

He'd apologised abjectly, asking her not to cry, had pleaded forgiveness as profusely as a burglar caught red-handed, had promised never to do such a thing again if she didn't wish. Nor had he.

Her respect for him had slowly rebuilt itself but lately she had begun to wonder if the reason for such self-control didn't spring from a cooling towards her, for all he professed to love her and wanted her to be his wife. You can't have it both ways, common sense told her, but it didn't help diminish the feeling that, engagement or no, he could be tiring of her.

'You do love me, don't you?' she asked as they left the restaurant.

His response was to guide her hurriedly to his car and having helped her in, run round to his side, slip into the seat to put an arm around her, pulling her to him. His kiss was ardent and lingering, without concern of anyone who, in passing, might see them.

'Does that answer your question, my dearest?' he asked gruffly, but she couldn't reply and in the dim light of a nearby gas lamp saw him frown.

'What must I do to make you believe how much I love you?' he asked. 'I've done my level best all these months to respect your wishes, refrain from doing what should be a natural thing between a couple in love. It's killing me, Geraldine, but you don't seem to understand I love you and I want you. How do you think I feel? You won't let me show you how much I do. Why? It almost makes me think it's you who doesn't love me and wants to back out of your promise.'

'No!' She clung to him. 'I do love you, my dearest. But if I let you do what you say is natural to people in love, you'll begin to think I'm not the sort of girl a man can respect.'

'I'd never think that,' he said. 'Never.'

She remained silent, head down, but detecting relief in his tone, she peeped at him from beneath the brim of her hat that all but covered her eyebrows, a lovely hat he himself had bought for her from Dickins & Jones in Regent Street. That he was always buying her presents, however, did not mean that he was sincere. Hastily she brushed away the cruel thought. He did love her, else he wouldn't have abstained all this time from overstepping himself.

'It's still wrong,' she said finally. 'Before marriage.'

'It's not.' And when again she didn't reply, he held her even closer, his voice a whisper in her ear. 'It will never stop me loving you, longing for you. I shall love you, Geraldine, until the day I die. It doesn't take a marriage to tell you that.'

And she wanted him too. Now she wanted him to, more than anything else in the world. She realised she'd lowered her head in the briefest of nods and, sitting very quietly, was aware of feeling an unusual breathlessness, of a heavy, steady pulsing somewhere below her heart as he took his arm away to tug on the starter button, coaxing the engine into life, and she knew then that she would let him take her back to his darkened shop and that when he kissed her goodnight she would be someone no longer virginal.

# Chapter Eight

Life for the Glover family had taken a moderate turn for the better. Mavis had had her baby, a bonny, eight-pound boy whom she christened Simon Thomas in their local church a month later. Fred was given a small rise in wage by the *News Chronicle* and according to his dad, didn't know where his arse was now, seeing himself one day as a full-blown sub-editor. Wally had found himself a girl and was going steady with her, and Evie, settled down to her job and ceasing to complain about it, was learning to tango, going with friends to every dance she could, wearing the shorter fashions; Geraldine made her dresses to save money, her hair bobbed and lips rouged, though not when Dad was around, who would have told her to 'Wipe it orf, yer look like a trollop!' – the totally emancipated young woman. 'Well before her time,' said Mum, though not too severely.

The only member of the family not to be looking up was Dad. His condition was steadily worsening and still he refused to go back to the doctor even though his gloomy prediction of strikes and being laid off hadn't materialised that summer.

Geraldine again confided in Tony knowing there was little anyone could do to help or advise her stubborn, proud father. But it did help release the tension she felt – those moments visualising her father no longer around.

Their wedding day was fast approaching and Tony thought long and hard about Jack Glover. The man didn't like him as first he had and it plagued him. If he could get him to accept his help to get better, Geraldine would be so happy. The only one who might persuade him to see sense would be the man's wife.

Against all odds Tony was determined to help the father of his fiancée. Besides, he'd recently had a bit of luck, a back door caller furtively displaying 'Somefink I just come by, guv.' Of course, no questions were asked and it proved to be a handful of jewellery no doubt *come by* from some loaded residence in the West End area. He'd found himself a good contact and had made a good bit out of the deal. It was easy money and if he couldn't help his own fiancée's family with part of it, who else could he help?

Feeling generous, he popped into No.27 for a social chat and an afternoon cup of tea with his future mother-in-law, this without Geraldine's knowledge; she was at work, no doubt her mind full of her wedding-day plans with only seven weeks to go.

He'd already paid for her dress to be made for her, a luxurious white creation in the shorter fashion but with a long veil, all enough to knock any other wedding in the area into a cocked hat, as they say. Her mother hadn't been too pleased when Geraldine had described it to her.

'They'll say yer showin' off,' was her emphatic comment. 'We ain't used ter society-like weddings round 'ere. You'll show yerself up proper.'

Geraldine was so excited she'd taken no notice. 'It's my wedding,' she'd said to him and he had agreed. But whatever thoughts her mother had on the wedding, she was still nice to him.

She was nice to him now as she let him in. Showing him into her best front room she set about making a cup of tea for him using her best china tea set, one or two rims of which he noticed bore tiny, age-darkened chips and made a mental note to buy her a fine, bone china tea set for Christmas.

'Nice of you ter call in,' she said, sipping too fast. 'Nice, you makin' yerself sociable like this.' As if it were royalty who'd condescended to visit.

'How's Geraldine's father keeping these days?' he ventured casually, setting down his empty cup and saucer on the somewhat scratched side table next to the armchair she had asked him to sit down in.

She'd chosen a hard seat, perhaps not wanting to get too comfortable in front of her daughter's well-to-do husband-to-be. Had Geraldine been there the woman might have been more relaxed and natural. The trouble was, with him sunk into this well-used, sagging seat and she on a hard chair, it brought her head just a fraction above his, putting him at a disadvantage. He moved forward onto the firmer edge of the armchair so that his face was now more or less level with hers. 'She tells me he's been rather poorly all summer,' he went on.

'She did, did she?' Mrs Glover's voice went on the defensive, guarded and annoyed. 'She's got no right ter discuss 'er dad's problems with . . .' She paused and he had the distinct feeling she'd been about to say strangers.

'It's because she's deeply worried about him. She was bound to tell me as her future husband.' Best to make that point.

'I suppose so,' she conceded. 'Even so . . .' and again she tailed off.

Now perhaps was the time to lay his cards on the table. Tony leaned forward in his seat, adopting a confidential attitude. 'I do understand. My own father had the same affliction but he's fine now. Completely recovered. Of course, he did have the money to be able to put himself into the hands of a Harley Street specialist, but you see I've money as well and if I can't put it to decent use, like helping Geraldine's father get better, I wouldn't be much of a man, would I?'

He had expected her to capitulate, to gnaw at her lip in indecision and to finally nod her head. To his astonishment she did nothing of the kind.

Her back became straight, bringing her head above his again, her face grown stiff. Seconds later she was telling him his fortune in no uncertain terms, that no matter what else he thought they had never stooped to borrowing from anyone in all their lives and didn't propose to start now. His protests that this wouldn't be a loan fell on deaf ears as she stood up, the proud matriarch in worn, old-fashioned skirt and blouse – her apron had been hastily discarded when he'd appeared at her door – and work-reddened hands.

Even as he came away thwarted, he had to admire the

woman's dignity, her refusal to be diminished by poverty or enticed by promises of money. He could see Geraldine in every inch of her mother. Pride without arrogance, determination without forcefulness, a quiet optimism in the face of adversity. He was so lucky to have found Geraldine. She might come from a slum area but she had the capacity to better herself and he not only admired her for that, he adored her. If only her family liked him better.

Even so, he was annoyed, hurt. How dare they treat him as if he were some interloper poking his nose into where it wasn't wanted.

'It's the last thing I'll ever try to do for your family,' he told Geraldine, and she got angry too.

'No one asked you to do it. I told you in confidence. I didn't expect you to go blabbing to Mum.'

'I wanted to help.'

'Well, you haven't, and you've made me look a fool too. What if she tells me dad about you going to see her? I won't be able ter look 'im in the eye.' In her anger she reverted in part to the way she usually spoke and he cringed inwardly, noticing it. 'I just 'ope she don't tell 'im, that's all.'

'I don't think she will,' he replied slowly and was gratified to see her temper abate. It served to moderate his temper as well, his tone becoming soothing. 'I know I was a fool. I promise not to interfere again.'

He saw her face go through several changes: understanding, sympathy, mollification, finally breaking down altogether as she moved nearer to him to end up in his arms, saying that she loved him for his kind intentions however misguided. 'You've got a lot to learn about people like us,' she whispered, and as he held her tightly to him the thought went through his head, Not if I can help it.

Soon he'd be taking her away from all that. If he had anything to do with it, she would have a life free from money worries, have all she wanted, be spoiled for choice in dresses and hats and shoes. All he had to do was keep from her the callers at his back door. What the shop itself earned him was peanuts to what he could make in other ways, and he intended Geraldine to have the cream.

Geraldine faced her mother unflinchingly as the words were spat at her.

'If your father was ter know what that fiancy of yours offered ter do for 'im in that patronisin' way of 'is, he'd 'ave a fit. I don't want 'im comin' 'ere any more wiv 'is money and 'is fine ideas.'

'He didn't mean to upset you, Mum.' At last she got a word in. 'He wasn't being patronising. He was only trying to help. Maybe he made a bit of a mess of it, but you can't condemn him for that.'

'I don't care what he thinks.'

Her mother had her back to her, was scrubbing furiously at one of Dad's sweat-stained collars before putting it in the copper with the rest of the Monday wash to be boiled, all her overwrought energy going on scrubbing. 'I felt that embarrassed I could of sunk into the floor. And what was yer doing tellin' a stranger about yer dad's illness? It's none of 'is business.'

'He's going to be my husband in six weeks, Mum. He'll soon be one of the family.'

'Over my dead body!' came the retort, Mum's back still turned to her.

If they hadn't before, Geraldine's hackles rose like the spines on those little sticklebacks she once fished for in the canal in Victoria Park as a child.

'What's that supposed to mean?'

'It means I don't want 'im ever coming 'ere again acting as if we ain't got two brass farthings to rub tergether, thinking 'imself too good fer us. No matter what Mr 'Igh'n'Mighty thinks, we ain't beggars. We pay our way. It might take a bit longer than others but we get there in the end – we 'ave to. Because we can't put our 'ands in our pockets straight away don't mean we 'ave to take 'umble pie from the likes of 'im.'

'He didn't mean it that way,' cried Geraldine, beside herself at her mother's unexpected venom.

'Well, I don't want 'im 'ere, acting as if we can't even pay our own rent or our own dues. We ain't never been be'olding to no one, so there!'

'It isn't like that,' she protested, but her mother rounded on her, hands wet, reddened from the soda she'd put in the water to soften it.

'*It isn't like that!*' The tone mimicked her better accent. 'All this posh talk. Why can't you talk like you used to? Drivin' you away from us, that's what 'e's doing. You'll soon be too good for us. Fine then, 'e can take yer places yer've never been to before, show yer a good time, make yer think yer someone you ain't. And when yer married to 'im – if yer marry 'im—'

'What're you talking about?' challenged Geraldine. '*If* I marry him?'

Her mother continued straight on, ignoring it. 'Yer won't want to come round 'ere ter see us. We won't be good enough for yer then, like we ain't good enough fer 'im now.'

'What did you mean, Mum?' she challenged again, '*If* I marry him? What about the wedding?'

Her mother gave a smirk. 'Are yer sure yer want us to your weddin'? Might we not be good enough?'

'It's being held here, Mum, in the church hall.'

'Yes, the church 'all, not 'ere in the house like your sister's was, where it should be – at 'ome. No, it 'as ter be in an 'all, proper posh. What d'yer think people will say? "Look at 'er," they'll say. And me in me cheap frock goin' to a wedding like that.'

Geraldine had begged her to let her buy her something better, Tony having given her money for extras. Mum had guessed that and up had gone her back. 'I'll pay me own way,' she'd said mildly, at that time not yet having reached the stage she was at now since Tony's offer to help Dad.

'In fact I wonder if yer really want us at yer wedding,' she added now. 'If yer do get married to 'im, it might be that we might not be there and yer could change yer mind about goin' through with it – makin' enemies of yer own family so ter speak.'

Fear gripped at Geraldine. 'Of course I want you, Mum. I want you all. What would I do without any of you there? I'll always want you.'

Her entreaty was thrust aside with a wet hand and the voice became saddened. 'That's what you say now, Gel. But you wait. You'll see. It's your choice, this weddin' of yours.'

'That's blackmail, Mum. You can't do things like that.' She waited but was met by silence, her mother apparently engrossed with her washing.

When she spoke again her voice was small and pleading. 'All he did was offer to help Dad get good hospital treatment if it came to that. His heart was in the right place, Mum. He only wanted to help because he could afford it.'

'And we can't.'

'Isn't that what you've been worrying yourself nearly into the grave about all this time? I just don't want you to have any more worries.'

Her mother turned to her, and the look Geraldine saw on her face took her breath away. It was a smirk, pure intentional derision.

'An' you can do that, can you?' she said with deliberate slowness. 'Yer can prevent your father being laid off because 'e 'as ter go into 'ospital and can't work, no money coming into the 'ouse? Not all your precious Tony's money can stop that 'appening. How long will your precious Tony be 'appy ter pay our rent and our food and all our other outgoings what can't be covered by what Fred and Wally and Evie can bring in until yer dad gets a job again – if ever 'e does, 'im being off work all that time being in 'ospital? You tell me that, miss! Men 'ave been laid off for less than that, what 'ave accidents through no fault of theirs but the docks' workin' conditions, and not a penny given to 'elp 'em but what their mates 'ave collected for 'em. An' that don't last five minutes with mouths ter feed. Tell me, is your Tony ready ter support us all the time yer dad's out of work?'

'That's unfair, Mum,' Geraldine blurted.

There seemed nothing she could do to persuade her, even less her father to see Tony in a better light. They were against his wealth and that was that. Nothing would change their attitude. In fact it seemed Dad would rather be an invalid, would rather die than accept help from someone like Tony. The people of the East End were a proud lot, a resilient lot, this she had to admit. They might steal, cheat, fiddle, but offer them a handout and it was like death to them. She came away wishing to God that she had never tried to tackle Mum.

'Why is he always at your parents' house?'

Alan Presley had been there all this Sunday evening, probably with nothing better to do, and Tony had sat in brooding silence for most of the evening. The atmosphere had been one quite capable of being cut with a knife even though Alan had chatted the time away in his usual loquacious manner, but she had put Tony's quietness down to the fact that he and her parents were not exactly on social terms – nothing at all to do with Alan.

She had been glad to come away from that strained atmosphere and spend some time alone with Tony. Now she held on to his arm, still down at heart, thinking of her parents and the wedding and how it would go with them being so hostile towards Tony when he'd done nothing to them except try to be generous and helpful. She was angry with them for their reaction and now all she wanted to do was to get married and live her own life.

They'd live above his shop at first, because of his work, he said, but after a while would move to a far nicer place. After all, he had the money.

Brightening, she glanced at him in amusement at his question as to why Alan Presley had to be at her parents so often. It was obvious he was jealous, this with only two weeks to go to their wedding, and in a way she felt flattered that he should be so jealous.

'Alan doesn't have many places to go these days other than his own family,' she said lightly, but Tony glowered.

'Alan, is it?'

Her amusement faded a fraction. 'I can hardly call him Mr Presley. We've known each other since we were youngsters. His family has known mine for years. They don't actually live in each other's laps – don't go round for tea or anything, but they're friends, like everyone around here. And now he's no longer with his wife, I expect he's lonely.'

'Lonely!' It sounded like scoffing and her back went up.

'Yes, lonely. Most people his age are married and it can't be easy for him on his own to intrude on old mates who have wives, can it?'

He didn't answer but she could see he was still displeased. There was no need to be. He knew of course that she had gone out with Alan Presley a few times before him, but she had promised herself to Tony and that should have been enough for him. He had no right to get all possessive.

A small feeling of rebellion came over her and her tone grew obdurate. 'He's my friend, Tony, and I'm not going to ignore him just because you and me are getting married.'

'You and *I*,' he corrected sharply, making her allow herself a small, irritated explosion of breath.

'You and I, then,' she said huffily, each lapsing into silence.

Geraldine thought about Alan. If Tony hadn't come

along she and Alan might have become closer, though thinking about it there wouldn't have been any future in it. Alan had since discovered how expensive divorcing someone was, way above his means at present even if he was doing well in his line of work. If he had the money divorce itself would be simple.

She sighed. It seemed so unfair that good, decent, hard-working men like Alan who had fought for their country should be denied the processes that to the wealthy were normal, should one or other spouse be caught playing around. If there were no grounds then they could afford to pay for hotel evidence and the divorce court turned a blind eye, but it cost money. For people like Alan, all they could do was grin and bear it, go their separate ways and if in love with someone else be forced to live in sin. Who could say even in her neighbourhood who was married and who wasn't, how many children were born within a marriage and who weren't, other than by the birth certificate kept tucked well out of sight?

Poor Alan, what girl would want to take that on, and not even his fault? Geraldine too felt a little guilty knowing she'd more or less made that the true reason not to further their association. Thinking about it, she forgot to be angry with Tony and cuddled close to him as they walked to his shop.

Up in his flat they would snuggle up close, not for too long because Mum would be watching the clock and if she hadn't returned home in twenty minutes she would want to know why, and stand her ground until she received some sort of plausible excuse. It made things very awkward and she couldn't wait for these next two weeks to pass and her life finally to be her own.

Only two weeks to go. Geraldine shivered deliciously against Tony's arm as they walked. Mrs Anthony Hanford – how wonderful that sounded. The Friday prior to her wedding day she would ask for her cards and never again have to cycle off to work every morning in rain, snow, fog, wind or even sunshine when she always begrudged having to spend the day under a dull roof, bent over a machine while outside the sun shone. She'd be a married woman and no longer expected to work.

# Chapter Nine

The wedding was so close – ten days to go. Tony sat in the back room of his shop, staring down at the almost blank sheet of notepaper. 'Dear Mother and Father.' That was all he had written so far and that at least ten minutes ago. How did one tell parents that one is about to marry a girl they have never met?

He had told them about Geraldine the moment their courting had become serious. His mother had written immediately, excited, inviting him to bring her to meet them straight away. Then his father had written telling him not to continue being a damned fool, to come home and stop playing blasted shops, to knuckle down to law, a profession he was intended to follow in the first place. No mention whatsoever of Geraldine. Anthony's back had gone up and he hadn't replied to either letter. He should have, but had been too angry and would have upset them more than not replying.

His mother had written several more letters, apologising for his father. 'He has always been brusque, you know that,' she wrote in one. 'You must forgive him. He is still so hurt by what you did. To turn yourself into a low shopkeeper after all the money spent on your education. I can see why you did it, my dear. The war, possibly shell shock turned your mind a little, but to cut us off as you did. And surely after two years you are recovered.'

She had gone on excusing his father. 'He hasn't been the same since the war took your poor brother. Frederick was your father's hope and joy, so easy-going, so different from you, my dear, who always did tend to kick over the traces. He feels his loss so deeply and is so bitter. If you were here, it would so make up for his loss. Please, my dear, I beg of you, come home.'

Another letter, again pleading for him to come home, had also asked to meet this girl he seemed keen on. But he knew his parents too well. They would immediately make her feel uncomfortable, especially his father, still of the old school and class-conscious to the last degree. Her upbringing flung in her face, not in so many words but by their very mannerisms, would be plain enough to her to interpret. It might even cause her to back out of their relationship at the eleventh hour – a term used these days to signify any abrupt, last-minute decision, stemming from that eleventh hour of the eleventh day of the eleventh month when the Armistice was signed and the Great War brought to an abrupt end.

He had almost been tempted to tell Geraldine of his mother's request, thinking she had a right to make up her own mind. He would forewarn her, explain the sort of people they were. He'd very much come to know Geraldine too – that she wasn't the sort to shrink from the harshness of others but stare them straight in the eye and say her piece. He'd found this was the way of the cockney – chirpy, as others like to call them, but in reality pure bravado, a refusal to be put down, a way to combat any barrier of disdain.

Geraldine possessed that trait too, would face his parents adequately enough, dealing blow for blow, but how would she feel inside? He couldn't put her through that. So he'd told her that he wrote regularly to them, that he'd told them all about her and that they had asked to meet her. He made much out of promising to take her to meet them, but let the time go on and whenever she'd brought up the subject he'd managed to put her off, saying his shop kept him so busy but that they would get around to it in time.

As time had gone on, even his parents had become impatient, for a while bewildered, then annoyed, asking to be given a reason as to why he hadn't introduced her, his father thus allowed no opportunity to approve or disapprove of her. As though he would promptly give up Geraldine on his father's decision anyway, just as he hadn't taken up the law to his wishes. That wish had become even more prevalent after Frederick had been killed, as though all his hopes for the older son's future had transferred themselves to his younger one, no matter what he wanted.

His parents' mounting frustration at not being allowed to view this girl he'd got himself entangled with brought demands to know what was wrong with her, phrased as though suspecting him of hobnobbing with some prostitute. Threats to come here themselves were the worst to deal with, at times making him scared of his own shadow or that he would see them drawing up outside his shop, but fortunately they never did, his mother being a bad traveller and not trusting motor cars.

When he'd finally plucked up courage to tell them of his engagement – he hadn't forewarned them lest his father came storming down demanding it be broken off – there had been entreaties from his mother as to why they hadn't been consulted or at least informed of his intentions. His father had penned a terse note to say that he had his suspicions of this person as being some sort of gold-digger, while his mother had clamoured to know why he hadn't given them any opportunity to organise any social celebration of his engagement as protocol demanded and that his reluctance to introduce her was arousing their suspicions fourfold as to her respectability.

Outraged, he had refused to reply to either until his father threatened to come himself to the East End to see this girl at first hand. He'd sent a letter and photo of Geraldine in a lovely dress and hat to match her lovely smile against a background of Hyde Park so as to appear utterly genteel.

It was a lie he'd soon be asked to face when they finally discovered where and how she really lived. That he'd soon be taking her away from it would cut no ice with his people – they'd forever see her as a working-class girl who had clawed her way out of poverty, using their son for a stepladder. Compounding it all would be his lying, though why should he care? All his life he'd had so little to do with his family – sent away to an expensive prep school as was the custom with the upper middle class before the war, then away to board at college, then on to university, then off to war. He and they had nothing in common. Geraldine was closer to her family than he had ever been to his. But soon she would be his life and they'd be together, always.

It wasn't his parents' annoyance, but her frustration that he'd had to deal with – why wouldn't he take her to see his parents? Was he ashamed of her, her background? Didn't he think she had enough gumption to take care of herself when she met them? She'd come up against people like this before (though he suspected she hadn't) and was as good as them any day. She'd show them. But if he *was* ashamed of her, then they'd better call it a day.

This more than anything served to frighten the wits out of him. The last thing in the world he wanted was to lose her. He'd rather never see his parents again. There had never been much love lost between them, his father to his mind an unbearable, verbal bully, his mother little better, meekly taking his father's side in everything.

Now the wedding was ten days off. He must send them an invitation even if they declined it and he must take Geraldine up to meet them before that. Who knows, he thought, his pen poised over the empty page, she might enchant them off their branch. She was an enchanter anyway. Had enchanted him. Even so, he shook in his shoes at the prospect of what could happen once there. He'd been a fool to leave it so long.

He bent his head over the blank page and began to write.

Tony drove steadily along the winding Berkshire roads and Geraldine's eyes were everywhere, never having seen so much countryside in all her life. She remembered little of that trip to Loughton given by the Children's

Country Holiday Fund, being only six years old, except for the clopping hooves of the horses pulling the brake and feeling scared of a sensation of being closed in – probably the trees.

Now she was travelling through changing vistas of countryside in her own car, or at least Tony's car – the same thing really, they being married next Saturday, just six days away.

He was taking her to meet his parents, a bit late in the day but better late than never. It was one of the few things that had made her angry with him, his refusal, or so it appeared, to introduce her to them. Now at long last she would see what they were like. She had begun to wonder about them, making a joke of it.

'Your dad hasn't got horns, has he? Or your mother got two noses?'

He hadn't smiled and she really had wondered for a second or two whether she'd put her foot in it, that there really was something wrong with one or both of them that he'd not told her about.

He'd shaken his head sombrely. 'They might as well have. If you can call one being full of himself and the other practically licking his boots and thinking the sun shines out of his backside an affliction, yes, they'd be more palatable with horns or two heads.' She hadn't asked him again.

That was all in the past now. She would get to know these people and once she got over these attacks of nerves she'd had all the way down here, life with Tony would be a path of dreams.

She wondered what sort of house they had. He'd said moderately big.

'Not one of your country mansions, but I suppose it's quite a tidy size. It was fine when we were all there together as little kids – myself, my brother and my sister. Us boys of course were sent away to school, Fenella was tutored at home. But now just the parents rattle around inside it. The place was made for large private soirées I guess, but they seldom do things like that.'

He had gone on about his family: Fenella married, his brother killed in the war, only him left and then not having been there for years; about the fun they'd had as little children before social etiquette caused them to be sent their separate ways. 'People where you live never send their children away,' was meant to explain things but would have put her back up had his chatter not served to dispel some of Geraldine's nervousness.

She'd never known him to be so talkative but put it down to nerves as well. After all, he was introducing his future wife to his parents – not easy at the best of times but having left it this late, and she a girl from a different background to his, she had to admit, he was bound to be on edge. Setting out he had been quiet enough, relaxed, just the odd comment. It had been she who'd done all the talking, mostly on the wedding next Saturday. But as the miles went by, his tension had shown itself and it had been she who fell silent while he chatted on.

She could tell they were getting nearer to their destination without his having to say so, as he grew quiet, his tenseness beginning to transmit itself to her. To dispel it, she took some deep breaths and told herself she was as good as they but that they had money and her people didn't; that they had to sit on a toilet and do their business same as her; that wind did make its presence known from time to time from either end as with everyone from the King and Queen down.

It was coming up to three o'clock. 'Almost there,' Tony said as the open countryside gave way to a sizeable village that he said was where his parents lived.

It felt to Geraldine as though they had been travelling all day, through small towns, isolated hamlets, dozens of tiny villages, stopping once at a country pub for a sandwich and a beer and to gratefully pop to its spider-web-infested toilet that straddled a gurgling stream visible through the bottom of the loo itself. Having started out at ten, even though they'd been doing a cracking thirty miles an hour most of the time, at times even reaching nearly forty whenever the twisting country lanes decided to straighten out, she was stiff, ready to stretch her limbs. Would they, she wondered, be invited to stay the night? They couldn't possibly make the journey back in one day. Perhaps Tony would suggest they stay at that village inn they were passing. Visions of him booking one room for them both brought a surge of excitement to her loins but she said nothing.

'This is it,' he said abruptly, swinging the car left to come to a stop before a pair of wrought-iron gates. She couldn't see any house for trees but it was one of several residences they'd glimpsed in passing, each apparently different to the next, all set well back from the road and hidden from view by shrubs and trees and all well separated by extensive gardens, every entrance guarded by wide, impressive gates, some open but most of them closed.

These gates too were shut, although Tony said he had written to say he'd be arriving about now. A brass plaque on one of the granite posts with the inscription Rosebrier House was the only welcome there seemed to be. Thankfully they weren't locked and Tony needed only to leap out of the car and push their iron latch down for them to swing open with ease, a gardener pausing to watch as he slipped back into his seat to give her a smile and squeeze her hand reassuringly before he drove on through, deliberately ignoring the fact that he had left them open as though to establish that this was his home even if he'd hardly ever lived in it. Geraldine even glimpsed a stubborn set to his expression as they motored slowly up a gravel drive that widened to an oval area at the main entrance of the house.

Though in good repair, the house was old, maybe around a hundred years, perhaps older – she was no judge of buildings but she could imagine this drive once full of carriages, the gentry assisted down by footmen and conducted into the house, itself bright with candle-light blazing from every one of the tall windows as the guests were welcomed in by host and hostess.

Today there was no welcome. Even the sky had clouded over. There might have been some staff, it being a sizeable place, but other than the solitary gardener there was no one about. Tony had to leave the car to ring the front doorbell before the door was opened by a young girl.

Geraldine watched him speak to her. The girl retreated, returning with a tall, thin, shapeless woman who leaned forward to kiss his cheek rather reluctantly. This had to be his mother, in her early fifties maybe but well preserved as to make her own mum in her early forties seem positively worn out. And why not? Mum had lived her life washing, cleaning, feeding a family in London's East End. This woman had done nothing all her life.

Geraldine felt her lip curl at the thought of the gulf that lay between her life and the one Tony's mother had led. She sat firmly in her seat in the car and waited. She wasn't going to let a woman like that put her down.

At a word from Tony, his mother looked beyond him to where she still sat in the car. She murmured something to Tony who left her to come and help Geraldine out. He smiled, asked if she was okay, took her arm and led her up the three wide steps to the porch and main door from where his mother hadn't moved an inch except to now extend her hand to be taken. Geraldine could hardly call it shaken because the very second she dutifully touched it, it was withdrawn. But the smile on that fine-boned face bore a trace of tension, uncertainty. Was Tony's mother, so self-controlled, just as uncomfortable in meeting her as she was in meeting Tony's mother?

'How do you do?' The ritual nicety was hardly audible, the voice low, the question indifferent.

'Very well, thank you,' answered Geraldine, realising that she should have merely echoed the salutation, but too late.

There came a polite inclination of that handsome head and, protocol observed, Mrs Hanford stepped away to allow her son to conduct his fiancée inside while the young maid closed the door on the outside world, effectively creating a sensation in Geraldine of being trapped, like a rat in a box, as she and Tony were divested of their coats and hats.

But this place was hardly a box. The trapped sensation fading as instantly as it had come, Geraldine gazed around the great hall with its central staircase leading up to a balcony on which she could see a row of doors, Mrs Hanford now leading the way to one side, the maid skipping ahead to open the door to which she was making.

A brief nod of the head on its elegantly long neck sent the girl away and Geraldine, with her hand still tightly clutched in Tony's, followed the woman into a huge, well-furnished room, a drawing room or reception room, she wasn't sure, her eyes now on a tall, somewhat thick-set man with a balding head and grey moustache.

Mrs Hanford, still on her mettle, went over to him, obliging her son and his fiancée to follow, and standing to one side of him, lifted an elegant hand.

'This is the young lady whom Anthony intends to marry, Miss . . . ?' The introduction paused at a question appeared to her to be deliberately couched to make her feel ill at ease.

'Glover, er, Geraldine,' she prompted, instantly annoyed at herself. She'd intended to greet these people with easy dignity, her tone direct and composed. Instead her voice came out small as if swamped by all this show of wealth, which she supposed it was.

'Miss Geraldine Glover,' repeated Tony's mother. 'Miss Glover, this is my husband.'

He nodded his acknowledgement of her and Geraldine nodded back, now gaining control over her actions. She was damned if she would speak if he hadn't the decency to address her.

She was asked how her journey was.

The conversation was polite, hardly that, she not knowing what to say, loath to speak of her background, theirs stilted, confined mostly to enquiries: how long had

126

she known Anthony before they decided to get engaged? Emphasis lay on the word *decided*; she readily replied that it had been about a year and in saying so detected not so much a look as a feeling that she'd apparently jumped in pretty quick. How long had they been planning the wedding? Mrs Hanford's eyes roamed towards her victim's midriff, immediately making Geraldine seethe that the woman dared to imagine that this wedding had been designed in a frantic hurry to save a girl's name. Was her father footing the bill for this wedding? And even as Geraldine lied with a curt nod, she knew that her inquisitor was calculating that the father of a girl from her background certainly wouldn't be able to afford much. And so it went on, over tea and little afternoon sandwiches and cakes brought in by the young maid.

'Who are you having as your groomsman?' his mother asked Tony, who grinned easily, almost rudely. 'None of my cousins, if that's what you're hinting, Mother.'

'I hardly thought you would after the way you have behaved towards us, Anthony, cutting yourself off from us in the way you did.'

'Tomfoolery!' his father broke in. 'All that education and you go and play the tomfool being a *shopkeeper*!'

'I wanted to enjoy my hobby, see if I could make it pay its way.'

'Hobby! Playing about with bits of coloured glass, like some child. You never have grown up, Anthony.'

'I grew up quick enough in France, Father.' Tony's voice had adopted an edge, but his father didn't appear to notice.

'France apart, it seems it didn't teach you anything.'

'It taught me more than I ever wish to remember.'

'Still tomfoolery – a fine profession laid before you for the taking and you turned your nose up at it. I've no understanding of you, throwing away a fine future after all the money we spent on your upbringing, your education. I wonder why I haven't washed my hands of you long ago. If it were not for you wanting to get married . . . If your brother was alive, he would have—'

'He isn't alive, Father. He's lying somewhere in some Ypres field and may not even be all in one piece.'

'Stop it, this minute, sir, I will not have you discussing your brother in this manner. We've had enough sorrow. This is about you.'

'Please, both of you!' his mother was holding out her hands, and in that instance Geraldine saw a submissive wife in place of the haughty matriarch she'd first met.

Haughty still, she saw the cracks appear in that lofty armour as the man turned a face towards his wife, not even needing to speak, and the woman instantly fell silent. She might rule it over others, went the thought through Geraldine's head, but in her marriage she cowed before this man, this important, learned solicitor of a husband whose intellect she would never aspire to; a woman of gentle upbringing, in her youth not deemed worthy to be taught as boys were taught, confined to learning the social graces designed to make her a good wife of a rich man and an accomplished hostess to his friends and business acquaintances. Geraldine felt almost sorry for her but seconds later she was looking directly at Geraldine almost as though venting her loss of dignity on her.

'Anthony should have told us much earlier about you.

The first we knew of this association was a week after he was engaged. It wasn't good enough. Would you like a piece more cake with your tea, my dear?' The unkindly remark was softened by an immediate display of etiquette so that she wasn't sure if it was unkind or not – an accomplished way of putting her down as she a moment ago had been put down.

Tony must have sensed the small drama being played out by his mother. He came and put a hand on her arm – Geraldine couldn't imagine him putting an arm about her shoulders as Wally did his mother, Mum giggling and after leaning towards him, straightening to give his cheek a playful slap before telling him not to be so sloppy.

'I've promised an old wartime chum of mine to be my best man,' Tony said lightly. 'Better than having four cousins at each other's throats because I'd chosen one above the others. I thought it best to be neutral.'

No one smiled at his little joke, and after a while Tony's mother reluctantly asked whether they would be staying for dinner normally served at eight, thus making it late for them getting back to London. If ever there was a broad hint that they wouldn't be staying the night, this had to be the one, thought Geraldine, glad when Tony said they had plans to eat at The Stag, the village inn they'd passed and that they'd stay there overnight and leave for London in the morning.

This was accepted without protest accept for a compressing of his mother's already thin lips as she envisaged them booking only one room and cared not to contemplate what that meant. But Geraldine couldn't have cared less what she thought, only too relieved that they hadn't been invited to stay. She couldn't have borne another hour under this roof.

She decided to be blunt as they took their leave of his parents. No point beating about the bush. She hoped never to see these people again.

'I don't like your people much,' she said, and was surprised but happy to hear his reply, 'Neither do I, much.'

# Chapter Ten

When Geraldine finally came downstairs followed by Mavis her chief bridesmaid and Evie her other brides-maid, it was to a house seething with relatives. At the sight of her, the buzz of voices ceased and instead came gasps of wonder while she, all smiles, gazed down at a sea of upturned faces.

'You look lovely, dear.' Dad's sister Lydia was first to break the spell. Instantly everyone began pushing out of the two downstairs rooms to get into the narrow passageway to see how lovely she looked. It was Mum who had to start ushering the bride back up the stairs.

'You shouldn't of come down yet, Gel. And you should of known better, Mave, letting 'er come down. Yer know it's unlucky for a bride ter be seen before she gets to the church.'

'That's the bridegroom, Mum,' said Mavis. 'It's 'im what can't see her.'

'Well, it don't matter, just you three get back up there. We all 'ave ter leave first. Then the bridesmaids, then yer dad'll escort yer to the bridal car.'

'Cars!' Geraldine heard someone say almost scathingly as she turned to retrace her steps. 'Fancy!'

And another voice in a whisper, but audible to her, 'Posh, ain't it?'

And yet another, obviously not caring who heard: 'Funny not seein' a weddin' breakfast laid out ready ter come back to. Bit silly if you ask me, 'avin' it in an 'all instead of in yer 'ome. Waste of money if yer ask me.'

Mum, who'd followed her daughters up to her own bedroom where they'd been getting ready as it was the largest, closed the door firmly.

'Don't take no notice of them,' she said. 'It's your day, Gel, you do what yer want.'

Now came the anxiety of waiting, with little else to do but prink herself while Mavis fiddled with the veil, making sure that the low circlet of wax orange blossom was sitting correctly just above her eyebrows, that the white satin skirt of her dress was falling properly just above her ankles, the scalloped hem of the tunic part lay just right, low on her hips, and that the V-neck wasn't revealing too much bosom, though that being as flat as the present fashion dictated would not cause too many problems.

Slowly the hubbub from downstairs died away as one by one the guests left. Mum came up to collect the bridesmaids who left before the bride. Now, with only Geraldine and Dad left to wait for the bridal car, the house had fallen silent.

Never in her whole life had Geraldine known it as quiet as this. At night when the world fell silent, the house never was, Dad snoring audibly through the thin walls, the occasional cough, Evie and Mavis breathing heavily next to her, sighing, stirring, the bed shaking whenever they moved in their sleep, springs faintly creaking, low, muffled tones from Mum and Dad whenever he was obliged to get up to relieve himself, Mum muttering, he replying, his voice deep and resonant. Even when everyone was out, there were always sounds from next door, but not even that today. In the silence she heard her stomach give a tiny gurgle. She hadn't been able to eat breakfast, but now she felt hungry.

The sun peeped out from a September cloud and shone suddenly as brilliantly as at any time in the height of summer. Geraldine glanced at her dad and smiled a little warily. He returned the smile equally as warily. They hadn't yet quite got over their differences of these past few weeks, but now he felt for and took her hand, his palm feeling calloused and hard against hers.

His light-brown eyes, faded now, but once, so Mum had told her, the most attractive thing about him, gazed into hers.

'You orright, Gel?'

She nodded without speaking and he looked down at the linoleum-covered bedroom floor.

'It's goin' ter be strange, not 'avin' you around – just Evie, Wally and Fred left. Funny not 'earin' your sewin' machine goin' any more. Used ter drive me ter drink cold tea, that thing rumblin' away over me 'ead. Goin' ter be very strange.'

'I ain't goin' far, Dad,' she told him. 'I'm only down the road. Hardly miles, is it?' But he shook his head.

'It don't 'ave ter be miles what takes people away.'

For a second she felt a chill like a cold flat shaft of metal go softly through her body. Why did Dad always have to put the kibosh on things? He'd never been much of a talker, but when he opened his mouth it was almost always some observation that for all its truth tended to provoke annoyance or evoke discomfort. What he'd just said, intimating that married she'd be too well off and fancy-free to have time for them, dispelled all of the fondness she'd been feeling towards him, and she had to force herself to be cheerful.

'Come off it, Dad, you'll 'ave me in tears in a minute.' But she still needed to get in a dig of her own. 'You won't miss me one bit, you and me's never seen eye to eye for years.'

'Probably miss that too,' he said in a low voice, then looked up almost in relief as a car's horn hooted down below. 'Right, then!' He surprised her by giving her a sudden, brief kiss, his face as hard to the touch as his hands had been. 'Come on, Gel, you knock 'em in the aisles, eh?'

Not much was said in the car. It was such a short journey to the church that a car was hardly necessary, but it seemed to take ages, the driver not rushing so that the neighbourhood got a good view of the bride. Geraldine could imagine the conversation spoken through pursed lips even as they waved to her: 'Showin' orf in a posh car – what's someone round 'ere want a posh car like that for? Ain't even five minutes walk from 'ere ter the church?'

Mavis on her wedding day had walked, same as most brides around here, unable to afford anything else, and Geraldine felt a little guilty knowing how much her wedding was costing Tony. It made her stand out like a sore thumb and she wished he hadn't done it.

There at last, Uncle Bert, Dad's brother, took a snap with his Brownie box camera of her on Dad's arm, then rushed back into the church ahead of them and to his pew. Mavis and Evie were in the porch waiting to receive her for a last-minute prinking of her headdress and she began her walk on her father's arm to the swelling of organ music while her heart thumped like an unevenly beaten drum inside her.

The air in the church felt cold on her skin. Faces looked up at her, smiling as she passed slowly by them. She recognised those of her family but couldn't truly see who was and who wasn't there, except to note vaguely that while her side of the aisle was full, Tony's seemed sparse of people. He didn't have the large family she had, but his parents had to be there.

At the altar rail she could hardly turn to see as Tony moved to stand beside her. He seemed very calm, confident. He felt for her hand, squeezed it, and as she managed a peek at him he smiled. She smiled back, feeling better. In half an hour this man would be her husband and all the earlier altercations between him and her family, her and his, would be over.

The service went smoothly. She could hear her mother's tearful sniff once or twice, and the rustle of wrapping paper – guests bringing their wedding gifts in with them – and once Mavis standing behind her gave a subdued little cough. Tony fumbled in putting the ring on her finger but his voice rang clear as he repeated his vows at the vicar's bidding. Her vows had not been half audible enough but her throat had gone dry.

It was after the signing of the register, the triumphant rising of organ music bringing them from the vestry to walk back up the aisle followed by the congregation, that she noticed the absence of Tony's parents. Glancing at him she saw a tightness on his face and knew he was thinking the same thoughts as she, only with more regret and bitterness. She wanted to comfort him but all she could do was walk beside him to the din of music meant to glorify their union.

Someone who looked very much like Tony, no doubt his sister, had been there with a man and a small child. Tony had said his sister was six years older than him and had a daughter five years old. Geraldine found herself wondering if Fenella's husband had been in the war – an idle thought that served to blot out the empty pew where Tony's parents should have been.

Outside for photographs, the sun now behind thin clouds but the air warm, Fenella came up to them during a lull in the congratulations and confetti-throwing. She was tall like her brother and angular like her mother but the angles were softer, revealing the beauty their mother must have been at her age, both she and Tony very like her in looks. Leaning forward she kissed first his cheek then Geraldine's, the kiss warm and friendly, the grasp of her arms conveying genuine delight for them and Geraldine felt instant friendship flow between them as Fenella introduced her husband Reginald and daughter Stephanie.

Waiting in the church hall to welcome their guests, Geraldine asked about the absence of Tony's parents only for him to snap, 'Later – I'll tell you later, darling.'

She knew even before he produced the telegram arriving moments before he left for the church that they had backed out. She felt angry for him, sad for him, knowing how he must feel, and through a dull ache made herself smile as people came to wish them lots of health, wealth and happiness. The anger stayed with her all through a day that should have been her happiest, but no one noticed as she laughed and chatted and danced to a tinny piano and a neighbour's accordian providing music.

The lack of Tony's guests was unmistakable. Her family, close workmates and friends, even Alan Presley, now established as a friend of the family, entirely swamped Tony's few friends from past years, who, with Douglas his best man, his wife and two small children, his sister and her family, were all there were. It was embarrassing in a way and she felt deeply grateful to Fenella for turning up, in some way making up for his parents.

As to her parents all differences of opinion seemed to have vanished, which was gratifying and she hoped it would continue. More worrying were most of her uncles getting drunk, and several aunts tipsy. She prayed there'd be no arguments breaking out as so often happened at weddings. It had happened at Mavis's – something one sozzled uncle had said that had displeased another, aunts having to separate them, something they had laughed over afterwards, as ever. But would she feel like laughing if Tony or Fenella or any of his nice friends saw such goings on to her lasting shame? Fortunately, with her lot probably being well behaved in the presence of a different class to themselves, there wasn't one squabble.

In fact there was a tension about the whole day that put Geraldine's nerves on edge, everyone trying to be at their best. But at least their send-off was enthusiastic, perhaps her own sort feeling relief that it was all over and the posh lot would go home, having to travel, while they lived only in the immediate vicinity and could go back and finish off the evening with a bloody good knees-up without feeling awkward.

With gales of laughter and shouts to the departing couple not to get carried away and that they had all their lives to 'do it', confetti was showered over them, a fine rain now making it stick to everything.

Wally and young Fred were thumping the groom heartily on the back, Mum cuddling the bride to her, telling her to take care of herself and make him take care too – 'Don't want ter start 'avin' babies too quick, give yerselves time.'

Fenella came forward to say not to lose touch and that they could meet in the West End sometimes for coffee. Aunts and uncles and friends took their turn to kiss the bride, Alan's slightly more lingering than she would have liked (it came to her that he must still be in love with her, a thought she brushed quickly away with a sort of sad feeling in her heart); the men to shake the groom's hand; and Dad who came forward, kissed her cheek and held her tightly to him for a moment, something very unusual for him to do, and in doing so managed to spoil it all by muttering in her ear, 'Don't distance yerself too much from us, understand?'

She was so hurt and shocked by the tone that she couldn't even whisper in return, 'Of course I won't, Dad,' the filial words sticking in her throat.

The motor car had borne the couple off to their flat over the jeweller's shop, Geraldine's new home at least for the time being, she had said. Once settled, they'd find a nice house to live in.

The car having left, the guests turned back towards the hall to finish off the evening. Mum did not follow for a moment or two. Her gaze now came to rest on Alan, who still remained where he'd been after kissing Geraldine goodbye. Even in the half-light she could see a look on his face that made her heart spill over for him. Quietly she went to stand beside him.

'Yer comin' back in?' she asked, and he turned as if struck but said nothing, merely shrugged.

For a moment Hilda hesitated, then continued in a quiet voice, 'Life 'as ter go on, love. It 'as to. Come back into the 'all. It's gettin' dark. Yer'll get cold standin' out 'ere, and it don't achieve nothink, do it?'

Now he spoke, his voice low. 'When did yer suspect?'

'Ages ago. Couldn't be off suspecting it. It shows on every inch of yer face.'

'She never noticed.'

'Oh, I think she did,' Mum murmured. 'And I think she loved you too. But 'e came along. Don't blame 'er, Alan. He's got money and she ain't known nothink but 'aving ter struggle ter make a livin' all 'er life, like we all do. It's bound ter turn any girl's 'ead. He's 'andsome, and he's got charm, bags of it. That goes a long way to makin' a girl fall in love. Ain't 'er fault.'

She began guiding him towards the now song-filled hall, but went on talking. 'I ain't saying you ain't got charm, love. But his is different. Yours is genuine and it don't make no breezes. It's like a calm day. A girl goes along with that quite 'appily. Then comes this gale what blows 'er thoughts away, and that's it. She gets blown along and she couldn't 'elp 'erself.'

'I 'ope he makes 'er 'appy, that's all,' he said slowly, and it was her turn to go silent as she guided him on into the hot, now rowdy little hall that smelled of beer and was filled only by their own, the posh lot having departed seconds after the happy couple had left, easing into their own vehicles and with gushing thanks for a lovely time, had sped off to their nice homes.

It was so wonderful being married. At times Geraldine could hardly believe she was, and to the most wonderful of men. At times it felt she was still being courted, he taking her here, there and everywhere: dancing, theatres, private parties where he delighted in showing her off.

'The prettiest girl on the set,' he'd say, and made sure she had the most fashionable clothes he could afford. It seemed he could afford it with ease despite an obvious dearth of customers in his shop; he in dinner jacket or evening suit. Dad had hardly laid eyes on one much less ever worn one.

Perhaps Tony was being quietly funded by his father to be able to afford such things. She did ask at one time if that was how he could afford to keep up such finery and take her places. He had given her a sly smile and though he hadn't voiced it, she took it to mean that was where most of it must stem from. His father couldn't be all that bad after all and perhaps he in turn was keeping his occasional handouts secret from his wife, thus Geraldine decided the least said the better and did not mention it again.

Even so, they were living comfortably enough. The

flat was small but one day they would move to somewhere really lovely. He still worked down in his back room, turning out bits and bobs to display in his window. These were times when she saw very little of him, and sometimes he would work well into the evening, the shop closed, but he not appearing.

She did ask on one occasion if she could look after the shop for him but he said no, very firmly. Of course she no longer worked and couldn't say she missed it. With time on her hands she still saw Eileen occasionally, at midday for a snack in some local café, making sure to dress down for her benefit so as not to look too opulent, and sometimes treating Eileen to a cup of tea and a sandwich – not going too over the top for rather than be grateful Eileen would have seen it as her being patronising and spoil their friendship which was tenuous enough lately. Eileen knew full well that her friend could more or less afford anything while she still struggled as Geraldine once had. She tried her hardest not to look too puffed up, but it didn't always work – Eileen saw things in every gesture that she hadn't intended.

Other times she went over to see Mavis or Mum, or sometimes popped in to see an aunt or two, but again there was a certain something in the air she couldn't quite put her finger on. Much more pleasant was meeting Fenella in the West End, and there she found a different air, as though the woman was making an effort to come down to her level. Apart from a faint sense of resentment Geraldine realised that it was exactly the way she was probably striking others. It was a painful eye-opener and she vowed to try to be a little more natural with them.

She remembered that first time two weeks after her

141

wedding, how excited she'd been to receive that telegram from Fenella to meet her in the Ritz in Piccadilly for coffee that Tuesday and a bit of shopping afterwards. She had asked Tony and he'd been all for it. 'It'll stimulate better interests,' he'd said, 'better than sticking around here with your old friends. You need to leave them behind.' He'd given her money to buy a few things while up there and she'd forgotten to be annoyed at the way he'd said that.

He was doing his best it seemed to stimulate her better interests.

Towards the end of November he'd taken her to a party at a large Kensington flat and the size of the rooms had taken her breath away. He seemed to be making friends with all sorts of society people, perhaps through his line of business, she supposed, though he said little about it. He'd warned her to watch how she spoke and when she had asked if she didn't speak well enough, he'd said, 'You speak marvellously, darling, considering how you were when I first met you. Just keep your ears open for the things they say, the small talk. You want to pick it up for when we are really rich and go to more places.'

'Oh, are we going to be really rich?' she'd bantered, and his earnest expression had melted into a grin.

'I promise you, one day we'll be filthy rich!'

The dress he'd bought her for that party had been stunning. A pinky-beige, silky and backless, the height of fashion these last weeks of 1920, so daring that she'd been almost scared to wear it, feeling practically naked – no bra, those straight bits of material designed to flatten the breast in a manner acceptable to young people of fashion.

But wear it she did, to his satisfaction, and after a while she got used to the feel of the air on her bare back, more concerned in picking up the jargon of the day so as to please him with it later. It was after they got home that he showed her a piece in a copy of *Punch* which he always had delivered. 'Have a laugh at that,' he said, and she read what the wit had written:

> *Mary, Mary, slightly airy,*
> *How do the fashions go?*
> *Scraped up hair and shoulders bare*
> *And vertebrae all in a row.*

She had giggled and he had burst out laughing and life was so carefree.

Now it was Christmas and she'd have to dress down to spend it with her parents. No point making them even more estranged from her than they had grown to be these last couple of months. To them she was apparently parading around mixing with what they saw as high society, seeing herself as part of it. The last thing she wanted was having them think she was putting on airs and graces in front of them. Better to be discreet.

'Do we have to go?' was Tony's first reaction when she said she must spend Christmas with them.

It had developed into the first quarrel of their marriage, she instantly huffy where normally she forgave him his speaking out of turn because her smallest frown would have him rushing out to buy her flowers so as to make up for upsetting her, and how could anyone be angry with someone making peace with flowers? Anger instantly soothed, she'd love him even more.

Accusing him of not trying hard enough, of being stand-offish and talking down to them, her anger hadn't been directed at him so much as an offshoot of anger at her parents. It hurt that despite the apparent armistice at her wedding, their attitude towards Tony hadn't changed one bit since his offer to help her father. Taking his generosity the wrong way, they wouldn't face the humility of saying that they had been wrong. After all, one can take personal pride only so far and it touched her as being grossly unfair.

Even Tony's parents, who'd made her feel utterly awful when she'd met them as well as not attending the wedding, seemed to have accepted her if only by making sure their son wasn't short of funds, she in turn benefiting from it. It had to be that funding that was helping him clothe her so finely, and himself too, as he could never have done it on what was coming in from his shop. It had to be his father's doing even though she never saw money arrive with the post. Probably being paid straight into a bank account. Tony never said, but of course that was his prerogative and so long as he was looking after her the way he was doing, she had no intention of prying. She was happy and content. But this evening she felt far from content.

This particular quarrel over her parents had escalated, ending with him flinging himself out of the room to go downstairs to his workroom. He often spent a couple of hours there after closing up, but not in anger before.

Normally she wasn't allowed in his workshop. 'Too dangerous,' he'd say, and on one occasion had added, 'and it upsets my concentration.' His expression as he said it had conveyed exactly what he was getting at, that when they'd been courting there'd been a couple of times when he'd hardly been able to control himself with her in that room.

This time, however, she was going to have to go down there, say how wrong she'd been to flare up like that. It wasn't his fault. After all, the way his parents had treated her that one time, she never wanted to go near them again, so why should he feel different about hers? She had to apologise. He would forgive her instantly, probably down tools and guide her back upstairs and into their bedroom.

There came a little shiver of anticipation at that prospect as she went along the darkened passageway. Gently she tried the workroom door. It was unlocked.

Calling his name softly, she came on in, her nostrils immediately filled with the smell of solder and hot metal, her roaming gaze taking in the usual muddle on the workbench, the curled slivers of metal all over the floor. But what pulled her up sharp was the sight of someone else in the room besides Tony – someone she'd never seen before.

She saw Tony start guiltily, his face angry seeing her standing there. 'What the hell are you doing down here?'

She was shocked into stammering, 'I – I came down to – to . . .' She tried again, this time with more certainty. 'I didn't mean to interrupt. I didn't know you had someone here.'

Her words died away, and so did Tony's angry stare. In fact he now gave her a smile, a somewhat sickly one. 'I'm sorry, darling, this is an old friend of mine, popped in to see me.'

Dutifully, she nodded. It was an odd sort of friend – unkempt, not too well shaven, grime under the fingernails, teeth none too clean as he revealed them in a response to her nod. He wore a shabby cloth cap, a grubby red choker, and the edges of his coat and cuffs of his sleeves were threadbare.

'My dear,' said Tony as she continued to stare. He never called her my dear; usually darling, or my sweet. 'My dear, go back upstairs. I've a little business to do. I'll be up in a few minutes. Go on now.'

Without a word she turned and hurried back the way she had come, mystified by the caller Tony had introduced as an old friend, not even giving his name. Possibly it was a down-and-out buddy from the trenches in France. There were so many of the poor devils trying hard to scratch a living, even begging half-eaten sandwiches off the people just slightly better off than they. She gave a quiet chuckle. Of course! Tony was ever generous, took pity of such people, had no doubt helped out many such old mates down on their luck. But they shouldn't come knocking on his back door. She would have to warn him against being too generous. But cautiously, for again that was his business and she could be in error in spoiling a good heart. So long as he didn't get too carried away.

# Chapter Eleven

Mavis was having a hard time of it with her Tom in and out of work.

'It's his own fault,' said Geraldine to her mother when she visited her, but Mum pressed her lips together in disagreement.

'It's the times we're livin' in,' she said, rigid in her opinions and ready to stand up to anyone when it came to speaking her mind. 'People like you don't understand.'

'What do you mean, people like me?'

'Well, you ain't got no fear of your 'usband being slung out of 'is job, bein' unemployed and 'aving ter tramp the streets looking fer work what ain't there.'

'He could go out of business,' said Geraldine hotly. 'If things got bad he could lose everything for lack of customers. We rely on people's custom, and if they stop buying because they've got no money, then we've 'ad it too. We'd be as down as Mavis is. We ain't got no guarantee, y'know.' Her posh accent as Mum liked to call it often slipped when she was with her family, made her feel more comfortable and less prone to ridicule.

'As it is, Tony's struggling. That shop brings in next to nothink.'

Mum gave a small explosion of contempt. 'Well, yer could of fooled me! You in yer nice frocks and yer fancy 'ats and shoes, and good food on the table, yer've no idea what yer sister's going through.'

Geraldine looked at her dumbly. Perhaps she didn't. A small shudder shook her body. There but for the grace of God . . . If she had married anyone else but Tony, she could be in the same boat now as her sister. Yet it could still happen and it would be all the worse for having known better things.

She must go and see Mavis to see if she could help. Unemployment had become alarming, over a million out of work and three-quarters of a million on short time; men queuing for hours for the unemployment benefit the Government had promised to put up from fifteen to eighteen shillings a week as soon as they could get the bill through Parliament amending the Unemployment Insurance Act; and even if they did, how could a man hope to support his family properly on eighteen shillings?

The King's speech had put it down to worldwide restriction of trade but all people could see was that it was they who were suffering. One could see them trudging away from some promise of a job because a hundred others had gone for the same one and perhaps only a couple were needed, coming away with faces tense with disappointment and what they could see looming ahead; strings of men dawdled along the kerbsides, cardboard boxes of whatever bits and bobs they could find to hawk hanging by a couple of bits of string from their necks as they tried to sell enough for a crust of bread for themselves and their families; more and more children in rags and without shoes – it was so pitiful to see.

The last thing she wanted was for Mavis's Tom to fall as low as that. Three years since the Armistice, people had expected the country to begin to enjoy growing prosperity. Instead it was slipping into even deeper depths than anyone could have imagined, and no sign of an end to it.

'Tom's lucky to still be in the docks,' she said lamely.

'Lucky?' echoed Mum, draining the teacup she was holding. 'You call 'im lucky? It's a pittance 'e earns, and 'im with a wife and kiddy ter feed.'

Geraldine couldn't feel as fair-minded, Mum making excuses for a man who had no gumption to try to get on.

'If he had some go in him, he might have got where Wally is now, working for a decent company. He hasn't even got himself in with a gang. Nobody wants 'im because he's always moaning. Wally told me, says no one in the docks likes 'im. So why don't he buck his ideas up. Cheer up a bit and put his shoulder to the wheel a bit more instead of going on about how badly life's treating 'im.'

Mum got up and took the empty teacups to the sink, not asking if she wanted hers refilled, and with no light hand put them in the galvanised washing-up bowl with enough force to crack something.

'Look, I don't want ter talk about 'im,' she said, but Geraldine was in her stride.

'Dad got him into the docks and after that it was up to 'im, but he's done nothink. Wally's got himself into a top gang now at the docks, and he's with a proper firm and getting regular work. If he can do it, why can't Tom?'

Wally was putting money away for his wedding next year. He and Clara had got engaged in February though with no ring as yet. He had said she'd have it as soon as he saved a bit more money and she had seemed happy with that.

'And Fred's doing marvelously at his newspaper office,' Geraldine went on. 'He's gone from being an office boy running around at everyone's beck and call to working in the Wire Room. He was hounded from pillar to post but he did it with a grin and a nice attitude, and now look at him, in a job that brings in much better pay.'

'And doin' shift work,' reminded her mother, waylaid from her earlier point. She was refilling the kettle to put it back on the gas hob. 'What's the good of promotion if he's comin' 'ome all hours and 'im only just sixteen.'

'Well, I think he got that job because of his cheerful attitude,' insisted Geraldine.

Her mother turned from emptying the teapot for another cuppa to look at her. 'And what about yer dad? He's always done 'is job with a smile – at least before 'e 'ad this trouble of his, but now 'e's more out of work than in.'

That was true. Geraldine felt for her father. He was having terrible difficulties and it was lucky that Wally and Fred were bringing in money, Evie to a lesser extent, or Mum would have been reduced to taking in washing or something equally paltry and humiliating. But what about when Wally got married and there was only Fred and Evie left to support the family? Dad wasn't getting any younger, and what with his illness, it was stopping him getting the plum jobs he used to, with complaints that he would frequently have to leave his work to rush off to the lav.

Mum would make up pads for him to wear at work – Geraldine had seen them sometimes when she visited, a small pile of flat, oblong things made from an old sheet, stacked on a chair, Mum having omitted to put them out of sight before her arrival. The humiliation of his affliction didn't help her temper or Dad's. But stubborn as a mule, he still refused to see a doctor, saying he'd aired his privacy to him once and wasn't prepared to get the same stupid advice again. His stubbornness must have irked Mum sometimes, but what she thought about it she kept to herself.

She was putting a spoonful of tea into the teapot she'd warmed with water from the partially boiling kettle. 'It ain't yer dad's fault, 'im bein' in and out of work, no more'n it's Tom's. It's the times we're livin' in.'

'Dad should see a doctor again,' put in Geraldine, only to have her mother round on her.

'That ain't nothink ter do with you. It'll be the same old thing – go to 'ospital? What work there might of been for 'im won't be there when he comes out. And is your rich 'usband still willin' ter put 'is 'and in 'is pocket ter keep us while yer dad's in there and coming out to no work? He's got you as 'is wife now. All 'e did it for then was to keep you fancying 'im.'

'That's not fair, Mum, and you know it. He offered his help with the best of intentions.'

'Oh, we know that!' came the retort, Mum still of the same opinion that all he'd done it for was to keep on the right side of the girl he was courting. Geraldine pushed the resultant resentment from her.

151

'Why can't you accept his offers? He wants to help, and he can. It's as if you'd sooner bite off your nose to spite your face so you can hold up your head and say you don't take charity. It's silly, Mum. Dad's ill, he needs to be treated. No one knows what he's got. It could be a tumour or somethink. It could be something really bad.'

'If it was bad, he'd of known it by now. He'd of collapsed and 'ad to be taken off to 'ospital whether 'e wanted to or not.'

'And be out of work anyway. So what's the difference?'

Geraldine stopped suddenly. She hadn't intended to come round here for an argument. She'd come to tell Mum her good news, and now it was all spoiled.

She allowed the ensuing silence to stretch out for a moment or two, just to settle things down while her mother poured boiling water into the teapot. Then, taking heart that no more contention seemed forthcoming, she got up from the table and began washing and drying the cups her mother had left in the sink.

'Mum,' she began, her back turned to her. 'Me and Tony's going to 'ave a baby. That's what I came round here for, to tell yer.'

She felt the ever-present veil of hostility fall away from her mother as though wafted away by a wind. 'You ain't, are yer? Oh, Gel, I'm so pleased for yer.' The voice was animated. 'When?'

Geraldine turned, her eyes glowing. 'I went to the doctor yesterday. He said I'm eight weeks.

''Ow long 'ave yer known?'

'I had a feeling about it two weeks ago.'

''Ave yer told your Tony yet?'

152

'Not yet. I wanted to see the doctor first, just to make sure. I thought I'd tell you first.'

She couldn't have done a better thing. Seconds later Mum's arms had encircled her. Mum who seldom demonstrated her feelings to anyone was holding her tight enough to smother her, she still with a saucer in one hand and the tea cloth in the other.

It felt wonderful. Mum who had been so chilly towards her throughout Christmas and had been ever since, two months now; who had made her displeasure felt in no uncertain terms when Geraldine hadn't come there to see 1921 in, but instead had made excuses and gone off to a party with Tony to celebrate it; now Mum had forgiven all.

'You must tell 'im straight away,' she said, loosing her hold and moving back, embarrassed by her uninhibited demonstration.

'I'm doing that tonight, Mum,' Geraldine said as she put the cups and saucers on the table ready for Mum to pour the fresh tea.

'It must have been after that New Year's party we went to. We both came home a bit tipsy, didn't we? It was a wonderful evening. And we made such wonderful love, didn't we? It must have happened then. Oh, darling, I'm so happy!'

'And I am too, delighted.' It had taken him quite a few minutes to recover from the surprise she'd given him as he sat back on the sofa, she leaning against him. Looking up into his face, Geraldine saw a thoughtful look rather than the ecstatic one she had expected to linger. She frowned.

'You are happy really, aren't you?'

He grinned down at her. 'Of course I am. It's just . . . Well, it's going to be strange, being a father.'

'I suppose it will be,' she mused, full of contentment.

He was silent for a while, then murmured, 'I don't know how we're going to manage in this place, just two rooms and a kitchen, once it arrives.'

This was what she'd wanted to hear. 'We'll have to move somewhere larger, won't we?'

'I suppose so. But it will mean my not being above the shop any more. It could make things awkward.'

'In what way?' She was confused when he seemed to give her a strange look as though he'd said something he shouldn't.

'Nothing special. I've come to be known here. Goodwill. Also it'll mean my being away from home rather than merely being downstairs. You'll miss me.'

She was prepared to suffer that to get her dream of a lovely home. For over five months she'd put up with cramped living, trying to put away the disappointment of not immediately living in style.

Not allowed to help him in the shop, banned from his workroom, she spent all her time visiting during the day. True he took her out a lot, but it was daytime that dragged with nothing to do. She would think about going to work and at times even found she missed it, yet at the same time thanked her lucky stars that she didn't have to drag herself out of bed at seven in the morning to be there, slogging away all day at a sewing machine.

She no longer made her own clothes. Doing so might have helped pass the time but there was no longer any need, all her clothes were store-bought now. The sewing machine was still at Mum's and would certainly have been of no use here. All the home-made clothes had been got rid of. The only one left was the blue dress that had been instrumental in her meeting Tony. Now scandalously out of date, why she'd hung on to it, she wasn't sure. Sentimentality? Or did it go deeper, some underlying wish to look at it from time to time and be reminded not to get too high and mighty? For somewhere inside her lurked a vague fear of losing touch with those she loved. Many times she shrugged off the notion as stupid, but it always came back, an almost superstitious belief that if the blue dress were to be thrown out, with it would go a lot of things that needed to be clung on to. Obviously it was daytime boredom that made her think such odd thoughts, compelling her to get out of the flat and visit as often as she could, at times probably wearing out her welcome, but what else was there?

'I'm so bored,' she told Fenella.

She and his sister had become good friends. Meeting every Tuesday morning for coffee and cakes in some nice restaurant and shopping together afterwards had become a small ritual. These meetings had helped some way towards compensating for the continuing frigidness of his parents.

'They are so utterly unprogressive, darling,' Fenella had said, the straight, thin nose wrinkling in derogation of them when Geraldine mentioned their attitude towards her. 'I hardly ever bother to visit. They are so tiresome.'

Geraldine had watched the dainty way the girl selected a Genoese fancy from the silver cake stand to take a tiny delicate bite of the small cake and made a note to do it exactly the same way in future.

'Never be bored, my dear,' Fenella had said. 'There's so

much to do in life. Join a club, darling, any club, a tennis club, make lots of friends.'

'I can't play tennis.'

'Then *learn*, darling! You'll soon pick it up. And I will show you how to play bridge or perhaps canasta – it's all the rage. But surely my brother does take you out sometimes, doesn't he?'

'Oh yes,' she'd said hastily. 'We're always out. It's the day that's so boring. That flat is so small – you can't swing a cat around in it.'

She broke off as Fenella gave out a tinkling laugh. 'Oh, my dear, I love that – can't swing a cat around.' Still smiling she went on, 'But now you're pregnant, you really cannot live any longer in that poky little place. You must tell him, my dear, you must.'

This is what she had told him and where previously he would have looked dubious, insisting that he needed to live on the premises, everything had changed. Snuggled next to him on the sofa, she saw herself in a nice house in a nice part of London, even though he still showed some reluctance about moving too far away.

'So long as it isn't too far from here,' he said.

A thought came to her and she sat up. 'We don't do all that well here with so much poverty, so many out of work. I know you love doing what you do, but we could find other premises in an area where people can still afford things like jewellery? Perhaps you could even start buying in supplies instead of making it yourself. I know how much you like making your own jewellery but you could sell that on the side. We might grow and grow and even end up in the West End and become—'

'Hold on!' He gave a laugh and she could practically

156

see his mind working. 'All this takes money. I don't have that kind of money.'

She calmed, but her enthusiasm didn't wane. 'I know this place hardly even pays for itself, and if it wasn't for your father we'd be—'

'Ah, yes, my father.'

The way he said it pulled her up sharply. 'You mean he might not continue to fund you if we move?'

The long silence made her start to wonder what she had said that was wrong. Tony pulled his arm away from around her shoulders and eased himself out of their comfortable position to wander about the small room.

'Yes, my father,' he said after a while. He turned to look at her, his expression somewhat strange. 'It's possible he'll continue to provide me with funds.' An odd emphasis fell on the word 'funds' but she overlooked it as he went on, 'But it might take a while for it to get going again. While we wait, we might need to pull in our horns for a time. With a baby coming as well.'

Geraldine brightened. She'd been worried that he might discard her suggestion of finding some other shop, but he seemed worried only about his father getting used to the idea of his son's intentions to become a high-class jeweller and not follow the profession he had set his heart on him doing, and that they must tread carefully for a while. But she was willing enough to go carefully if that was what it took to get out of this hole and into a lovely house.

'With a baby coming,' she said, full of excitement now, 'I don't think I shall be in any fit state to go gadding about anyway.'

She saw his smile return, confident now. He was

thinking of course that his father would soon come round and they'd be off again as the new shop, wherever it would be, began to pay for itself.

Anthony closed the door quietly on the fellow, and returned to examine what he had brought – a couple of gold rings, one ruby, one emerald, one gold necklace, one gold pendant, two jewelled neck brooches, and some silver trinkets, no doubt from a woman's jewellery box, the petty criminal not daring to venture further – not bad for forty shillings, the man registering the usual look of disappointment at reaping so small a return for a risky night's work. But such people couldn't be choosers. Anthony had discovered that in Paris while on convalescent leave, when he had first tried to get rid of a bit of stuff he'd come by from someone needing a drop of whisky to help calm his shell shock.

Now to break down the stuff and dispose of it elsewhere in the usual way. He'd developed some decent contacts in the time he'd been in this shop. He gnawed the corner edge of his lower lip as he thought of Geraldine and her desire to move away. It meant having to pass the word that he was going elsewhere, make sure it was his present contacts only who'd know his whereabouts. Had to be careful. Couldn't risk the crime squad coming down on him.

He set to work on the rings. Mustn't be too long about it or Geraldine would start asking why he was being so long down here. He had put aside a stock of the cheap imitation jewellery he still made to show her in case she insisted on seeing the fruits of those labours.

Meantime, he must get to work prising the stones from

their settings, wrapping them in velvet ready for disposal, the empty settings to be melted down. He knew a chap who took the resultant small ingots of gold and silver, no questions asked, who gave him quite a decent price so long as he could always promise more. There was another who specialised in good gems, but a harder man to deal with and Anthony didn't entirely trust him.

He glanced at the clock on the wall. Five to eight. Time enough to smelt down the metals, pour them into their separate moulds. The smelter he had wasn't large, didn't hold a lot. If this game were to expand he'd need a far bigger one. Geraldine's suggestion to buy a larger place had come at the right time and he nodded happily to himself. A larger place, a bigger area to 'work' in, secreted maybe in a basement – yes, Geraldine falling for this baby had been the best thing that could have happened.

So long as she never discovered what he did. He didn't care to think what her reaction might be; but whatever, good or bad, he couldn't risk her letting the cat out of the bag to a friend or one of her blasted relatives, not seeing the danger in her eagerness to boast. Loose tongues weren't what he needed.

He smiled grimly to himself. His was an entirely different face when dealing with these people. He had learned to be tough in France, had learned to look after number one without it being too apparent. The only way to stay alive. He'd even got a medal for staying alive. For bravery, but it was the two dead soldiers who'd been brave. Required to go over the top to rescue an injured superior officer, he'd taken two men with him. He'd led the way at first, but as they drew enemy gunfire, the three of them had dropped to the ground, crawling through thick mud to reach the stricken officer. Somehow the two privates had reached the man first, the mud seeming to impede his own progress. Getting to their feet well before he reached them, they had attempted to lift the injured man whose right leg had been torn completely from his body by an exploding shell.

Standing, the injured man being dragged heavily between them, they'd made a good target and as he reached them, still crawling, they had fallen dead. He had felt the impact of the officer tumbling across his shoulders. Unwittingly shielded by the man, he had twisted round and had crawled back the way he'd come, had toppled back into the trench, medical orderlies coming forward to get the rescued officer to a field hospital, noting how his rescuer had risked his life to save him. He hadn't enlightened them with the truth.

For a while he'd felt guilty of deceit but it had opened the way for an existence he'd never anticipated. Men, trusting him, came to confide their worries and anxieties, even on occasion entrusting him with a valuable or two, to be given to a wife or a fiancée or a mother should something happen were they to be ordered over the top, superstitiously deeming him invincible after what he'd done in the face of enemy fire. There had come others, not so honest, who, also having come by such items of sentimentality, had hung on to them and now approached him looking for a few fags in exchange. And after a while, not knowing to whom these valuables belonged, he, to his shame at first, had flogged one or two bits to someone who in his turn had given him a few francs, he too playing the game. This way they had become buddies in crime, if it could be called that.

Wounded in the thigh, he had spent a little time in hospital and had somehow managed to be sent to Paris to convalesce. He'd had a good time there and it had been there too that he'd been able to unload himself of a fine gold pocket watch and a signet ring that had come his way via some cad or other. He hadn't got much for them from the Parisian fence he'd found, in fact not a fifth of their true worth, but he'd glimpsed what could be earned were he to get into this lark for himself.

On being returned to the front, the idea had faded. But with the Armistice, his father looking to rule his life, and he needing to kick over the traces and achieve something by his own merits, something that would keep his hands occupied and stop them shaking so much from the odd attack of shell shock, he discovered a hidden gift for designing nice things from metal – having occupied himself during quieter moments of the war by twisting softer bits of metal he found into interesting shapes and becoming absorbed by it.

He'd hit on the idea of trying to design jewellery. This shop and the sideline that had ended up going with it had been the result. And well paid was that sideline that still went with it.

So long as Geraldine never found out.

# Chapter Twelve

It was one of those deceptively warm March afternoons that made people feel that summer would come early. If it didn't lift the heart of the man standing in the dole queue, the down and out begging in the gutter, or the mother trying to feed her family on fifteen shillings a week unemployment benefit, it certainly put a spring in the step of the well-off – like Geraldine for instance.

She had just remarked on how good the fresh air made her feel, though it didn't feel that way to Mavis as her sister took in a deep and appreciative lungful of the balmy March air of Victoria Park, the sun's warmth on both their faces. Mavis breathed too, but shallowly and only because she had to and for no other reason, and sod the fresh air.

Pushing little Simon in a second-hand, somewhat dilapidated pram, she gazed down at him, the nine-month-old baby, face pasty, his skin spotty from not getting the best of food. But he was well dressed in a little coat and bonnet Geraldine had recently bought for him. Mavis, learning fast, wasn't one bit insulted by her sister's gift – why shouldn't she accept a present or two from someone to whom a few shillings didn't matter?

Tom was out of work and she was worried out of her life with possibly another baby on the way, at least she hadn't had her period for two months and that could only mean one thing. Nor was she too proud to take the few shillings Geraldine had begun handing her since Tom had been laid off. Desperate measures had no time for pride, even if Mum and Dad stuck to theirs like jam to a blanket. They'd have rather seen themselves in the gutter than accept money that Dad himself didn't earn. Principles – you could stick em!

But she did need to cling to a little self-respect. 'Please don't tell Mum,' she'd pleaded when first she held out her hand for the five shillings Geraldine practically had to force on her four weeks ago. There had been such an argument about it but finally she had to give in. 'You won't tell them, will you?'

'Of course I won't.'

'They'd be so upset with me. I wouldn't take it but I need ter pay the rent and we ain' got it. We 'ave ter feed ourselves, and Simon more than either of us needs to eat.'

'I know, Mavis, I understand, and if I can be of any—'

She didn't want to listen to the words of charity that would make her feel worse than she did. 'Last week,' she cut in, 'I could 'ardly afford milk for 'im. I don't want ter start owin' on the rent. It builds up and finally yer don't know where you are and next thing yer know, they're slinging you out. They don't care, them landlords, so long as they get their money, they don't care who suffers.'

Since then, Geraldine had upped her handout a little – six shillings this week when she'd come to visit.

Mavis felt her smile stiff on her face. 'This'll pay the rent at least,' she said. And Geraldine, almost as embarrassed as she, had said, 'Look, Mavis, don't say any more about it. I'd rather you just take it.'

It wasn't just the money, but little things she brought for Simon, like the coat and bonnet, and not even his birthday. She was embarrassed and hated herself at times for the feelings of resentment that stole over her when Geraldine bid her a bright, careless goodbye that she could do things like this, fling money about, while she herself was reduced to taking it.

Monday was when Geraldine always visited Mum. She'd have a cup of tea with her and eat a piece of the cake she always brought along. She'd have brought much more, knowing Dad's work these days was erratic, but Mum so regularly spurned her handouts as she liked to call them, leaving Geraldine to take them back home, that she had learned never to overdo it. But a piece of cake was just a token, a little gift. Even so, Mum would cut a piece for her and never for herself. It was so obvious sometimes that more often than not Geraldine came away quietly seething. Her parents were the limit and there was no reason for it. Yet she always brought the cake.

Today Mum met her at the street door, her face tense and stressed. 'Yer dad's bin taken to 'ospital. Accident at work this mornin'. Some crates gave way while they was being hoisted or somethink, so 'is mate what came ter tell me said, and a metal strip from a crate went through yer dad's arm right ter the bone, 'e said.' Despite her expression Mum's voice was toneless. 'Another knocked unconscious 'e said. Concussed. The bloke what told me went off ter tell the other one's wife. They got an ambulance an' took 'em ter the Poplar.' It was the hospital to which most men hurt in the docks were taken, but it was quite a way from Mum's house. 'I'm on me way there now.'

Geraldine hesitated hardly a second. 'I'll dash home and get Tony to take you in the car.'

Mum lifted her head. Quite suddenly it seemed as though she saw herself as having been insulted. 'No you won't!' she snapped. 'I can walk!'

'Don't be silly, Mum.'

'It ain't far.'

'But you'd be there in two ticks in the car. It'll take you nearly half an hour walking.'

'Time he gets in 'is car, gets it started up and gets it round 'ere, I'll be 'alfway there. I can nip through the back-turnings, a car can't.'

'Time you get there you'll be worn out,' retorted Geraldine.

Her mother glared at her. 'I don't want no car, thank you!'

Geraldine stood at the door as Mum disappeared inside the house to get her hat, her coat and her handbag. The shock of the news had stunned her. She would go with Mum of course. But as her mother came out she brushed past her as though she didn't exist, or as if she'd been insulted by her, starting off at a brisk pace leaving Geraldine standing for a moment, shaken by her attitude before galvanising herself into action and racing after her.

'Mum, please. What's the matter?'

'Yer dad's in 'ospital, that's what's the matter.'

'I don't mean that, Mum.' It was all she could do to keep up with her, her mother's step so rapid, and before long she was out of breath. Mum couldn't carry on at this pace, but she knew it wasn't so much an urgency to reach the hospital as a wish not to be beholden to Tony, even for getting into his car. It was so ridiculous. 'Mum, slow down, you'll kill yourself. Why are you so against Tony? He's never done you any harm – not consciously.'

Her mother stopped suddenly to glare up at her. 'Your 'usband acts like we're paupers. Offerin' this, offerin' that. Don't he know what accepting money makes yer feel like? I expect he's always bin able ter put 'is 'and in 'is pocket and don't know the first thing of what it's like ter worry where the next ha'penny's coming from, without 'im making us conscious of it. No, Gel, you tell 'im we don't want 'is 'elp if all 'e can do is look down 'is nose at us. It takes more'n money to 'elp others, like just being neighbourly fer one thing.'

'But—'

'And I don't need you with me neither.'

Anger blazed up inside Geraldine. Her hands tightening into fists at her sides, she glared down at her mother, whose naturally proud stature still didn't increase her height above her daughter's eyes.

Recrimination tumbled uncontrolled from Geraldine's lips. She was a child again, being wrongly accused and not knowing how to combat it. 'Why don't you want me with you, Mum? He's my dad and I don't want to see anythink 'appen to 'im. I love 'im, and I'm as worried about 'im as you are. I'm scared for 'im knowing what's 'appened. I don't care if you don't want me with you, I can walk behind you. But you can't stop me going to see me own dad. And I hate the way you and Dad treat me and Tony, Mum.'

Her mother's voice was steady. How could it be so steady? 'If you and 'im was ter come down off yer 'igh 'orse once in a while, I might be better inclined to the pair of yer. But ever since yer met 'im, Gel, yer've made us feel as if we ain't good enough for yer no more.'

'That's not true, Mum. I love you. I love you both.'

She blurted it out in desperation but Mum gave a mighty huff and turned away to walk on almost as fast as before. Now Geraldine remained half a dozen steps behind her but not once did she turn round, leaving Geraldine to stare at that straight, proud back for the rest of the way.

Even when they got to the forbidding entrance of the hospital with its blackened brick and its windows staring out like sightless eye sockets, she strode on as though her daughter wasn't there.

All this from being offered a lift in a car – Tony's car. So unreasonable, so pointless and so stupid! It was hard to control the sickness that lay in her heavily beating heart, even harder to subdue the anger accompanying it.

By the time they'd walked endless, cold corridors, and climbed endless flights of stairs, every part of the place an unrelieved cream and green, and that dulled and pockmarked by time and open fireplaces, an ancient hospital to say the least, she and Mum were worn off their feet.

What Geraldine had expected to find as they finally

reached the ward and a nurse directed them to the bed at the far end of the long, busy hall, she wasn't sure, but her mind saw a man, grey-faced from the loss of blood, body limp, the drip making hardly any difference, the expressionless face of the doctor sadly shaking his head in silent commiseration at the doomed man's loved ones. Instead there was a nurse, all bright and cheerful, saying, 'Mrs Glover? Ah, yes, your husband's fine. All successfully stitched up but he is swearing a lot.' It was a jovial admonition, a hinted request to try to curb the man's bad behaviour in a crowded ward with nurses around.

'I bet they've heard worse than your dad,' Mum said, smiling grimly, seeming to have got over her resentment, possibly borne out of anxiety, Geraldine imagined, now forgiving her and only eager to see her father.

Making their way down the ward, passing bed after bed of men, some lying limp and ill, some sitting up and grinning at the visitors, they finally came to Dad's bed, two from the end. He was sitting up, his arm swathed in a pure white bandage and in faded cotton, blue-striped, hospital pyjamas, though his cheeks and greying dark hair still had traces of dust and grime from the hold he'd been working in at the time of the accident.

He made a face as Mum approached to bend over him to ask how he felt and how serious was his injury and did he need anything.

'I need ter get back ter work, that's what I need. The quicker yer bleedin' get me out of 'ere the better. All this bloody muckin' about with me.'

Geraldine was sure she detected an 'f' rather than an 'm' in that word 'mucking' and looked hurriedly at the nurse who was with them, but the young woman's expression remained impassive.

'Mr Glover can go home later today, if you would like to come back to collect him, Mrs Glover.'

Hilda straightened up in alarm. 'I can't go all the way back 'ome and then come all the way back 'ere. I 'ad ter walk all the way—'

She stopped sharply with a furtive glance at her daughter. Geraldine looked down at the floor, fighting back a retort. This wasn't the place to start another argument.

'In that case,' said the bright nurse. 'I'll see if he can be discharged while you are here. Where exactly do you live, Mrs Glover?' On being told, she smiled knowledgeably. 'Then you could get home by tram. The sixty-five and sixty-seven pass by here and you can change at Commercial Street to take you to Bow Road.'

'I walked 'ere,' returned Hilda sharply. 'I can walk 'ome.'

'I think not, Mrs Glover, not with your husband. He has a very nasty cut on that arm and will be in no condition to walk all that way.'

'He looks orright ter me.' She glanced at her husband who apparently had enough go in him to lean over and with his left hand help himself to a drink from the water glass on the wooden locker beside his bed.

'He would soon feel the strain walking so far,' said the nurse. 'We can get him to the hospital gates for you. The tram stop is just outside. That is of course if he is allowed to leave. So if you and your daughter would like to stay with your husband, I'll go and make enquiries about that. I shan't be two ticks.'

Left alone, there seemed little to say. Geraldine sat quiet while her mother asked exactly what had happened, her father answering tersely that she ought to know by now how quick things did happen, that it had and there was nothing else to be said. In the docks accidents were a daily occurrence, men could be injured, men could lose their lives and there was nothing one could do – a whip round among the injured man's mates if he had to be off from work for any length of time, or if someone was killed a whip round for the widow; in neither case could those putting in the collection afford more than a shilling at the most; these days of short time it was usually even less.

Few had the means to pay out weekly for sick benefits or any hospital savings cover, and many a man injured just had to rely on what he might get in the way of social help. It was all part of working in the docks and just had to be accepted as such. There had always been heated talk about compensation, even talk of a strike for better conditions, but nothing ever came of it, nor would now with all this unemployment and the chance of being laid off at the slightest whim, with someone always there to leap on any vacancy there was.

The nurse returned accompanied by a doctor, a grave expression on his face though all doctors seemed to bear grave expressions. Geraldine, sitting beside Dad as the doctor took her mother to one side, tried hard to hear what was being said, but with Dad going on nineteen to the dozen about working conditions in the docks and if unemployment wasn't as bad as it was they'd strike for better conditions, she couldn't hear a thing.

She expected Mum to come back with a face drawn

with anxiety by what she'd been told. Instead she was smiling.

'The doctor said you've been tiddling the bed while you've been 'ere. He wants ter keep you in another day so's he can take another look at you.'

Her husband's eyes widened, glinting with belligerence. 'Like bloody 'ell 'e does! No one's keeping me 'ere any longer than I need ter be. I've got ter be back at work. I ain't losin' any more pay. We can't live on air.'

'There's no question,' the nurse butted in, 'of your returning to work today or—'

'What d'you know about it, yer silly bitch, with yer reg'lar income an' nice clean 'ands? Anyway, I ain't 'aving no one poking around me like I was a bleedin' guinea pig. Tell 'im ter go and frig 'imself.' At least he hadn't come right out with it, thought Geraldine, still wondering at Mum's smile.

Mum sat down again, the doctor standing a little apart from them. 'It's yer waterworks, Jack. The doctor thinks yer trouble is yer prostrated glan.'

'Prostate gland,' corrected the doctor, coming forward. 'I'll explain it.'

'I don't need no bleedin' explanations,' Jack Glover roared. 'I 'ave ter get back ter work. I'm losin' money lyin' 'ere.'

'I'm afraid you won't be able to work for at least a week, Mr Glover, not until the wound has had time to heal, if only partially. Working will break the stitches and you'll be brought back here. It must heal before—'

'Don't tell me what I can and can't do,' Jack belted

at him. 'You ain't the one what's goin' ter lose yer livelihood if yer don't work.'

'I'm sorry, Mr Glover, work is out of the question.'

'Jack, listen to the doctor,' urged Hilda. 'Take advantage of what he's saying. Let 'im look at you. He might be able ter make you better regarding yer trouble down there, Jack.'

'What we will do,' went on the doctor in smooth tones and completely unruffled, 'is examine you to find out what is causing the problem.'

'I know what the perishin' problem is – I can't 'old me pee too well.'

'Then we'll find out the cause and we may be able to remedy that,' the quiet voice went on. 'It's nothing to be scared about—'

Jack glared up at him. 'Oo says I'm scared?'

The doctor ignored the challenge. 'It may be that your prostate gland has become enlarged. We can sort that out for you quite easily.'

'You mean operate! I ain't 'aving meself cut open.' But some of the belligerence had dissipated. 'What if it turns out ter be somethink else?'

'I doubt it is anything else. As I said, probably the gland is enlarged and has been left unchecked for quite a number of years. It's a common enough condition in men.'

'But what if it ain't just that?'

Geraldine stared at him, ready to forgive his spurning of Tony's offers of help to tide him and Mum over while in hospital. The truth was, he was terrified of something awful being discovered, would rather not know than find out the worst. It was rather like someone walking a cliff edge, eyes tight shut so they wouldn't have to see the danger, no matter that they could fall.

'Dad, you've got to let him have a look at you,' she spoke up. Her reward was a baleful glare, but one that was tinged with an animal fear.

'You mind yer own bloody business! I ain't 'aving you stickin' yer toffee nose into my concerns. This ain't nothink ter do with you. Go 'ome.'

'Dad!'

'Go on, sod off!'

'Mr Glover, please!' intervened the doctor, his command sharp and stern. 'I insist you listen to what I have to say. We need to have a look at you. And while you are here I think we should.'

But he too had seen the fear in the man's eyes. Turning to his wife, he said quietly, 'I think I need to have another word with you, Mrs Glover – if you would come with me.'

This was accompanied by a curt nod to her and she was compelled to proceed a little ahead of him. Unable to bring herself to remain with her father, Geraldine followed at a short distance, pausing when the two people stopped some way down the ward.

What were they saying? She could see the tall doctor bending toward her mother, her mother's head nodding up and down, her eyes trained on his face, her own expression stiff. Finally he gave a nod of dismissal, touched her arm briefly and gently and returned for another word with her father, passing Geraldine with a small acknowledging smile and a tilt of the head.

Mum was moving off towards the exit. Geraldine sprung into action and followed, catching up with her as she went out through the doors and into the corridor.

'What did he say?'

Mum's face was still stiff. Her voice was small. 'He said it could be something more serious, but they 'ad to examine 'im before they could be certain what exactly is causing your dad's incontinence.'

She seemed to be talking more to herself, quoting the doctors words, words that would never have come from her own mouth. 'Until they do that they can't be sure if it's only this swollen gland thing. If it is somethink more, and he won't say until they've examined 'im, it could be very serious indeed. But we're not ter say anythink to yer dad. It might upset 'im. We've ter behave as if everythink's orright. We've got ter look cheerful and not let on what we've bin told.'

She pressed her lips together with forced determination, lifted her shoulders and took a deep breath. 'But then it might not be anythink like that at all.'

Geraldine couldn't feel that confident. What had been intimated was that there could be a threat to Dad's life. What if they did find some sort of growth, a tumour or cancer? Could they cut out something that had been left to go on for years undiscovered, unchecked? Though after all this time wouldn't he have had some pain? He'd never complained of any. Even so, he was a fool not to have accepted Tony's help all that time ago just to save his stupid pride – she ignored her earlier surmising of it being fear and not pride that had made Dad spurn the offer. Now it was too late, Dad would have to lose time at work, maybe lose his job, maybe worse. Geraldine shuddered at the thought that refused to become words.

'We'd best go back an' see yer dad,' Mum said suddenly.

Turning, she went back up the ward. All Geraldine could do was to follow but remained a little apart, sitting on a chair near the foot of the bed while Mum sat urging him to take the doctor's advice. She couldn't hear all Mum said, speaking so low, but she saw the tension on his angular, work-lined face, the chin begin to jut as Mum slowly convinced him that it was for his own good, nothing else he could do, that things were out of their hands now and he'd be a fool to turn his back on what could no longer be avoided.

Each in their turn they dropped a kiss on his cheek. He didn't smile and they came away. Nor did he respond as they turned to wave goodbye. At the far end of the ward he looked a lonely figure. Geraldine could have cried.

With their view of him finally obstructed by some screens surrounding another bed, they left, and the tram ride home was made in silence.

# Chapter Thirteen

Two days later Dad had his operation. Declared successful, the next day he was sitting up, his arm still bandaged from the accident but well recovered from the operation on the *other thing* as he described it to his wife.

'I ain't all that chuffed at the way they pulled me about though,' he confided to her when they were alone after a cohort of relations had been to see him to his utter humiliation, they aware of the reason for the operation.

Hilda looked amused. 'How'd you know? Under the anaesthetic yer wouldn't know if yer was pulled about or not.'

He grimaced. 'If yer saw the colour of me whatsit under that bandage, yer couldn't be off seein' as 'ow I've been pulled about. It's black an' blue down there. All bloody colours of the rainbow. I told the doctor what came round and 'e took a peek ter check and said it looked orright to 'im – in fact 'e said it looked very nice. Nice! Cheeky bugger! I told 'im, "If yer like that sort of fing, maybe it do look nice ter you but it don't look too rosy ter me." Cheeky young sod, just 'cos he's a

176

doctor, don't give 'im no call ter stare at me whatsit and tell me it looks nice to 'im.'

'The thing is,' Hilda said, offering comfort, 'it 'as done the trick. You won't 'ave no more trouble down there. And them bruises'll fade in no time.'

'Yeah, but I don't want no doctor peeking at me and smirking and saying 'e thinks me lower parts look nice – bloody cheek.'

'It's what doctors 'ave ter do. Just be glad it weren't a nurse.'

'I've 'ad them gawpin' at me too. I can't wait ter get 'ome where I can keep me private parts ter meself. Yer body ain't yer own in 'ere.' His averted face peevish, Hilda hastened to soothe him.

'Well thank Gawd it weren't nothing more serious. An' you be thankful too. I don't know what I'd of done if it 'ad been somethink really bad and you'd been . . . well, you know what I mean.'

Giving a cough to cover the fluster that had come over her at having nearly revealed her deepest fears of losing him and in that way inadvertently declaring the love that the habit of twenty-five years of marriage had long ago decently buried, she got to her feet and in a crisp tone said she'd see him tomorrow. Asked equally as tersely if there was anything he wanted brought in, he gave a short list of clean socks, a couple more handkerchiefs and a packet of fags for when he was allowed to leave the ward. On this she made a mental note, kissed his cheek and left.

'So we didn't need your Tony's 'elp after all,' said Mum when Geraldine popped in to see her after visiting Dad.

He had said very much the same thing: 'So now your Tony can keep 'is money, can't 'e?'

All she could say to that was, 'I'm glad you're better now, Dad. We were worried for you.'

'No need to've been,' had come his reply. 'P'raps now I can 'old me 'ead up in front of people like 'im what crows about 'is money in front of people like us.'

She had been affronted and had shown it. 'He's no different to anyone else. All he wanted was to help. He has no intentions of crowing. And what d'you mean by *us*? There's no such thing as *them* and *us*, Dad. Things are changing. And if he could have helped you out of a spot, why couldn't you have let him? You might still need some help till you go back to work.'

Her father had irascibly raised himself up on his pillow, wincing as he did so at the stab of pain at the tightening on the stitches on his still very tender wound. 'I don't need no 'elp from no one,' he'd rumbled, and thus chastened, Geraldine cut short her visit and came away angry.

Now she was getting the same treatment from Mum. 'Sometimes I almost feel I'm not wanted here,' she said, close to sudden tears that made her angrier than ever, against herself as well as Mum.

Her mother sat solid and dry-eyed, that back of hers as stiff and as proud as ever, impervious to her daughter's glistening eyes. 'I don't know where you get that idea. I've never turned you away, 'ave I?'

'You don't exactly make me feel that welcome.'

'But 'ave I ever turned you away from me door?'

'No.'

'There you are then. Never let it be said that I'd turn a daughter of mine away from me own door. And if that's what yer implyin', Gel, then all I can say is, it's casting aspershuns on yer own mum.'

'I didn't intend it that way, Mum.' Tears welled in her eyes, filtering her view of the light from the kitchen window as though seen through the facets of a splinter of glass.

Her mother busied herself pouring the obligatory cup of tea offered to any visitor to an East End home. 'Well, be that as it may, 'ow did yer find yer dad when yer went in ter see him?'

In Victoria Park where they'd gone for a stroll, this part of March remaining warm enough for it, Geraldine told her older sister of the doctor's findings about her being two months pregnant. She'd said it with all the pent-up joy inside her but Mavis merely pulled a face as she pushed little Simon in his second-hand baby carriage that had certainly seen better days.

'Lucky ter be able ter crow about it. All right fer you. Your old man's got a business. Yer can afford to be pleased about 'aving a baby.'

It wasn't what she'd wanted to hear. 'His business doesn't bring in all that much.'

'Enough from what I can see,' said Mavis, eyeing the dress Geraldine was wearing, shop-bought and certainly not cheap, even if it was the oldest one she had.

Geraldine always took care in picking her dresses according to whom she was seeing. For Tony's sister, of course, it was the most expensive day dress she could find. For her family, it was one that wouldn't put their backs up. She would even take a wander round the market stalls in Roman Road to find something cheap just to wear to visit them. Though contrary to her purpose it had often caused Mavis to remark that surely with her money she could afford better than that. 'It makes it look like you're patronising us, pretending yer can't afford much when we know yer can,' she'd once said.

There was no winning either way. Even today. All she'd wanted to do was impart her joy to Mavis at finding herself pregnant, and even that was thwarted with her sister already casting aspersions on her happy news.

Mavis had looked so dowdy, the carefree young girl gone forever. In her place a housewife, worn by worry over an unemployed husband, a mother stewing how to keep her son properly fed, and now with her son only nine months old she was worried sick that she had missed two full months' periods.

'I don't know 'ow we're goin' ter manage, Tom out of work an' all with no money comin' in.'

'He might not be for long,' said Geraldine, trying to offer solace, but as she might have expected, Mavis gave her a scathing look.

'You don't really believe that. You only 'ave ter take a look at the length of them dole queues. My Tom ain't goin' ter walk into a job this year nor next as far as I can see. Him with no skills, oo'd want 'im? An' now me with another kid on the way possibly.'

'It might still be a false alarm – all the worry about Tom.'

'What, an' me always regular as clockwork? Or used ter be. Not the way he . . . well, you know, it's 'is only bit of comfort nowadays. He can just about afford a packet of fags now and again, and an occasional pint to 'elp keep 'is chin up. What else 'as 'e got if he ain't got me ter give 'im his bit of comfort at night?'

Geraldine felt little sympathy. It was their fault if Mavis was pregnant this quick after having Simon. They should have at least tried to be careful knowing their circumstances. To her mind people often brought their own troubles on themselves, but she thought better than to say so to her sister, already down in the mouth. In fact she wished she hadn't spoken so quickly about her own condition, but she had been so happy about it that she hadn't paused to give it proper thought.

If only there was something she could do – like Tony offering Mavis's husband a job. But doing what? There was no call for an assistant in the shop as it was seldom busy. She still wondered how Tony could make so much money when it was never busy and he still hedged about his father seeing him all right, as if he felt it put him down to admit it. There was no way in which she could offer Mavis money even though Mavis wasn't as proud as Mum at taking it, but there was the same atmosphere there. She had offered her a dress or two in the past and Mavis had accepted them, grudgingly, as if to retain her sense of pride by making the giver feel put down rather than the other way around. It wasn't a nice feeling, to offer help then immediately to be made to feel awkward where she should have felt nothing of the sort. Perhaps Mavis was saying that being given some cast-off dress wasn't going to put food into her family's mouth, that she had less need to dress well as a greater need to see her family fed. Yet even when she did chip in with something edible, as Mum did, there was the same negative response, a sideways look even while it was being accepted.

Mum's offerings – maybe a small basin of stew or a home-made cake, something she too could ill afford while Dad was in hospital – were always readily accepted above anything Geraldine had to offer and which she considered far better quality than Mum could ever give, and more of it.

Time and time again she came away vowing not to bother any more, yet she could no more visit Mavis empty handed than fly in the air. If only she'd be a bit more grateful, or at least try to show it sometimes. But then, Mavis had always been hard to get along with.

Only one consolation was that on one occasion Mavis accepted something from her with her usual begrudging thank you, but added, 'You won't tell Mum about this, will you?'

Reassuring her that of course she wouldn't, she had seen relief on her sister's face. Mum's enormous and at times senseless pride touched even Mavis into being wary of handouts from what Geraldine could only interpret as the better-off playing Lord and Lady Bountiful before their less fortunate relations, when all the time she was only trying to do her best for them. It hurt. It hurt very much, almost making her vow to let them get on with it.

Geraldine let out a little giggle as, clinging on to Tony's arm for support, the two of them stumbled into the flat. Three-thirty in the morning with the first grey glimmer of a late May dawn just beginning to show, and still the party when they'd left it had been going strong, probably wouldn't break up for another hour at least.

The party had been in Chelsea, Tony invited by a jeweller whom he'd dealt with from time to time – someone wealthy with a lovely apartment, beautifully furnished, a hired jazz pianist, a spread to die for, and drink coming out of their ears.

'Why can't we live somewhere like that,' gasped Geraldine, ceasing to giggle as she let her handbag fall to the floor, struggled out of her hat and coat and flopped down into an armchair without hanging them up.

She gazed a little bleary-eyed about the flat. After the brilliance of the party, the beautiful frocks, the rich décor, this place struck her as decidedly drab, cold and uninviting, for all the fine furniture it held. She shivered.

'How much longer are we going to stay here?' she asked, accepting the brandy and soda Tony handed to her.

'Here?' His gaze followed hers about the small living room and he grinned, taking a sip of his own brandy. 'It is getting a bit cramped, come to think of it.'

She stared up at him, trying to focus. 'Then when are we going to remedy it? When are we going to move to something worth living in?'

'I was going to talk about that some time or other.' He was still grinning inanely through his drink. 'But your father being laid up, you've had your mind more on that, so I thought I'd delay things until you asked again – sometime.'

It was true, she'd been taken up with the state of her family with Dad not able to work after being discharged from hospital, and when he was well enough to go back to work, finding it hard to get back into the docks with so many men clamouring for jobs. It had been Wally who had managed finally to wangle him back in. In all that time, his family had lived virtually from hand to mouth and if it hadn't been for Wally and Fred and Evie bringing in something, God knows what they'd have done.

Geraldine had managed to dissuade Tony from offering his help. 'They won't thank you for it, darling,' she told him. 'In fact they might even get nasty about it. Best leave well alone and let them weather it out.' His reply had been to ask whether she worried about them and he'd been taken aback when she'd flared at him that of course she was worried, but it hadn't yet come to hand-outs. Tony had gone silent on her after that and the air had been a bit strained for the next few days.

But that was all passed. Dad, back at work, was the one angering her now with his remarks that he'd got himself right without help from *other people*, that he didn't need *other people's* help in looking after his own family contrary to what *some people* thought, that he managed all right before *they* came along and would continue to do so. All of which she knew was directed at her husband who had done nothing to him except to make the mistake of offering a few quid or so to help him along. So as far as she was concerned, Dad could sink or swim and the rest of them along with him.

She let out another little giggle and slipped down a fraction in her chair, returning her gaze to the room around her.

'Then let's talk about living somewhere really nice,' she said. 'So as to be all nice and settled by the time the baby arrives.'

Anthony regarded her as best he could through the

haze of the cigarette he had just lit. The baby. Coming up to five months, fortunately she wasn't the sort to show her condition too much and had taken to wearing loose, flowing frocks, but soon she would and that would put a stop to their social life for a while. A couple of months from now she wouldn't be able to kick up her heels as she did at the moment. He wasn't unhappy about a baby and they could always get a nanny for it once she'd had it. He made enough to afford one. So long as Geraldine didn't go all motherly on him – he liked her just as she was.

She'd lit up too, one of her favourite Abdulla cigarettes, having fitted it clumsily into its ivory holder and even more clumsily lit it, blowing out a cloud of fragrant smoke to waft all over the room. He loved seeing her tipsy. It turned him on no end. It was turning him on now.

'Let's go to bed,' he suggested and getting the message instantly, she stubbed the Abdulla out into a figured glass ashtray, drained her brandy glass and got uncertainly to her feet, laughing as she staggered.

'You'll have to carry me, darling,' she murmured, which turned him on even more.

After it was over, he heard her whisper into his ear, 'We will start looking for somewhere nicer to live soon, won't we?'

He nodded into the darkness and felt her turn over, contented, ready for sleep, leaving him more sober now to think over what she'd said.

They did need to find somewhere more fitting than over this shop. It would be difficult though, because this was where he was known, becoming more known by the day, the people he dealt with knowing where to find him. He would pick the best from the stuff they bought to his back door, discard the rest, pay them and get down quickly to the task of breaking the stuff up before it could be traced to him, if indeed it could be. Precious metals melted down into less traceable ingots, jewellery suitably parcelled up for trading on to one of the several dealers he knew and had become friendly with, like the one at whose party they'd been this evening – he was becoming well respected by them – he would await the next caller.

He told no one where he lived. His card bearing an address of some nondescript jewellery shop in Bow was all they had to go on – maybe a false address – so no one had any inkling that he actually resided above it, and let them continue to think of him as someone who lived well but preferred privacy.

Since starting up this game he had become something of a mystery. He liked that. A couple of years ago people had begun to ask about him and his beautiful wife with the somewhat strange accent. He could sense the inquisitiveness as to what shadows the two of them melted into after leaving a party, a dinner, the theatre or nightclub. It was better that way, safer.

But now he was beginning to sense a different atmosphere: was he after all not as kosher as he'd led them to believe? Had he merely come into a bit of money, maybe by unsavoury means? Not that such a thing bothered the sort of people he mixed with but did this mystery of where he lived mean he couldn't be trusted? The time had come to find a good address to invite his friends to, and Gerry's request had come at the right time. Tomorrow he'd start putting out feelers, perhaps look at one of the nicer London squares to see if he could afford it. Of course he would have to step up his other business as the shop wouldn't provide. That had become a mere front. It was just as well to move, keep Gerry away from where she wouldn't need to ask questions for it was only a matter of time before she did. He'd have to be there in the evenings, of course, which meant being away from home, but if she wanted to live somewhere nice, she'd have to make some sacrifice.

'We'll be moving, Mum, about two weeks' time.'

Mum eyed Geraldine's thickening midriff with some scepticism, quite unaffected by the news itself. 'Yer around seven months, ain't yer? Not a good time ter go moving 'ouse. Yer won't do yerself any good, strainin' yerself an' getting all churned up. You 'ave ter be careful around seventh months. Don't want ter do 'arm to yerself or the baby.'

Geraldine had told her early in June that they had begun looking for somewhere better to live and that too had been received with the same indifference as now. She had expected a more ready response such as 'About time too,' or even 'That'll be nice for you,' but Mum had merely nodded and got on with brewing up the usual cup of tea she'd give any caller.

It was now July and having found a suitable place far quicker than Geraldine had expected, one she had instantly fallen in love with, it seemed Tony couldn't wait to move in.

'I can let everyone know where we are, have parties, invite everybody.'

'Hold on,' she'd laughed happily. 'By the time we're settled in it'll be nearly time for me to have this baby.'

She was beginning to feel her condition now, though not as big as she'd expected coming up to seven months. Tony had remarked last week that he wondered where she was keeping it. 'I'm beginning to think you've got it in a case somewhere in a cupboard!'

The dry quip made her laugh, in fact made her proud of herself as though she and not nature had achieved something quite remarkable. She thought about Mavis whose missed period had indeed heralded the start of pregnancy, who was already as big as the half side of a barn and she a few weeks behind her. It meant having to suffer baleful glances at her own sylph-like figure with its little round football of a lump and the snide – and to her mind quite unreasonable – remarks that why should she have all the luck while her sister looked like a bag of doings, almost as if Mavis saw it as stemming purely from her sister's more comfortable circumstances.

'If you 'ad ter put up with what I do, you wouldn't be so chirpy about lookin' like yer do', she said, again without foundation. It wasn't her fault that she was carrying better, nor that she was comfortably off where Mavis still struggled with Tom not yet in work. She hadn't planned it this way, it just happened to be.

She had stopped offering Mavis bits and pieces. All she ever got lately was a begrudging 'Thanks' and down-turned lips. Just a couple of weeks ago she'd made another attempt to help with a hat she'd had in a cupboard for ages, almost new but Tony had said it was out of date now; a neutral beige, large-brimmed, deep-crowned, just right for the hot summer weather and Mavis's face looking flushed and mottled from her condition. Again, her own skin had remained unblemished, pale but for a gentle glow that increased Mavis's jealousy, for that was all it was – jealousy.

Mavis seemed to delight in appearing shabby as though seeking to draw attention to her wretched life, wheeling her dilapidated perambulator almost with pride, a bold statement that cried out, 'Look what I've got to put up with while my sister flaunts her money left, right and centre!'

'I don't want your silly 'at,' Mavis had said, the unexpected venom of the refusal knocking Geraldine back a step or two. 'What would I look like pushing this pram, me in clothes what's come off a second-'and market stall, and wearing an 'at what looks like it's come straight out of some fancy West End store like 'Arrods. People would laugh at me, say I've gone off me nut!'

The gift thus flung back in her face, Geraldine had vowed that Mavis could go to pot for all she cared, she wouldn't offer another thing to her.


Geraldine sat next to Tony in his car and watched the furniture van in front of them move slowly off.

'Soon be there, darling,' murmured Tony as he pressed the starter button and they too pulled away from the kerb. 'Excited?'

'Mmm!' Geraldine accompanied the sound with an energetic nod. Her stomach was churning and it had nothing to do with the gentle kick she felt from the baby inside her. What a wonderful life she had. It occurred to her to feel thankful for just how lucky she was as she cast her mind ahead to the day Tony had taken her to see the house he'd chosen for them.

It was the most delightful house she had ever seen, much less ever hoped to live in, painted white, terraced, narrow but with four storeys, oval doorways set behind railings, and with lovely narrow Georgian windows to the second floor. Mecklenburgh Square off Grays Inn Road was wide, quiet and withdrawn from the London traffic and adjacent to some delightful gardens. Inside, the hugeness of the rooms had taken her breath away, coupled with something like alarm.

'But the cost! What's the rent on this place?'

'Let me worry about that,' he'd said without the flicker of an eyelid.

But alarm had refused to go away. 'We can't possibly afford anything like this.' She'd gazed around the huge drawing room that would take a fortune to furnish, and had turned back to him in disbelief as though he'd lost track of his senses. 'The shop can't possibly pay for all this. Even I know it doesn't earn enough to maintain anything near a place like this. Where are you going to find the money?'

'I'm taking care of it, darling.' He cuddled her. 'I shall take care of everything.'

Somehow his patronising got to her and she broke away. 'Don't treat me as though I've got no brains, Tony! I know and you know we can't afford this on what the shop brings in. Where are you getting the money from?'

For a moment or two he studied her, his face tight, then it relaxed. 'I'm borrowing it.'

'From your father, I suppose.' She gave him no time

to confirm or deny but ploughed on, angry at the time, angry and fearful. 'How can you go on letting him support you? And how you let him go on financing you when we both know he and your mother have never liked me, believing that you married beneath yourself. Knowing that, how can you keep going to them cap in hand asking for support? Haven't you any pride?'

Her mind had flown to her own family who would never take a penny that wasn't theirs. Suddenly they soared in her estimation, they had more respect for themselves than he could ever have, and even though she loved him dearly she had felt oddly ashamed that he could take off his father so lightly.

'It doesn't matter where I borrowed it from,' he'd grinned at her, pushing away her accusations. 'Maybe from the bank.'

Obviously she'd judged him wrongly, but she'd still been unsettled by what she could only see as foolhardiness, trying blindly to impress her and going over the top about it, not realising how he was jumping in out of his depth. In all logic, she'd demanded, 'So what collateral do they want?'

He continued to grin. 'Or maybe from a friend.'

'And when do they want paying back?'

'Or maybe I've had it secretly stashed away.'

He'd been bent on teasing her, enjoying her anger. She'd told him to be serious, had asked again where the money was coming from and he'd replied, growing serious, that it was purely a business thing. When she'd asked what business thing, he had startled her with a glare, telling her that it was none of her affair.

'Be content that I know what I'm doing, Gerry,'

he'd snapped. 'You're my wife and it's my job to conduct a transaction and not for you to stick your nose in.'

'Tony!'

'I mean it, darling. There's only one head of a family, one man to do the worrying, and I don't intend to explain myself to you. It's enough that I provide you with nice clothes, a decent roof over your head, and a social life you can be proud of. What more do you want?' When she'd fallen silent, he went on more gently, 'Leave the business end to me. I'll do the earning, the supporting of you and the baby when it arrives. Isn't that enough for you?'

'Yes, of course it is,' was all she could say, telling herself she was indeed a fool not to appreciate what he was doing. In future she would try not to question him but just be thankful for the pleasant life he was giving her. Silly to rock any boat that was on an even keel.

Now they were leaving their cramped little flat, going somewhere where she could hold up her head. Perhaps that was why Mum and Dad hadn't popped round to see them off but had stayed solidly ensconced in their own home. Perhaps she should forgive them – she was only moving a few miles away, not the other side of the world. Even so, she knew that for the few times they would ever visit her posh new home, it might well have been.

Why did they act this way? What was so wrong about having a bit of money? She'd been lucky, that was all, it wasn't a disease, yet they treated her as if she was a pariah. It was so silly, and it was hurtful, and there was nothing she could do about it. Try as she might, she had never been able to shake them off their lofty perch into which was forever burnt the indelible words '*Them and us*', still living in the era when the gentleman would not dream of mixing with the common man except to slum for fun. To Mum and Dad she was now *'Them'*.

Taking in a sharp, deep breath through her nose, Geraldine cast the questions from her and turned her thoughts to the life opening up before her. If that was how they wanted it, then sod them. She'd tried to do her best and her best had been spurned. So all right, then, sod them!

# Chapter Fourteen

Life couldn't have been sweeter. With five weeks to go before the baby was due, Geraldine was happy to stay at home rather than socialise and her new house was so lovely she was as content as a pig in swill, as Mum would have put it. Roaming from room to room, gazing over and over again at all the lovely furniture and furnishings Tony had managed to fill the rooms with was pure joy from which she never tired.

Fenella came often to see her and they'd sit talking about babies and clothes over coffee and cake. And Geraldine nearly passed out when a letter came from Tony's mother, after months of silence following her letter to them saying she was expecting their grandchild. His mother hoped that her daughter-in-law would go through her delivery safely and without too much trouble, and though there was no invitation to visit, Geraldine wasn't as concerned as once she might have been, vowing to take it all with a pinch of salt. They were the losers, not her. She was ecstatically happy.

One fly in the ointment was Mum and Dad. So far

they'd deigned to set foot in her new home on one occasion only, the Sunday afternoon after moving in, and then to sit on the edge of the green brocade sofa in the elegant living room with its Georgian windows as though they were visiting a stranger. The conversation had been equally stilted and after a while Tony had excused himself saying he had to go to see someone. Left alone with them, her own parents, the conversation hadn't relaxed one bit as they sipped their tea as though she'd poisoned it. Invited to stay for tea, they had made an excuse that Mum's brother Frank and his wife and kids were coming to tea with them and they had to be back in time.

As yet Mavis hadn't come at all, but then it meant paying out for the bus fare which they could ill afford and Mavis too was nearing her time. She could discount Evie and Fred – they were young and visiting was a chore for them, but she hoped their hearts were with her.

Wally and Clara, courting strong and probably needing to find places to go to while the time away quicker to their wedding next spring, came on several occasions, Clara gazing around enviously but not unkindly, her small face full of yearning, saying how she wished this was all hers and Wally earnestly promising that one day they might have a place like it.

Aunts and uncles had up to now been noticeable by their absence, maybe expecting to feel uncomfortable by what they saw as their jumped-up niece lording it over them in her grand home. But then they were far enough removed not to concern her. The only one who came had been Dad's eldest sister Aunt Jess. Widowed and at a loose end, she'd turned up unannounced one Monday with her unmarried daughter to sniff a lot as her eyes roamed about the place, while she made a point of saying that of course *all this sort of thing* wasn't to her taste.

'I like a place ter be more homely,' was her chief remark, repeated several times. 'I couldn't never feel comfortable in a big place like this.'

To which Geraldine couldn't help thinking, that's because you don't have it – if you had, the boot would definitely be on the other foot, wouldn't it?

Cousin Doreen said little, but kept picking up this ornament, that vase, this and that piece of porcelain, to peek surreptitiously at the base as if looking to detect some rare mark that might establish some vast worth, though why she needed to at all was beyond Geraldine's comprehension. Watching with growing irritation, she was sure that were she to discover anything costing a fortune, she wouldn't have recognised it anyway.

Apart from Mum and Dad's one and only appearance so far niggling at her, Geraldine found herself perfectly happy being at home on her own. It wasn't exactly wise at this time to go socialising and she was content to let Tony go off on his own knowing he quite often combined it with business, as he'd made a lot of business friends this last year or so. She would go to bed early with a warm drink and a couple of biscuits, perhaps a few chocolates, and read. She was often asleep by the time he came home tired and just a little tipsy, though quietly so, every business deal hardly expected to be conducted without a round or two of brandies to finish off the champagne that usually went with dinners out.

Obviously he was away during the daytime at his shop, and some evenings would work on in the back room of the shop after closing up, fashioning more jewellery to show in his window, though these days the settings were gold and the gems real. Also he was beginning to deal in already complete jewellery.

'Don't you think,' she said after a couple of weeks of his staying behind for hours after the shop closed, 'that place is rather like trying to make a silk purse out of a sow's ear? It's in the wrong area for the kind of stuff you're making now. Surely no one around Bow can afford to buy any of it. Might it not be a good idea to get rid of it and find somewhere slightly better? Nothing too grand, but certainly somewhere better than Bow. Hackney would be nice – it's quite a nice area.'

He'd grown oddly stubborn, telling her she didn't know what she was talking about. But three days later, he surprisingly relented.

'I've been thinking over what you said,' he told her, coming home around midnight, apparently from dinner with a colleague. Geraldine was already in bed when he entered the bedroom.

'I've been talking to someone I know and he agrees I should get out of the East End and set up somewhere more suitable.'

Sitting there in bed, she couldn't help but feel a little irked. He'd had the conceit to dismiss her advice as not worthy of note yet had taken the same advice on board from a man, a casual friend no doubt. That he and this person probably knew more about the jewellery trade than she did cut no ice with her – common sense should have told him that she knew what she was talking about. It was belittling, emphasising a man's opinion that she was just a woman not worthy of being listened to.

'So I've decided,' he went on, slowly undressing, 'to look for a place somewhere in the Bond Street area.'

Geraldine experienced a brief flashback to the day she walked down that street and found the dress she'd copied, thereby getting to know Tony for the first time. But she pushed away the lovely memory, still indignant.

'Don't you think that's jumping the gun a bit?' It was impossible to keep the sarcasm out of her voice. 'The rent on that old place is a fraction of what you'll have to pay on what you're looking for. *And* the landlord won't be too happy having to find someone to take it over with the present state of the country.'

'No bother. It's already been arranged.'

She stared at him. 'How can it be? I only spoke of it three days ago.'

'I've been toying with the idea ever since we moved here and a few weeks ago I began getting the wheels turning.'

'Then why put me off when I mentioned it? You were positively offhanded with me. You dismissed out of hand what I suggested.'

'I didn't want to get your hopes up. I had to see if things could go through OK. Now they have and so I'm telling you.'

'After someone else has advised you the same as I did,' she added sarcastically. She was confused. He'd said he'd already got the ball rolling, yet had kept silent about it when she'd made the suggestion. Then someone had apparently advised him this very evening and he'd said he'd taken up the suggestion, yet had apparently already started the ball rolling. Something felt wrong, none of it making sense. But he was a little drunk and probably wasn't able to string his sentences together accurately. He'd explain it better in the morning, no doubt, when he was sober.

She forgave him his drink-garbled information and snuggled down under the covers as he crept in beside her, the brandy on his breath wafting spicily across her face as he kissed her goodnight and her silent forgiveness grew in volume.

Yet the way he had told her nagged on well into the early hours. How had he found someone for the shop so quickly? And even with that out of the way, where was he going to find the rent for premises in a place like Bond Street, even the tiniest corner. The rent being asked for West End premises was sky-high even in these days of unemployment, and though it was true that while the poor grew poorer the wealthy continued to thrive, even so, how was he going to afford such rent, on top of what he was paying for this place?

Surely he wasn't thinking of going to his father yet again? Tony was seeing it as all too easy for her peace of mind, taking from his dad just as and when he fancied. Naturally she didn't wish to see him – and of course herself – lose all the things they were enjoying, but to expect his father to finance him forever . . . what if one day he ceased to? Where would they be then? Common sense told her it must stop now before it got out of hand and they took an even greater fall.

Tomorrow she'd write to his father, a decision that made her tremble beneath the bedcovers while Tony began to snore gently, contentedly. It was a daunting thought, contacting his father who still saw his son as having married beneath him and had no regard for her whatsoever. But something had to be done. For Tony's sake she must try to nip this cadging lark of his in the bud. On the other hand, if Tony's father took her advice and put a stop to the allowance, which it appeared to have become, she could be the loser, all this grandeur she'd come to enjoy disappearing overnight. Not only that, Tony would be furious with her. He might never forgive her.

Perhaps she should speak to him first. Then perhaps not. He'd be just as angry and there'd be such a devil of a row.

Perhaps if she asked his father to cut down on the money, not to such a degree as to see them reduced to going back to the Bow area, but at least enough to stop Tony continuing to assume it still grew on trees and from stretching to even greater hare-brained ideas. And she must make a point of asking his father never to let him know the source of what had prompted him to be more frugal with his allowance.

But what if Tony's father, disliking her as he did, told him about her letter? Dare she risk writing at all? Yet if she didn't do something now, could they very well find themselves heading for a terrible downfall one day in the future? On and on the questions nagged until finally she fell asleep.

Somewhere in her sleep her mind had made itself up. The following morning after Tony had left for his work, she found herself sitting down at the small bureau in his study, writing furiously, as though someone else was guiding her hand. Encouraged by the way she was able to word the letter she let her hand run on. That Tony was becoming far too reliant on the money his father sent, and the fear it was bringing to her, was enough to keep her hand moving.

Filling an entire page, she finally signed off, rapidly folded the paper in three, pushed it into the first envelope she found, a long business one, sealed it, the gum sickly sweet against her tongue, and addressed it. There, it was done. Giving no time for second thoughts, she threw on her hat and coat and hurried out into the morning drizzle. In her haste the heel of her shoe slipped off the wet top step of the three down to the street and she landed on her back with such a wallop as to shake her from head to toe.

Several men going off to their places of work came rushing to her aid, seeing the pregnant woman in distress. Some bent over her, one asking if she was all right, had she had hurt herself, and started to make an attempt to help her to her feet, but another told him to let her find her breath before getting up.

It was so embarrassing that she got up, practically leapt up, unaided, hastily reassuring everyone that she was quite all right, that it was just a silly tumble, that she should have looked what she was doing. Before they could do anything she was virtually running down the road to the post box with her letter, anything to get away from them and the gazing intrusion of their eyes. And if she did pause to reflect on her action before popping the letter into the narrow opening of the letter box, she did so with little thought other than how foolish she had felt lying flat on her back on the pavement with men staring down at her as if she were an imbecile, at the same time openly taking note of her condition.

She hadn't been hurt, just very shaken, though the thump of landing flat on her back was still with her, as if something heavy had gone right through from her back to her stomach. There was a small pain there but as she made her way back home, the back of her coat still wet from the damp pavement, it slowly diminished. All she wanted to do was to get back indoors out of the way of any prying eyes from other windows in the square, hoping that no one but those off to their various businesses had witnessed her stupid fall.

Two days later, with always two or three posts per day, came a letter from Tony's father, addressed to her. Fortunately it arrived after he'd left and thanking God for that, Geraldine tore it open. The letter could not have been more terse, half a page, no more.

*In reply to your request that I send my son no more money, or at least less than you assume I have been sending him, I have to tell you that I have never sent my son any money from the day he gracelessly turned down my offer to have him with me in the law firm of which I am a partner. As far as I am concerned he chose the bed he preferred to lie in, and further confirmed it by his marriage.*

*If I hadn't washed my hands of him the day he walked away from my generous offer to set him up in a thriving law firm, then I certainly did so on the day he married without the courtesy of asking our opinion, and to someone, and I am sorry to have to say this, of whom we would never have approved had he sought it.*

*Therefore, he forfeited any prospect of my ever sending him any money. If he gets himself in severe straits then he will have to get himself out of it, as we all have in our time. I do congratulate you both on the coming birth of your child, and may send a little something for it on its birth – but as for forwarding my son any funds whatsoever, I never have, nor ever shall, finance him in any way connected with this foolhardy pursuit of his.*

*I see that you have been labouring under a misapprehension all this while, but hasten to put the matter right.*

*Please let me know when the child is born.*

The letter hadn't even addressed her by name, much less any word of endearment, nor did it end with any signature, a direct snub to her standing if ever there was one. But if it rankled, that rankle was smothered by the shock of knowing that Tony's money was not coming from his father.

Yet Tony had money – he had to have in order to afford this house, and apparently for the exorbitant rent that would be asked for West End premises, and for seeing that she remained well dressed and to continue to be taken out socially to fabulous places. Where was he getting it, and from whom?

All day she stewed, waiting for him to return home. He came home late as she had expected, remaining behind after closing the shop. She wondered why he should bother working on his beloved lapidary knowing full well that more and more his trade involved buying in and selling the real thing.

He came home around eleven. She was still up, despite now aching all over as the muscles stiffened from the fall she had taken. She hadn't yet told him about that because it might have meant mentioning the letter she had posted to his father. Now it was different.

Conscious of her aching limbs and of a small pain in her stomach, she sat very still in the armchair as he came into the living room. Waiting until he had come over to kiss her, and then offering only her cheek, she held the letter out to him as he stood back in some surprise at her cold reception.

'This arrived today from your father,' she announced, and in case he thought something bad had happened to his parents, added quickly. 'It was addressed to me in answer to one I wrote to him.'

'You wrote to him?' he queried as, innocently, he took the open sheet of paper.

'I felt a need to. Read what he says, Tony.'

She remained very still while he read, mainly because the movement of her muscles was so painful. She watched his face closely, saw it change from smiling bewilderment to concern then alarm. She was still watching his face as he looked up, a silly grin beginning to spread across his features.

'So you've caught me out.' He even managed a chuckle and put his hands above his head, elbows crooked, the letter still clutched in one hand.

'Fair cop! OK, I confess!'

'Please do, darling.' Despite the endearment, her tone was frigid.

Sitting down in the other armchair, he studied the letter again, she suspected so as not to meet her steady

gaze still trained on him. Seeing she wasn't to be messed
with, his tone when he spoke had become thoughtful.

'I know what you're thinking, that I've got money by
borrowing.'

'Have you?'

'Well, yes and no.'

'What does that mean, yes and no?'

He was gnawing the inside of his mouth as though
trying to make up his mind how to reply.

'Well?' she prompted and he gave a start, looking up
at her for the first time.

Still she waited while he scrutinised her face, taking
his time about it until she felt she wanted to scream at
him. Yet she sensed he was trying to define her mood,
debating whether it was safe to divulge whatever secret
he held for being the possessor of all this money that
had not come from his shop or his father. Finally she
could stand the scrutiny no longer.

'Well, what do you mean by yes and no?' she repeated.

Again he started, seeming to come to life rather like
a clockwork toy suddenly switched on. But when he still
made no answer, this time she moderated her tone. He
needed to be coaxed and anger wasn't going to do that.

'Is that all you've done, Tony, borrowed money?'

His responding nod struck her as unconvincing. There
was something he hadn't yet told her, she was sure of
it.

Something was slowly dawning on her. As the wife
of a jeweller, even a small-time one who fashioned much
of his stock from bits of glass, scraps of silver and semi-
precious stones he himself would cut and grind and
polish, she was aware that there might be the odd petty

thief or two appearing at his back door with something to sell.

She'd always seen Tony as one hundred per cent honest. A dishonest man would never have done what he had – offering to help her parents out of trouble when Dad had been ill, even in the face of Dad's rude and ungrateful rebuffs. Yet her mind sped back to the time when she'd come downstairs and found him with a scruffy, furtive-looking man, the pair of them startled and alarmed by her entrance, Tony recovering himself, passing the caller off as an old army chum looking for a handout. Had that man been looking to lighten himself of his haul for a bit of cash, a burglar, one of several? Many a time she had heard that back door to Tony's workshop open, but had never thought much of it. Now it all made sense.

'You haven't been dealing in stolen goods, have you, Tony?' she accused outright, instantly wishing she hadn't asked the question and wondering why she had.

To her utter surprise and some little shock, Tony nodded, crestfallen, and she leaned quickly towards him, wincing from the sharp pains the movement caused. She ignored them. 'How often, Tony?'

'Quite a bit.' His voice sounded small. Then he seemed to make up his mind, almost eager to talk. 'I suppose I ought to have told you, darling. But I thought you'd never want anything to do with me again. That shop was never going to make money, and when you and I began going out together I knew I had to do something. Under no circumstance was I ever going to go back to law and have my father tell me what to do and what not to do for the rest of my life, especially as my parents would never have accepted you, never understood that I loved you down to my very soul and that I could never give you up.'

Despite what she'd discovered, Geraldine's heart leapt at those words.

Tony's features, however, were contorted and he seemed very near to tears from the emotion inside him. He leaned towards her, the letter crushed between his fingers.

'That first time, I thought buying a few bits off an old mate couldn't be that bad. He needed the money and I didn't ask where the stuff had come from. I named a price and he was happy and a few days later I sold the stuff on to another dealer. Somehow word got around and I found it was too late to start refusing stuff. Some I resold, some I melted down and remade into other jewellery to sell myself. It was money for old rope. I found it becoming quite lucrative and it enabled me to buy you things I could never have afforded before. Then one day a man came to me and spoke about doing a deal – big money.'

Tony was talking faster and faster as if eager to get it all off his chest. 'I said I didn't want to get in that deep but the things he said made me certain he'd go to the police if I didn't comply. I was scared, so I did. It's that which started all this. But it hasn't been as bad as I thought it would be. I'm in with these people now. They are professionals and so long as I deliver and don't ask questions there's nothing they wouldn't do for me. They promised that. And they've now proved it, by giving me . . . not lending me, darling, but *giving* me the money to furnish this place. That's why it's so beautifully furnished.'

She had wondered about that, had thought his father

must have been mad to give so much to him. Now, of course, she knew better.

'It's they who are paying the rent on this place. They are the ones who have been inviting us out, all those people I've introduced you to at parties, at the theatre, at restaurants. I actually feel I can call them friends. They have been very good to us. They're really nice people, darling. You said yourself that you liked them, and they like you very much.'

She'd wondered many times about that too, how he had come to find such a prosperous, fun-loving set.

'The times when you've not been with me,' he continued, 'they asked after you, thought you were ill and could they do anything for you, and when I told them you were expecting our baby, they sent their good wishes and said they will buy the best for it as birth presents. As for my new shop, they will pay the rent on a prime position in Bond Street. Not too ostentatious but respectable. It's they who arranged my giving up the old shop. And I'm also to find a site in the suburbs where I will be able to operate a smelter.'

Geraldine came to life. 'You mean for melting down big stuff, bullion?'

'Well, precious metals of course, but I don't think it'll ever go as far as bullion. I really don't know what it'll be. They've not said.'

'Of course you know,' she spat out, the effort hurting her, but her reaction was now one of anger at him. 'You're not daft, Tony. You know the score. They've got you wrapped around their little finger and you've let them. You've walked right into it, haven't you? People like that know a greedy man when they see one.'

'I'm not greedy, darling!' He too had grown angry.

'Of course you are, you want everything. If that's not greed—'

'And so did you,' he cut her short. 'You wanted everything too. That's why you married me, because I was your way out of the muck you lived in.'

'That's not true!' she burst out, indignant. 'I fell in love with you.'

But was that really true? She had wanted to escape the life she'd led, had wanted something better, and he had been her way out. That she had fallen in love with him had been an added bonus . . . no, that had come first. Or had it? She was confused. The truth batting against her brain was rebounding from side to side like a hard rubber ball. It almost hurt. She hurt. Her stomach was aching too.

'I fell in love with you, Tony,' she persisted, trying to calm herself.

He had calmed down too. He put out a hand and touched hers. 'I know. And I loved you, still do, with every part of me. But please, darling, please understand. I admit I was a fool, but I've got myself in too deep to get out. I have to go along with it. So long as I'm protected, and these people protect their own – they don't kill the goose that lays the golden egg – we'll be OK. I know there must be other people handling their stuff, but so long as I am trusted I'm all right and I'll be well looked after.'

She had a sudden frightening thought. 'This isn't the Mafia, is it?'

He gave a little chuckle, almost of relief. 'I don't think so. If it was they'd keep things to their own, not some failed country lawyer like me. I think they're just a firm who needs someone like me, that's all.'

'What if you get caught?'

'I shan't, not so long as they're OK.'

'What if any of them get caught?'

'People like them have a code of honour, Geraldine. No one squeals.'

He was talking like a gangster, and she suddenly realised that she too was talking as though she was colluding with him. He was all smiles now, his hand tightening hers reassuringly. He was at ease, glad to have it off his chest at last and her on his side.

'Don't worry, my darling,' he was saying. 'Everything's going to be fine, and you and I will be living in the lap of luxury, don't you worry.'

# Chapter Fifteen

On the face of it he was self-assured; inside he was full of unease and had been so for months. How could he have been such a fool to have this creep up on him without seeing the consequences? He was almost glad Geraldine now knew the truth.

And she was right. If he were honest with himself it did all amount to greed. From that first innocuous knock on his back door by an army chum down on his uppers and turning to crime as the only way he could see to keep from poverty.

So easy, so bloody easy, offering a couple of quid for the lot, the man's face lengthening with disappointment, but before he could up his offer out of pity, the poor bugger grabbing the cash and bolting.

He'd enjoyed the experience of prising the stones from their settings, real gems these, the gold melted down and refashioned, the result sold on to some other jeweller he knew. Days later the army chum back with another haul – it had gone on from there.

The contact he'd met in a local pub, a chummy sort

of chap, had quietly remarked that this was the business to be in, accompanied by a sly look, half a wink. Anthony knew what he was getting at; had felt the greed surge through him. Longing to get on in this trade he began to see profit with very little outlay and hardly any risk – just small-time stuff but enough to live comfortably on.

When bulky stuff came in he simply melted it down into small ingots to sell on to the outlets named by his contact in the pub. Where it ended up after that he didn't care, it was off his hands. Money for old rope.

It was a few months ago that things began to escalate, someone calling himself Dalkener entering the shop with a proposition. A small-time crook, he nevertheless made the eyes glitter at the promise of even more fine rewards for very little effort, and now he was beginning to see it come about. Now those he'd never thought to be dealing with were jovially shaking him by the hand, slapping him on the back, their wives and lady friends kissing his cheek on meeting, calling him darling, he being assured that any problems whatsoever, not to hesitate to ask for help and they'd be sorted out for him.

Geraldine too had been received with open arms, delighted by all the attention. But he knew the score. Clever people these, recognising his weaknesses and leaping in, tempting him with promises, promises they would keep, no question of that, so long as he held to his part of the bargain. And while he did there was no height to which he might not aspire, slowly being given an ever larger piece of the cake, in the process, however, sinking in deeper, and always underneath the feeling that if one day he did not toe the line, their retribution would be felt in no uncertain terms.

Did all of those in the world in which he had poked a toe, then a foot, then an ankle, feel as he did? Was this part of the price, knowing the end product might be to be caught, to go down for a stretch, one's family left to suffer? He'd heard criminals usually look after their own so long as the one going down could be trusted, so long as that person did not turn informer; a kind of insurance, of being part of a family. But if they were ever done down, he could imagine that were this family to be wronged, rather than a silent snub or a sharp word, there could be the silent blade or the sharp crack of a bullet to the head by some hired killer. Pleased as he was with his good fortune, he trembled at the consequences were he to fall foul of these people.

But he was being overimaginative. He pulled himself together and grinned at Geraldine, showing her a cool, calm and collected face. In her condition she mustn't be upset. Things would be fine so long as he did what was asked of him and that was simple enough – just do the job he was being paid handsomely for, handle the stuff that came in, send it back in different form and let them get on with disposing of it all. Couldn't be simpler.

The benefits had begun. This nice house, the next would be fine shop premises in a respectable area even if it was a front for illegal activities. He had nothing to worry about. He was being a bit jumpy, that was all.

As shock or surprise often does, the impact didn't truly hit home until much later, the next morning in fact. After a good sleep Geraldine awoke to find herself amazed that she could have taken what Tony had told her so calmly, even to discussing it as if going over some ordinary daily routine. Watching him getting ready to go to his shop as he would until new premises were got for him, realisation flooded over her that she was the wife of a criminal, not just a petty criminal but getting into the big time.

Lying in bed, which she often did of a morning, she said nothing as he kissed her goodbye, told her to take things easy.

'What are you doing today?' he asked casually as he straightened up.

'I'm supposed to visit the doctor at eleven. Just to be checked over.'

'Tell him about the pain you've been having in your stomach all day yesterday,' Tony advised, she having told him of it without mentioning the tumble she'd had. 'Have you still got it?'

'Just a twinge. It'll be all right. It'll go off.'

'Well, tell him anyway.'

He'd been concerned but she had passed it off as indigestion. No point getting him all upset. What he didn't know wouldn't hurt him. 'Yes, I'll tell him,' she obliged.

At the door to the hallway he paused, turned and looked at her. 'I am worried about you, you know.'

'Yes, I know,' she smiled at him, though the vague ache had returned to her stomach.

It was a strange ache, a pain yet not a pain, the baby like a heavy sack seeming to be sitting full square on her lower parts. Just lately it had hurt to walk at times even though she did not seem all that big compared to

214

some she had seen the last time she'd gone to the doctor to be checked.

It had been a different doctor to the one she had now. She had still been living in Bow and had automatically seen the same doctor her parents saw if ever they needed one. She'd had to see a doctor prior to booking up for a maternity nursing home when the time came.

Mum had scoffed that idea. She'd had all her children at home, but Tony had been adamant about going into a proper nursing home.

'I want you to have the best,' he'd said. 'If I can afford to give you the best, why shouldn't I?'

This retort was because Mum had said in his presence, 'Load of old nonsense goin' into 'ospital just to 'ave a baby! Women 'ave bin 'aving babies without all that fuss since anyone can remember. You youngsters are too soft. 'Aving a baby is the most naturalest thing in the world. Yer don't need an 'orde of doctors and nurses fiddlin' about round yer. 'Orspital! Huh!'

Geraldine had gone to that doctor only the once. With several other mothers-to-be in his waiting room as well as a full complement of patients with an assortment of coughs and sneezes and sore throats, sore eyes, sore spots and stomach pains, he'd given her the most cursory of examinations and had announced her in good health and perfectly normal with nothing untoward to be found. She'd left full of confidence in her well-being and hadn't gone again.

What a difference her new doctor was, one whom Tony had secured for her and whom she had so far seen only the once. Charging Mecklenburg Square fees, his surgery's décor tasteful, the furnishings expensive and unbelievably comfortable, everything had been so quiet and peaceful. She'd reclined onto a softly padded table, her dress above her abdomen while he, beaming, sociable, round-faced, slightly balding, and impeccable in white coat, pressed her stomach in several places with cool, smooth hands, all such a far cry from the first doctor's ramshackle surgery, and had listened through his stethoscope to the baby's heart, announcing all was perfectly fine, that it was beating nice and loud.

So what point of going to see him again, paying out several needless guineas when she had more on her mind to worry about, remembering all that Tony had told her yesterday?

He was looking at her with deep intensity of concern in his dark-grey eyes. 'I do love you, you know.'

She nodded and sent him a kiss through pursed lips. But still he lingered.

'I didn't get much sleep last night for thinking about what I told you. I shouldn't have said anything. With you in your present condition I shouldn't have said anything to worry you so. Being as I feel a lot better about things this morning, I wish I'd never said anything.'

'I'm glad you did,' she said more easily. The ache seemed to be dying away again. It couldn't be the start of anything yet – she was still only eight months.

'Are you all right?' he was saying.

'Quite all right.' She felt a prick of impatience at his hanging back. 'Off you go, darling. I'll see you tonight.'

'You sure you won't get bored or anything.'

'I've got lots to do.' She would sort out the baby things, gaze at them lovingly and tidy them gently back into the drawer, all the little things white so that, boy or girl, they wouldn't be caught out with blues or pinks.

While she looked them over, studied them, played with them, she'd think of her baby who would be in her arms four or five weeks from now. Her heart gave a leap of joy at the prospect, visualising Tony leaning over her shoulder, gazing down at the little face of their first child. It was a joy hardly to be contained. He seemed to read her thoughts.

'Take care today, won't you? Look after our baby.'

'Of course,' she laughed at him.

'And you will see the doctor today.'

'Yes. Now off you go, darling.'

'And you won't worry too much about what I said yesterday, about what I've been doing and—'

'NO! Tony, go!'

'And you will mention that pain of yours—'

'Yes, I will. Tony, darling, sod off!'

She laughed as he vanished as if plucked away by some unseen hand. But after he'd gone and the love his concern had burnished inside her began to fade, all that he'd told her yesterday came flooding back again. Sighing, she got out of bed realising that the heavy ache in her tummy had lightened considerably as though making room for this renewed anxiety. Slowly she went to the bathroom, relieved herself for the third time since waking, the baby squatting squarely on her bladder, then washed, dressed, combed her hair, powdered her nose and went into the kitchen to try to eat something.

Appetite seemed to have vanished. Gazing down at the one slice of toast she had made, she debated whether to keep the doctor's appointment or not. What she really wanted to do was to go and see Mum. Mum was the one person she most wanted at this moment, to pour out this new worry to her, have her give advice, at least share the weight that was fast descending upon her rather like some light fluffy cloud high in a blue sky; the way she'd felt on waking this morning began to darken and spread and lower itself down to the very crown of her head.

Geraldine pushed the toast away from her and gulped down the nearly cold tea she had poured ages ago. She had decided. She'd drop a note into the surgery saying she couldn't keep this appointment and would make another for the next day instead. Then she would take a taxi to Mum's – too near her time to fight with buses, nor was she prepared to be rattled around in a tube train.

She felt much better as she left the house, apart from the somewhat painful weight of the baby lying on her bladder all the time and feeling as though its main aim inside her was to prise the top of her legs apart.


As always, Geraldine made her way around to the back door of what had once been her home.

There was no horrid smell now. Dad was better, had been back working with his old gang in the docks for months now. Where there was still a million unemployed, Dad was bringing in decent money – not enough for what he'd like, but reasonable with so many lay-offs, though that had always been accepted in the docks.

Mum was able to keep the outside lav and its surrounding area as fresh as a daisy without having all her hard work thwarted. Apparently Dad was no longer compelled to creep down in the middle of the night, the chain being pulled to wake up the entire neighbourhood. Mum could now hold her head up with pride before all her neighbours.

Geraldine tapped on the back door, opened it a fraction, calling, 'Coo-ee!' and heard her mother call from the back room, 'Oo's that?'

She came fully into the kitchen. 'It's only me, Mum, Geraldine.'

'Oh.'

Mum appeared from the back room, broom in one hand, a battered, black metal dustpan in the other, full of grey fluff from odd corners and from the rug in front of the fire grate and brownish-white breadcrumbs from her family's usual hurried breakfast taken in relays as each got ready for work. Now she was the only one left in the house and well into her chores for the day. On a clothes horse folded clothes hung airing, having been ironed the day before and now ready for putting away in drawers and on shelves.

Geraldine leaned forward and kissed her mother's lined, narrow cheek, touching both arms in an apology for an embrace, aware that Mum with her hands full could not embrace her in any way, though even if she had been able to, she wouldn't have done so. As usual Geraldine could feel the coolness emanating from her into her own body.

'How are you, Mum?' she asked as she took off her deep-crowned hat and dropped it onto the kitchen table, already cleared, the plain deal board already scrubbed and clean. 'Been keeping well?'

'Since yer last came, yes,' was the reply, stiff, cold,

indicating that Geraldine hadn't set foot here for nearly three weeks.

'I'm finding it a bit of a job travelling,' she said by way of excuse.

'Yer managed today, though.'

Geraldine gave a laugh and took off her jacket in a gesture of her intention to stay awhile. 'It's still a bit of a job. Shall I put the kettle on, Mum?'

'Your Tony could of dropped you off in 'is car – he comes this way.'

'He left early, well before I was up.'

'When I was 'aving you kids, I was always up before yer dad, makin' sure I got 'im off ter work proper. I didn't 'ave anyone ter tell me ter lie around in bed 'alf the morning.'

'Tony just worries about me, says I need me rest.' Automatically she'd slipped into the old speech. 'D'yer want me to put the kettle on, Mum?'

'If yer like.' Her mother went to the back door, beyond which stood a pockmarked, well-battered steel dustbin. There came the clash of metal on metal as the debris of the dustpan was emptied into it, the crash of the dustbin lid being replaced, speaking volumes to the listener as though Mum was working herself into a confrontation with her daughter.

Geraldine, with the kettle balanced over the sink, its lid taken off for the tap water to trickle into the aperture, listened to the sounds with a heart that grew heavier by the second. Why did Mum always have to be this way? How could she ever tell her what Tony was up to and hope for sympathy?

Tea was drunk in virtual silence, she asking the

questions. How was Dad? How were Fred and Evie getting on at work? Mum's monosyllabic, monotonic responses. And were Wally and Clara doing all right?

For a moment or two Mum came to life, forgetting to remain on the defensive. Yes, they were fine, these days talking of nothing but the wedding next spring, saving every penny they made but still hadn't as much as they wanted and they yet had to find somewhere to live.

Another hiatus during which Geraldine sipped her tea and nibbled a biscuit she didn't really want. The house smelled of yesterday's ironing and the washing and drying of the day before. It seemed to hang around as though seeping from the very walls – a damp smell. There lingered a faint odour of yesterday's dinner too, unidentifiable yet persistent, and mingling with it a faintly pungent scent of mothballs.

She asked after Mavis, saying she'd not been able to get to see her, being near her own time as she was; was told Mavis was bearing up as best she could, that she (Mum) went round there several times a week to see if there was anything she needed to be done. This brought a stab to Geraldine's breast that Mum never hopped on a bus to her to see if there was anything *she* might need, but then of course she was further away and it meant a bus ride, and being *comfortably off* as Mum would have it, she could afford to pay for help, and didn't need her – all hurtful in its intimation.

She asked after Aunt Tillie, Mum's brother Frank's wife who hadn't been too well just lately with breathing problems, and was told she was a lot better; asked after Aunt Vi, Dad's sister who also hadn't been too well, was told she was no better, her husband Bill said it was her heart, which had got Dad worried. 'If she goes, it'll be 'is first sister ter go. It won't 'alf upset 'im.'

Appropriate nodding of agreement, another cup of tea offered which she refused politely. She'd been here long enough trying to force conversation.

'I'm going to have to go, Mum,' she said as her cultured tones returned. 'I need to go off home and rest.' She gave a little laugh. 'I'm supposed to rest in the afternoons.'

'I worked right up to the last minute with you lot,' said Mum, also getting up as Geraldine got awkwardly to her feet. 'And I didn't 'ave no trouble bringing you all inter the world.'

Geraldine smiled and nodded compliance. Mum had had one still-born and two miscarriages from what she'd heard. Perhaps if she hadn't had to work up to the last minute she might have saved those babies. Then of course her family would have been bigger still to have to cope with, the mother worn out before her time. Again, she, Geraldine, the third oldest child now living, might never have known this world, might never have been where she was at this moment, enjoying her life, worrying over Mum's attitude towards her, her parents' attitude, might never have known heartache or pleasure – ironic, but not to be thought of, in fact too fleeting to be clung to. In her place now, Mum might not have had so many children anyway.

'I've got to go, Mum.'

'If yer must.'

Geraldine, gathering up her beautifully tailored jacket and her hat from Dickins & Jones in Regent Street, donned them, went to the back door and opened it. Mum asked out of the blue if she was keeping well, almost an afterthought, not having asked all the while she'd been here, and all the more hurtful because of it.

'I'm fine, Mum,' she replied.

'Well, you take care of yerself. Ain't got long ter go now.'

Geraldine searched her mother's face. 'You will be there when I go into hospital, won't you? You'll be there to see the baby?'

''Course I will. What makes yer think I won't be? It'll be me second grandchild. Mavis's won't be born till a month after yours. 'Course I'll be there. Soon as yer start yer labour, get yer 'usband ter send us a telegram. We'll be waitin' for it.'

Always *your husband*, seldom Tony, almost on purpose, spoiling the heartfelt sentiments she'd just uttered.

''Course, bein' in 'ospital yer won't 'ave need of yer mum fussin' around. Not like at 'ome.' Again the barbed remark spoiling what sentiment there had been.

Her mother gave a deep sigh as she saw her out to the yard. 'Don't really expect I'll be able ter get around ter seeing you before then. Might not see nothink of yer at all, unless yer 'usband wants ter bring yer in the car ter see us. It wouldn't 'urt 'im. Of course we'd like ter see yer before the baby arrives.'

All this was the longest Mum had spoken all morning. As if attempting to make up for the time lost, all in one swoop. She leaned forward for her daughter to kiss her goodbye but didn't accompany it by an embrace, and this time her hands were not occupied with broom and dustpan.

223

'I'll give yer love to yer dad and tell 'im yer was sorry to 'ear about yer Aunt Vi. Take care going home. Don't walk too fast. 'Ope yer don't 'ave ter wait too long at the bus stop.'

Once in Bow Road she would find a taxi outside Bow Road Station to take her home. But with thoughts of what that would cost possibly making her mother turn from her as seeing money thrown needlessly away, making enemies again, she said nothing.

Nor had she said anything about what Tony was up to these days. She came away feeling she had mislaid something or rather that which she had wanted to unburden herself of was still up caught inside, leaving a strange empty feeling. She wanted to cry, very weepy these days, but not here in the street. This empty feeling was probably hunger. She was hungry and it was midday. She hadn't even thought of staying with Mum for a bit to eat. Mum wouldn't have begrudged her that, her tongue sharp, bitter at times, but she was never vindictive. Geraldine remembered that she hadn't had breakfast either and she was now feeling famished. Famished and faint.

She would have to find a coffee shop in Bow Road just to eat a bun, before finding a taxi. Bow Road seemed miles away yet it was only little more than a quarter of a mile.

There would have been somewhere in Grove Road but it meant going past Tony's shop. The last thing she wanted was for him to see her. It might be better to have gone the other way to Roman Road, plenty of coffee shops there, but that would mean retracing her steps. She felt confused, consumed by misery. The weight inside her was bearing down on her bladder, hurting her, making her want to wee again even though she'd been twice at Mum's.

With vision misting from the tears lying along the lower rims of her eyelids and her nose threatening to start streaming, she pulled her deep cloche hat even lower over her brows, thanking heaven for the current fashion and a now overcast sky that shielded her from passing glances.

# Chapter Sixteen

By the time she reached the corner of Coborn Road with Bow Road she had a great need to sit down. She was beginning to wonder if she would indeed get as far as a café when she thought she heard her name being called as if from some way off.

At first she thought it to be the coalman she had not long passed, rasping out his trade above the trundling of his laden coal cart as he led his horse down the road. She remembered the coal-dust-streaked face, the cap back to front with its leather shield draped over neck and shoulders, the trousers tied below the knees with leather thongs, the thick boots, the loose coat all black with coal dust. As she passed him her nose had filled with the salty tang of coal and the warm odour of his horse. But now above his rasping call was a lighter voice, distinct now, hailing her.

'Geraldine . . . Wait! Geraldine!'

Damn! The caller would see she'd been crying. They would want to stand and talk, and the way she was feeling at this moment, she'd more likely pass out in front of them, make a fool of herself.

Blinking away the moisture in her eyes, she turned to the voice, ready to smile and make the ubiquitous excuse of having something in her eye, or maybe having a bit of a cold, and then say she was in a rush and, sorry, she had no time to chat.

She was making up her mind about that when she realised it was Alan Presley belting towards her, raincoat flying, one hand holding his trilby firmly onto his head. It was he who'd called to her – all the more reason to make an excuse for her tearful appearance.

In seconds he was beside her, just the tiniest bit out of breath from running. 'I 'ad ter run like mad to catch you up. I saw yer from some way off an' thought it was you so I broke into a sprint and it was you, thank God. I didn't want ter be caught chasing after some female I didn't know—'

He stopped abruptly, for the first time noticing her dejected features. His grin dissolving, he bent to gaze into her face, still half hidden by her hat brim. 'Are you orright? Yer've been crying. What's up?'

'Nothing's up,' she said tersely but her throat rasped painfully.

She couldn't stand here. She felt she couldn't stand at all. Her legs were beginning to go wobbly on her.

He must have seen what was about to happen because his arm came around her, drawing her to him, taking her weight. 'Fer God's sake, Gerry, don't faint on me. Yer as pale as a ghost.'

She was leaning against him, her head drooping without strength on to his shoulder. Yet in the midst of her faint she was vaguely aware of the fact that they must look like two outrageous lovers, and out here in the street would draw disapproving looks from passersby. This was not the done thing. That thought helped to return her to her senses, the receding world bouncing back as she became aware of how this must seem to others.

She made an effort to take her own weight but he held on. 'No, take it steady. Give yerself a bit of time,' he was saying, so she let him continue to support her until she was slowly able to stand without support. He was gazing into her face, now unobstructed, her hat having been pushed up from her brow a little when her head had sunk onto his shoulder.

Hastily she readjusted it but still he regarded her with concern. 'Yer colour's beginning ter come back, thank Gawd. Yer gave me quite a turn, yer did, collapsing on me like that an' me just meetin' yer after ages. But yer look all in, Gerry. What's 'appened. You ain't 'ad bad news or somethink?'

'No,' she replied. 'I'm just overtired – tired and hungry. I've not had anything to eat today except for a biscuit and a cup of tea.'

'What, no breakfast? No dinner?' In the East End the midday meal was always called dinner, where she now called it luncheon. His brown eyes were studying her closely. 'Ain't broke, are yer? Down on yer uppers? You ain't broke up wiv yer old man or anythink, 'ave yer? I can lend yer—'

She laughed in spite of herself, but it was a weak little sound. 'No, not broke. And me and Tony are fine. It's just that . . . it's just . . .'

Without warning she burst into tears, they never being far removed from laughter, the two emotions travelling hand in hand like twins. This time they came in great, uncontrollable gulps. And again she was in Alan's arms, being held tightly, and damn what passers-by might think.

'It's because you're 'ungry and weak,' he was crooning through her great, hiccupping gulps. 'Should of eaten breakfast, you in your condition. If yer can make it, we'll get yer somewhere where yer can get somefink inside yer. Yer'll feel a lot better. Then yer can tell me all about it.'

She was being guided along, his arm still around her until she could eventually walk unaided, if unsteadily, merely holding on to his arm. Even in her state she'd felt uneasy about him having his arm around her waist out in the street as though he'd just picked someone up, and in broad daylight too. Not only that, they'd not touched since she had decided between him and Tony and it felt strange just holding his arm, if only for support.

The nearest café was but forty yards off, where Bow Road became the Mile End Road. It felt more like forty miles, each step an effort, she fighting weakness the whole way. It was a working men's café, grubby, stinking of the all-pervasive smell of fried onions and sausages and overused frying fat, but to her it was a haven as Alan eased her down on one of the wooden benches, a couple of none-too-clean road menders moving up to make way for her.

Feeling slightly sick she rested her elbows on the stained, green, baize-covered table top, her head bent on her two fists. Like this she could see her protruding stomach, and it occurred to her to wonder what the men in here must think – not that a pregnant woman had entered, but that a woman was sitting here at all, a café like this normally used by working men and far too grimy for any woman to eat in. Not only that, her clothes spoke of a well-groomed lifestyle. They must be wondering what she was doing here, the unsteadiness of her entry, the way she had been helped into a seat by the man who'd brought her in, the waxen colour of her cheeks making them wonder even more. They were probably having a field day. Well let them, she didn't care; all she wanted was to be home, to sink down on her soft sofa, close her eyes and sleep in quiet surroundings away from this echoing boom of men's voices, the clash of plates, the shouts from the counter hand – 'Two 'Oly Ghosts' (for years she'd known the rhyming slang for toast) 'and two Rosy Leas!' (this for tea) – and the nauseous smells coming from a probably foul kitchen with everything caked with fat residue. The very thought of that kitchen from where her tea and toast would come made her want to vomit.

By the time Alan returned with the two cups of tea in thick china cups and two massive rounds of toast, often known as doorsteps, sitting on equally thick plates, she felt she couldn't have taken a single bite.

He sat down opposite her, obliging another customer to move up a little, and leaned forward, peering into her wan features.

'I know it ain't no Buckin'am Palace, but it was the nearest in an emergency. Just take a couple of bites and drink the tea and yer'll feel better and then we can find a decent place and talk. Yer need to talk, Gerry, yer really do, the state of yer when I saw yer. Now eat up, gel. Get yer strength back.'

He was kindness itself. She thought of the time she

had told him she did not want to see him again, how she must have hurt him, what he must have thought of her chucking him over for a man with money. Yet here he was behaving as if none of that had happened. She felt humbled.

'You're being very kind,' she mumbled.

'Oh, bugger that!' He gave a small chuckle. 'Damsel in distress – wot bloke wouldn't come to 'er aid?'

Geraldine took a small bite of the toast, found it palatable, even tasty, realised how hungry she was, as though she hadn't eaten for a week. She took another bite and another, then a sip of tea, making certain to wipe the rim first in case it hadn't been properly washed. The tea was hot, short of milk, bitter and strong enough to stand a blessed spoon upright in, Mum would have said.

Normally she'd have pushed it aside in disgust but she gulped it down gratefully, finally putting the cup back on its saucer to lift her eyes to Alan.

'I don't feel hungry any more.'

He was sipping his tea and thoughtfully eyeing her over the rim of the cup that looked more like a soup bowl it was so wide. He dropped his gaze to the half-eaten round of toast. His had already gone.

'You ain't 'ad much. Go on, get yerself stuck inter it. Yer need a bit more ter get yerself all the way 'ome on. 'Ow yer getting 'ome anyway? D'yer want me ter come with yer?'

'No, I'll get myself a taxi.' She saw his chin tilt a little, one eyebrow raise itself slightly, and she realised what a snob she must have sounded and hurriedly tried to rectify it. 'I don't think I could get on a bus.'

'No, I don't s'pose so, like you are.' He paused,

231

apparently reflecting on their meeting, for when he spoke again it was to ask what she had been doing stumbling along on her own and in tears.

'Yer seem in some sort of trouble, that's fer sure. Where was yer comin' from when I caught you up?'

'Me Mum's.' It seemed easy to fall into his way of speaking.

All of sudden she found herself pouring out all that she had wanted to tell her mother and couldn't. He listened without interruption. The men sitting talking to each other next to Geraldine, seemingly oblivious to her, eventually left. The one sitting next to Alan lingered on, quite obviously ear-wigging as Mum again would have put it, for all Geraldine tried to keep her voice low. Until Alan gave him a long and deliberate penetrating look so that, clearing his throat noisily, the eavesdropper hurriedly got up and made his departure. Geraldine found herself quite suddenly admiring Alan for his strength of character in facing the man. She felt oddly protected and within her something reached out to Alan, a sensation she quickly stifled but which over the next half-hour kept arising.

They didn't seek another place to sit and eat in better surroundings. She said she just wanted to go home, even as she felt a strange longing to stay with Alan. Not that he'd said much, had offered no advice – simply listening had been enough – beyond saying that she must be careful to whom she spoke of the things she had told him.

'It's not the sort of stuff yer should be bandying about,' he'd said quietly as the man who'd been sitting next to him left. 'There's big ears everywhere and someone always around ready ter make a bit of mischief. Yer never know 'oo's listening.'

'I didn't think,' she'd returned, colouring a little, aware of the man with ears virtually flapping like an elephant's and pale blue eyes widening every now and again despite his obvious attempt to look nonchalant and interested only in his double helping of egg, chips and sausage.

'But I see what you mean,' she'd continued in a whisper even though the man had left and the table had become empty for the while, less working men around these days able to spend even in a cheap working men's eating room. 'I'm going to have to keep it all to meself in future.'

He must have seen the loneliness register itself on her face for he'd leaned forward and, taking one of her hands between his, said softly, 'If ever yer need someone ter talk to, I'm always 'ere. Yer know where I live.'

It could have sounded like some overt invitation such as a man might give to a girl he fancied, but she knew that this was purely a warm offer of help and friendship, and again that strange flutter had made itself felt inside her, and again in a kind of alarm she hurriedly quelled it.

He stood with her by the kerbside to hail a taxi, at one time pulling her gently back as a one-armed busker, a war veteran, trudged by playing a cornet, quite skilfully and tunefully, with his left hand.

Automatically Alan reached into his trouser pocket and drew out a coin which he tossed into the box hanging by a thin string from the man's neck, and on which a placard was pinned:

'WOUNDED AT MONS – WIFE, FOR KIDS AND NO WERK'

The gesture brought yet another pang to Geraldine,

but this time she ignored it. She was feeling backachy, a dull throbbing that was beginning to take up all her thoughts. All she wanted now was for a taxi to hove into sight and get her home to that quiet room and soft sofa.

'Are you on your own still?' she asked by way of diversion while they waited for something to come along.

He inclined his head in a wry sort of way. 'I got me divorce, finally, but still on me own, yeah. Looks like that's me future as far as I can see, bein' on me own.'

'You'll find someone,' she tried to console him. It proved the wrong thing to say for he turned his face to her and the look in his eyes pulled her up sharply, reading that look as plainly as though he'd spoken. 'There's no one I want,' it seemed to say, 'but you.'

A split second later the look had vanished leaving her wondering if it had actually been there, that she must have misread what it had said to her as he quickly turned away in catching sight of a vacant taxicab rattling along the road. His hand shooting into the air, he signalled to the ever-alert driver who swung his vehicle over to the kerb.

'There y'are,' he said cheerily, and she thought for a moment that the cheeriness sounded false. 'Soon be 'ome. And remember what I said, keep shtum! Certain things shouldn't be talked about. But if yer need ter talk ter me, I'll be there. Remember now.'

She didn't know why she did it, but as he helped her into the taxi, she awkward at getting in, she turned and kissed his cheek. 'Thank you for everything, Alan, for listening, for being there.'

He seemed taken aback, but said calmly, 'Remember what I said.'

'I'll remember,' she promised.

'And good luck with the baby,' he called as she closed the door. 'And maybe yer'll let me know what it is.'

'I will,' she called back as the taxi bore her away.


By the time she reached home her back was killing her. How had it come on so quickly and what did it mean? Her mind harked back to the fall she'd had a couple of days ago – had it been that?

If only she'd gone to see Doctor Bailey-Sutchens this morning instead of chasing off to see her mother. Nothing had come of that. It had been a waste of time, though meeting Alan Presley had been beneficial. She knew now that she had the hard task in front of her of keeping her husband's illegal activities to herself – not easy when one's insides were squirming with anxiety and fear of his getting caught.

Geraldine got herself onto the sofa, gingerly, trying to concentrate all her thoughts on diminishing the slow ache in the middle of her back, and awkwardly because of her lump which, when she lay on her back, resembled an overlarge football and was just about as hard.

If she had seen the doctor, whatever it was that was creating this ache might have been sorted out and she'd be feeling comfortable now. She had so longed to spend a restful afternoon getting over this morning's escapade, now all she was doing was suffering. Slowly, Geraldine allowed herself to relax and a huge sigh to escape her lips at the relief lying down afforded.

Without warning there came a piercing pain in her stomach so that the sigh became an abrupt cry. Geraldine struggled to an upright position as the pain died away.

But she was left rigid with a new fear. The baby wasn't due for weeks. So what was that pain?

She had little idea of childbirth. No one had ever explained it to her. Her mother had kept it very quiet as if it were as private a function as going to the toilet. All Geraldine could remember of it was being told as a child to go off next door to a neighbour, tell them Mum's time had come, then to be taken into the neighbour's house to be fed and put to bed there for the night, she and Mavis and Wally. They'd return home next day to be taken upstairs to their parents' room, Mum in bed looking tired but smiling, in her arms a tiny baby, they being told to say hello to their new little brother – that had been Fred, another time to their new little sister, Evie. There'd been a couple of occasions when coming in they'd been told there wouldn't be any baby this time, and all questions would be harshly dismissed.

There had been no more babies after Evie and Mum had never spoken about it. So as for knowing what went on prior to a baby being born other than Mum growing stouter around the waist, beginning to waddle and finally to hold her back with both hands as if it ached, this was all Geraldine had ever known about childbirth.

Now it was her turn. There came a mounting sense of panic arising from an inborn animal instinct that needed no prior instruction or handed-on knowledge. Instinct too told her that she was about to give birth and that it was too early. Something had to be done. And she was all alone.

There was a telephone in the hall Tony occasionally used to talk with business people. She'd never had need to, was too terrified to ever try using the thing sitting there on the polished mahogany side table, tall and elegant in all its black, menacing glory, it's technology there to confuse, the round, metal dial with its finger holes showing letters and numbers, its yawning mouth-piece at the top, all making her fearful of touching it and doing harm.

What would she do if she lifted the earpiece from its hook on the thin black stem to hear someone speaking to her? What would she say? But now a fresh bout of grinding pain got her to her feet in a panic and sent her stumbling to the hall and the thin, upright instrument.

With the earpiece jammed against her ear she heard that dread voice. It was asking for the number. What number? What was she supposed to say?

'I don't know any number,' she gasped into the mouth-piece that sat at the top of the stem.

Her tone must have sounded frantic for the voice that had been so frighteningly efficient, now grew concerned. 'Who are you wishing to call?' it asked gently.

'I need the doctor.' In one breath she poured out his name and the street where he had his practice and that she'd not used a telephone before and didn't know how, ending, 'I'm about to have my baby!'

The voice became urgent. 'One moment please. Don't hang up.'

'Hang up?' Geraldine queried idiotically, not knowing the phrase.

'*No, don't* hang up! Keep holding the receiver to your ear and wait.'

Geraldine did as she was told, despite the beginnings of another pang coming on. It was an immense relief to finally hear the doctor's voice asking who she was.

Nothing had ever sounded sweeter. Quickly she gasped out her name, and to his question, her address, just able to add her need of him before the contraction had her breaking off with a cry of pain, dropping the earpiece to sink to her knees in an effort to help it subside.

She remained there, unable to think what next to do, the earpiece still dangling by her side, until a rat-a-tat on her door made her struggle to her feet. She got to it, opened it as yet another contraction had her falling into the doctor's arms.

'Please help me,' was all she could whimper ineffectually, then, 'I 'ave to tell Tony, my 'usband,' refined speech gone out of the window, still but a fine veneer over what she truly was.

After that it was all a blur – being helped back to the sofa, the doctor making a telephone call while she lay moaning; people coming in to help her down the stairs and into an ambulance, being wheeled through the entrance of the private nursing home and into a white-painted single ward; examined by a doctor then being surrounded by nurses, and of pain, mounting pain that had her screaming, uncaring of who heard her, and pleading for all this to be over.

The midwife glanced up at the doctor attending and the silent message that passed between them was brief but significant, accompanied by the midwife giving an audible click of the tongue. This was plainly a breech, the bottom being presented rather than the head as in a normal birth.

Fortunately, being an eight-month baby, it was small and manageable and hopefully wouldn't cause too many complications. Confidently they set to work to deliver the child as skilfully as possible while the mother, crying and moaning, needed to be coaxed or bullied as the case may be into doing whatever she was told to do as best she could. The doctor stood by, his presence required at any complicated delivery. Trying to turn the child at this stage had proved useless, so a breech delivery it would be though he didn't foresee any real problem – the baby was small, the mother strong, and his nurses some of the best.

Even so it took several hours of the mother's strength to push the little buttocks clear of her young and strong pelvic girdle, positioned with her body balanced over the foot of the bed so that such a delivery could be handled easier. But when the child finally decided to come into the world, it was far swifter than even their training had prepared them for.

All were well aware that a baby's head, the largest part of its body, would stretch the pelvic girdle enough to let the rest follow easily, but a child's bottom had no such girth, the child shooting out far too quickly.

It was exactly what happened, a nurse leaping forward with a cry of alarm to hold the tiny body back before the head could appear. No breech baby could be allowed to enter the world so fast that the head, face up, became caught while still inside the mother. The method was that with her pelvis on the edge of the bed, her child could be eased out and down giving enough room for the head to emerge without harm.

Seeing the danger at the same time as did the nurse, the doctor too sprang forward, automatically and instinctively, ready to hold back the eager child before the pull on its tiny head could rupture fragile blood vessels.

Between them neither did their job well. The head had already popped out, being jerked in the process. Both faces registered alarm as the nurse took the child and laid it on the waiting side table. Then came a cry every midwife dreaded – thin, high-pitched, unnatural, like the cry of a seagull – often called a seagull cry. What they feared had happened. Already the little face was turning blue and rapidly darkening. There was nothing they could do. In less than a quarter of an hour the child would be dead.

Instantly relieved of pain, Geraldine lifted her head in relief and anticipation to the group standing around her baby, their backs to her.

'Is it all right?' she queried. 'What have I got? It is a girl or a boy?'

A nurse turned and came over to her, a bleak expression on the woman's face, the hand slightly outstretched as if to allay something.

'A girl,' she said simply, flat-toned.

Lying back, tired from her ordeal, Geraldine dismissed the almost non-existent sense of foreboding that solemn look brought to her, and smiled. Nurses, especially older ones like this, could be dour. Soon she would be taken back to a private ward and Tony allowed in to view his daughter lying in her arms, all clean and wrapped in her new shawl.

The doctor had come to join the nurse, was peering down at her, angular face so serious she wanted to laugh. Perhaps to him delivering children was a serious business.

But her laugh had become nervous, the doctor's

expression bringing slow awareness of something not being as it should be. 'What's wrong?' she asked. She was being silly; what could be wrong?

'I'm very sorry,' began the doctor, but she was now ahead of him.

'What's the matter with her? What's happened?' Her voice sounded high-pitched to her own ears.

He was still staring down at her. He had taken one of her hands between his. 'I have to tell you, you have lost the child,' she heard him say as from a long way off. 'I'm so very—'

But already she was screaming her disbelief, struggling against his pacifying hands so that the nurses had to hurry over to help calm her.

She knew little else but for a sharp prick on the skin of her upper arm until coming to her senses much later to have reality press in upon her with all its cruel weight, reducing her to feeble weeping, aware of Tony beside her, ineffectually smoothing back her hair from her forehead, gazing into her tear-filled eyes. His own too were full of tears.

# Chapter Seventeen

'Gerry, my love, it's been more than four weeks. You must start making an attempt to get over this.'

Her only reply was to look at him as though he were speaking some foreign language. It was like this the whole time and was driving him mad for all he tried to see things from her side. Granted, it probably did not seem that long to her since the loss of the baby; granted, it was still all too fresh in her mind to grasp that life had to go on; granted, that had the baby lived it would be lying in its crib, but all the grieving in the world wouldn't alter what had happened. Yet she seemed to think that it would.

The crib had been put up in the loft along with the box of baby clothes, the fluffy toys, the teething rings, the napkin squares, the little baby bath – all at his insistence in a vain attempt to stop Geraldine moping, going endlessly through the stuff and weeping at each unused item, and especially in an effort to try to stop her referring to her lost child by name as though it were alive – Caroline this, Caroline that. He wondered how much longer he'd be able to put up with it.

By now she should be coming to terms with her loss but really she was no better than the day he'd brought her home from hospital, her face expressionless with grieving, and should he mutter so much as one word, be it in sympathy or sorrow, her face would close and become vaguely hostile as though she were entirely alone in her grief.

Couldn't she see how keenly he felt it too? When they'd come home from the hospital he'd expected it to be in joy and triumph, she seated next to him, her face radiant, tender, bending over the little bundle she held so lovingly, so proudly. No one could begin to know that feeling of coming home that day – the emptiness, the silence cocooned only by the low rumbling of the car's engine as he drove.

But all that had been a month ago. It was time she made some effort towards recovery. She wasn't the only one grieving. He was as disappointed, as devastated as she, but it wasn't as though they'd known the baby. She should never have begun choosing names before it was born. Arthur it was to have been called had it been a boy, Caroline for a girl. He'd been happy to let her do the naming, himself having none in mind. She'd said that giving it a name made her feel as though she knew it already.

'Almost,' she'd said, 'as if she's already a little person,' having made up her mind it would be a girl. No doubt that too had added to her grief. And now look at her.

He felt angry, frustrated, impatient, not knowing how to deal with her. Life had to go on. He was learning to face it and so should she; he needed to get on with his business.

Seated opposite her in the quiet sitting room, taking a moment after breakfast to be with her before leaving for work – she had eaten nothing – a thought made him pause. He had his work. What did she have? Nothing. Nothing to help her combat her loss.

She saw little of her family and that was her fault, cloistering herself in this house day after day. They saw nothing of his, had received but one card of condolence, leaving him to rage silently against his father and to harbour contempt for his mother who followed her husband in every way.

Only Fenella had visited, several times, and once with her husband; and even with her, Geraldine's only friend it seemed, she was distant, cold.

Maybe if he gave her something to do, something connected with the business, to keep her mind occupied. Provided it were harmless, it would make her feel needed and useful while not bringing her into too close contact with the seamy side of what he did. She knew of course, for he had told her that once, but not so as to frighten the life out of her. All she needed to do was manage the shop once in a while. And she'd look good behind the counter: she was attractive, had a good figure – a bit thin of late but the current fashion called for a slim figure – had a pretty smile, when she began to learn to smile again of course. People liked being served by an attractive person, especially in the jewellery trade.

Maybe she could do some bookkeeping as well, at home, the set of books he kept for his legitimate trade. She needn't know much beyond what he had told her some time ago now. If he remembered rightly, what he'd said to her had only been in the form of a brief confession,

244

a little vague even. She still didn't know the real extent of it, that it could increase as time went on if he was lucky. What was the saying? Least said, best mended. And now that he had his smelter outside London where it was safe, not far from East Ham, he'd need an assistant he felt he could trust. And who better than his wife?

The smelter had been set up in an unused, derelict, single-storey building that had once been part of a farm, long since gone, and more or less hidden away on a piece of marsh waste ground with no one interested in it but himself. The position was just right for what he did. But he couldn't be there and in the shop, and Geraldine was perfect for the job, not asking too many questions, prying into things she shouldn't know about. On top of that she'd have his best interests at heart. After all, if he went down the pan, so would her fine lifestyle and she'd be well aware of that. It was just perfect.

He would suggest it to her, say in a couple of weeks, after she'd had a little more time to get over the loss of the baby so that she wouldn't turn him down out of hand because she couldn't think straight.

He now had his new shop, not very large, not too pretentious, in Old Bond Street, the slightly narrower extension of New Bond Street before meeting Piccadilly. It wasn't much larger than his old shop with just a single window, but the glass display unit on one wall, the narrow glass display counter on the other side and a shorter one at the end held far finer merchandise, much of it the genuine article.

It had been a struggle, the rent asked for this site as well as that being asked for the place he'd bought to live in. Despite coming up in the world with the help of his other dealings, as he preferred to call it, he was finding it a struggle. How he was going to afford the upkeep of this place in Mecklenburg Square was becoming a real headache. He should have thought it all out more carefully but he'd been carried away by success, by the lure of what he could see coming in from his other dealings. He now knew he had stretched himself too far and was becoming a worried man.

Last week, however, Geraldine herself had solved his problem.

'I don't think I can stay here any more,' she had wept in one of her more grieving moments. 'I want us to move, darling. Everywhere I go here I keep seeing little Caroline, and it's so lonely here, no one to talk to, no one here of my sort, all of them stuffy and terribly correct. I wish we could move away, Tony. I know you did your best but since losing Caroline I hate this place.'

He'd tried to reason with her, but now, growing alarmed at his dwindling resources, it was a wonderful chance to get himself off the hook.

The premises above his shop had become vacant some weeks ago – two storeys and not bad-sized rooms. She'd said how she felt lost in that large place where they lived now that there were no little feet to run around in it. He would suggest they give it up and take possession of the premises above the shop. That way there'd be more money to spend on finery for her, taking her out and about, and maybe she'd put her loss behind her. It was a wonderful idea. She'd said herself on the rare occasion she put more than two sentences together that already mid-September was driving indoors those few people she did see.

He'd leave it a few more days then pop the question. How would she fancy moving in above the shop premises? Two floors, good-sized rooms, windows looking down on busy Bond Street, a far cry from the quiet square where they now lived, he with her most of the time, his shop just below – she would have to agree it was far better than here.

Tonight he rose from his armchair. 'I'll be back as soon as I can.'

That evening, as he closed up for the night, there had been a visit from an impeccably dressed man in a dark overcoat, homburg hat, spats, gloves and carrying a heavy-looking black bag. Experience told Tony that his caller was no rep eager to display gold chains and the like nestling in that large bag in the hope of securing orders. Tony had said nothing, but guided the caller to the rear of his shop, having first securely bolted the front door and pulled down the blind. The bag being opened, he'd glimpsed the glitter of gold ornaments, cutlery and place settings before the bag was closed again.

Nodding to the instructions given him, the lot to be melted into ingots, the caller returning in a day or so to take away the results – where it all went after that was none of his business – he'd be well paid for a job well done.

Coming back from the hall in hat, coat and gloves, mid-September tending to be chilly in the small hours with a creeping dampness rising from the East Ham marshes, he bent to kiss her cheek. It felt stiff and cold. Straightening up, he gave her a final glance, aware of a small stab of impatience, laced with resentment when she did not look back at him, and went downstairs to his car sitting at the kerbside.

Seven-fifteen. He'd eaten out before coming home. There was a woman, Mrs Stevenson, who came in to clean, to make a meal, Geraldine still doing little these days, and certainly not up to cooking. Mrs Stevenson was always gone by the time he got home, so he'd taken to having something to eat out – more pleasant than having to stare across the dining room table at his wife's bleak face, she merely toying with her food.

In the car he stashed the heavy black bag in the rear and pushed the starter button of the still warm engine. It would be dark by the time he reached East Ham. He would spend his time there turning the contents of the bag into small ingots, no doubt to be sold in Hatton Garden by a purported dealer in gold and silver bullion. Its many workshops turned precious metals into beautiful jewellery, all meticulously worked by hand and soon there'd be nothing left of the booty to be traced. He never asked questions, did his job, kept his mouth shut, received his share and got on with his legitimate trade until next time. Whoever these people were, and however they came by the stuff they brought in at night, was nothing to do with him, and the less he knew about it the better.

When he got back home after his night's work as dawn was coming up, Geraldine was fast asleep. She did not stir at all when he crept into their bedroom and for a moment he gazed down at her, her features in repose, which they never were when awake.

She looked like a child, her face smooth, her eyelids gently closed, her mouth soft and untroubled, and for a moment his heart leapt with love, but then hardened with the knowledge that on waking in a couple of hours' time, that mouth would adopt a thin, hard line, the eyes with the lids now covered so gently would stare into nothing, would flick towards him should he speak as though resenting the very sound of his voice; the face would work as though she were about to burst into tears, though tears seemed now to have dried inside her, and he would crab up inside, hardly able to wait to get away to his shop. Breakfast would be eaten in silence unless he spoke, to be responded to monosyllabically and in a monotone, until he wanted to shout at her to buck herself up for God's sake! Sometimes he didn't even stop for breakfast but fled the moment he was washed, shaved and dressed.

Geraldine watched him go without bothering to acknowledge him. It was an effort to do anything. Only occasionally was she given to an outburst of any kind such as last week when she had told him vehemently how much she hated this house with its big rooms and its isolated position.

She had recollections of when she lived with Mum and Dad, the poky little two-up-two-down house when as few as three people together made it seem crowded; the comings and goings of family and other relations, the back door ever open to anyone calling in; its scrubby back garden, its tiny three-foot patch of grass out front; the noise from the other rooms travelling through the walls, including every bump, every word uttered from the house next door. How she longed for that life now, but she'd moved on.

Sunk in the armchair where she'd been most of the afternoon, she hadn't even looked up when Tony told her he'd be going out for a while, promising not to be too late. She knew he would be, returning in the small hours. She'd be asleep by then, having dragged herself to the bedroom, not bothering to wash or tidy her hair, the effort of undressing for bed enough in itself.

Odd how she could sleep so soundly. She'd not had to take medicines to make her sleep except for the first two days after coming home. She had never needed it again. Needing to mentally flagellate herself, it disturbed her that her sleep was never fraught with dreams of her poor dead baby coming to further torment her already guilty conscience in not looking out properly the day she had fallen, practically killing her child by her very own carelessness. Instead hers were sweeter dreams: of pushing Caroline in the park or of her running around on the grass; of holding her in her arms one minute, a tiny baby with trusting blue eyes, the next a young girl full of vitality, glancing at all the boys and they glancing at her. Geraldine knew she smiled in her sleep and a joyous voice would tell her that losing a baby had been the bad dream. She was unaware of the reversal for those sleep-visions had such reality that, on waking, the real world would assault her like a clenched fist so that she was never sure whether sleep was a curse or a blessing.

The memory of her stay in hospital was still vague, as was the one of seeing Mum there, holding her hand, her thin face gaunt with sorrow for her. Tony had telegraphed her parents about her being taken into hospital and Mum had hurried to be with her. She remembered Mum's voice coming through the cotton-wool world in which her loss had left her suspended, talking trivia as though to fill a void by the sound of words – something about already having been alerted to her urgent and premature rush to hospital; something about Alan Presley having come to the house to say that he had met her daughter Geraldine in the street, that she had been crying and that she had looked terribly ill.

Through a pall of grief, Mum's words had drifted on, saying how concerned Alan had been, how he had urged her to go and see her daughter straight away but to her shame she had ignored that advice until Tony's telegram had come.

Geraldine stirred herself briefly. She thought of Alan Presley. That he should put himself out going round to her house – her old house, she corrected – to tell her mother of their meeting. Somehow it seemed he had been affected by seeing her. Geraldine found herself smiling. He was the nicest man she had ever known. Of course she loved Tony, couldn't imagine life without him and appreciated all he'd done for her, and thought that no one could be nicer than Tony, yet a small admittance crept into a tiny corner of her brain that the man she had turned down might have been the one to make her happier for all his lack of money. Geraldine pulled herself up in the realisation that she hadn't been thinking of Caroline, her lost baby, for at least several minutes, knowing a surge of guilt at the fact.

She became aware of someone ringing on the newly installed doorbell. Mrs Stevenson no doubt, come to do her morning chores and cook lunch for her, a lunch she would toy with before pushing away, barely nibbled at. Mrs Stevenson would be gone again by then and thank-fully wouldn't see her culinary efforts thus wasted.

With an effort, Geraldine got up and went to let the woman in, turning away with a desultory good morning when a voice in the street hailed her.

'Don't close the door, darling!'

Glancing towards it she saw Fenella flying down the street towards her, a bright vision under a leaden sky, brown and orange umbrella flapping wildly and almost hooking off her low-brimmed hat; below the French seal-fur coat with its snug collar and huge cuffs, slim legs going like pistons while Cuban heels echoed like castanets tap-tapping on the shiny wet pavement.

She arrived with a final flourish of silk-stockinged legs at the top of the three stairs. 'Darling, simply couldn't find one taxi in Oxford Street that wasn't being used.' She sounded as breathless as if she had been running the entire length of it. 'It's this atrocious weather, my sweet, everyone using them. So I thought I'd walk – I had an umbrella – and walking helps keep one slim, darling. Then down came the rain again, and I had to run for it.'

Inside she pumped the umbrella vigorously, flapping the silk in and out, then closed it, dumping it in the hall stand to drip to its heart's content. Geraldine had leapt back to avoid the cold splatter of rain on her legs from the flapping of the brolly. Mrs Stevenson with hers had already gone towards the kitchen.

'I'll have Mrs Stevenson make up some coffee,' Geraldine said.

'Oh that would be absolutely divine on a day like this!' Fenella replied a bit too loudly so that Geraldine felt the curl of her lips in an amused smile.

Fenella was at last making this happen; had ploughed

through many a dreary visit with the tenaciousness of a farmer ploughing some claggy field by hand, and was finally reaping the results: to see her smile, no matter how brief or thin.

Coffee brought in, and a plate of small, assorted sweet biscuits from Harrods, Fenella continued talking. For the most part Geraldine listened, aware of life seeping back into her as it always did when her sister-in-law was here. Fenella *was* life. She felt its gradual transference into her as one hour went past, then a second and it was time for lunch. She was even joining in the light conversation: how the décor of the living rooms in this house could be made far more modern at little cost, 'unless you use the services of a really good designer – I mean art deco is all the rage and these rooms are so old-fashioned!'; the growing problem of keeping domestic staff happy, 'They walk off the moment you're horrid to them, not like when I lived at home, servants knew their place, but now . . . so independent!'; the cost of house repairs, 'Simply soaring through the roof since the war – skilled labour demanding enormous fees, yet there are still hundreds of ex-soldiers parading the gutters – one would think some of them might turn their hands to *something* or other!'

Geraldine, remembering her own background of struggle and poverty, merely nodded as she had more or less nodded to everything Fenella had said, too weary to argue but content to draw strength from her prattle. Sometimes Fenella could prattle endlessly, other times she could be quiet and thoughtful. Obviously this morning was one for prattling.

So Fenella continued bounding from subject to subject:

her husband, Reginald, came under fire about his work, a solicitor like her father, 'That's how we met, you know, Gerry'; the clothes she'd just bought, taking them from thick paper bags with names of well-known shops to display a green tweed skirt, fashionable jumper, maroon and white-striped cardigan. Geraldine hadn't noticed the additional encumbrance of bags as well as the umbrella.

'I need a complete new wardrobe with winter coming on,' Fenella chirped. 'And look at this, Geraldine dear – don't you think it's simply marvellous?' She unfolded layers of tissue paper to reveal a gold-embroidered, taffeta evening dress, the skirt cut to resemble the petals of a flower, the hem at least eight inches above the ankle.

It was all light-hearted. Mrs Stevenson having finished her morning chores and prepared lunch came and placed plates of egg and cucumber sandwiches, cake, fruit and coffee hot in its pot before making her exit for the day, after asking if there was anything else Mrs Hanford needed and receiving a negative shake of the head and a mumbled, 'Thank you, Mrs Stevenson.'

Persuaded to show Fenella her wardrobe so that Fenella could make comments about what she should be wearing this coming winter, she felt more lively than she had for days. But Fenella always had this effect on her after a while of being there, bless her heart.

'With Christmas less than three months away, Geraldine, you simply must prepare for it. I've still loads to do as well as buying presents for all and sundry. Mostly I'm ordering Harrods hampers to be sent, as you know. So convenient. But my own family is different – I'm buying Reginald one of those darling gold wrist-watches that have become all the rage. His pocket watch is so old-fashioned. And you and Anthony of course will have special presents, and naturally, mother and father, and for little Stephanie I'm choosing . . .'

That's when it happened – all Fenella's efforts wiped out in a word.

She knew Fenella had been talking so brightly, not because she was in any way shallow but because she felt that by remaining so there'd be no danger of unwittingly penetrating to the thick layer of grief lying just below the so-thin armour of normality. Then, this single unguarded moment. Even as she cut off abruptly, Geraldine, on the point of going to the occasional table where lunch had been laid, sank back into the armchair.

Without warning, huge gulping sobs welled up from deep inside her to choke in her throat, the name of Fenella's daughter reminding her of how she'd been robbed of the joy of buying for her own daughter. There would be no buying of baby presents, no baby, no Caroline.

'Oh, Fen!'

Her sister-in-law was leaning on her with her whole weight in a vain attempt to undo her last words as Geraldine crumpled into the armchair to double up in misery.

'I'm so sorry, Gerry. I didn't think,' she kept saying, over and over.

It was ages before Geraldine could get out the words, 'It wasn't your fault,' and force herself into recovering. But lunch had been spoiled and lay untouched; she sunk into her chair, Fenella on the padded arm, one arm around her shoulders, and her voice low and soft but insistent with restored confidence.

'Darling, you must let go. I know what you must be going through, but you can't go on like this.'

But what did Fenella know of the loss of a child? Maybe her mother did, having a son killed in the war in his youthful years. But what did Fenella understand of the inability to cast Caroline from her mind. She'd say it to herself over and over, hearing herself addressing the infant as though it lay in her arms. She knew she should not be doing it, that she would drive herself mad doing it, but she couldn't stop. She had once spoken the name to Tony but he'd flown into a rage, told her she must try to forget, not keep harping on it, life had to go on. Easy for men. Men didn't feel these things like women did, especially a grieving mother.

Tony's parents hadn't come. For all she saw or knew of them, he might not have had any family at all. But she lacked the will to criticise even as Tony spent energy alternately apologising for them, feebly defending them or being angry with them on her behalf. For all the good any of it did he might as well have said nothing at all, she not having the go in her enough to respond.

'I know,' she answered limply, not caring enough to control that occasional spasmodic sob left over from her outburst of tears. 'I try, I really do. Tony gets impatient with me but somehow I can't bring myself to remedy it. It's like being held by an invisible rubber band that stops me going forward. I can't help weaving little scenes around Caroline – what she would be doing now, what I'd be doing – preparing her morning bath, seeing the water wasn't too hot, feeling her soft silky skin all slick with lather, lifting her out, drying her, dressing her, and her all clean and sweet-smelling ready for her ten a.m.

feed. My milk has now dried up, but if I squeeze a nipple long enough there's a sort of pearly drop of watery milk that oozes out, and the sight of it only makes me cry again to think it had been meant for her, to nourish her, my little Caroline. Instead—'

Fenella cut her short. 'That's what I'm getting at, Gerry dear, you mentioning her name and referring to her as though she were here. You mustn't. Gerry, darling, I know this must sound callous, but you've done enough mourning. You gave her a lovely little burial even though the church hadn't officially christened her. Stop trying to resurrect her. She's buried in the ground. She must be buried in your mind too, covered, and time given to let the flowers grow over her. You'll never forget her, but do you think that little baby can rest in peace while you are constantly bringing her back? My dear, be kind to her. You loved her all the while she was being made. Now let her rest.'

Geraldine had lifted her eyes to her sister-in-law, one thought in her mind that surprised her – she'd never thought of Fenella as being religious. Perhaps she was. Perhaps from that great house of hers not far from her parents' home, she sometimes attended church on Sunday mornings. Fenella could be full of surprises at times.

'Can you do that, my dear?' Fenella was begging. 'She really should be left to rest. Can you do that? For her sake.'

Geraldine's stare, drying now, was still on her as she nodded. How simply she had put it. The last thing she wanted to do was to have Caroline's peace of mind disturbed – no loving mother could do that to her child. For Caroline's sake she must return to sanity.

'I'll try,' she said in a small voice, and Fenella patted her shoulder and rose from the arm of the chair as though the problem had been solved satisfactorily.

'Now then, darling, let's find you a drop of brandy.'

'There's coffee in the pot.'

'Brandy and coffee – perfect.' Her observation was interrupted by the trilling of the doorbell. 'I'll go,' she chirruped.

Left alone, Geraldine sat without being able to form one thought. She heard Fenella query, 'Yes?' then a man's voice, a small hesitation, followed by Fenella calling, 'There's a Mr Alan Presley here, wants to see you, Gerry.'

# Chapter Eighteen

'Sorry to intrude.' Alan Presley stood in the centre of the lounge where Fenella had brought him in the same manner in which she might have brought in a stray cat, unsure of its genus, much less its pedigree.

He looked quite out of place yet it was only his clothes that made him seem so and as he turned his face towards Geraldine, firm and calm, she saw a natural dignity that appeared to give him height. It was a dignity she'd never noticed before and she experienced a surge of pride for him. In the right clothes he could fit in anywhere.

'Didn't mean to,' he was saying. 'I ought ter go.'

'No, you're not intruding, Alan.' She glanced across at Fenella, who for once was silent, hovering to one side of the room, eyes switching between her and Alan as if to ask incredulously, 'You know this man?'

'Fenella, this is . . .' Geraldine began and stopped. How should she introduce him? Who as? 'Fenella,' she began again, more firmly, 'this is a family friend. Alan, this is Fenella Grading, my sister-in-law.'

He had turned to the other woman, gave her a small nod. 'Very nice ter meet yer.'

Fenella returning the nod without speaking, Geraldine found herself cringing at Alan's untutored accent. 'Well,' she said brightly, and realised this was the first time she had sounded anywhere near bright since Caroline died.

She turned away from the thought. 'It is nice to see you, Alan. I think there's still some coffee left. Would you like a cup?' It sounded so trivial and she could see he was feeling awkward. She felt awkward too. A look flitted across Fenella's eyes and she knew exactly what she was thinking.

Fenella made a move, coming forward as if struck from behind. Her voice was overbright. 'I'd best be off, darling. Things to do, you know. Sorry I have to go but I hope our little chat . . .' she grew guarded and secretively confidential, 'I hope it has been of some help, my dear. I expect I'll see you on Wednesday. Now keep your chin up, Gerry darling, remember. I'll see myself out.'

'No.' Geraldine followed her. 'I'll come to the door with you.'

With Fenella putting on her coat and bending to gaze critically at herself in the hall mirror so as to adjust her low-brimmed hat properly on her head, the now dry umbrella retrieved from its stand, Geraldine added rather foolishly, 'I'm sorry about that. I was surprised to see him. He's never come here before.'

It occurred to her that she must appear to be defending herself. And indeed that was just what she was doing, even a trace of guilt in her tone. She could hear it and so had Fenella, who touched her arm lightly.

'Don't worry about it, darling. He's as you said, an

old friend of the family. Well, I must be off. See you on Wednesday, okay?'

'Yes,' supplied Geraldine, wishing she could say something to vindicate herself from her sister-in-law's obvious assumptions.

They were without doubt mild ones – many a wife enjoyed a bit on the side in these new, heady days of broad-mindedness, non-conformism, freedom and frivolity among the social set with the opening of a new decade. Plainly Fenella saw her as no different, might herself have had a dabble though she had never let on, wasn't even indignant on her brother's behalf, and quite definitely wasn't showing any embarrassment.

Fenella leaned forward and dropped a kiss just short of her cheek. 'See you later, darling, love to Anthony. I'll hail a taxi in Piccadilly, still have a little more shopping to do!' and was off.

Long legs twinkling down the three steps, at the bottom she paused to glance up at the still leaden sky, winced at the splatter of rain on her rouged cheeks and up went the brightly coloured umbrella like a flower popping open to greet the morning sun.

Geraldine stood watching her departing figure, slim, busy, leggy, her narrow Cuban heels going tap-tap-tap on the shining pavement, her brolly swaying mightily, her handbag and paper bags swinging from her arm. She waited for her to wave before turning the corner, but she didn't.

Geraldine went back inside and closed the door. Returning to the lounge she found Alan still in the centre of the room where she had left him. He turned to look at her.

'I shouldn't of come. I saw straight away you was embarrassed. I saw the way she looked.'

Defiance suddenly flooded over Geraldine. 'I don't care how she looked. You're a friend of mine and I choose who comes into my house and who don't.'

'It's what sort of friend,' he answered. 'That's what she was querying. I saw it the way she looked at me. And you, I embarrassed you.'

'No you didn't. I'm really glad to see you.'

She needed all the friends she could get at this time and Alan had proved himself one of them on the day he had taken her into that café for her to recover herself. So damn what Fenella read into his arrival. Fenella's few words of wisdom had made her think a little. And now Alan's presence was adding to all her sister-in-law had said to her – that the time must come, if it hadn't yet come today, when she must learn to face the world again, that she was only destroying herself as well as impeding the release from the child she had lost. Now Alan had turned up and his presence was already adding to the healing process.

She went over to the armchair where she was wont to sit the day long and, hesitating, moved away to an upright chair. 'Alan, come and sit down.' She indicated the sofa. 'Would you like a drink? Brandy? Whisky?'

He shook his head. 'Too early for me.'

'Coffee then? Or tea? It won't take me a second to make it.' Again she wondered at her enquiry. It was a chore even to stir to make a cup for herself, or even to pour herself anything stronger – probably her salvation from drinking herself into a stupor at times, this inability to bother. And now, suddenly, here she was offering to make tea.

Alan was shaking his head. 'No, but thanks. I ain't stayin' long. I just come because yer mum told me 'ow low yer've bin. She's worried for yer.'

Mum? Worried? Mum had come round here several times, but her attitude had always been distant as if the visit were a chore she'd rather have done without.

'Takes blessed ages on that blinkin' bus. I 'ate the noise and rush of the West End, never could abide it. No one gives yer a second glance even if they bump inter yer.'

The nearest Mum came to showing any affection lately was a peck on the cheek, and when Geraldine burst into one of her frequent weeping fits in front of her, longing to be cuddled, to be comforted, there was only a cold, hard hand patting hers and a toneless encouragement to keep her chin up.

Mum had gone through this in her time, but rather than soften her to the pain of others it had hardened her to their weaknesses; if she had held up under the loss of a child, then so could another – no allowances for the fact that everyone was different. Mum's life had taught her to be hard, and equally as hard on herself. But how wonderful it would have been to have just one small cuddle to say she cared.

Alan was leaning forward, his brown eyes full of regard. 'You orright, ole gel?'

It was a simple enquiry, loosely encompassing a world of probabilities as most simple enquiries do for want of something more specific, and could have sounded inane, but coming from him, she knew instantly what he meant. She nodded wordlessly and the next second he was leaning towards her, taking her hands in his and there was pressure and warmth in those hands.

'I wish I could take away yer sufferin', Gel. I wish I could take it all on meself so's yer'd be free of it.'

She found her voice, heard the tears in her throat, tears that stemmed from having someone feel for her. 'You wouldn't want this sort of suffering.'

'Any sort,' he said, his voice low, 'so long as it freed you.' He let go of her hands suddenly and moved back a fraction, gazing down at the hands that had previously held hers. 'P'raps I shouldn't say this, but I've got to. I ain't just bein' kind to yer. I've been wantin' ter come and see yer for a long time but thought it best not to. But yer Mum seems upset so I promised meself I'd come.'

'It's good of you,' Geraldine managed, controlling her tears.

'It ain't good of me.' His tone had become harsh. 'If I came reluctant-like, then maybe it would be good of me – like charity. But I came because I wanted to. Because I had to. I don't want ter lose touch wiv yer.'

'And I don't want to lose touch with you, Alan,' she said, still fighting the tears his kind sympathy had provoked. 'We'll always be friends.'

He sat very upright now. 'No, you don't understand, Gel. It's more than that, more than just bein' kind. It's . . . I've got ter say it. It's . . .'

He seemed to collapse a little within himself, the rigidness melting and he was leaning forward again, his gaze grown intense. 'I still love yer, Gel. I always will. That's why I ain't found meself anuvver gel since I packed up with me wife. I'm bein' stupid, I know, and you're 'appily married, and I wouldn't want ter see yer any ovver way, but it don't alter how I feel about yer.'

Geraldine was staring at him. Deep in her heart she knew he loved her but to have it come out like that shook her and she didn't know what to say to him. Was there anything to say?

'Well, I've said it,' he went on as though she had spoken her thoughts aloud. 'All I want ter say now is, I 'ate seeing yer so un'appy. If only I could do something ter make yer better, but there ain't nothink no one can do. The only one what can do anythink is yerself, and that takes time. Maybe it'll take forever though I just 'ope and pray it won't be forever, that in time all this pain and emptiness yer goin' through will go away. I know the memory won't ever leave yer, but just that in time it won't hurt so much. And I feel sure it will go away, Gel. I know you. You're made of strong stuff and yer will weather it. Just one fing – don't let it change yer. Don't become all crabbed up and 'ard-'earted against the world. I couldn't bear ter see that lovely nature of yours get lost in a twisted, bitter way. Think about it, Gel, think what I've said, or tried ter say.'

She sat silent, and a warmth seemed to be flowing from him into her, yet they were not touching. All of a sudden, Alan gave a low, almost self-conscious chuckle. 'I fink I've said enough, yer know. I didn't really come 'ere fer that. I just come ter . . .'

He stopped, and got slowly to his feet, yet it was as though he had left the warmth to continue flowing into her as she looked up at him.

His voice had lightened. 'I 'ad no idea what I was going ter say when I come 'ere. I never intended . . . Never mind, forget what I said. Look, I've got ter be on me way.' He stepped a little nearer, gazing down at her. 'Will yer be orright?'

Geraldine's smile was tremulous. 'I think so.' Now she too got to her feet. Her voice had grown suddenly strong. 'Yes, Alan, I think I will be all right.'

'Good.' He turned and made for the door, with her following.

It was two people who were mere friends once more as she said goodbye, thanked him for coming, told him that he'd done her a great deal of good by doing so, and watched him depart, striding through a steady downpour as though he couldn't feel it. But in her heart as she watched him go, she knew she'd never be the same. A declaration had been made and although she hadn't returned it, she had accepted it, taken it to her and would never view him in the same light again. Unexpectedly she felt strong again – a goal had been reached and surpassed.

Going back indoors, she glanced in the lounge at the armchair where she'd sit for hours on end, then continued on to the kitchen to make tea.

The look on Mum's face as she opened her street door to see Geraldine there was a picture to behold.

'Well, blow me! What brings you 'ere?'

Geraldine gave her one of her brightest smiles, still somewhat stiff but after three days of thinking about what Fenella had said to her, then Alan, her mind was learning to cope again with the world.

'I thought it was time I came to see yer, Mum.' She'd automatically lapsed into her old way of speaking, but there was no disguising the veneer of culture she'd acquired, and she saw her mother frown as if she viewed her as slumming it.

'Well, yer'd best come in.' Mum stepped back to allow her entry, closing the door behind them to instantly dim the narrow passage. After months of not setting foot here, Geraldine's unaccustomed nose took in the smell of washing, yesterday's Sunday dinner, and all the other little smells that had once made home while hardly noticing them. Now they struck her as quite unpleasant, not even a welcoming feel to them.

'So what did yer come 'ere for?' her mother asked, leading the way to the kitchen where the inevitable cup of tea would be offered to anyone who entered: friends, neighbours, the man coming to empty the gas or electric meter.

'I thought it was time I came ter see you rather than you coming to see me.'

'That's nice of yer.' Noisily Mum filled the kettle and put it on the black-leaded gas stove, applying a match to the gas ring which gave a little plop as it ignited. 'But I didn't come that often.'

'As you said, Mum . . .' She sat down at the table. 'It was the buses.'

'Blooming long trot, that's why.'

'Yes. Well, I'm here now.'

Mum turned and studied her. 'Yer look a lot better than when I last saw yer. More perky. Getting' out, at last. Must say it took yer long enough.'

Didn't Mum notice how her words could hurt, or was it deliberate? Geraldine forced cheeriness.

'Everyone orright? Dad? Fred and Evie, Wally? And Mavis?'

The last name was an effort. Four weeks ago Mavis's baby had been born, a lovely little girl as ever there was, Mum put it when she'd visited just afterwards. Her lips had tightened when tears had flooded Geraldine's eyes at hearing it, her testy remark, 'Ain't you over it yet? You ain't the only one ter lose a baby,' stinging like a scab ripped from a half-healed sore.

Now Geraldine asked the question, managing to stay dry-eyed and without her voice wavering, 'And the baby?'

'Doin' grand,' Mum said casually as she put two cups and saucers out on the kitchen table, giving herself the worst chipped one, and began ladling a spoonful of tea into the brown teapot, that too somewhat chipped – no money to buy such luxuries as a new teapot the second a chip or two appeared on the lid or spout.

'Lovely little thing, she is. Barbara. Barbara Hilda, after me. That's nice, I thought. But of course it's another mouth for 'er ter feed, and 'er Tom on the dole again too. She could of done without 'aving another baby at the moment, way things is going. But then, babies take no 'eed of people being 'ard up, do they? They just come, money or no money.'

It seemed to Geraldine's sensitive mind that Mum was delighting in rubbing it in, but she fought back the threatening tears that would only irritate her mother, seeing her as the one with the money and therefore with no cause to feel sorry for herself.

Ironic though that the one living from hand to mouth with a husband out of work still should have another baby to feed, a bouncing, bonny girl with nothing at all wrong with her, while she with everything to give a baby should lose hers. It seemed to her that Him up there enjoyed playing games just to see how a body reacted – 'Like playing chess with us all,' came the bitter thought.

It must have shown on her face for Mum stopped pouring hot water into the teapot to glare at her.

'What's the matter now?'

'Nothing.' Geraldine shook her head vigorously to clear the moisture misting her eyes, but Mum was already ahead of her.

'You ain't cryin' again, are yer? Is that why yer've come 'ere ter see me, fer a bit more sympathy?'

The moisture dried as if by magic. If she'd wanted sympathy, Mum was the last one she'd have come to. She had come from a sense of duty and all she seemed to be reaping was a hard, unforgiving reception.

'Yer'd be more upset,' Mum was going on, 'if yer was in yer sister's boots. We're 'aving ter 'elp her out these days with a bit of this, a bit of that, 'er Tom gettin' just a day's work 'ere, a day's work there, if he's lucky. On the dole fer months on end and 'er not knowing where ter turn for 'er next penny. You should count yerself lucky, 'aving a bit of money around yer, and count yer blessings instead of moping all over the place, and p'raps put yer 'and in yer pocket to 'elp 'er out a bit. Yer can always 'ave another baby any time, but money never do come easy – except fer some.'

The tea drawn, she began pouring it into the two cups, adding milk from an opened bottle, adding sugar. Geraldine had gone off sugar but had no will left to stop her.

True, she hadn't given her sister anything to help her these last couple of months, but she had been ill, had lost a baby, hadn't been herself. On the other hand the last time she'd tried to give her something, Mavis had turned on her savagely saying she didn't want people's charity, other people's handouts. Yet she was happy enough to accept handouts from Mum who was just as hard up as she at times, and from Wally desperately saving to get married. The odd thing about not having to fight for money was how to give to others without appearing superior and patronising.

'What yer doin' fer Christmas?' It was the inevitable question, November always the month for Mum to ask what you were doing for Christmas, more or less demanding an appearance.

'I'm not sure yet,' she hedged, looking across at Tony whose expression remained blank and she knew what that meant – he had no intention of spending Christmas with her people. To his credit he had no intention of spending it with his own, they keeping no contact at all.

It was Saturday evening and she and Tony were at Mum's. So was everyone else, her brothers and sisters and one or two relatives on Dad's side, each with a present for Dad's birthday as well as a little something to supplement the birthday tea for which Mum had made a cake with icing on.

Mavis sat with her new baby, Barbara, on her lap. It had been an effort of will to go and sit beside Mavis, smile and force herself to admire her baby and not let herself be seen as resentful, an emotion that still churned within her, threatening to surface if not carefully guarded. Even so, she was sure Mavis saw through her bright façade and would alternately show pride in her achievement where her sister had failed or draw back from appearing too pleased with herself.

Either way it nibbled away at Geraldine's resolution to remain strong, made her feel a complete failure, even though Mavis had a wan and weary look and the baby clothes were obviously second-hand, as were the clothes her eighteen-month-old son Simon had on. Mavis's own best dress with its cardigan was little better than everyday wear, Tom looking equally poor, the little family enough to wring the heart of the sturdiest onlooker.

Geraldine ached to suggest giving them something to buy themselves a decent outfit each and put a bit of good food on their table, but again drew back from the possible reaction she might reap.

Dad of course was in his Sunday suit, still able to hold down his job and bring in a little money, if erratically. He sat amid his family, stiff in his buttoned-up jacket and waistcoat with its silver-plated fob watch and chain, his collar and tie stretching his neck, though they would come off later when he'd had a drink or two.

Everyone was dressed in their best such as it was, although Geraldine, knowing the quality of what they considered their best, had deliberately sought to wear something modest. Even so, she was aware of the glances towards the green wool dress with its fashionably lowered waistline, and read envious disdain into those glances. Even Tony's quite ordinary suit drew looks at its cut and quality.

'Well, yer'd better make up yer mind,' Mum said, as she passed the sandwich plate across the table around which they were all crowded. 'So's we know what yer doing fer Christmas. Unless of course yer planning ter spend it with some of yer *friends*.'

Mum's intimation was glaringly obvious, that she saw her family not good enough for her any more, and yet it wasn't like that. How could she command Tony to spend his Christmas with her family if he had other plans. She had to follow him or cause a row, and she hated rows.

'It's not like that, Mum,' protested Geraldine, taking a couple of fish-paste sandwiches from the plate that was being offered her, but Mum didn't answer and her refusal to reply rankled still more.

She was glad when the evening was over, with Dad nodding almost casually to her birthday present to him of a pair of leather gloves, a white scarf to wear with his Sunday suit and a large tin of pipe tobacco, nothing too grand to embarrass him. She'd had a disconcerting sense that he'd looked on the gift as meagre considering her circumstances, yet had it been grander she was sure he'd have taken it as being ostentatious and belittling to one in his circumstances. It seemed to her that there was no way she would ever win.

As for Tony, he seemed heartily glad to be home, hadn't once referred to the evening or to spending Christmas with her family, and she knew that if he hadn't so far made other plans he would be going out of his way now to make them. In that respect she felt she couldn't care less what they did over Christmas so long as the months following it would speed by so as to heal her still raw sense of loss the quicker.

Maybe in a few months they might try again for a baby and the next time it would be successful.

# Chapter Nineteen

Last month Tony had suggested she manage his shop. 'It might help to get your mind off all you've been through,' he'd said.

It had made her angry. First, that he should think helping him in his business was the answer to what she had gone through, and second, the very words 'all *you* have been through,' rather than *we*, as though her loss had been hers alone, nothing to do with him. Yet she knew he was trying to help, and now, a month into 1922, she felt she was at last turning the corner, if not completely.

Every now and again, even as she joined in the spirit of this new year, being invited to house parties, dinner parties, accompanying others to the theatre – all those new friends Tony was making in his astonishing rise to prosperity – the ghost of her dead child would reappear, she would hear that strange haunting mew and remember the moment that little life became extinguished and all the pain would come flooding back even as she laughed and smiled with those in whose company she was at the time. Sometimes it felt worse than the initial sense of loss.

Tony would never be capable of feeling what she felt for all his efforts to help her get over it. He was making money hand over fist and the more he made the more he strove to make, so that in his haste to rise up in the world little Caroline, dying at birth, held no place in his heart. He'd not seen her alive, had not heard her cry, so how could her memory ever mean anything to him? And if she mentioned their child or appeared to slide into a moment of moping, he would grow impatient with her, these days demanding bluntly that she snap out of it.

'I'm trying to give you a good time. Why can't you appreciate it? All the moping in the world isn't going to change things. What's the point of my trying to provide you with the good things in life if you can't appreciate them and throw all that I'm trying to do back in my face? You couldn't have had a better Christmas.'

They'd had a lovely Christmas and a simply wonderful New Year, she and Tony invited to spend both with some of Tony's friends with whom he was beginning to acquire a place in their social hierarchy.

She'd met a couple of them last year at a party, Yvonne and Terrance Gallsworth, he too in the trade but far larger than Tony with jewellery shops in Birmingham, Chester and Gloucester. Of the other people, one introduced as Douglas Timmerson apparently had a small factory, another, George Grieg, seemed to be engaged in some sort of business dealership – all rather obscure though they seemed to know a lot about Tony. Both were some-what intimidating: Timmerson was heavily built, fat and overbearing, Grieg large and raw-boned with a scowl that showed even through his broad, handsome grin. Their wives, however, were both slim, very beautiful, expensively dressed and made up with powder, mascara and lipstick, their hair fashionably bobbed or marcel waved. Learning to mix easily with them, it seemed to her that she was living two lives – this and the one she took on when going to see her parents.

She'd gone there, without Tony of course, on Christmas morning with presents for all the family: a soft, thick cardigan for Mum, a warm pullover for Dad – she'd have loved to give something more expensive but feared to in case they were misinterpreted as usual. Even what she gave were received somewhat coldly, a nod and a thank you, to be left on the table without even being tried up against them. A pair of humble, home-knitted gloves given to her in return had brought home both how hard it was for them to pay out for presents at all and the guilty fact that these days she would never be wearing such things, that they would lie in a drawer unused except to be displayed on the times she went there during the colder months of the year.

Wally and Clara, with both of whom she felt far more comfortable, had been pleased enough with theirs, something for the bottom drawer. Clara had admired the set of Irish linen sheets, pillow cases and the embroidered cushion covers, had unpacked them and held them up for display, coming to give her future sister-in-law a big thank-you cuddle while Wally beamed, no doubt seeing himself lying back on that linen with his wife beside him.

Evie and Fred too had been genuinely pleased with theirs: a fashionable dress for Evie, now a pert young lady, and a silk tie for Fred to wear in his intended upward climb in the newspaper world, their exuberant thanks conveying no animosity at all.

She'd popped to Mavis with something for all of them: clothes mostly, a warm skirt and jumper, a shirt and pullover, clothes and toys for the children, maybe going a little over the top, but Geraldine felt they needed all they could get.

She had asked if there was anything Mavis wanted, anything she could do, and at first Mavis had said no, then almost rebelliously said, 'Yes, yer could, such as get my Tom a job so we won't 'ave ter keep going cap in 'and ter the likes of them what's better off than we are.'

It was a stinging reply that had thrown her for a moment, then Mavis had added as if regretting her words, 'Or else a few quid ter get us over the next few weeks till he does find a proper job.'

A pathetic entreaty and Geraldine saw the tears spring as Mavis broke down, blubbering while her husband looked on in wretched embarrassment.

'We're in debt. Tom did a bit of borrowing. They want it paid back and he ain't got the money ter pay it back and we owe on the rent, four weeks in arrears, and the landlord's threatening to evict us if we don't pay something. We don't know where to turn. I daren't tell Mum, and Tom's family can't 'elp us. They're as 'ard up as we are. Thank God we're 'aving Christmas dinner at Mum an' Dad's, else we wouldn't be 'aving nothink.'

'Why in God's name didn't you tell me?' Geraldine had exploded.

She'd delved into her purse and brought out the paltry

sum required to cover the four weeks back rent: twenty-two shillings in all, plus a couple of pounds to see them over what should have been for them a festive season. When the banks opened after Christmas she had taken out money from her allowance which Tony always made sure was very substantial to hand to her sister prior to New Year's Day, saying she didn't want it paid back and would be upset if she tried to do so. But looking around the poor living room with its tatty, second-hand furniture, its scuffed linoleum, its lack of ornaments, just some home-made Christmas paper chains and on the mantel-piece over a tiny flame of a fire a few Christmas cards, including her own, she knew there was no likelihood of Mavis ever paying the money back whether she'd have intended to or not.

It was agreed to say nothing to Mum about it. But even though she felt Mavis was on her side again, her sister seemed to continue bearing resentment towards her from the fact that she'd had to ask for her help at all. It was an odd situation, the sisterhood that had once existed between them no longer there.

As expected there had been no card from her. One had come from Mum and Dad saying love from them including Evie and Fred, and one from Wally and Clara, a few from relatives and one from her old workmate, Eileen Shaw – not a word since her marriage and then, typically, a Christmas card enclosing a note saying she was married, living in South London and expecting a baby in six weeks time, which immediately brought such an agony of emptiness to Geraldine's stomach that she thought it would rip itself out through her very flesh.

There had been one from Tony's parents, an

insignificant, postcard thing that struck Geraldine as hardly worth posting, wishing him Happy Christmas, her name not mentioned. There'd been a great ostentatious one from Fenella, full of Christmassy sentiments, and the cards from the many friends Tony had made over the past year stood in a double row on the shelf over the fireplace of the flat. (Geraldine had settled down well in the flat with its cosy feel and in the hub of things. Tony had been right in that it had helped lay the ghost that had haunted every corner of the house they'd left.)

There was one card that did not sit alongside all the others, a small, unpretentious card from Alan Presley, wishing her every happiness in her new home and that her life would be easier and more contented as time went on. It held a note of nostalgia that made her want to cry, almost feeling his loneliness, and had borne the words, 'With all my heartfelt love, Alan.'

She'd sent him one in return, saying she hoped he'd have a happy Christmas, knowing that it probably wouldn't be, refraining of course from mentioning his admission of love the day he'd visited her. She couldn't help wondering what sort of Christmas he would have with no family of his own but his parents. By now a man his age should have had his own family.

Much to her surprise it had been a year of fun, 1922 simply flying by. But it would soon be September and Geraldine found herself hard put not to dwell on thoughts of the anniversary of the loss of her baby.

To some extent memory had dimmed where once she'd thought it never would. She'd hoped they'd start another family in the spring but it hadn't happened. Maybe because she'd tried too hard, on edge, which some maintained could prevent a woman conceiving, or maybe Tony's heart hadn't quite been in it. He was often distant towards her, though she put that down to work – perhaps a hidden tension that what he did at times could rebound on him one day. It had to be a worry for him though he never shared it with her.

She would take over during those frequent absences of his, he saying it was business. There was never any need to question him. She knew full well what he did and what could she do but accept it, grateful for the lovely life it afforded them as she mused where they'd have been without it. So it wasn't kosher, but not exactly criminal, those who stole were the criminals, and what Tony didn't know couldn't hurt him. In the meanwhile they lived well.

There had been the New Year party, she and Tony and some friends joining the jam of revelling bodies at the New Year Ball at the Albert Hall. She felt she hadn't a care in the world as they milled around with crowds in fancy dress, streamers trod underfoot or entangled around necks and heads, balloons bursting continuously as twelve o'clock chimed until the air seemed filled with explosions – drunk on brandy and champagne and cocktails with by then unpronounceable names, cavorting with men divested of their once immaculate evening shirts, while quite a few girls boldly displayed a bared breast or two, men leering, sidling up and maybe sneaking off with them.

Too tiddly to care, she had come home asleep on Tony's shoulder in a taxi. She thought he'd made drunken love to her because next morning, awakening with a thumping headache, she noticed the signs on the bed clothes, and not once had she thought of her family and their own humble celebrations. Only the next day, with her brain finally unscrambled, did she wonder if they had thought of her.

March saw her in Paris, her very first trip to that lovely city that had her giddy with adoration as well as with the view from the top of the Eiffel Tower, blushing at scantily dressed artistes and naked statues at the Folies Bergères and at the strange behaviour of some Parisians in that quarter.

In June there had been another trip abroad, to Deauville, to sit under a sunshade on the beach in a bathing costume, test the warm sea or join in beach recreations.

At home more parties, more balls, vying with other women to appear the best dressed, the most elegant, the liveliest, the most brilliant in a new age of escapism, kicking over the traces in the question of morals, manners and taboos. All so marvellous. How could she have ever dreamed of all this only a year or two ago? This year she was soaking it up, a once dry sponge wallowing in the moisture of wining and dining and rubbing shoulders with the rich and famous.

She may not have spoken with any of them but at times was close enough to feel their breath on her bare shoulder or draw in the smoke from their cigars and cigarettes, she puffing her own cigarette smoke in their direction, sporting the perfumed cylinder on the end of the long, ivory cigarette holder that Tony had bought her, jangling her long earrings and ropes of pearls while striking fashionable poses.

She said nothing of this to Mum when she found time to visit. Mum would have been horrified, seeing her as little more than a social climber – to those of her part of the world not far removed from the women who paraded the streets. She was critical of her daughter's rise in circumstance instead of being pleased for her; what would she have said had she known of the escapades she and Tony were indulging in?

Of course, Wally and Clara's wedding was in May, and for a while, attending the church and reception in Clara's parents' house, she became once more part of that old life she'd known. After a couple of false starts, at the church having to meet sidelong glances at her splendid beige outfit and Tony's well-cut suit, she was soon letting her hair down with the best of them at the party afterwards in the parents' house, drinking gassy beer, sherry and the odd gin, while Tony sat apart, isolated for most of the time, glancing again and again at the clock on the mantelshelf.

With the others she saw the happy couple off to their honeymoon in Margate, Wally having been able to save well in his new job as a stevedore in the docks. Tom's luck too had taken a good turn and he was in steady work at last.

At Wally's wedding, plans had been laid for the whole family to have a day in Southend on August Bank Holiday. 'Just like old times,' Mum said.

'Shall we?' Geraldine later queried of Tony but he shook his head.

'Too much business to do.'

'Not on a bank holiday, darling.'

'I don't think so.'

281

When nothing would persuade him to join her family, she grew angry. Too beneath him, she interpreted, though she didn't say so, except to snap, 'Then please yourself! But I'm going!'

That was it. He was sullen, she was stubborn as she packed a picnic lunch on the day to eat on the beach along with the others who could never afford a meal in a restaurant. Cups of tea from a beach kiosk was their limit, all they needed brought along with them – sandwiches, cake, lemonade, biscuits, a bit of chocolate, a few apples, a flask of tea already sugared and milked so as not to have to lay out on another cup of tea – the money going instead on the luxury of an ice-cream cornet or even a wafer.

The day was warm and sunny, and even though it clouded around late afternoon, nothing could dampen the Glover family's fun.

'Fancy a paddle?' suggested Mum to Mavis, sitting on a coat on the gravelly sand, wiping chocolate from little, nine-month-old Barbara's mouth with a soiled hanky. Evie and Fred were already in the sea, Evie's all-enveloping bathing costume, knitted by Mum, sagging a little with the weight of water so that she was spending most of her time up to her waist in the sea while wringing out the waterlogged knitwear in case it revealed her young breasts to the general public. Fred in a shop-bought bathing suit had no qualms and with one foot on the bottom made an effort to look as though he were swimming.

Dad was standing at the water's edge in his shirt sleeves, his trousers rolled up to his calves to avoid getting wet, his head shielded from the strong sun by a knotted handkerchief. Wally and Clara, who'd also come along, had gone off together along the promenade with plans to look in at the Kursal funfare.

Mavis stopped wiping Barbara's face clean, jumping up at Mum's suggestion. 'Why not? I've bin longing ter get me feet wet. Let's see if the kids like it. I 'ope they do. If they don't, I'll 'ave ter take 'em back up.' She already sounded prematurely disappointed.

Mum glanced at Geraldine, still sitting on a small beach rug. 'Ain't you goin' ter put yer toes in the sea?' she queried. 'Or don't yer do them sort of things now?'

But it was too nice a day to let such remarks offend her. She should know Mum by now, and, 'I think I will, Mum,' was all she said.

With Mum beside her and Mavis carrying Barbara on one arm while dragging a toddling, half-reluctant two-year-old Simon by the hand, she made her way painfully and gingerly barefoot over the stones to the warm, brown wavelets with their mottled yellow lines of foam that had a doubtful look as to cleanliness. But wiggling her toes in it, the sand here and the first traces of mud uncovered by an outgoing tide soft underfoot there, gave pleasure in the sensation.

Little Barbara, her tiny dress held high, took like a duckling to water and to having her bottom without its napkin dipped into the briny, gurgling with delight, although Simon at the first touch of a slightly larger than usual wavelet on his legs, yelped and backed away and there was nothing Mavis could do to persuade him to go back in. Finally she took them the few yards back to where their towels and other paraphernalia lay un-attended, to rub both her children dry.

Later, with Dad watching the kids, they walked out onto the mud after the tide had receded to almost a mile from the shore to do a spot of cockling, digging toes into the clinging, black mud where a tiny jet of water was seen to spurt to ease up the small, fan-shaped shell-fish to fill their buckets and be taken home to be boiled for tea – delicious, if slightly gritty, cockle meat, straight from the sea to be eaten with bread and marg.

Dad came out from another dip of his toes to help eat the sandwiches and cake and drink hot, Thermos-flask-tasting tea, later to go and pay out for fresher stuff from the nearby kiosk with hard-earned money. Evie and Fred had dried and changed under towels held up by Mum, then went off to buy an ice cream. Wally and Clara returned after a while, obviously weak from laughing and bearing a little, garish, pink, celluloid doll, a cheap prize from a shooting gallery, while Mum, Mavis and Geraldine spent a frustrating ten or so minutes trying to dry wet feet and wipe the clinging sand from between toes.

There had been a frantic five minutes looking for Simon who had wandered off unsupervised for a moment. They found him with another toddler in a shallow pool some child had dug in the flattest, muddiest piece of beach, his clothes grey with mud, he in his element with no waves to scare him. It had taken ages to get him clean, using buckets of whatever cleanish seawater they could find in different pools left behind by the receding tide until he was relatively decent again. All the time Mavis was screeching at him, he bawling out crying in protest with the whole beach looking on. It was a dishevelled, grubby child they took home that evening, Mavis explaining the reason and her resultant shame of him to everyone on the train interested enough to listen.

The hem of Geraldine's dress had got wet in looking for water and all the while they were on the beach kept clinging uncomfortably to her legs, even when she eventually got back into her silk stockings, in the process noticing Mum's askance glance at their richness.

'Make an 'ole in them and that'll cost yer a pretty penny,' came the acid remark, going on when Geraldine gave a small grimace of agreement with, 'Don't suppose that means too much ter you. Lucky ter be able ter afford 'em, I s'pose.'

But she was still enjoying her day out too much to care to retaliate. Nothing Mum said could have spoiled her day, for the first time maybe since her marriage feeling one of them, and Dad had been really friendly towards her, as if Tony didn't exist.

A month had gone by since then but the joy of that day remained with her as sharp as if it had been yesterday. They'd laughed at characters paddling: thick-waisted, middle-aged women with their dated dresses held high, so that the elastic hems of their knickers showed; men revealing bow legs normally disguised by decently rolled-down trousers in the street; picture postcards of roly-poly, shiny-cheeked women and equally roly-poly men with glowing red noses and leering expressions at the near-the-knuckle captions beneath; kids on the promenade roundabouts and swings, young girls in summer dresses and little else on the bigger see-saws, the wind blowing their skirts up above their knees, the men, especially the older ones, ogling them; kids' faces smothered in ice cream, kids laughing, kids crying, getting a smack and told they'd come here to enjoy themselves and enjoy themselves they would, if it killed their mothers!

It had been so like old times when she'd been younger and that one day out in a month of Sundays something to recall for the rest of the dreary winter. All the jaunts to Paris and Deauville, the house parties, the race meetings, the air shows she'd attended, couldn't hold a candle to that Bank Holiday Monday, and it was just as well Tony had cried out of it, not only because he would have made her feel silly, but when she got home with them all, weary and satisfied, Alan had popped round. He'd become very much a friend of the family, whether by their design or his own, she didn't know or care to ask, but these days he seemed to be included in much of what the Glovers did.

Much against her better judgment, seeing him had been like the icing on the cake of her day out. They had talked over a tea of bread and cockles and some shrimps Dad had bought on the way home, and it had been like talking to an old friend. She told him about her day from beginning to end and he had seemed so interested, saying he wished he'd taken up the offer to come but had felt he might seem to be pushing in. If he'd known she would be there he would have definitely come along.

He'd popped round all dressed up for visiting and he had looked so nice. He had smelled nice too from the brilliantine on his smoothed-down hair, though no amount of brilliantine could keep down its persistent waviness. She'd felt a distinct reluctance to leave.

To get Alan out of her mind, when she did arrive back home she tried telling Tony about her day but it seemed he didn't want to know and went off to bed early, leaving her to stay up for a while longer on her own to think about it all, but most of all to think about Alan and how nice it had been to see him after such a wonderful day.

# Chapter Twenty

She should have learned by now not to spoil a quiet evening at home with Tony by alluding to their dead daughter. But it seemed so right, playing dance tunes on the gramophone, in fact getting up to dance to the last one, the tune a bit old now, two years old in fact, but one of his favourites: 'I Left My Heart In Avalon', a smooth, smoochy, love song.

The music coming to an end, he'd chosen another, something brighter, and had come to sit down in the armchair. Beyond the closed curtains a motor car or two rumbled their way faintly to wherever they were going or coming from, adding to the peace within the flat.

Contented, drawing slowly on his cigarette while she fitted her own into a long ivory holder, they were both in casual evening garb, the first time in weeks that they'd shared an evening like this together, just the two of them. And then she had to say it, didn't she?

'Do you realise, darling, it's thirteen months since we lost Caroline.'

She hadn't mentioned it on the anniversary of that

dreadful day. It had been too painful. But now she felt she could, it being no special time. But as soon as she came out with it, she knew she'd said the wrong thing.

She saw him wince, not with pain but irritation. But thirteen months on – surely she could speak of it without seeing his lips grow tight and his expression harden. A stab of anger made her plough on.

'I was thinking, darling, why don't we try for another baby? This time in earnest.' They had tried, he only at her insistence, but so far nothing – almost as though he had no enthusiasm for it, or secretly had no wish to have children.

The tight expression had become one of impatience. His tone when he answered had grown harsh. 'I've got more on my mind just now. We'll talk about it some other time.'

Her anger too was up. He'd hedged on this matter long enough. How much longer were they going to go on, no family, just the two of them? How could he be so selfish? Him and his work! That's all he cared about, that and enjoying himself, dragging her along with him, going here, going there, in the company of this friend and that, not one of them genuine, not one as good as they ought to be; they with whom he did his shady deals, who used him, and if one day they were done with him would drop him like a hot potato, or – she dreaded the thought – would shop him at a moment's notice if they looked like getting into trouble, leaving him to carry the can.

He couldn't see it, refused to see it. He thought he was in the money forever, seeing himself as well in. He'd play cards with them, well into the early hours, leaving her alone while he gambled. There'd been a number of times too when he had shut her out of a conversation with someone, making her feel she was not to be trusted, an outsider. Sometimes she felt so alone. If Caroline had lived she wouldn't have felt so alone. She wanted a baby, wanted it desperately, and this hedging of his served to infuriate her, and frustrate her, as it was doing at this moment.

'No, Tony, I want to talk about it now!'

Startling her he leapt up, stubbing out his cigarette in the ashtray on its stand beside him. In a split second their pleasant evening had changed.

'I'm sick of hearing about babies!' came the roar. 'Can't you ever be satisfied with what we have? I do all I can for you, work myself into the ground for you, even put myself at risk and all you do is carp. I'm sick of it!'

Before she could stop him even to say sorry had she wanted to, he'd stalked out of the room. She thought of following him either to have this thing out with him or make some sort of appeasement but instead continued to sit there seething. He wasn't worth trying to appease.

She listened to him moving about in the bedroom. Later, dressed for outdoors in overcoat and trilby, he passed the lounge without glancing in. The door of the flat closed with a thud, his footsteps raced down the stairs to the shop and then came a fainter thud as that door too shut behind him.

Where he was off to Geraldine had no idea. Maybe to see some friend, someone she didn't know, maybe to join a card game in that person's home – not a club, for gambling was illegal though she wouldn't have put that past him, his life so on the edge of the law since their marriage. He seemed always to have enough money to gamble with, to take her places with. But it did worry her, his apparently bottomless pit of ready money. How much longer could it last? Would it all come to an end one day? Suddenly, perhaps with him being caught and found guilty, sent to prison. What would she do then? How could she ever face her family knowing what they'd say – have to hear those inevitable words, I told you so.

She sat surrounded by thoughts while the gramophone played the cheery one-step 'Ma, He's Making Eyes At Me' running down for the want of winding, the lively song falling in pitch to become a dismal, diminishing wail, then a growl, finally falling silent before the record had reached its end.

Tony glanced at her over the newspaper he was reading at the breakfast table.

'What would you say to a trip to Egypt, darling?'

The suggestion, coming out of the blue, made Geraldine look up from her own meal.

'What?'

'Egypt. Let's say sometime in April.' He leaned forward and passed the newspaper to her, now folded at the appropriate place for her to read.

'They're saying that people are flooding out there to see the tomb this Howard Carter chap discovered last November,' he went on as she read the piece indicated. 'Said to be filled with treasure from this pharaoh, what's-his-name, Tutankhamun. Everyone wants to see it. So what d'you say, shall we? Can't find ourselves left out in the cold when others start asking if we've seen it when they already have.'

291

That was Tony these days, killing himself to keep up with others. Of course she wanted to go. Who wouldn't? But all this spending as if money grew on trees, it worried her.

'Can we really afford it? It could be awfully expensive. Should we be spending out so much?'

A peeved look had come over his face. 'Of course we can afford it!'

'Well, we do get through quite a bit. Too much. I just feel it can't last.'

Reaching over he grabbed the paper from her in a small show of temper. 'You let me be the judge of what we can and can't afford. Trouble with you, Gerry, you've never got over those penny-pinching times you used to know. It's about time you forgot all that.'

'Old habits die hard, I suppose,' she snapped, though she hadn't intended to retaliate with quite that sort of retort, practically affirming what he'd said. Any reference to her upbringing rankled and made her say stupid things.

It seemed unbelievable that in three days she and Tony would be sailing off to Egypt. April already, April 1923, so much had changed in her life since marrying him two and a half years ago. She had only two regrets: no children, and the gulf that still lay between her and her own family. In a way she was glad that a similar gulf lay between Tony and his, for the very opposite reason to hers, but in a way they were both in the same boat. He'd not had a peep from either of his parents last Christmas, and one would have thought being so estranged from them, he might have looked to hers to compensate, but he seemed not one bit inclined to.

At her insistence they'd spent Christmas Day with her family, but he had been so cold and distant, his all-too-obvious, bored manner making the atmosphere so uncomfortable that all she wanted to do the entire day was to sink into the ground with mortification.

He had wanted to go to a party where it had been planned for them all to listen in to this new fad, the wireless. He'd been so eager but she'd played up, insisting in no uncertain terms that it was time her own parents had a look in until he finally conceded with a churlishness that foretold the sort of day she would have and she had ended up wishing to God that she'd gone with him instead.

That had been almost sixteen weeks ago and she hadn't seen them since. Just after the New Year she'd gone to Mum's on the off chance, looking to make up for his behaviour and for going with him to a New Year's Eve house party instead of to them. Mum hadn't been in.

Going on to see Clara, not daring to face Mavis although her sister seemed to be doing better these days for money and was expecting her third baby, she at least found Clara at home.

With no axe to grind with Geraldine's more than generous wedding present to them of a whole year's rent in advance on a little terraced house in Belhaven Street, just the other side of Grove Road, her sister-in-law had welcomed her warmly.

She had gone there a few days after they'd moved in to find it in a dreadful state, the previous tenants not at all finicky as to cleanliness. She'd taken off her coat and hat and got down to help with the scrubbing of floors, washing of walls and windows, even to cleaning a most revolting outside loo, all the while trying not to retch at the sight and smell of it. Clara had been so grateful, and in her she knew she had an ally against Mum's constant insidious remarks that had never really diminished in their smarting results.

With Clara's house, the first time she'd been there since helping to clean it, as neat a little home as anyone could wish for and as bright as a new pin, even to the well-scrubbed window frames and door as well as the doorstep, Clara had told her that Mum was at Mavis's where she always went on Wednesdays. Geraldine had forgotten that but was glad she hadn't chosen to go to Mavis's and have the two of them to cope with.

It was a nice afternoon with Clara offering a lovely cake she had baked and her tea like nectar. She promised to tell Mum that she had gone there and Geraldine had no reason to doubt that she wouldn't, but Mum had never responded, hadn't come nigh or by her flat. Over the weeks of silence Geraldine experienced a rebellious reaction. Why put herself out to go and see Mum again if Mum couldn't be bothered to come and see her?

Even a little note to Mum had reaped no response, probably still seething over Tony's attitude on Christmas Day. But surely such a small scratch should have healed by now. It was typical of Mum to pick and pick at it until it continually bled! Thus with her nose put out of joint by those weeks of silence, the weeks had blossomed into months and the gulf had grown wider.

She hadn't even told Mum she and Tony were off to Egypt, something she would normally have ached to spread around and see eyes open with envy and awe. The eyes of those friends she imparted it to in this present existence of hers wouldn't widen a thousandth of an inch. They'd all done it at some time or other – going abroad to those of the giddy set to which she now belonged was completely commonplace, perhaps only to awaken interest if one said one was off to chart some new undiscovered jungle or follow in the footsteps of Scott or Amundsen across the still much-uncharted Antarctic.

It seemed no matter who she spoke to, they had all either been already or were about to go and discover Egypt. To be in Egypt had suddenly become fashionable. But wasn't she too about to join in the fashionable rush for the place? She could hardly wait, and Mum, if she continued to be the way she was, would be the loser by not being told!

It was the first time she'd ever sailed on a proper ship. There had been those bobbing little packets going between England and France, the route to Paris or one of the resorts popular with society types.

This huge ship had her in awe, filled with excitement, hardly able to believe that she was about to travel in it to somewhere she'd never even dreamed she'd ever see. It was like a great floating hotel. The grand, ornate, central staircase you could watch people ascending and descending all day long. The high-ceilinged, brightly lit ballroom with its magnificent clean lines of art deco echoed dance music from an impeccable orchestra while men in their evening clothes and women in fashionably short, glitteringly beaded dresses that far outdid hers glided about the small dance floor or else kicked up their heels to the brand-new dances like the Black Bottom, the Jog Trot, the Vampire and the Shimmy.

There was the most fantastic lounge and an almost intimidating dining room where cutlery tinkled gently and voices droned with such a richness of quality that she felt she only dared to whisper to Tony in case her humble origins were detected, despite the odd explosion of some light ripple of laughter or high-toned, refined exclamation. There were people who milled about with names like Ponsonby and Fotheringay and Lord this and Lady that. And all the while came the regular thumping of the ship's engines until finally she got so accustomed to it she forgot to hear it, the only time to be aware of it was to lull her to sleep at night, listening to its subdued beat with knots reduced for the benefit of slumbering passengers.

Of course they were well segregated from third class – Tony had seen to that, spending money on this trip that had frightened the wits out of her and made her wonder just how much money he did make other than legitimately, and again what would happen to her if he ever got caught at what he was doing. But she forgot all this once on board, the big ship gliding out into the English Channel and on to the Bay of Biscay.

She'd heard ghastly tales of the Bay of Biscay ever since Tony had decided on this trip, of storms that induced violent bouts of seasickness. But it seemed almost for her benefit alone that those terrible waves remained virtually pond-like the whole way, giving her not one single moment of discomfort.

There were parties and dancing, the Captain's Dinner, deck games by the score, endless entertainment, then relaxing in deck chairs, a continuous round of eating such delicious food as she had never before tasted that she was sure she would be quite fat by the end of the trip with her breasts far larger than the accepted flatness of the day. But for now she would enjoy every second and everything that was thrown her way and damn the pounds she put on and damn the cost of it all. It seemed the motto 'Live for the moment and forget tomorrow' was the normal pursuit of everyone on board, so why not join them?

With the ship moving steadily towards the Mediterranean, there were warm night breezes that merely ruffled the hair so long as one kept well out of the stiff wind created by the ship's own progress and she felt like a film star. Again and again she needed to pinch herself to see if this was really her participating in all of this, and every now and again a twinge of utmost excitement and elation would deal an unexpected punch deep in the pit of her stomach until she wanted to leap for sheer joy, though of course she never did. And show herself up among all these seasoned travellers to whom sailing the high seas was probably commonplace? Never.

Tony, however, was treated to it nightly in the privacy of their cabin and took great delight in hearing her explosions of joy.

'I just can't believe it's me here,' she trilled, cuddling up to him as they lay in the somewhat narrow bed of their cabin, its narrowness bringing them closer together.

'You wait until you see Egypt,' he promised as though he'd been there before, although he hadn't.

'I can't wait,' she sighed. 'To think – me going to Egypt!'

They made love as they had almost every night on

board, with pleasurable abandonment, like during those early months of marriage. Unless too weary from dancing and parties so that they fell straight to sleep on hitting the pillows, they continued making love with such passion as the ship sailed on its way she was sure she must conceive, then wondered if she really wanted to – a baby would put a stop to all this sort of life, enjoying it so much that all she wanted at the moment was for it to go on and on. They could always have a nanny, but there'd be months during which she would slowly get fatter, finally too fat to go anywhere. She decided it be best left to fate and to make the most of what she had, as Tony had so often advised in his more provoked moments.

Egypt, when they finally reached it, took her breath clean away. The heat was so dry it was like the heat from an oven. Wearing a sun helmet and needing the constant shade of a parasol, she began to wonder what mad idea had made her want to come here, except that both she and Tony had been totally innocent of what this sort of heat could be like.

Consuming what seemed to be virtually gallons of water from leather bottles, they motored from Alexandria in convoy for more than one hundred miles between a vast expanse of dun-coloured desert with often hardly any horizon and nothing to see but dust devils and occasionally incongruous and wavering glimpses of distant water, seashores and green trees which their Egyptian escorts said were mirages – illusions she'd never bothered to think of, far less expect ever to see – on a road that was almost dead straight all the way to Cairo and often narrowed by blown sand. The journey had begun late in the day, necessitating they bed down for the night in tents. Then at last Cairo itself.

What a contrast to the silent majesty of the desert with just the odd camel caravan being passed or passing in the other direction. The din of Cairo was alarming, everyone seeming to need to yell above everyone else, whether talking, arguing or bartering, all against a background of a strange wailing of flutes supposed to be music.

There were so many people, so many beggars, so many starved-looking children with tangled hair and sore mouths and wide black eyes around which flies congregated for the moisture they contained; so many women shrouded from head to foot in some strange, shapeless garb; so many carts pulled by camel, donkey or human-power, the men as well as the poor creatures so thin that Geraldine felt her stomach turn as she wondered what sort of place Tony had brought her to.

And the smell! Invading her nostrils, an overpowering miasma of sickly perfume, strange cooking and, in passing many a back alley, stagnant odours of both animal and human excrement. As her dad often remarked at any not-too-pleasant smell: 'What a rotten effluvia, what an 'orrible stink!' Amid the sights and sounds and smells of this city, Geraldine had to smile.

After a trip to view the Pyramids they were soon boarding the paddle steamer taking them down the Nile to Luxor, once more back to serenity and peace as Egypt seen from midstream regained its romance.

Even so there were still the flies, millions of them, tiny, tormenting little horrors that seemed to follow the boat, and her in particular, with vicious glee; she wielded without mercy the flywhisk she'd bought, or during the evening fluttered a fan. There were the mosquitoes too, whining beyond the netting put up around their bed at night. But having brought along medicines lest she got bitten, she had no fears of malaria.

The food, though, was sumptuous, the staff soft-footed and polite-toned, the accommodation, though hot even at night, was spotless with cool white sheets and crisp mosquito netting, and the double doors leading to a tiny veranda could be opened to a pleasant breeze created by the boat's progress upstream.

Once again she began to relax and enjoy the sparkling company, the good food, the soporific rhythmic pulse of the engine turning the paddles, the romance of slowly passing banks with their ever-changing scenery. Here groves of date palms, there huge, deep-green trees she was told were mangos – she'd tasted these the first night on the boat and wasn't too impressed, the taste strange with a slightly, somewhat unpalatable creosote flavour.

On deck, under a sunshade, sipping tea from fine china cups, she'd watch a finger of desert probing down to the very water's edge, or some local village sliding by with the faint, excited cries of children at play drifting over the river towards her. Now and again would be a drifting mass of lotus plants with a few flowers sprinkled among the light-green fronds, or a low bank of reeds among which people laboured, at what she didn't know. All so removed from the elegant and civilised life on board this sedate paddle boat, a world away, and again she must pinch herself to be sure that she wasn't dreaming all this.

It took days of leisurely gliding to reach Luxor and the Valley of the Kings where Carter had made his wondrous discovery. Here Europeans appeared to outnumber the locals at last, a couple of hotels brim full of visitors and she and Tony – he with his quiet wit, his natural charm and his ease of conversation – began rapidly to make friends as people will on holiday.

They went the next day in a fleet of cars bearing a horde of visitors, first stopping off to admire the Colossi of Memnon, taking turns posing for photos dwarfed by the huge, crumbling statues, the men hardly reaching above the plinths. They spent so much time there that by the time they arrived at the Valley of the Kings, Geraldine already felt worn down by the heat.

She'd never seen anything like those towering cliffs of sand, brilliant under an unforgiving sun. Standing about as the marvellous discovery of the boy king Tutankhamun's tomb was explained to them all, Geraldine began to feel strange. Not exactly sick or faint, but that the brightness of the sand began to grow brighter, more glaring, almost white, the heat more intense. Despite her sun helmet, her parasol now wavering a little, despite drinking desperately from her water bottle, the glare grew in strength before her eyes.

'I've got to find some shade, darling,' she whispered to Tony. The heat was battering her body. Her breathing had grown rapid and oddly shallow, yet she seemed not to be sweating though tiny shining particles of salt on the back of her hands when she looked at them told her she must be, the moisture drying as fast as it seeped through her pores, its salt loss betrayed by those tiny crystals on her skin.

'I have to sit down.'

301

The way she panted her request brought Tony's gaze. 'Are you all right, darling?'

She tried to focus on him. 'I – don't know. I feel . . . funny.'

As her body gave way she felt herself being lifted, carried, aware only of shade, of the heat of the sun diminishing as people bent over her, but she felt no better for it.

'The heat has got to her,' came a woman's voice. 'She has been drinking properly, hasn't she?'

'Of course.' This was Tony's voice. 'Just as we were instructed.'

'It could be heatstroke. We must find somewhere cool. Let's splash her face with water. It might help cool her. Look, use my handkerchief. It is clean.'

After a while, with cooling water dabbed on her fore-head, the back of her neck, the backs of her hands, she recovered slightly to find herself in the shade of a kiosk that had been set up by wily locals to dispense soft drinks to wealthy foreigners flocking there in their dozens these days, foolish people with more money than good sense, paying more than such drinks were worth – piastres simply for the asking – and these people called them foreigners and natives!

A drink of indeterminate flavour in a cool glass was being applied to Geraldine's lips. She drank a little then opened her eyes to see a pretty young woman kneeling over her, a glass of pale liquid in her hand. Above her stood Tony with a lost if concerned expression.

'How do you feel now?' queried the woman.

Geraldine sat up slowly, needing to gather her wits, needing to dispel the embarrassment she felt. 'A lot better. I'll be all right in a minute.'

The woman laid a gentle hand on her shoulder to prevent any attempt to rise to her feet. 'Don't hurry. Just stay sitting for a moment.'

'I just came over all unnecessary,' she excused herself in confusion of having a complete stranger seeing her in this state, and saw the woman smile at her colloquialism, but it was a smile that also carried a look of recognition.

'I'm sure I know you, my dear, both you and your husband. Didn't I meet you at some party in London? I forget whose, but it was at a party, I am sure.'

'I can't recall,' said Geraldine, now more in command of her wits.

'Well, I certainly know you from somewhere.' Enquiring their name and being told, the china-blue eyes opened wide in triumph, the red lips parted to reveal small, perfectly white teeth. 'Of course! Geraldine and Tony! Yes, of course I've met you. I still can't remember which party it was, a house party I'm sure, but which?' She gave a little shrug and turned to look up at Tony, pointing a finger of recognition at him. 'You're the jeweller, aren't you?'

What that statement meant with particular emphasis on the jeweller, Geraldine wasn't certain. But apparently his reputation had gone before him even here.

She had begun to feel forgotten as the beautiful young woman stood up to extend a hand towards Tony who promptly took it.

'I'm Diana Manners. Not *the* Diana Manners, daughter of the Duke of Rutland, now Lady Diana Cooper.' She gave a tinkling laugh. 'I wish I were as famous, but I'm not, just happen to have the same married name as her

maiden name. I was married to someone called Billy
Manners but he died last year. Now I'm fancy-free, you
see, so I came out here to soak up the atmosphere and
find my feet. I'm mostly known as Di.'

Tony still had hold of her hand but was looking
bemused. Geraldine spoke up quickly from where she
still sat on the ground. 'I think I can get up, darling.'
She was feeling even more of a fool sitting here. 'Darling,
can you help me?'

Di Manners turned back to her, but speaking to Tony,
'I think she ought to go back to the boat to rest. You
never know, it might be heatstroke, and one has to be
careful. I'd get a doctor to look in on her if I were
you.'

It was almost as if she wasn't there, or too far gone
to comprehend if spoken to directly. 'I'm fine,' she
blurted out. Struggling to her feet, she made a play at
brushing down her dress, adjusting her sun hat, looking
for her parasol, but the change from sitting to standing
made her stagger a little.

Both Tony and Di Manners grabbed her arms. 'We
must get her back to the boat,' instructed Di, 'then I
expect she might have to spend a day or two in the hotel
we're all going to when we reach Luxor.'

Luxor was on the other side of the Nile. The more
expensive rooms, one of which Tony had paid for to
Geraldine's concern that he was spending far too much
on this trip, looked directly across the river and the
golden cliffs of the Valley of the Kings, each morning
made even more golden by the rays of the rising sun.
The reverse was seen at sunset, the cliffs black against
a dying light, the temples of Luxor and Karnak watching

the sunrise depict the afterlife of those buried there and proclaim the death of the worldly body.

Why such thoughts should invade her mind as Tony, with this young woman's help, got a driver to take them back to the boat, she didn't quite know, except that her mind was still in a whirl. Waiting for the rest of the company to return, the three of them sat with her leaning against Tony, a thumping headache now making her want only to lie down and sleep.

'I'll be all right,' she said, 'now that me Tony's here.' She felt too out of sorts to care how she sounded, until she saw that quirky little smile come to the woman's lips once again and could have bitten her tongue, showing herself up again. 'If you want to go,' she ended lamely.

'No, I'll stay,' came the ready offer. 'I've had enough of milling about among barren rocks in full sunshine. I'm happy to stay.'

Geraldine saw a look pass between her and Tony that her befuddled mind saw as kindness and concern on the woman's part and gratitude on his, no doubt wondering how he would ever have managed her on his own.

# Chapter Twenty-one

Egypt was six months ago now and great chunks of it were beginning to fade from her memory. Only those moments of special note stood out – that first sight of Cairo with its crowded thoroughfares and its smells and all that. The journey there she still remembered vividly but not a lot of the trip down the Nile that despite parties every evening did become a little bit too much of the same old thing as the days flowed slowly on like the river itself. Only the odd snatch of memory of some village lingered, a certain tree or two, some portion of bank somewhere or other, a young girl, a child of about eight years old, driving a couple of huge bullocks with a stick as she walked confidently behind them, they obeying her every command.

What she recalled most vividly was the way she'd passed out in front of dozens of people who unlike her were quite unaffected by the heat, and coming back to consciousness to find a young woman who actually knew her bending over her.

What had the woman really thought of her despite her

attractive smile? Had she gossiped about her later? And how many people had witnessed it and hurried forward to offer help, discussing the incident long afterwards, debating if she were in fact normally poor in health?

She hated the mortification of having made such a fool of herself, even after all this time with a damp and cold English October crowding in on her, often with not even Tony's company to soothe away the shame of it. But he seemed always off somewhere, making an excuse not to take her with him.

They still went to nightclubs, dancing until all hours and having fun with the people they knew, went to the theatre on occasion, had gone once to the cinema to see the acclaimed film *The Ten Commandments*. But there had been no summer holiday, Tony having spent far too much in going to Egypt.

Geraldine knew he was short of money and struggling. How could he have been so silly as to put someone in charge of his shop while they were away? She hadn't queried it then, being so excited at aping the wealthy. There had been no complaints about the man, a friend, he'd put in charge, but he'd had to pay him an exorbitant wage, taking up any profit there had been, and of course while he was away there was no other work done.

In fact it recently reached her ears that those he dealt with hadn't been too happy and, in the words of her informant, a spidery little woman named Kate who owned a nightclub and was herself involved in all sorts of shady goings on, were leaning on him so that he was spending endless time away endeavouring to make up for it and ingratiate himself once more into their good graces. Without what he did for them, it was obvious the shop on its own, with its large overheads, would never keep himself and her in the style they'd grown used to.

'He should have spoken to them first,' said Kate darkly, as they sat together in a corner of her nightclub, Tony having disappeared somewhere into a back room with his cronies, not saying why, but she guessed, either to play cards or discuss something she wasn't meant to hear.

'People aren't very happy with him at the moment, you know. But don't despair, darling, it'll all come out right if he behaves himself.'

Geraldine gazed at the unglamorous figure seated across the table from her, spidery fingers toying with a small glass of absinthe, a tatty velvet cape draped about her skinny shoulders, a dowdy dress hanging on her thin frame, the sharp eyes in a sharp face regarding her with a meaningful glint. The look had all the semblance of a gun pointed at her and Geraldine shivered.

The woman had strong links with the underworld, knew everyone, did questionable deals, had bribed the police when necessary, even though in the short time of owning this club, an ill-lit basement beneath Gerrard Street and a far cry from law-abiding places like Quaglino's or Sovrani's or Lett's, it had still been raided by them several times. They'd have had a field day were they to know all that took place behind the front the club presented. People came here solely to enjoy the possible danger of a raid so that she still managed to bounce back, aware of all that went on as well as she was aware of the back of her own skinny hand.

Gazing at the dingy surroundings, Geraldine thought suddenly of the easy life she had led before her marriage.

They had been dingy too but not like this. There had been dignity in such dinginess, people striving to make a better life from it. She too, with little money, had had to work often nine hours a day, Saturday morning included, to make ends meet on piece work. But the stress of that life could never compare to the stress of this one, hobnobbing with society, and not such high-class society at that, not what she had once imagined herself as being part of.

It had got worse these days, she left alone while Tony stayed away far more than the demands made on him seemed to warrant. But she realised he needed to make money. His excuse was always plausible: a business dinner, no women allowed; a card game he'd been asked to take part in; a business meeting that might go on late into the night; and of course that pressing need to spend sometimes a whole night working at his smelter.

'Big job,' he'd say. 'Very important. Can't let people down. I'm going to make bloody good money on this one.' And so on.

He'd been quite distant ever since Egypt and that faint of hers – attentive, yet something had been lacking. In fact he appeared not to be unduly worried by his long absences from her. Even when she was confined to her bed in the hotel for two days with a thumping headache, though he had been attentive and full of concern for her, she'd detected a longing to get away, to carry on enjoying himself.

People had felt sorry for him stuck there with her, had invited him to spend a few hours with them, *to take his mind off it, and leave her to rest!* He'd asked if she minded. 'Just this once,' he'd said, and she, feeling guilty, had urged him to go along.

The once had become twice, then three times, but how could she complain when he'd paid out so much money on this trip, and there was she ruining everything for him. To venture out of doors in that heat would have been even more disastrous. The following day they'd journeyed back on the boat, she doing her best to join in the fun but eventually having to retire earlier than anyone else, Tony staying on *just so as to appear sociable* and so it had gone on, returning to Alexandria by train, then boarding the ship home.

The Bay of Biscay hadn't been so kind on the way back, not savage but rough enough to make her in her delicate state faintly seasick and again Tony had joined in the general pleasures without her, *being sociable*, the couple they'd most made friends with, Vivienne and Ronald Fairfax, and who had previously taken him under their wing after her touch of the sun, only too pleased to have his company, just as they also had included the one female on her own on this trip, Diana Manners.

Kate's voice floated back to her. She heard her say, as the woman leaned forward in a confidential manner, her nasal voice dropping in volume, 'Look, darling, I don't often say this to people, but you have a little talk to your Tony, my dear. Tell him to be careful what he's doing.'

'Why?' cried Geraldine, alarmed by her tone.

Kate straightened up. 'No reason. No *apparent* reason. Just a feeling, dear.'

Draining the milky-looking absinthe in its glass, she stubbed out the Abdulla cigarette she'd been puffing all the while, and stood up as several people, chattering and laughing, entered through the curtained door. Small uneven teeth were revealed in a warm smile in their direction, and not glancing again at Geraldine, her eyes trained solely on her customers, she added in passing, 'Just watch it, dear, that's all.'

Geraldine gazed after the woman, now with those who'd come in, two couples in evening dress, all four exuding wealth and obviously members, speaking with her as though she were a queen. Kate had that effect on all who knew her, commanding attention despite her notorious lack of glamour.

But Geraldine's thoughts were not on the little cameo. What had Kate been intimating? What was she supposed to watch? Tony? What was he up to that she'd not been told of? Was he in trouble or likely to be? What did Kate know that she didn't?

Stubbing out her own cigarette beside the still smouldering Abdulla in the ashtray she got up, suddenly angry – with Kate, with Tony keeping her in the dark, with her life, with something she so often felt was missing in it. Hurrying over to the cloakroom girl and grabbing her evening coat from her, she swept out of the '43' Club to hail a taxi, leaving Tony to his own devices. She needed to escape, just for a while. She needed to be somewhere where she wouldn't be forever on tenterhooks about what could happen to Tony and to her life. She needed to find some sanity.

There was only one place. She fled to her parents. No doubt they'd receive her coolly, as always, but she was used to that now. Even that would be a breath of fresh air, the lesser of her two problems, and she needed time to think. Her plan was to ask if she could stay there overnight or even a couple of nights, she'd see.

At home she left a note, saying where she'd be, that she needed a break from their constant social round that lately was wearing her down, just a short rest, then she'd be back. What Tony would think of that she did not much care. At the moment it seemed her life must constantly revolve around him. Well, let his revolve around her for once, if only for a brief while.

Hilda Glover stared in bewilderment at the small overnight bag. 'What you up to?' were the first words to come from her mouth although she'd already interpreted the reason for its presence.

Her daughter stood on the broken pavement below the single doorstep as though expecting already to be evicted from there. 'I just thought I'd pop over to see you.'

'Just pop over,' Hilda repeated woodenly, nodding as she spoke. She couldn't help feeling sceptical, this daughter of hers with her high and mighty attitude towards them, seeing herself above those roots she had once been part of, staying away not for weeks but often for months on end but whenever something wasn't going right, there she'd be on the doorstep looking for a bit of sympathy. What was it her Jewish neighbour often said? 'Kids – they want you, you live only around the corner, they don't want you, suddenly your house is the other side of the world!'

How true that was in Geraldine's case. She thought handing out a few expensive presents, like when she'd got back from Egypt, made it all right. Well it didn't!

She'd had no time for Gel's stories of the lovely time she'd had, boasting about it as if she'd become one of the aristocracy. She'd let it all go over her head, unimpressed, seeing it more like money being slung out of the window just so's she could show off. That last visit was five months ago. Gel hadn't been nigh or by since.

No doubt she'd brought lots of nice things with her this time like she always did when finally deciding to come here, looking to vindicate another long absence, and that would put it all right. Well, it didn't!

If she popped round even once a fortnight, like Mavis who had to cart three kids with her every time, she'd have felt more disposed towards her. Even Wally came more often and you don't always expect boys to do that all that much, they working, caring for a family. Even Clara, just a daughter-in-law, came regularly with her baby, Vera, now seven months old. Gel had seen that baby just the once to her knowledge, when she was a month old. Seeing her, Gel had immediately wiped her eye, while trying to hide it, over the baby she'd lost.

Crocodile tears, that's all they were. She should know the cure without having to be told – knuckle down to reality and get stuck in to trying for another one. But as she saw it Gel was having too much of a good time to have a baby, or else didn't want to spoil her nice figure. No, her with all her money, she preferred going here, there and everywhere – *abroad!*

Hilda felt a sneer rise up at the word. What was wrong with this country? What was wrong with Southend, or Margate or even Eastbourne? They all had nice scenery and could be warm if you went the proper time of year and if you were lucky. It was still the same sea you saw which went all the way round the world so why go all that way to see it, throwing away good money you probably couldn't really afford? No doubt about it, being in the money had turned her daughter into a right snob.

She didn't begrudge Gel her fine life, was glad to see her settled so well, but she'd never liked Gel's husband, jumped up little maggot, and what he was had rubbed off on her daughter – snobs, the pair of them, she, silly cow, thinking she knew which side her bread was buttered, not realising the butter itself was rank, spoiled by her so-called fine living.

Hilda stood her ground. 'So what's it this time, 'ad a bust-up wiv yer ole man?' She deliberately made her cockney accent more pronounced, and dig that into you, you jumped-up la-di-da!

'No, Mum. I just thought I needed a break from everything.'

'And thought yer'd 'ave it 'ere, wiv us, yer dad and me.'

'No, I just wanted ter come and see you.'

Just wanted. Well, well! It was nice to hear that tinge of Cockney in her voice still, but the pleasure was marred by a slight suspicion that Gel was putting it on so to speak, the other way around so to speak.

'So what's the attaché case for?' she asked.

She saw her daughter blink quickly. 'I wondered, to save rushing off back home, an afternoon visit being so short after all this time' – so she was· aware how long it had been – 'I might stay the night and go home tomorrow. We could have a longer time together. It'll be nice.'

Nice! Fully expecting to stay the night, just like that, after all these weeks, no, months of silence with not even a note, and so blinking matter of fact with it too.

It wasn't right to feel like this. She loved Geraldine

314

as much as she loved all her children; it was just that she wasn't demonstrative by nature. She would have thawed more towards her, if only Gel would thaw towards her in turn instead of taking her for granted, turning up only when she fancied to. Where was the warm, loving daughter who'd been brought up to have a care for her parents?

'We'll see.' She stepped back. 'Yer'd best come in then, 'adn't yer. Standin' 'ere on the doorstep in the wet.' For it was beginning to rain a little.

Geraldine's tenuous smile grew firmer. 'I thought you'd never ask!' came the quip and Hilda allowed an answering huff as she turned on her heel, leading the way, leaving her daughter to close the door behind them.

'What she doin' 'ere this time of night?' Jack whispered in the kitchen as he dragged off his well-worn and wet overcoat, his soiled jacket, muffler and frayed cloth cap, also wet from a now steady evening downpour.

'She's been 'ere all afternoon,' Hilda whispered back as she took the damp things from him ready to hang around the kitchen fire. 'She wants ter stay the night. And don't do that!' she paused to hiss in irritation as he lifted the lid of the kitchen range lit against a miserable October evening to spit into the flames, first clearing his throat of the dust from a day unloading coal from a ship's hold. 'Not in front of her.'

He scowled. 'She's in the uvver room, ain't she? I ain't doin' it in that fire, am I?'

'Just make sure yer don't when yer do go in there! Just mind yer p's and q's, that's all.'

'Was a time,' he said slowly, 'when p's and q's

didn't matter. Now we got ter keep our collars an' ties an' jackets on in case we don't come up to 'er measure, an' make sure we don't break wind by accident in 'er company.'

'Don't be so blessed crude, Jack.'

'Why not?' He didn't wait for a reply. 'So what's she doin' 'ere, then? Don't she like the rain? Mustn't get wet, even runnin' to a taxi? I don't suppose 'er 'usband brought 'er then. Never comes near us unless 'e 'as to.'

Hilda understood how he felt. Since the days when he'd refused the offer of the man's help with that affliction he'd had, he seldom had a good word to say to him. Another's help he would have accepted, but it had been the toffee-nosed way it had been offered.

It might have been that Gel's husband couldn't help the way he sounded. Maybe even now he had no idea how he'd come to offend. Perhaps it was just his way. But it caused Jack to feel that his dignity had been undermined, to see himself less than a man by the fact of the other seeing him as one unable to support his own family, and that never made any man feel good.

'I'm wonderin',' Jack went on, 'if them two ain't 'ad a bit of a bust-up. No other reason why she'd want ter come ter spend the night 'ere.'

In fact, Gel had been very tight-lipped about why she'd wanted to stay the night. Several times she thought she was about to say something, but each time Gel clammed up again, and she wasn't going to ask her. Let her come out with whatever was bothering her. But in the end all Gel did was make small talk the whole afternoon.

Geraldine lay beside Evie, listening to her sister's gentle breathing. Evie had been happy enough to see her even if Mum and Dad hadn't or made it seem that way.

After a tea of cheese on toast, a bit of cake left from what Mum had made last weekend, Dad having a proper dinner after working all day, Dad had gone and sat in his chair in front of the fire. Quite a decent fire as well as the one in the kitchen, Mum not short of coal at the moment with Dad unloading the stuff at the present time.

This family, like the families of most dockers, nearly always benefited from whatever hold the man was working in at the time: a handful of sugar in the paper bag his lunch had been in and stuffed under his cap; a couple of tins of fruit or a bit of meat at the bottom of his haversack; a pocket full of nails to mend a broken part of a pigeon loft, for lots of men in the East End kept pigeons for recreation; a short length of material torn from a broken bolt of cloth brought out wrapped around the stomach for the wife to make a dress out of. It all depended on what came off the boat. Not every time, for any man caught pilfering could lose his job and not get back so easily into dock work – it was a case of biding your time, watching out for whoever was on the gate, any alert one spotted from a distance and whatever you'd come by having to be ditched, or march through brazenly if you recognised the sloppy one lounging there. Worthwhile if you could make mates of some blokes on the gate too.

Geraldine knew the drill as good as any in her family. This week for the Glover family it was coal, brought out lump by lump wrapped in the old morning newspaper kept especially for the purpose; and Dad had made best use of it after tea, settling back in his wooden armchair, feet on the brass fender, nose in the evening paper, finally falling asleep, probably much needed after nigh on twelve hours of backbreaking unloading.

It had been quite nice around the tea table with Fred and Evie there, Mum doing the rounds of family news: Mavis's three children; Clara's baby; Granny Glover not doing too good these days, getting old; Uncle Bert hadn't been too well, chest trouble of some sort; Aunt Jess with a terrible cold she couldn't shake off and it being so early to get colds, what would she do if it was still there come wintertime? Young Fred doing well at the *News Chronicle* newspaper; Evie still working behind the counter at the Co-op and promoted to the dairy counter where she was learning how to work butter into pats for customers, quite a skilled job. Mum had finally dried up, not seeming to want to hear anything Geraldine had to say.

Thankfully young Fred had taken up the subject of his work, how much he was liked there, how he had high hopes of promotion, advised to go off to night school a couple of nights a week learning journalism, shorthand and train to be a reporter one day. 'Get all the best scoops,' he vowed, 'and see me name there at the top of what I write.'

Evie too had been relatively loquacious, talking about her current boyfriend, Stephen, with whom she had been going out for several months now. But after tea she had left to go and meet him while Fred had gone off to meet his mates. That was when the conversation had tailed off until Dad, retiring to his chair having said little around the table, had fallen asleep and Mum had got on with some darning leaving Geraldine to stare into the fire.

She had wanted to confide in Mum about Tony and the warning Kate Meyrick had given her regarding the possibility of his getting in too deep with those he hung around with and which was beginning to worry her no end.

But how to confide her worries to Mum? As poor as she and Dad were, as much as there were shady types, vicious characters, dark dealings in the alleyways of the East End, they were themselves above board, apart maybe from Dad helping himself down at the docks occasionally, which everyone did if the coast looked clear. They knew nothing of this much darker side of life in the sort of society Tony had got himself in with; from what reached her ears now and again, there was far more evil than even the odd murder reported in this deprived area, for much of what went in the West End was big time – the crooked gambling with high stakes that went on in clubs like the '43', vicious deals concerning drugs, extortion, protection, big names involved, which often the police would miss even when raiding nightclubs, maybe bribed, who knows. And Tony, a tiny cog in that huge evil wheel, could be one of those who would get caught one day.

She'd never told anyone except Alan where his money came from. The fewer who knew, the safer it was, and besides it would give the impression he was thoroughly dishonest. He wasn't dishonest. Those who brought the stolen goods to him were. All he did was give a service. True, one by which he made good money. He'd formed friendships with some of them, got invited out by them, and yes, maybe he did other deals with them, but what they were she didn't know and he wouldn't tell her.

It was hard to tell who was crooked and who wasn't among his friends – nice people many of them, polite people, people who drew her into their circle with open hearts: people like Samual Treater, Sam; Ernest Bulwalk, known as Ernie; William Schulter; and a man called 'Fruity' Hicks, seldom seen without an apple or a banana or a pear he'd be eating. They treated her as if she were someone of importance; their wives too, Lily, Cynthia, Dolly, Dotty and lots of others. There was also Kate who'd warned her of some danger to Tony. With no husband, she flirted with every one of the men, dowdy though she was, with her warm smile. And there was Di Manners who had more or less come on the scene since that first meeting in Egypt. She was usually escorted by a very thin young man called Jimmy, but didn't seem particularly fond of him though he hung upon her dazzling smile.

All this Geraldine thought on as she lay beside her sister. Evie hadn't been too pleased coming home to find she was to share her bed, Geraldine's old bed long since got rid of to make the tiny bedroom roomier for the one girl left in the house.

Made to feel awkward by her sister's lengthened face at the news of having to share her bed, Mum's lack of conversation during the evening, and being more or less ignored by Dad, she finally burst out on impulse that it might be better if she went home after all. Mum had looked at her as though she'd committed some sort of offence.

'But yer've asked if yer can stay, and I said it was orright. So why change yer mind? It's raining cats and dogs out there, can't you 'ere it?' Beyond the drawn brown curtains rain was pattering on the windowpane like something gone mad. 'Yer'd get soaked findin' a taxi. One ain't goin' ter be waiting outside the door for yer. Yer'll 'ave ter walk all the way to a main road and even then there mightn't be one this time of night. We ain't the West End, yer know. Don't be so blessed silly. Yer'll 'ave ter stay 'ere now.'

That last was said as if it was begrudged, they'd just have to put up with her. She'd capitulated, and so here she was, lying here, the rain now ceased, and going over all sorts of thoughts and wishing she was back home in Tony's arms, perhaps confiding her worries to him, with him comforting her.

# Chapter Twenty-two

It was as though last night's rain had washed the world clean. Though cold, everything had a polished look about it, positively glittering in the early morning sunshine as Geraldine walked towards the main road, looking to catch a bus home if there were no taxis around. If only she felt as bright and cheerful as this morning was.

She'd got up early. Not right to stay in bed once Evie was up, getting ready to leave for work at eight-fifteen. Besides, she'd had no wish to stay there any longer than need be. In the kitchen, Evie refused even a bite of toast, keeping herself slim, her bra-flattened breasts even flatter in her present quest for the boyish craze, and cheerfully moaned on about another boring day working her insides out. Serving behind a counter even if it meant having to spend hours on her feet couldn't be all that grinding, Geraldine thought.

Fred, who had devoured his couple of pieces of toast and jam almost before Mum had time to spread the margarine on them, hadn't been able to wait to get out of the house and off to work, loving his job, calling a careless 'bye' as he went off to join the flood already making their way to work, banging the door behind him.

Dad had left the house while still dark outside, needing to be with his gang early although his work was more steady with a proper company, Slaters. Now she and Mum were alone.

'So what was the reason fer you coming 'ere yesterday?' Mum had asked, making toast for the two of them. 'You and 'im ain't 'ad a row, 'ave yer?' She seldom referred to Tony by name. It was always ''im'. Geraldine had ignored the reference.

'No. I just wanted to see you for a bit longer than I usually do.'

It was all she could think to say. Mum had given one of her humphs.

'And I can't say that ter be all that often either!' Then perhaps to compensate for sounding a little too sharp, she'd added rather more gently, 'I know yer didn't 'ave a chance ter say much last night with all us lot here, but is there somethink worrying yer? Yer can tell me now we're on our own and quiet like.'

So Mum did have some feelings for her, was concerned, wanted to help, advise. It sent a warm glow through her even now as she made her way towards Grove Road. Even then she hadn't been able to bring herself to say what had been on her mind. It had been there trembling on the edge of her breath but her throat had closed against it, refusing to let the words pass and she had merely repeated her earlier excuse, that she thought she'd pay them all a visit and had thought staying a bit longer would be nice.

Now it weighed all the more heavily on her for it had

remained unsaid. There was no one she could talk to, not even Kate Meyrick, for despite her covert warning that they were all tarred with the same brush, she would regard her with amusement and shrug it all off. A deep, amorphous fear still gripped, unrelieved, persistent and overwhelming.

She was in Grove Road, passing the shop Tony had once had, now a tobacconist's. Memories assailed her – the first time she'd met him, the flurry of excitement when he'd first looked at her, when he'd asked her out, that pleasurable warmth when he'd proposed. Where had it gone wrong, if indeed it had? More likely it was her, with no cause to worry where the next penny was coming from, whether she'd always have a roof over her head, it seemed she had to have something to worry about, building up imagined fears.

She passed the shop, head down to avoid looking at it. But the corner of her eye caught a familiar figure coming out of it and halted her.

'Alan?' She was conscious of a wave of relief washing through her body as his name burst from her lips.

He looked up from stuffing a new packet of cigarettes into his jacket pocket, and seeing her, his mouth broke into a wide smile. 'Gerry!'

Quickly he wended his way towards her between passers-by. 'Fancy seeing you! What you doing here this time of morning?'

'I stayed at Mum's last night,' she offered over the noise of people.

'Stayed? What, you and Tony?' He glanced up and down the busy street for him, the gesture portraying surprise, instantly assuming something in the Glover family must be amiss, needing both their presence at a time other than Christmas. Geraldine hastened to put his mind at rest.

'I went there on my own actually.'

She was conscious of that stupid word *actually*, tending to use it casually and often as the people she knew did. She hurried on before Alan could enquire further. 'I felt like a bit of a break. Me and Tony's been going out such a lot lately and he's so busy, I just felt like it. You know, a bit of a break, sort of?'

She was now consciously toning down that affected accent. The last thing she wanted was to put Alan at a disadvantage, though it seemed to her his speech had improved, or was it because he was talking to her? Though he'd never watched his speech before when with her.

Maybe she'd been talking too fast. Maybe something in her tone had arrested his attention. He was scrutinising her from under his brows, the gaze questioning, a discerning gaze. 'Is everythink all right, Gerry?'

Foolish tears began to flood her eyes. Unbidden, they stemmed solely from the way he'd said it, the words so tenderly spoken that they flowed like gentle water all about her.

'No, Alan.' Her throat constricted but the need to unburden herself proved stronger, issuing from her in a trembling sob, altering the tone of her voice, lowering it, strangling it. 'Everything ain't all right.'

His hand was on her arm. 'Not here. Let's go across the road fer a cup of tea, and if you want, you can tell me about it – only if you want.'

She didn't reply but allowed herself to be conducted

across the road, he watching out for the morning traffic, cars and vans mixed up with horse-drawn wagons, milk carts, bread carts, bicycles.

By comparison the café was quiet, no one wanting yet to eat or drink. By dinner time it would be full up, but now was empty apart from an elderly woman in one corner with fingers in ragged mittens clasped around a sturdy mug of tea.

Geraldine watched her in her worn coat and shapeless hat, threadbare mittens, old boots and scrap of a scarf about her neck as Alan went to get their tea. What right had she to be miserable and in fear when people like this could only seek solace in a mug of tea, just as she was about to? But for them this was all they had, a mug of tea bought with a coin that had been tossed at them and a forlorn hope of any sort of roof over their head on a freezing, foggy or rain-soaked night.

She felt a fraud sitting here. But Alan's eyes when he returned with two mugs reflected the fact that he wasn't regarding her in that light, that he saw her fears were real to her and that he was ready to do all he could to allay them.

'Now,' he began after taking a sip or two of the dark brown, almost undrinkable brew. 'D'yer feel like telling me what's bothering you, Gerry? Only if you want to of course.'

It felt the most natural thing in the world to slowly unfold all those anxieties that had been eating into her for so long. But hearing them coming from her own mouth they seemed to her to be dreadfully trivial: still pining the loss of her baby after all this time and taking second place to Tony's work even though she'd thought that herself being in the shop would bring them closer, but how close did she expect to come? He took her out and about, they went on fabulous holidays together, had a vast number of wealthy friends, he always paid her compliments, saw to it that she was nicely dressed, gave her presents of jewellery, clothes, flowers, chocolates – what more did she expect? What if he was often away, she ought to expect that if she wanted to live well. Perhaps not so trivial was her wish for another baby, one that Tony pushed aside time after time. And even more important, that his work – his *other* work – could be leading him into danger.

She was chary about telling Alan too much about this last grievance but it was precisely this that had him sitting up, looking at her.

'You really suspect he's in trouble?'

'Not in trouble,' she prevaricated. 'Just that I get worried sometimes.'

'With cause,' he said so succinctly that she couldn't escape.

'It's just what I've been told.'

'So it must hold some substance, mustn't it?'

The elderly woman had got up, was shuffling out. Geraldine let her eyes follow the woman's departure and for moment wondered vaguely where she lived, more like existed.

'You must think it holds some substance?'

Tony's repeat of the question dragged her mind back to him and she nodded miserably. That woman who'd been in here taking a little comfort from a mug of practically undrinkable tea, what were her fears? Maybe she didn't have any beyond the uncertainty of how long before she died of cold, or for want of food or from some illness, or probably she was too dim even to give it a thought but lived from day to day no more than an alley cat or a stray dog roaming the streets might. Who was the luckier? Quickly she shrugged off the dreary thought. There was no comparison. She pulled herself together and looked at Alan. 'I'm just being silly.'

He held her gaze as though physically compelling her to look at him. 'You're not being silly. What your husband is doing is bloody dangerous. Not just because of *what* he's doing, though that comes into it, but because of the people he's in with. And you could be too. You're his wife. You assist in his shop. You could be seen as knowing everythink he does. If somethink went wrong, Gerry, all sorts of things could 'appen. To him, to you.'

'Nothing's going to happen.'

'Then why are yer so scared?'

'I don't know.' She dragged her gaze away from his and concentrated on slowly pushing her still almost full mug of tea from her. Then she turned her gaze to him again, this time adopting a look of confidence, even a little smile. 'I'm all right, Alan, really. I just feel a bit down in the dumps. End of summer, I suppose. Only winter to look forward to.'

'With parties and celebrations and loads of socialising and Tony to buy you everything you want?' It rang of scepticism, he fully aware she was putting on this act, avoiding reality. He sounded almost angry. 'Don't give me all that rubbish, you're bloody scared stiff,' he rushed on savagely, then suddenly mellowed, leaning towards her, his hand reaching out and covering hers. 'Look, I don't blame you fer feeling like that. I would be too. And I've got a

feeling your Tony is too but he won't let you see it. I bet
he's bluffing it out all the time, but underneath . . .' He let
the rest go unsaid, then with his fingers tightening about
her hand, he went on slowly, 'Listen to me, Gerry. If ever
you felt the need to get in touch with me, you know where
I live. If things ever get a bit dicky, don't ever hesitate fer
one second to let me know, you understand?'

He was being so earnest that Geraldine at last found her
voice. 'I don't know what you could do,' she said lamely.

'Neither do I. But I'd do something. I'd never sit back
and say, oh, what a pity she's in trouble, I wish I could
'elp. I'd do *something*!' His tone lowering so considerably that she could hardly hear it, he added, 'There ain't
nothing I wouldn't do for you, Gerry, no matter what it
was. Please remember that.'

She found herself nodding her assent. 'I'll remember,'
she murmured, suddenly aware that she had an ally at
last, that she could go to him with anything that might
be worrying her and he would listen.

She went home with a far lighter heart and something
else besides. Was it knowing she had someone she could
trust in this world of mistrust she seemed to live in? In this
make-believe world where those she mixed with were basic-
ally false, cultured like some of the pearls Tony sold to
those not able to afford the real thing – peal away the layers
to find just a thin nacre about a man-induced piece of grit
in the oyster – Alan was an anchor. Or was it something
more. Love? She could have loved Alan, quite easily.

Despite Tony's obvious reluctance, Geraldine insisted
that Christmas Day would be spent with her family.

'I don't want to spend it with a lot of strangers,' she

burst out, on the verge of an argument about it when he told her he'd already planned to go to this huge house party in Chelsea and that everyone would be there.

'They're not strangers,' he shot back, his voice impatient as he put down his pen from the accounts he'd been doing. 'They're our friends.'

'Your friends.'

'*Our* friends. Mine *and* yours. We've been invited and I've promised now. I can't break it. I can't let them down.'

'Then *you* go!' Fear as well as anger made her shout.

It was only a party after all. They wouldn't be missed. But the very words 'promised' and 'can't let them down' sent shivers up her back. 'Can't' she interpreted as 'daren't', as though he was obeying an order rather than an invitation, as if he was in the grip of these people he called friends. Yet she always found them nice, enjoyed their company when she was there. It was only afterwards, or when invited to join them that she'd experience this vague sense of dread. No doubt she was being silly but in her mind she could still hear Kate Meyrick's oblique warning.

This time, however, she pushed disquiet aside for the more needful determination to have her way. 'I don't mind if you want to go off with your own friends but I intend to be with my family on Christmas Day.'

'Why don't you stop saying *my* friends?' he snarled. 'They're not *my friends*!'

She looked at him thinking, you've said a mouthful there, my dear, even as, going back to his account books, he added sullenly, 'They're *ours*.'

Tony had capitulated. He'd telephoned the hostess who'd invited them and made his apologies and now this

330

Christmas night sat in a corner of Mum and Dad's crowded front room, showing off as it were, looking visibly bored, declining conversation, except perhaps with Wally, drinking too many whiskies – and her parents ill able to afford someone taking more than his share of drink even though Dad may have come by a few extra bottles.

To her earlier annoyance, he'd hardly said anything at both the dinner table with its chicken, stuffing, pork and all the vegetables with Christmas pudding and custard for afters, or later at the tea table with its slices of cold pork, pickled onions and gherkins, the usual shrimps and winkles, its fine Christmas cake, mince pies, jelly and tinned fruit, much of that saved over the year from what Dad brought home from time to time.

The meal table had been quite a squash, Tom and Mavis and their kids, Evie, Fred, Wally and Clara, her baby mostly in her arms so that she had to eat one-handed for much of the time, Mum, Dad, Granny Glover who always had her Christmas here, Tony and herself. Despite Tony's unsociable attitude she meant to enjoy herself and ignoring the looks, be herself for once, dropping aitches to her heart's content.

By evening more family turned up as well as Evie's new boyfriend, a few of Fred's friends, a couple of them girls, and close neighbours Mum had known for years as friends, they now with no immediate family, no children, both sons lost in the war. The place was soon full of people. So was the kitchen where the beer was kept, bottles and a small barrel balanced on the draining board that kept a constant stream of men supplying themselves with beer or whisky, sherry or gin for the womenfolk; while with backs tight against the milling menfolk in that tiny space, several women helped to cut bread to spread with marge, and fill with pressed ox tongue or more cold pork for sandwiches with pickles to be washed down with a drop of drink, and later as the small hours crept up, fortifying cups of tea for the weary.

There was music in the two small main rooms. An uncle, as usual, was playing his squeezebox, to which his wife loved to sing in an uncertain soprano, not always on key on the high notes but which went unnoticed as all joined in, each priding their voice over others.

Interspersed with the music were games, some a little rude, such as Kiss The Blarney Stone with each of the unsuspecting young friends of Fred, certainly the girls, cajoled into being blindfolded in the passage and led into the room to kiss the 'stone'. To gales of laughter a boy would roar, a girl squeal, as the soft, cleaved flesh was felt by searching lips and, whipping off the blindfold, would reveal a man completing the pulling up of his trousers. In reality it had been the crack his forearm formed when doubled up to his upper arm, the girl finally relieved to be told the truth, shrieking happy indignation at those who'd duped her. There was Buy the Donkey, again using the innocent, led in to bid for someone on all fours under a sheet, who when bought, was given the string to lead it away, but the string was attached to a chamber pot hidden under the 'donkey' and drawn into view with its 'contents', everyone in fits to the degradation of the buyer, the contents merely a cooked chicken neck in light ale, but in its container most unsavoury-looking. The same was used for Find the Treasure, a blindfold girl's hand guided to the 'treasure', her horror as fingers closed around it, the object often violently flung across the linoleum to shrieks of amusement.

More music from the squeezebox, the talented airing their tonsils or indulging in lengthy Rudyard Kipling monologues or a saucy piece of poetry, even a funny joke or two. Geraldine lapped it all up as though it would be her last time. By now Tony's disapproval of it all no longer bothered her. But she was glad to see him several times engaged in chats with Wally who, with quite broad interests, could talk to anyone no matter who they were on quite a few subjects.

In his spare time, what little there was for him working as a stevedore, Wally had taken to studying, according to Clara.

'He's always reading books from the library on all sorts of things, science things about birds an' animals an' about the Earth an' that sort of thing an' what he calls astromony or somethink. He knows the names of all the stars.' A brief look of pride faded. 'Then he starts giving me lectures about it. Honestly, Gel, it bores me stiff – goes right over me head. Just lately he's got interested in how to run a business. Gawd knows why. I don't want ter know. All I want is to get on with me life and look after 'im and this little'un.'

She bent her face to bury it in her daughter's fair, curly locks. 'Why should I want ter know about business and things? We ain't never going ter 'ave one. So why's he reading stuff like that, wasting 'is time?'

Listening to her, Geraldine wondered vaguely if her

brother harboured that secret wish. After all, Tony was in business, and young Fred was doing so well in the newspapers, in collar and tie and a nice suit, never getting his hands dirty.

Clara was still rabbiting on. 'He was talking to Alan Presley the other day. You know him. He often comes ter see Mum. He's still on his own, yer know – never got married again. It must be lonely sometimes, just 'is mum and dad. He don't even live with them. Got 'is own place. It do sound like a miserable life, stuck in a place all on yer own. But as I was saying . . .' she paused to take a sip of her sherry. 'Wally was talking to him the other day. He runs his own business, yer know, a builder's yard. He even employs a couple of blokes though Wally says he works alongside them 'imself selling building stuff. Wally said it'd be nice if we did somethink like that instead of him having ter go ter work before it's even light and working all hours fer the sort of wage he gets.'

'You've got to have capital before yer can start a business,' Geraldine broke in knowledgeably. 'That's not easy. It'd take years to save up enough.' She avoided adding 'on what Wally earns', instead continuing with what she knew. 'Then you might have to go to a bank in the end ter borrow money to help yer get started, and you have to have collateral so as to convince 'em.'

She was aware of Clara looking at her as though she were speaking a foreign language, the word collateral no doubt going right over her head, though Wally would have understood. Clara had probably never been in a bank in her life, nor probably had Wally.

It was, however, as if she hadn't spoken a word as

Clara picked up exactly from the point where she'd been interrupted.

'I expect he's spending today with his mum and dad. By now I'd of thought he'd of been spending it with a wife and a family. Funny life fer a man if you ask me, living all on 'is own all these years.'

Geraldine let her thoughts wander. What *would* Alan be doing at this minute? Perhaps he wasn't with his parents at all but surely he wouldn't be sitting on his own? Perhaps he had gone to friends. He must have friends. One of those could even be female and unattached. Geraldine felt her skin prickle with sudden jealousy. He was still a young man, a handsome and confident young man now with his own business who, despite all he'd said, could still attract young women and one day would be attracted by one, forgetting about her, laying her aside as futile, married, inaccessible, out of reach, to be given up on. That he'd once said he would never forget her intimated he would wait for her forever, yet he was eligible to be snapped up one day.

But this was silly! To put a stop to the idiotic pricking of her skin, Geraldine leapt up from her chair.

'I just need a word with Tony,' she said by way of excuse to a startled Clara. 'Be back in a moment.'

It helped sitting herself down next to him, Wally having gone off for another beer. She needed to be near Tony to disperse the inane jealousy that was invading her. She spent the rest of the evening at his side, and he in turn seemed relieved to have her there, giving her to realise that she had been guilty of ignoring him. Maybe that was why all this time he'd been sitting with a long face. Alan

Presley faded into oblivion as she saw Tony buck up immediately.

From looking bored out of his head he didn't say once about leaving early, which he might have done had she continued to leave him on his own, and she took heart that with a little encouragement from her maybe he might come around to her folks. Thus she vowed to do her utmost in future to bring him and her family together again. They'd been estranged too long and it was her fault, not theirs.

# Chapter Twenty-three

It hadn't lasted – maybe for the first couple of months into 1924, consenting to have the odd Sunday dinner with her family, though she could see Tony was never truly at ease with them, nor they with him. It was more trouble than it was worth and soon she had stopped pushing him to go.

Now, six months on, he was back to his old self, eager to socialise with his own friends, glowering if she as much as mentioned their seeing her people, but apparently not too unhappy if she in turn cried out of seeing his friends. It was as though it no longer mattered to him whether she went with him or not.

True, they'd spent that Boxing Day on their own, which in one way was nice and cosy but in another rather worrying: firstly because she could have enjoyed it with her family eating up the cold meat with pickled onions and leftover potatoes and sprouts mashed together to make tasty bubble and squeak; and secondly because they'd not been invited anywhere by anyone who mattered, almost a punishment of a sort for Tony not taking up that earlier invitation to Ernie and Cynthia Bulwalk's Christmas shindig in Chelsea – to Geraldine's mind containing an almost ominous message.

New Year, however, made up for all that, and she was conscious of breathing a sigh of relief in spite of having chided herself. It had been a wild time, after the Chelsea Ball going on to Sam Treater's substantial place around three in the morning. The house party had continued into the next day, everyone awash with fatigue and too much to drink but no one willing to be last to fall down. She and Tony had got home, or rather staggered home, Tony's driving appalling, in the early hours following New Year's Day, everyone having spent New Year's Day itself flopping about the place that in the cold daylight stank of cigar smoke and stale perfume, indulging in idle, mostly meaningless chatter, coming out with silly quips no one particularly listened to, much less appreciated; picking at smoked salmon and caviar and drinking champagne the moment they'd sufficiently come to and getting sozzled all over again, only half aware of where they were but quite content to be there; falling into armchairs or on to some bed to doze beside whoever already occupied it.

Geraldine wandering around looking for Tony, had found him spark out beside Di Manners, she also dead to the world. She remembered standing in the centre of the bedroom trying to take in the scene. At first there had been shock seeing them together like that, then hurt, but after a while it receded as it came to her that while Di was under the bedclothes, he lay on top of the covers, fully dressed, probably with no idea of the person next to him. Diana too was still clothed, one arm flung above the covers to reveal the glittering strap of her dress still in place. For a while Geraldine had studied that pretty face, composed even in drink, eyelids delicately closed, rosebud lips soft and yielding. Had he kissed those lips?

She had shrugged off the thought as ridiculous. Radical thinking had returned, or at least she had thought it so – though today, six months later, she wasn't so sure but still shrugged away the thought as impossible, Tony still loving and thoughtful towards her – as she had tiptoed from the room.

That evening at the nightclub he had been so attentive, now and then she'd caught him giving herself sideway glances that had made her smile. He and Di? Not a chance. Besides she'd noted that he didn't once glance towards the refreshed and by that time vivacious Diana.

At home she and Tony had fallen into bed utterly exhausted and very much dishevelled. Next morning it was she who'd had to pull herself together to go down to open the shop, feeling well out of sorts, and realising for all her high time that she hadn't enjoyed herself half as much in the company of her so-called friends with their society manners, their rich food, haute couture dresses and expensive jewellery as she had having Christmas with her own family with their ordinary ideas of enjoyment, in clothes to make Tony's friends turn aside in horror, but their common manners princely beside that of the people Tony mixed with. It wasn't beyond any girl in those circles to entice a man not her husband to bed. And in the early hours of New Year's Day she too had been propositioned by Paula's fiancé Harry Sullivan, his paws all over her despite those around them.

'That dress y'nearly wearing,' he'd purred, well oiled by that time, 'it's getting me going no end. Mus' be hard keeping it from falling down, my dear. So what d'yuh say we get together somewhere and I c'n help make you more comfortable? So what d'yuh say, eh? Yeah?'

Tony had bought her the dress for Christmas, spending far too much money on it. She hadn't dared to wear it at Mum's and draw disapproving looks at such a daring thing – the back of the heavy silk satin in electric blue draped so low that it was a marvel, even to her, how it didn't slip off her shoulders but for the skilled cut of it, the draped edges held together by a huge bow resting on her left buttock. Harry Sullivan's roving hands had almost had it off one shoulder at one time, her breast in danger of exposure, such a plunging back not tolerating a brassiere.

Managing to get away from him, she'd been glad Tony hadn't seen him, though Tony had gone missing much earlier, spark out on the bed Di had already found, or so she'd assumed at the time. It was Harry Sullivan following her everywhere that had made her go seeking protection from Tony, only to find him fast asleep with that Diana Manners beside him.

Again, thinking back on it, she hated this constant agonising over whether what she'd seen hadn't been as innocent as it had first appeared to her. Over these months the question had raised its vile head more than once and more than once had been dismissed as foolish. It was wrong. She had nothing to suspect Tony of. He was always attentive, so nice, so generous, bought her little presents, took her out and about. He hadn't changed towards her.

True, they didn't make love as often as once they had but that was how marriage became, and when they did make love she always hoped that this time she would become pregnant. So far that hadn't happened and she now wondered if perhaps she couldn't have another baby, that something might have gone wrong when she'd given birth to Caroline. The fall she'd had prior to giving birth, had it done something inside?

True also that Tony was away from home even more often than he used to be. It was the growing frequency of demands being made on him, he told her. More than any other suspicions she might have had that concerned her, the dowdy Kate Meyrick's sinister hints concerning Tony, which should have faded long ago, still surfaced from time to time though Kate had never spoken of it since.

Chiding her vivid imagination, Geraldine spent the rest of the summer determinedly shrugging it off as she shrugged off thoughts of any possible infidelity on Tony's part.

'Gerry, darling, there you are!'

The voice assailed her from a little distance away, necessitating Geraldine, with her cloche hat pulled low over her eyes both for fashion sake and to protect them from the bright sunshine, to tilt back her head to see who was calling her.

It was Easter. She and Tony were at Brooklands for the motor racing, picnicking with friends beside their two cars, as was everyone else. Family tourers were everywhere, their tops down on such a lovely day, parked higgledy-piggledy on the grass by the stand, picnic tables set, cloths spread, their owners lolling contentedly eating the goodies they'd brought along.

It was good being with the two they were spending the day with. Rex and Maggie Drake weren't of the usual crowd Tony mixed with, the man merely in the same line of business as he, a jeweller. They'd met them last year at the 1924 Paris Olympic Games. A casual exchange had revealed the man's business and naturally he and Tony, discovering a common bond, had struck up a friendship that still continued. Rex Drake's business, however, was in Birmingham so the friendship was mostly by telephone or letter. The couple, who had two growing-up children, had come down on a visit a couple of times since, and she and Tony had gone up there once. Today, Rex being keen on racing cars, they had met up for a picnic here at Brooklands. An extremely nice couple, Geraldine was sure they were 100 per cent above board, totally honest. Completely at ease with them, she wished all Tony's friends were like this.

It was Tony who by stretching his neck caught sight of Paula Griggs, the one who had called out, dragging her new husband along behind her. Now Paula Alcott, she and Jimmy Alcott had finally got married the week before Christmas, a wedding that she and Tony had attended, the whole thing very Christmassy.

The usual crowd had been there. The usual crowd seemed always to be there no matter where she and Tony went: at every house party, at nightclubs, at functions, at the Grand Prix motor racing circuits abroad, abroad again to spend a fortune in the casinos in the South of France after bathing, sun-lounging and wolfing down heaps of food.

Being summoned to a huge Christmas party last year

had prevented her going to her parents, to their chagrin, which still rumbled on a good three months on. But Tony had been firm on that, they were expected to be with their friends for once, which had meant Christmas Day itself.

Paula, coming up to them, flung herself down beside the four of them uninvited while Tony got up to stand beside an impassive-faced Jimmy Alcott who appeared to see it beyond his dignity to squat on the grass.

'I was told you were here, Gerry darling,' Paula gushed. 'William Schulter and Sam Treater are here too with their wives. Cynthia said she caught a glimpse of you earlier on but you disappeared . . . Do you mind if I have one of your delicious sandwiches, my dear?' She was helping herself even as Geraldine glanced across at Maggie for confirmation.

Taking a large bite, Paula closed her eyes in pleasure. 'Mmm! Smoked salmon. Jimmy and I had such a silly little luncheon, all salad and airy-fairy egg-things – cost him the very Earth but couldn't have sustained a flea!'

She was settling herself down for a long session. 'We're all going on to a restaurant after this.'

'What, now?' exclaimed Geraldine, which caused Paula to laugh raucously.

'No, my sweet! After the racing's finished. We're all planning to eat there this evening – a rather delightful old hotel place down the road from here. I forget which village it's in, but it's there. You are coming, aren't you – you and Tony and your friends? We haven't been introduced yet, have we?'

'Paula, this is Rex and Margaret, Maggie,' Geraldine leapt in. 'We met last year at the Olympics. This is a friend of me and Tony's, Paula Alcott, and,' she looked up at the thin, dour figure standing over her, 'this is Paula's husband, Jimmy.'

There came nods and how-d'you-do's, Rex smiling, about to stand up to offer the man a sociable handshake, but his smile falling away as it was met by a curt nod and an unbending expression. So Rex stayed seated, resuming his earlier position of one knee bent, one arm resting on it, the other supporting himself in a sitting position on the grass. Geraldine noticed him give Jimmy Alcott a bewildered look that he switched to Tony and herself as though he was deducing what Jimmy Alcott was and searching his thoughts as to why she and Tony associated with such a person. As Paula prattled on, Geraldine felt herself grow hot with embarrassment, knowing exactly what the Drakes thought of these inter-lopers to their erstwhile peaceful picnic.

'I don't think we'll be coming,' she burst out on impulse. Paula's grey eyes widened in a somewhat offended way. Above her Jimmy Alcott cleared his throat in a small double cough, the cough sounding significant.

'Oh, but you really must come,' Paula was saying. 'You'll be the only ones out of us all not there.'

'Yes, of course we will,' came Tony's voice from above her.

Paula's eyes resumed their normal size. 'So that's settled then. We'll be off around six after a drink at the bar here.'

She gave a glance at the other two, though refraining from addressing them to their face. 'You can invite your friends along as well, of course. The more the merrier!'

The Drakes having left earlier than intended, saying they had enjoyed their day and hoped to do it again but needed to get home to their family and it was a long drive back, the evening was spent at the restaurant Paula had indicated. Last to arrive, the others there already, immediately put Geraldine ill at ease.

She had been sorry about the early departure of their Birmingham friends, feeling they might have felt a little put out, though their goodbyes had been cheery enough. They'd been a breath of fresh air in the dim world she had come to know. Now she was again with people she held mistrust for, especially Jimmy with his narrow, immobile features and eyes that had a tendency to hint at unremitting hostility, unless he was cracking jokes of which he had a vast store, most of them crude. Even then there was never a smile as everyone else dissolved into laughter and to which his diminutive wife squealed with merriment, crying as she clung to his arm at the table and later at the bar, 'Isn't he a scream?' then kissing him in full view of them all.

Watching him, Geraldine experienced an inward shudder. Not a man to be crossed was Jimmy Alcott, for all his jokes. It was towards the likes of his sort that Tony, to her shame, seemed to act as though the sun shone out of their arses. Or was Tony also afraid under his show of chummy bravado? Whatever, he never let on to her, scoffing if she so much as even partially admitted to uneasiness about these so-called business friends. How deeply he was involved with them sometimes seemed to her more than she knew.

Jimmy was telling one of his jokes, hunched over his brandy at the round table where the eight of them now sat in the bar after their meal, the joke crude in the extreme. Geraldine, appearing to listen intently, had her mind more on her life, on a year that had simply sped by.

Where had the last eighteen months gone? Hers was a life many a woman might envy yet even the wild social round could become humdrum by its very frequency. Then there were the evenings of real boredom when Tony was away, *doing business* from which she was excluded – in the way, not to be trusted, the less she knew the better, and so on. If only she had a child it might be easier to bear, someone for company. Why had all the times she and Tony made love never produced a baby?

Geraldine let her mind wander dismally. It seemed she lived two lives, divided between the normality of her own family, and this swaying tightrope life on the edge of a society with its probably dishonestly come-by wealth, looking to ape the real elite yet never quite succeeding. The real cream of polite society, the nobility, the upper crust and famous names, the well brought up to wealth rather than the suddenly rich, would never have tolerated people like these. They too knew how to kick up their legs, did things decent common people would never dream of doing, maybe there even existed an undertow of illegal dealings, but they had real elegance, good manners, whereas the people of money she knew didn't even profess to loyalty except that which crime and crooked dealings no doubt held together.

The company exploded into laughter, pummelled her from her thoughts and, thus prompted, she laughed along with them, despising the wide-open red mouths of the guffawing women, lips no longer the rosebud shapes the rouge had painted them.

The men were beginning to sweat a little after the heavy meal and too many brandies and glasses of champagne. Tony had loosened the knot of his tie for coolness. He was still grinning away at the last joke. Cynthia, patting her prominant collar bones to cool herself down, gave a little hiccup.

'I simply must go off to the ladies. If I'm not careful I shall wet myself. Anyone coming with me? Lily? Paula? You, Dolly?'

Each in turn shook her head, Paula again convulsing into laughter at an aside from Jimmy whose own face remained immobile. Cynthia's eyes switched to Geraldine. 'How about you?'

It would be good to escape the incessant laughter, the men's sweaty faces, Jimmy's steel-eyed stare. Tony must never get on the wrong side of him.

Only two other women were in the large, ornate cloak-room with its pink and gold décor, but they very soon went out. It was peaceful in here after the roars of inane laughter that had invaded the other bar users' quiet conversations.

Geraldine drew her powder compact from her bag and dabbed the puff around her nose while Cynthia went off to relieve herself. Geraldine had been earlier, needing only to escape. The chain was pulled and Cynthia emerged to wash her hands, dry them on a pink towel, then to plaster more rouge on to her already bright red lips, carefully tracing the cupid's bow shape.

'We should have worn something nicer to come here, had we known,' Geraldine said, staring into the mirror at her outdoor clothes.

One of the most enjoyable things she knew was dressing up in the lovely clothes Tony gave her, latest fashions complementing her now almost Eton-cropped hair, jewellery, long ropes of pearls, dangly earrings, those new slave bracelets, the best his own shop provided and often admired by others.

Cynthia nodded concurrence to Geraldine's statement, if somewhat absent-mindedly. Leaning closer to the large gilt-framed mirror the easier to study the rouged cheeks and painted eyes, the reflected eyes switched to the mirrored ones of Geraldine. There was a light of admiration in them.

'I do think you carry it all off so marvellously well, Gerry,' she said in reply to Geraldine's questioning look.

'Carry what off well?' Her mind half on clothes, she automatically assumed her companion had referred to style, fashion.

There came several rapid blinks of the reflected blue eyes. 'Why, the way Tony's carrying on with that Manners woman. I do admire you your composure over it all. Some wives would have gone berserk, darling.'

The regard slowly grew cautious, guarded, almost seemed to shut down as Geraldine's stare continued somewhat uncomprehendingly.

'Darling, you must know!' Cynthia burst out, and then, realising the faux pas, whispered, 'Oh, God, you don't! Surely you must have suspected. It's been going on for over a year. Everyone knows about it.'

Cynthia seemed fixed in her bent forward position, her stare now completely confused. 'Hasn't anyone so much as hinted? Oh, Gerry, I'm so sorry. I don't know

348

where to put myself, I'm simply devastated, really I am.'

She wasn't the only one. Geraldine could only stare at her as though mesmerised, at once overcome with disbelief and shock, even to returning her powder compact to her bag as though it had to be the most important thing to do. Then without warning came anger, a flood of anger, like a river bursting its banks.

'How can you make up such lies?' Fine words fell away. Tears of rage filled her eyes. 'You'd all love me and Tony ter fall apart, wouldn't yer?'

'No, darling!'

'Yes you would. Well, I don't believe one word of it. They're rotten lies. Tony's—'

The door bursting open to admit a diner stopped the flow, but the woman had already heard the raised voices. With awkward glances towards Geraldine's flushed and contorted face, she hurried on past the two of them and into one of the toilets. Reluctant to be overheard, Geraldine closed her mouth as Cynthia lowered her painted eyes.

'I had best be getting back to everyone. They're most likely thinking we've both fallen down the loo.' She gave a nervous half laugh then stopped and looked directly at Geraldine. 'Are you coming, Gerry?'

Without knowing why, Geraldine nodded, picking up her little bag from the shelf under the gilt-framed mirror and following her out as though she were some little puppy called to heel.

Mum was glaring at her. 'Why come ter me? I could of told yer so, Gel. Yer made yer bed, love, an' yer messed it up. What d'yer expect me ter do?'

'I don't know,' she answered lamely, then in renewed anger, at herself, at Tony, at Mum for taking it all so calmly, not one hint of sympathy, only blame, condemnation, a shrugging of the shoulders, burst out, 'I don't know what ter do, where ter turn.'

'So yer come cryin' ter me,' Mum was going on. 'Don't want us when things is going on orright. Ain't got time for us. But the second yer get a spot of bother, its, "Where's Mum?"'

'That's not true, Mum. I do come to see you, any time.'

'When it suits.'

'And this ain't a *spot of bother*, Mum. Tony having it off with another woman ain't a spot of bother. It's the end of our marriage. He's been lying to me all this time. He's been unfaithful.'

'It takes two, my gel. And I don't mean another woman, I mean the person what could of drove 'im away in the first place.'

'How could I have driven him away? I've been a good wife to 'im. I've never gone off the rails.' She thought suddenly of Alan and how easily at one time she could have done just that except that it never came up, he'd never approached her in that way, merely said he loved her and always would. It broke her heart thinking of the way he'd said that. 'I've been loyal and loving and caring – what more could he have asked for?'

'Fer you to of give 'im a baby.'

'I did. But she died, Mum, remember?' Fresh tears collected in her eyes but her mother didn't even blink.

'Then yer should of tried again instead of gallivanting around dressed up like a dog's dinner, stinkin' to 'igh heaven of scent, yer face all plastered with paint, you drippin' with jewellery, yer 'air cut like you was a boy because it 'appens ter be the fashion.'

She hadn't paused to think that Evie too had cut her hair almost as short. 'Too blessed 'igh an' mighty ter go in for a family. Would of clipped yer wings too much, spoilt yer enjoyment.'

Anger was bringing more tears. 'Don't you think I've tried?' she was blubbing. 'God knows I've pleaded and prayed for another baby but it just ain't happened. I don't think I *can* 'ave any, Mum. I 'ad that fall just before Caroline was born. Maybe it twisted something inside me – I don't know. But it ain't my fault I ain't had another baby. And I've tried so 'ard to.'

Mum was regarding her with just a fraction more sympathy, was even looking surprised. 'I didn't know you 'ad a fall. Yer didn't tell me.'

Geraldine too had calmed a little. 'I didn't give it much thought at the time. It wasn't a bad fall and I forgot about it, until much later, until I never seemed to get pregnant. Then I began putting two and two together, and that's all I can think of – the reason why I ain't been able to start a family.'

Mum's shoulders appeared to drop as though the short moment of sympathy had already drained away. 'Well, it could be one reason, I s'pose. Maybe it ain't your fault not 'aving babies. But when a woman can't keep 'er man, somethink's wrong somewhere.'

'Something certainly is wrong,' Geraldine burst out, angry again. 'And it ain't me. It's that woman, with her bleeding enticing eyes and her bleeding seductive voice, and her—'

'Don't swear.' The admonition, totally divorced from the pain she was trying to convey to her mother, shocked and enraged her. How could Mum be so unfeeling, concerned only that her daughter was resorting to swear words?

'You don't bloody care at all, do you, Mum? You've never 'ad to go through what I'm going through and you can't even be bothered to put yerself in my place just for a second. I'm losing my husband, Mum!'

'And blessed good riddance.'

'You can't say that. I love 'im! What d'you know about love?'

The question was ignored. 'Yer'll just 'ave ter learn ter fall out of love, won't yer?'

Before Geraldine could retort to that unfeeling remark, Mum said, dropping her voice and speaking as though to herself or to a child not quite comprehending her words, 'If yer 'usband died this very day, yer'd 'ave ter get on with life, learn ter survive, pull yerself up by yer boot straps and get on with it.'

Mum was wandering about the back room, picking up vases and the small, framed photographs of family members, studio photos and seaside snaps, and carefully replacing them as though they were the sole objects that mattered to her at this present time.

'When God takes our loved ones there ain't nothin' we can do about it but get on with things, even when we're in grief. So yer've got ter look at this, Gel, the same way as yer would if yer lost 'im proper like.'

'It ain't the same, Mum. Someone dying can be taken as God's will if yer like, but this 'as been done by Tony 'imself, and the bitch of a woman who doesn't care who she hurts, only interested in stealing someone else's husband for her own pleasure.'

'It is the same. And if you can't see it, then it ain't worth talking to yer. You're a fool to yerself. You're determined to suffer like some blessed screen heroine and pull yer 'air out, an' make life a misery fer yerself and fer everyone around yer, as if other people tearing out their 'air on your be'alf will cure what you're going through. Well, it don't wash, Gel. It's only you what can make things better. If yer can't entice 'im back ter your bed, then best forget 'im, like 'e 'ad died, and get on with yer own life. It's the only way. It's the only advice I've got ter give yer.'

'You can't even give enough to cuddle me, can you?' Geraldine spat.

'What's cuddling goin' ter do?' came the reply. 'If I cuddled yer, yer'll feel better for a time, but it'll all come back, an' I can't be 'ere cuddling yer forever. Yer've got ter see ter yerself. No one else can do it for yer.'

Mum was wrong. She couldn't see how alone she felt, had no feelings; if she lost Dad, or if he walked off and left her, would she be spouting the same platitudes, taking her own advice?

Geraldine came away from the house filled with anger and remorse and quite understandably sorry for herself. Alone in her world, she thought of Clara and went to seek her out. Mavis was too like her Mum to tell her woes to, and Evie was too young and in love to understand. And besides, she'd asked, pleaded with Mum not to tell anyone why she had gone there, and Mum, to give her credit, would honour that plea. Even if she thought it herself – 'I could have told you so' – she wouldn't want others to have the privilege of thinking it, to her own humiliation, not even Dad.

Clara was all sympathy, crying along with her, holding her to her bosom and for a while it did help. But Mum was right after all. When she finally came away from Clara's home, her sister-in-law standing at the door, eyes filled with concern and sorrow as she watched her go, all the cuddling in the world hadn't changed anything one iota.

# Chapter Twenty-four

There was one person who might make a difference. More or less by instinct her footsteps turned towards Alan's place of business.

Some time ago he'd told her where it was, not too far to walk, on the corner of Roman Road and Eden Street by the Grand Canal, though she had never been there before. Soon she was standing at the open gates to the builder's yard, gazing in, unsure whether to go through or not, whether he'd be at all pleased to see her there – in fact, what on earth was she doing here at all? But she needed an ally, needed someone who might understand.

Still unsure of herself, Geraldine walked in, stood gazing at the piles of brick and timber, the ramshackle main building, little more than a shack, at a couple of men moving to and fro shifting something here, something there. Someone passed her trundling a wheelbarrow full of something. She moved aside for him and saw the odd look he gave her. This was no place for her, she was in the way.

What if Cynthia had been making it all up, thinking it funny to tell a silly fib about Tony, then stand by and watch her get in a state, bursting into peals of laughter at the game she'd played on her when it all came out that Tony was as loyal as the day was long? And now she'd made a fool of herself with Mum and with Clara. It could get all round the family, everyone grinning behind her back, except Mum, angry with her. Now she was about to make another a fool of herself to Alan. Better to leave.

'Want some 'elp yer, missus?'

The voice held a challenge. Geraldine turned on her heel to see a big man in cloth cap, heavy boots, trousers and jacket splashed with plaster over a soiled, blue-striped shirt and stained pullover. Instead of a tie he had a polka-dot choker, once plum-coloured but now dark from sweat.

'What yer want?' Again challenging, her nice clothes being eyed with something like hostility – what was a woman like this doing in a builder's yard? She could almost imagine the question: if she needed work done on her property, she should be sending the man who was working for her? She must either hurry away or face the man.

'I . . . um – I . . .'

'Yus?'

Geraldine gathered her wits and faced the man squarely, her voice becoming positive. 'Is Mr Presley around?'

'Oo wants 'im?'

'Is he here?' It was her turn to be hostile. There was enough on her plate without this.

'All depends.'

'On what?' Her tone sharpened considerably. She wasn't happy. The man was being openly uncivil, certainly no way to treat a potential customer, though of course she wasn't, was she?

'On wot yer wants 'im for.'

'Now listen!' she burst out, ready to rant. 'I've come here on specific business and I will not be treated as if—'

'Gerry?' The voice stopped her in mid-flow. 'Gerry, what're you doing 'ere?'

Turning to see Alan in his working clothes striding towards her, she immediately began letting off steam. 'Alan! This man! All he's done so far is to treat me with not one spark of courtesy. I've come here . . .'

She paused, confused. What exactly had she come here for? This wasn't the place to be if she hoped to tell him her problems, appeal for sympathy. 'Alan, I . . .'

He was laughing, waving the man away who moved off with a brave show of indignation at being dismissed when he'd no doubt expected his boss to uphold his defence of his yard against stupid women in posh clothes who thought to invade it, and him not even alerted to the fact she was someone his boss knew.

Still chuckling, Alan repeated, 'What *are* you doing here?'

She couldn't even raise a smile. 'I needed to see you, urgently.'

That put an immediate stop to his amusement, his brows knitting together at the way her face was beginning to distort. 'What on earth's wrong, gel?'

Geraldine caught her lips between her teeth to stem

ready tears. She looked round, certain that the few men in the yard were watching her, the man leaving with a horse and cart, the man who'd been rude to her, even a housewife maybe looking out of her bedroom window nearby.

'I can't say anything here, Alan. I need ter talk to yer, but you're busy. Perhaps later, after you've done work. I don't want to be a nuisance and it's probably nothing at all but . . .' She was gabbling. 'I don't want ter get in yer way. I'll wait till yer finish work and then—'

'Want, be bloody damned!' He took her by the arm, gently but firmly. 'You're in a state. Yer've come ter me. Bugger the work – I want ter know what's upset you to come 'ere and find me, and I want to 'elp, if I can.'

He looked round the yard. The men watching immediately turned to what they'd been doing before staring with utmost interest at the cameo.

She shook herself mentally to push away the thought as he took her arm and led her from the builder's yard, and her thoughts returned to Tony and what he'd done, was still doing if what Cynthia had said was true. Was she jumping to conclusions after all? At this moment it seemed she must be. How was she going to confide this to Alan? He would think her mad. Even she didn't know what to think now as they made their way together round the corner to the café he'd indicated.

She stirred yet another cup of strong, almost black tea in thick, stained china, keeping her eyes on what she was doing. Why was it always over strong, dark tea, in horrid cups and chipped saucers that she must tell Alan her troubles?

He was sitting opposite her, as always. Came a wild

thought – if only they were seated on a sofa, his sofa, his arm around her, his hand warm on her shoulders, face close to hers. How much more comforted she would feel. Instead of this place.

'So what is it, Gel?'

'Don't call me Gel,' she burst out irritably. 'Gerry or Geraldine – not Gel, please!'

'Sorry.'

Silence fell between them. It was relatively quiet, not much going on in the place, most having had their midday snack and gone back to work, those who had work; and all that could be heard was the sound of washing up in the kitchen area. Clara had asked if she wanted anything to eat with the cup of tea she had made, but Geraldine had felt that the last thing in the world she needed had been to eat anything. She still wasn't hungry, felt that even a biscuit would have choked her.

After a while, Alan said quietly, 'Whatever's on your mind, Gerry, you can't keep it to yerself.'

She found her voice; it sounded husky. 'I always seem to be running to you. I shouldn't be bothering you like this.'

'Who else should you bother?' There was no amusement there though the question had the element of amusement.

'I don't know,' was her lame reply.

'Then tell me.'

No, she couldn't tell him. What she'd heard about Tony wasn't true, a made-up joke played on her by an unscrupulous woman, like all of that unscrupulous lot. Yet deep down she knew it was no lie said for fun and suddenly she was crying, silently, head bent over her cup, a tear falling into it.

Alan's hand reached across to cover hers but she couldn't look up.

'Let's go somewhere else,' he was saying. She was sure he'd said these same words once before, somewhere else. She was aware of herself nodding agreement and being helped up by him, led out, their tea left untouched.

Back at the builder's yard, now with her eyes dry, he led her into his office and sat her down in his chair, a decrepit thing with scuffed arms and torn padding, but like his messy office and jumbled yard, suitable for what he did.

Perching on the edge of the desk beside her, he said, 'Get yer wind, then we'll go in me wagon to my place. They can do without me for a couple of hours. It's the afternoon. Ain't that much goin' on once the morning's finished – not what Bill can't cope with anyway.'

Before she could ask where they were going, he was out of the door for another word with Bill, his foreman. She could see them outside the one dusty window pane of the office, Bill, squat, merry-faced, in his forties, with fading ginger hair and heavy ginger eyebrows, nodding attentively to what Alan was telling him.

'Go where?' she asked, getting to her feet as Alan returned.

'To my place?' It was a question that begged no answer. 'We can talk better there. I've got the old wagon I use ter pick things up in. Engine ain't all it should be but we ain't far away. If yer don't mind being bumped about.'

She shook her head and was soon sitting beside him in the wagon that though repainted green looked as though it had seen plenty of service during the war. It was ancient and battered but she supposed good enough for the work he did.

Before long she was following him into his home, a small terraced house squeezed between similar homes each with a door and window on the ground floor with two small windows above, of the two-up two-down type but much smaller than her parents' home. She supposed this was all he really needed on his own.

The front room was tiny, an armchair, a settee, a sideboard, an upright chair and a tiny writing bureau filling it fit to burst. An empty grate with a bit of carpet in front of it, the room retained a bare look even so, a look of utility, any sense of cosiness not a prime aim. There were books everywhere – books and magazines on building, carpentry, plumbing, all sorts, scattered on the sideboard and in heaps on the floor, only adding to this lack of comfort.

'I'll get some tea,' he said as, standing in the centre of the room gazing about, she automatically took off her hat.

'No, I don't want any,' she stopped him. She wasn't even sure why she was here – wished she hadn't let him bring her but then she'd been so dispirited and at a loss as to what she really wanted to say to him. She was still at a loss, seeing herself a fool, certain he would also see her as one.

Taking her at her word he asked her to sit down, which she did, on the edge of the settee as the armchair held several newspapers, as did the far end of the settee. Because of these Alan came and sat beside her.

'Right then, Gel . . . Gerry,' he corrected hastily. 'I 'ope you don't mind being 'ere, but yer looked so terrible it made me feel yer really need a shoulder ter cry on, and a café ain't the sort of place ter do it. Nor is me office. So . . .' He paused, then went on. 'Tell me, Geraldine, what's it about? What's made yer look so sad, so ill?'

'Do I look ill?' she queried idiotically.

'Yes, yer do. I want to 'elp, if I can.'

He sat in silence while she fought with herself whether she really wanted to say anything or not. But to just sit here was meaningless. She must say something.

'It's Tony,' she began, then, drawing strength from those two small words, began to talk of the absences she had assumed were his business taking up his time, of the odd instances when she thought she imagined he no longer felt any real affection for her.

'I always thought it was my imagination. Since we lost Caroline I've felt so isolated even in company. Tony says I think too much, but when I talk of trying for another baby he shies away, says there's time. Nor do I seem to be capable of . . . well, you know, starting a family.' It was hard talking of these sort of things to him, yet they had to be said in order to make it clear. 'Then over Easter, someone I know, someone we both know well – Cynthia – let drop that Tony was seeing some other woman.'

In a flurry of words she blurted out what had been said, adding, 'She could have been making it up, playing a rotten joke on me.'

Alan's voice was low and sombre. 'I don't think so, Gel.'

This time she let the offending diminutive pass over her. His arm had gone round her and he gently pulled her towards him. With no will in her, she let him, laying against him in a welter of misery. 'What am I going to do?'

She felt him shake his head. 'You'll have to talk to him, Gel.'

'I can't,' she whispered, but trying to find hope in the midst of this sense of wretchedness, went on, 'If it was a joke, I could make such a fool of meself. He'd be hurt, me making him feel I don't trust him. No one wants someone ter think that of them. It could even break up our marriage and it'd be my fault.'

'It wouldn't,' he said, his tone soft.

'I ought to ignore it,' she offered. 'Forget it.'

'Yet it's still there, eating into yer, making yer unhappy.' He thought for a moment. 'If yer was ter say what this . . . Cynthia?' She nodded against his chest. 'This Cynthia said and tell 'im yer thought it was a rotten joke on 'er part, maybe yer'd feel more certain and with no harm done.'

He was offering crumbs of comfort. Yet she was slowly beginning to know that it had not been a joke, only her heart wanting it to be.

He seemed to read her thoughts. 'You don't think so, do yer?' She shook her head vigorously and let herself lie even closer to him. 'I wish I could take all this away from yer,' he was saying. 'I want to, so much.'

'There's nothing you can do,' she whispered. 'You holding me is comfort. Makes me feel I've got a friend I can turn to.'

'Yer can always turn ter me.' His tone was washing over her. His arm about her had grown firmer. She felt his lips resting among the hair on the crown of her head and as she lifted her head a little, it brought those lips close to hers.

'Alan . . .'

She hadn't known exactly when their lips touched but for a moment was lost in the sensations rushing through her body at their warmth, their pressure, the hunger that had begun to race from him to her. Seconds later reason came flooding back. She drew away in alarm.

'No!' It wasn't repulse. Had things been different this would have been wonderful. But she was married, no matter what Tony had been up to. Two wrongs could not make a right and for all she was totally in distress at what Tony was apparently doing, she couldn't start doing the same thing and then think to condemn him.

Alan had released her the moment she drew away and it occurred to her in some disembodied way that another man might have pressed his needs if he felt as she had in that moment, which she could see by the tension in his face that he had. A strange love surged through her at that knowledge, one that she curbed instantly.

'I'm sorry, Alan. I shouldn't have . . . I didn't mean to . . .' She got up from the settee. 'I'd best go. I have to go home.' She would have to confront Tony, she knew that now.

Alan got to his feet as well, looming over her. Without her leave he grabbed her to him, bending over her to kiss her hard on the lips.

'You know how I feel about you, Gel,' he rasped as he put her away from him. 'I love you. I'll always love you. I'll always be here if you ever want me, want help from me, anything. I shan't push meself on to you, ever. But don't hesitate ter come ter me if yer need 'elp, you understand? No matter what it is. Do yer understand, Gel?'

'Yes,' she said simply.

There were no more words to be said as she fitted her cloche hat awkwardly on her head, her short hair disappearing beneath it. In silence he conducted her to the door, saw her into the vehicle then got in beside her. He said nothing as he drove, she sitting next to him, her head in a whirl of muddled thoughts – about him, about Tony, about this need to see her marriage stay firm, be mended if it needed to be; about what she'd do if it couldn't. If Tony had been unfaithful, would she pretend, try to make it work for appearances' sake? She could hear Mum saying, 'I told yer so,' and, 'People like you don't mix with people like him, but yer wouldn't listen, and now you've come a cropper.' Mavis turning up her lips in a sneer if she didn't come right out with it like Mum would; Dad embarrassed, not saying much, but embarrassed; neighbours looking sideways, wondering, pointing fingers. 'Marriage broke down, y'know. That's what yer gets for trying to get above yer station.' Clara looking sorry for her, which would be every bit as bad to her mind as any sneer might be.

Lastly there was she and Alan, the feelings that had passed between them, sealing something, declaring something that should never have been declared. How could she go to him now? Her conduct had lost her a good friend. Though had it truly? It remained to be seen. But above all she did not want her marriage to fall apart. She wanted to think of Tony as honest, loyal, the vicious rumours about him just chaff in the wind, going to show what piecrust friends he had if they could spread rumours like that, happy to see her marriage fall apart.

Alan didn't take her back to his yard. Instead he took her as far as Liverpool Street and put her on a bus to go along Oxford Street where she could get off and go back home to her flat.

'Don't forget,' were his parting words. 'I'll be here if you need me, always.'

# Chapter Twenty-five

Tony wasn't in when she arrived home. To some measure it was a relief – the way she felt at this moment it would have been impossible to speak to him.

With both he and herself being away, she still helping out now and again, the part-time assistant he'd recently employed for when he had to go out appeared to be coping well enough with just one customer studying the necklaces and pendants behind the glass of a display cabinet. As Geraldine paused to look in on her way to the door that led to the flat, the assistant, Mr Bell, glanced up. 'Afternoon, Mrs Hanford.'

His tone was full of cheer. She smiled wanly and came into the shop. 'I take it Mr Hanford isn't in?'

'Went off around lunchtime. Said I was to give you this note.'

Fiddling briefly around the edge of the till, he extracted a folded note and held it out to her. She unfolded it, read the few words Tony had written, very scrawled as though he'd been in a tearing hurry.

'Had to go out suddenly. Not sure when I'll be back. Could be late.'

No word of endearment, no explanation. She looked up, keeping her expression bland. 'Did Mr Hanford say where he was going?'

'Afraid not. Said for me to close up at the end of the day.'

Again she nodded. 'Thank you, Mr Bell.'

The customer was approaching the counter, one arm raised in the direction of the cabinet he'd been gazing into, indicating that he had made a choice and wished to view it and perhaps purchase. With the assistant's attention diverted, Geraldine made her exit without another word. She now needed to be alone, to think.

The flat lay silent. She hated coming home to this sense of emptiness. Even when here on her own all day it never felt this way, and definitely not when she and Tony came home from being out together. There would be the feeling that it had been alive in their absence, a living thing waiting only for them to come home. But coming in all by herself always brought a sense of being unwelcome, a chill as if the whole place had died – utter deadness.

Geraldine shivered and hurriedly turned on the gas fire. It wasn't a chilly day but the small warmth would help take away some of the empty feeling. In the kitchen she busily filled the kettle, put it on the stove, lit the gas, chinked together the cup and saucer she'd got down from the cupboard, banging the cupboard door after her – anything to fill the vacuum with the sounds of life.

While the kettle boiled she went to wind the gramophone, selecting a cheerful tune, put it on the turntable and set it going, fitting the needle into the record's groove.

The room instantly filled with music. That should make her feel better – but it didn't.

After a cup of tea, having to force down a couple of biscuits because she hadn't eaten all day and felt a little weak, though not at all hungry, she sat in the once more silent living room with no will to fill it with music from yet another record. Her head ached from all that crying; her eyes were heavy, her whole body heavy, her throat aching each time she swallowed. If she didn't have this business out with Tony the second he came home she would die.

But Tony didn't come home. He came in around six the next morning saying he'd been out of London, had been detained on business and had to put up at a hotel. But she knew instantly where he had been. A hotel? Certainly. Alone? Definitely not. And as he passed her to go off to get ready to go downstairs to his shop, she caught the faintest trace of perfume.

Intent on her purpose, Geraldine followed him into the bedroom, there to stand gazing at him. It did the trick. He began to look uncomfortable.

'Something wrong?' he queried, a sickly grin on his face.

'Maybe you could tell me,' she offered tartly and saw him frown as if perplexed, then saw his face clear.

'Oh, if you still mean me being unable to get home. I'm sorry, you must have felt lonely last night. You did get my note of course?'

'I got your note.' Again she let her response fall tersely, flatly.

'Good.' Tony sat on the edge of the bed, bending down to lace up his shoes. A good ploy so that he wouldn't have to look her in the eyes. 'I'm sorry, darling, it was quite unavoidable, too late to get home by then. I did want to come home, but . . . well, you know how business takes over.'

'What sort of business?'

'I can't explain at this moment. It was a bit involved.' Shoe laces tied, he got up, still avoiding her eyes and began adjusting his tie, doing up his waistcoat.

'Was your accommodation all right?' she persisted, arms folded as she stood in the doorway, to all intents and purposes barring his way.

Seeing it, Tony gave a silly laugh, his hands gesticulating ineffectually while making small oblique movements of the head meant to convey some unavoidable situation, much as people do when at a loss for words to explain something or other. He turned casually, too casually, to explain how unbearable the hotel had been, how poor the food, how wretched the room, how lumpy the bed, and he all on his own with nothing to do.

Geraldine said nothing. She remained facing him aware that her lips and cheeks had grown stiff, and could almost feel the guilt and the need to bluster oozing from him like treacle from a spoon.

She felt she couldn't much longer stand that fixed smile of his, that effort to appear at ease with himself, and blameless. Any minute now she would burst out, 'Liar!' and confront him with all she knew. It must have been the way she was staring at him, the tense way she was standing, her refusal to move from the doorway that was alerting him to the fact that she knew he'd been keeping something from her, for he began to frown, his lips grow tight. He stood rigid before her, a creature on the defensive but ready to fight if needs be.

He'd had no idea that hot midday in Egypt that Geraldine fainting would change his life.

He'd seen the girl somewhere before, realised later that it had been at some party in London months back. Having noticed her from afar he dimly recalled a passing thought on how stunning she looked, much as any man might, but after that had given it no more thought. Until that day in Egypt.

She'd appeared as from nowhere and as she bent over Geraldine's wilting form to help him hold her up, he'd caught a whiff of her perfume. It had gone to his head. Afterwards, when they'd got her into the shade of the refreshment kiosk, bathed her forehead with a handkerchief soaked in water and given her something to drink, she had spoken of possible heatstroke and of getting Geraldine back to her hotel room. The sound of her voice had been like a tinkling stream in that parched place they called the Valley of the Kings. He'd been captivated by the sound of that voice.

When Geraldine had been compelled to remain in her room for the next two days, a couple taking pity on him had suggested he join them for an hour or two in the evening – such a shame coming all this way only to sit in a dull hotel room and surely his wife would prefer to be alone to rest, and would understand. Geraldine had understood, had preferred to be alone, had urged him to take up the couple's offer, saying she'd feel guilty otherwise. So he'd gone with them.

Diana Manners's company had been enervating.

She had the most fascinating, tinkling laugh that washed over him and almost made him feel giddy. Her hand stealing into his as they went with the others to dine at a nearby restaurant had felt so small, so warm, and he hadn't withdrawn his because of Geraldine. In fact he forgot to think of Geraldine at all as the conversation sparkled around the table.

Later, the couple who had invited him went their own way leaving him to return to the hotel. He had returned but not until a couple of hours later. Being in Diana's company was so terrific that he hadn't wanted it to end. She had such a scintillating way with her, made him laugh, and the way she snuggled up to him as they walked made him feel like he owned the world.

It had meant nothing, he told himself, a holiday thing, an hour or so of enjoyable company. They'd done nothing underhand, hadn't even kissed though he had wanted to as she leaned close against him while he talked of this and that. It was the following evening, the one before they were due to leave for home, that Geraldine, needing to have an early night, told him to go out and make the most of it, so he and Di, as she wanted to be called, did kiss, or rather he kissed her and she allowed it, seductively teasing, saying he was a very naughty man. That kiss stayed with him the whole way home.

He hadn't seen Di Manners again until he saw her come into the hotel bar where he'd been with a couple of his so-called business friends. She was with another party and as their glances met she'd smiled across at him just as though no one else at all was in the room – such a meaningful smile that as he returned it, he was conscious of a movement in his groin, an excited twinge down there.

Her short fair hair was secured by diamanté head band and she was wearing an orange-coloured dress that should never have gone with fair hair but oddly did with her. The loose front panel of the dress was caught into a band on the hips to drop away in folds below, the whole thing kept up by two of the thinnest shoulder straps imaginable. Slave bangles adorned her upper arms and long pendant pearl earrings brushed the bare flesh of those shoulders with an almost seductive touch whenever she moved her head so that he'd squirmed anew.

It had been difficult to present a calm face to his companions as he went on nodding to what they were saying. Even the nature of their talk, concerning a heist in which he was expected to eventually play his part, being truly in their hands and worried though he always did well out of it, even that failed to quench the excitement he'd known seeing Di Manners again.

When he came down into the hotel foyer ready to go home, there she was, seated on a sofa, having obviously ditched her own company so as to make herself available to him. Seeing him she stood up. A gauzy, orange cape with a large, black fur collar dangled from one hand, it's hem dragging the floor, he remembered, as she came towards him. The other hand held a tiny black and diamanté evening bag by its thin gold chain. He even noticed that her shoes with their sharp toe points and high heels matched her dress perfectly. Black and orange – dramatic. She'd looked the true society girl.

They'd gone on to another hotel for a drink together, he driving a little way out of London in case he was recognised. It would make it late before he got home, but it hadn't seemed to matter – Geraldine would be none the wiser as she was used to him returning home late, though at that time he hadn't bargained on how late.

He couldn't remember what he and Di had talked about, but he could still recall his eagerness for her – that very first time. His need of her became so strong he'd hardly been able to contain himself as she too indicated some willingness. He could still recall how hard his heart had pulsed, the pulsing being matched thump for thump down below, as still happened whenever he knew what he and Diana were about to do. With her clinging to his arm he'd booked a room, he laying out a veritable stack of pound notes to acquire the best one, and in the luxury of a bed with soft sheets and a silk coverlet, he'd exploded inside her.

There had never been anything like it, not for him, not even in that first flush of love for Geraldine. It had been Diana, with her beautiful, shapely, naked body wrapped around him. Those breasts, once free of the restrictions of the fashionable, flattening bra bursting onto his naked chest and burying his face to almost smother him, as she had transported him into the realms of ecstacy. So it had gone on, going to this hotel and that, stolen hours when he'd told Geraldine he'd been playing cards all night or had been sweltering at his smelter alone in the barn of the derelict farmhouse on the marshes, or had been talking business into the early hours. He'd always make sure to be home before dawn unless he could use the excuse of being too far from home to get back, as he had done this morning. But this morning something must have alarmed Geraldine. Was it something someone might have said to her?

He'd been very careful in the past, but there was always someone with a nose too long for their face, always the chance of a slip-up. There had been a couple of times when he'd been stupid enough to let himself be seen with Di when Geraldine hadn't been with him. Now and again he'd noticed the raised eyebrows and had vowed to be more careful, keep his eyes from wandering too often to Diana, stop appearing too attentive; but being absolutely head over heels with her, it was difficult, he wasn't the best of liars, had convinced himself that it was probably his imagination, that he would never be found out so long as he remained careful and that the odd glance wouldn't matter.

Then only a few weeks ago Paula had made a flippant remark loud enough to carry across an entire room as she was wont to do when she'd had a few, always enjoying the act of seeing someone ill at ease in any sticky situation, that there was a handy bedroom in her house he and Di could use if they felt that strong about each other. She'd quipped that if Gerry were to see them making eyes at each other, she'd be after him with a hot iron for his private bits and that'd cure him of his habit!

Surely being seen with Di Manners on occasions wouldn't have been enough to cause evil tittle-tattle. But Geraldine must have caught wind or why was she behaving like this, staring at him as if she knew every last thing that had been going on. He dared not let his fears show.

'What's the matter with you, darling?' he blustered as

she continued to bar his way. 'I said I was sorry not getting home last night. What else can I say?'

Geraldine half turned as if to walk off but then turned viciously back. 'No, Tony, I want to know where you really were last night, and who with.'

'Who with?' He tried to sound aggrieved but his voice sounded squeaky. 'What the hell are you talking about? I was with some business people. I know you're not always happy about those I associate with, but I don't see you shying away from the money it brings in, the good times I give you, the holidays, all this.'

He flung his arms wide to encompass the luxurious, art deco bedroom furniture, the fine furnishing, the two original paintings on the wall, the silky Chinese carpet, her dressing table with its litter of gold bracelets, rings, necklaces, earrings, expensive perfumes, his with its ivory-backed brushes.

She hadn't even blinked, thrusting aside his counter argument. 'Tell me who it was you spent the night with.'

It was he who blinked before rage overtook him, rage borne of fear. 'Blast you! Are you accusing me of going with another woman, of having it off with some tart or other?'

'You could say tart.' Her tone was cold, like ice, and as unbreakable – not even fractured by tears. 'I definitely say tart. That's what she is.'

'Who're you talking about?'

'You know who I'm talking about.' Her voice was beginning to shake a little. Perhaps if she broke down he could go to her, pull her towards him, cuddle her to him. He could tell her, soothingly, that she was a just being a silly, imaginative little fool, and she would melt into his arms, crying gently on his shoulder, and soon all would be well again. What vain hope.

Her voice pierced those hopes like a spike through a cotton sheet. 'It was Cynthia who told me. She said everyone but me knew about it . . .'

'How could Cynthia have known, the bloody vindictive gossip! And you're an idiot to take notice of what she said.'

Too late he realised that he had lain himself wide open by a few simple, unconsidered words. Even as he had blustered on he knew he had inadvertently revealed more than intended, what he'd said screaming out confirmation rather than denial. Geraldine instantly picked up on it.

'*How could Cynthia have known?*' she echoed. 'I take that to mean she knows and you're not sure how she could. Is that it?'

'Don't be ridiculous.' He had no time to think what else to say. 'You know what she's like. And you're a fool to take notice of damned wicked rumours like that.'

'Am I?' It was a challenge more than a question, said so quietly and for no reason it promptly promoted something akin to panic inside him.

'You're bloody mad!' he yelled at her. 'What d'you think I am? I'm not standing for this!'

Leaping towards her, he swept her aside with one arm so viciously that she fell against the wall as he raced on past her. Flinging open the door of the flat he tore downstairs to the shop below, in his haste almost missing a step and taking a tumble. It took ages to calm down enough to unlock the shop door in preparation for the day, praying that no customer would detect the sick thumping in his chest as they looked into his passive face.

But then, customers hardly ever looked at the one behind the counter, even when asking about something outrageously expensive.

It was an awful half-hour, he expecting her to follow and continue her accusations. When she didn't appear, he spent the time until Mr Bell came at nine, hardly able to apply his mind to anything other than making all sorts of contingencies against whatever might now raise its ugly head, dreaming up excuses to vindicate the mess he'd obviously but innocently, he told himself, got into. He almost deluded himself into believing that he was the wronged one, the falsely accused, the one who ought ultimately to be begged forgiveness once Geraldine came to see how misguided she'd been to listen to idle gossip.

When Bell did arrive, he yapped at him that he had to go out and to mind the place, and with that jammed his trilby on his head, flung on his coat and fled, glad to be out of danger. In the car he furiously pushed the throttle, stamped on the accelerator. The vehicle roared into life and swept down Bond Street in the direction of Knightsbridge and the apartment where Diana would be, most likely sleeping off their night of passion.

Some time went by before Geraldine felt able to move from the spot where she had been pushed by Tony's retreating arm. She stood against the open door as if needing its support.

The truth now glared at her. It must have begun soon after Egypt. All this time – two years, two whole years and she'd had no inkling. Those times he'd been away on his so-called business he'd been with her, Di Manners. How could she have been such a fool as not to ever suspect what was going on? He'd even had the disgusting cheek to come home here to make love to her. It made her feel sick thinking of him inside that woman then inside her. Her stomach suddenly heaved making her fling herself away from the door and rush to the bathroom, but little came up except bile as she crouched over the toilet. Pouring a glass of water to wash away the taste, she went into the kitchen, automatically putting on the kettle for a cup of tea.

As she stood waiting for it to boil, slow anger began to consume her. His parting shot as he'd flung open the door to leave had been to bellow, 'So what're you going to do about it?' but not even waiting for her reply.

The anger was like a coldness rather than heat, induced by not being able to reply what she was indeed going to do about it.

Questions – she could divorce him for adultery, a long and painful business, her name dragged around her society friends, her family with their inevitable I-told-you-so attitude, the humility of proclaiming herself the betrayed wife, it all following her around like a ghastly shadow.

She could keep quiet, say nothing, endure in silence, hope that one day he'd tire of his lover and come back to her. Would she still want him then? Did she still want him now despite everything? That was a hard question. Not easy to shrug away love that until a few days ago had felt so strong, so enduring, so comfortable. But her marriage was broken and did she really want to mend it at all costs or would she be prepared to see it go?

Tony's words as he left the flat had thrown down the gauntlet, she could either put up with it, fight for him or divorce him. Was it the third option he was really looking for, freedom to marry Di Manners? It was that thought which decided her. She wouldn't give him the satisfaction. It was only later that the thought came that, divorced, she'd be free to marry Alan. He'd said he was in love with her. But did that include marriage? He had proved himself to be a confirmed bachelor since his own divorce, a once-bitten twice-shy attitude. Otherwise he would have suggested she divorce her husband and marry him. And he hadn't, had he?

It was then there came a fourth option. With no one to turn to who could truly offer her sanctuary, not Mum, not Alan, certainly not her society friends, this fourth idea came like the opening of a door onto bright sunlight. Revenge.

How easily she could wreak revenge on him, he with his underhanded dealings, he on the wrong side of the law most of the time. When she'd asked him to be careful he had so many times taunted her with all it bought her – fashionable clothes, the fine jewellery, the good times, the fabulous holidays and great parties, her comfortable home; had flayed her with her own greed. But not any more. To get back at him now she would walk the gutters. To see him brought down after blatantly taking her for a fool with his affair was now her main aim. She'd come to mean nothing to him and he hadn't even had the decency to tell her so, or even to cease making love to her between making love to Diana Manners. He was vile, filthy and he sickened her.

Again the bile rose in her throat making her fight to control it. Yes, all she wanted was to pay him out. But how? To shop him, that was how.

*The Factory Girl*

Her mind in a turmoil, still in shock, but slowly beginning to think straight at last, she took the now boiled kettle off the hob and with purely automatic movements began to make herself some tea.

# Chapter Twenty-six

The interior of Charing Cross Police Station struck dim to eyes that a moment earlier had battled with bright if chilly sunshine. With her heart stifling her by its thump-thump against her ribcage, Geraldine approached the desk as the middle-aged constable behind it looked up.

'Yes madam?' he enquired, and when she continued to regard him dumbly, added, 'Can I 'elp you, madam?'

'I . . . yes, I think so,' she stammered. How to explain? What did she think she was doing anyway? But then a vision assailed her of Di Manners with her bare legs wrapped about Tony's body. This was her revenge.

'I want to report . . . my husband receives stolen goods, has been doing it for years and . . . and I want to report him. He's . . .'

The man didn't even blink, reached for a form and looked at her, pen poised. 'What's the name, madam?'

'Tony . . . Anthony Hanford, he . . .' She paused seeing the man begin to write.

'And this is your husband. You are Mrs Hanford. Christian name?'

'Do you need my name?' she asked, panic beginning to mount.

The question was ignored 'You're saying he's a receiver of stolen goods?'

'I—' She broke off, fear taking hold. She couldn't do this. 'Look, it don't matter.' Fear broke down her grammar. 'I shouldn't of come here. I made a mistake.'

The man was now blinking rapidly, obviously thinking her mad. 'This is a serious crime you're reporting, y'know. I must make out the report, madam. I can't just let it go, y'know.' He was beginning to look stern. 'We can't 'ave people walkin' in off the streets saying their 'usband's a criminal – that's what you're saying, isn't it, madam? – and then saying it don't matter, they've made a mistake.'

'Yes, I understand, but—'

'Do you know if your 'usband works with a known criminal gang?' He was now giving her an amiable smile. 'Do you know any of their names?'

'Yes, but . . . No, please, I'm sorry.' Realising what she was getting herself into, she began backing away. 'I don't know what got into me.'

Seconds later she had turned and bolted from the building, hurrying away until lack of breath forced her to stop. She was shaking and despite the chill air, her forehead under the cloche hat was damp with sweat. Her hands were too, under the gloves she wore. She tried to think but nothing would come; tried to think of what to do but again nothing came into her head.

People were looking at her in a strange way, or was it merely her imagination? The thought of revenge was one thing, carrying it out was entirely another. And still she couldn't stop the trembling, as if her very blood and nerves were jiggering about of their own accord.

One thought began to penetrate her muddled mind. That was to run to Alan. He would help her to calm down. He'd probably tell her that no harm would come of her actions, the police wouldn't investigate such flimsy information from an apparently distraught woman – not even an address given, she remembered. He'd tell her not to worry. But she needed *him* to tell her that even though she had already come to those conclusions on her own. At this moment she wanted Alan more than she'd ever wanted anyone in her whole life.

Collecting her wits, she hailed a passing vacant taxi, waited for it to rumble to a stop at the kerbside and got in, giving the address of Alan's place of business.

The man at the desk watched the departing woman narrowly. Even after she had gone he continued to stare at the exit, his eyes still narrowed to slits, the amiable smile he'd presented to her having faded to leave the lips to form a contorted, contemplative, almost malevolent slit in those square features.

It was only when an elderly woman entered to enquire about her missing dog that the benign smile returned and he came to life to jot down the particulars being given concerning the animal, this time with far more meticulousness than the information from the previous woman.

When the lady with the missing dog had departed, he looked again at the uncompleted sheet concerning Mrs Hanford, Mrs Anthony Hanford, then with a slow, knowing smirk, he took the sheet and, folding it carefully in four, slipped it into his breast pocket before continuing with his desk work. Rather than being sent for police information this was destined to reach entirely different hands.

For the second time this week Geraldine sat on Alan's sofa, his arm about her shoulders. He had told her exactly what she'd expected him to, but coming from him rather than her own mind, it gave masses of comfort.

'I couldn't go through with it,' she sighed yet again. 'I thought I could. I thought I could be tough, but I can't. I'm hurt, desolate, I feel betrayed, wronged, but in the end I wasn't able to do something like that.'

'I know,' came the whisper. 'You just ain't got that sort of heart.'

His lips were buried in her short fair hair where the waves fell gently over her forehead. 'You ain't got a vindictive bone in yer body.'

She allowed the lips to remain where they were. 'But I can't just stand by and let him go on making a fool of me. I felt I had to do something.'

'P'raps now 'e knows you know, 'e might give 'er up. Come back.'

'I don't want 'im back!' The words burst from her and she sat up suddenly. Turning her face towards him, she knew her expression was one of appeal. 'It's done, our marriage broken. It'll never be the same again. I just couldn't, not now, knowing what he'd been up to. It's not as if he went off the rails just the once or even twice. You know, his head turned by a ravishing face and he made a mistake. This has been going on for nearly two years and after he's been with her, he's been coming back to our bed . . .' She couldn't say it. 'And knowing he's been lying to me all this time,' she went on. 'Me kept in the dark while he . . . while . . .'

Visions of it all contorted her face and she sank back into Alan's arms, felt them tighten about her as she let herself weep against his chest. 'I feel so powerless. I feel so hurt, and so angry because there's nothing I can do. I hate him. How could he be like this towards me? I feel shunned and ugly and unwanted.'

If it was possible, Alan's hold tightened still more. 'You ain't at all ugly, Gel. You're—'

'He always told me,' she cut in, 'that he thought I was the most beautiful girl he'd ever known. He'd loved buying lovely clothes and things just to show me off to everyone. I want to know, when did I start becoming plain and miserable? For a couple of years he's been saying I'm miserable and making myself ugly by it. It was because we lost Caroline. I tried to—'

'Listen,' Alan interrupted. 'You're the most beautiful girl in all the world. Don't listen to what he says, you are ter me. Always 'ave been. Always will be. Don't ever let anyone tell yer that you ain't. You take my breath away sometimes.'

His lips had slid to her neck exposed by the scooped neckline of her dress, her hat and coat discarded when they'd entered his house. The touch felt so tender, so comforting, she reached up a hand to lay it on the nape of his neck. How warm it felt.

She heard him murmur against her flesh. 'And I love you, Gel, yer know that. Always wished yer'd choose me.'

'I should of.' Her voice too was a whisper. Had she chosen Alan she wouldn't be in this mess. She wouldn't have been any the wiser about the life that was now hers. By now she might have had children, never have had a baby die, the baby she'd called Caroline not known to her and thus not grieved for. How strange was fate. She would have been moderately well off with Alan, he now with his own business, not as excessively well off as she was with Tony, but there would have been contentment, she knowing no other life. What a fool to have been blinded by Tony's fine prospects, those promises of them going places, living the high life, how empty they were. Mum was right. She'd got out of her depth and now look at her.

With all these thoughts flashing through her mind, she only slowly became aware of Alan's lips, having travelled to rest against her cheek, were moving towards her lips. Feeling so betrayed and forsaken by others, and so very much in want of honest affection, she let them rest on hers, lightly at first but her hand still on the back of his head was pressing down, strengthening the contact with a sudden, desperate need to know herself loved.

It was with a strange mix of emotions that she returned home. In the taxi these emotions had refused totally to come together into one whole, and even when she'd let herself into her empty flat, still they didn't fuse into any solid decision but persisted in bouncing off each other.

What she and Alan had done was totally out of character, he normally so decent in his behaviour towards her to such an extent that she had laboured under the idea that he hadn't ever fancied her in that way despite professing love for her. Today had proved otherwise. He'd been masterful, decisive, taking her with a strength that still shook her. But she had been the one who'd allowed it to happen, hadn't protested, if she could rightly remember, though those more fraught moments only came hazily now to mind, had begged him to make love to her.

Afterwards she had lain limp in his arms on the sofa, incapable of thought. Normality returning only slowly, they'd got to their feet, not looking at each other as they'd adjusted their clothing. She'd said something about having to get home, though why, she'd had no idea except for a need to put distance between them, not because she'd been ashamed of what they'd done – she still felt that way – but that she'd had a need to think about the fact that she was no longer quite the innocent party in this broken marriage of hers, having done exactly what Tony had been doing this past couple of years behind her back. Except that he'd seen fit to let it go on, even planning his meeting with his mistress whereas what had happened today with her and Alan had been entirely unexpected.

Almost in shock she and Alan had avoided each other's eyes as she got ready to leave, their words stilted, she half expecting him to whisper how sorry he was to have let it go that far and how could she ever forgive him.

He'd not mentioned it at all and had driven her to Mile End station where she could get a tube train home, chiefly in silence with her finding it hard to think of anything to say to him and suspecting he felt the same. Once he had asked if she was all right. She'd merely nodded confirmation and he'd grunted acceptance of that. The short hop to where she had decided to get a taxi had seemed endless.

When they finally stopped, he'd said, 'There'll be one

along in a minute. I'll hang about until you're safely in one.'

Making ready to get out of the rickety old van, she'd hesitated, had looked at him, silently begging some word beyond the few he had offered and when he remained silent she'd fumbled with the handle that would open the door, but he had reached across and covered the hand.

'I want ter say somethink.' His eyes held hers as she looked at him. 'I'm not a bit sorry about what 'appened. Per'aps I should apologise but I ain't going to, because I love you. Maybe I shouldn't of let it 'appen but it seemed right and I think you felt the same. And I'm going ter say it again, I love you, Gel.'

She'd leaned back into the seat, her gaze downcast. When he asked, 'Do yer love me too, Gel?' she had nodded fiercely, unable to speak and, not knowing what to make of her emotions, had escaped his grip and moving forward had pushed open the door in her haste letting her flat, envelope-shaped handbag slip from her grasp to fall under the scuffed seat.

As he bent to retrieve it she gazed at the mass of dark hair and suddenly found her voice. 'I do love you, Alan. In a way I'm glad what happened, but in another I'm frightened. We mustn't do it again.'

He'd glanced up at her, the handbag caught between his fingers, and the stunned protest on his face had all but torn her apart. She had made an effort to explain herself, though not a terribly successful one, it seemed to her.

'I don't want what happened today to ruin things between us. I want to keep on seeing you, but two wrongs don't make a right. Just because he's been cheating on me don't mean I have to do the same on him. But at the same time

I don't want you to think that what happened between us happened just because I wanted to get back at him.'

'I know that,' he'd said simply as he handed back her bag but it hadn't struck her as that convincing and she'd striven to enlarge on it.

'If we're caught, he could divorce me.'

'As you can divorce 'im now, at any time. Ain't that what someone in your position would want, seeing what he's done?'

'But I've committed adultery too now,' she'd said and because that sounded so stupid, added, 'Besides, I can't give him the satisfaction of getting his freedom at the drop of a hat. I've been hurt, Alan, two-timed. I can't take that lying down, have him rubbing his hands, laughing at me. I want him to squirm. I want to see him beg.' Venom had crept into her voice, she recalled. 'I want to see his face when I say I'm not prepared to give him his divorce, no matter how much he asks.'

The look on Alan's face had given her a fright, a sort of crushed look. It still tore at her heart to remember that look of disillusionment.

'I don't see why I should be the little woman ready to fade into the background,' she'd gone on. 'I'm made of more than that. It's why I went to the police. If he was caught and convicted it would give him the shock of his life. He doesn't think he's ever going to get caught. Well, this time he's gone too far thinking he can get away with everything, including adultery. The only way I could see to get even was to make sure he suffers for what he's done to me. Only . . .' Her voice had then begun to tremble and she had felt her face pucker. 'Only, I couldn't go through with it.'

Alan had stared at her like a rabbit mesmerised by the light of a torch and it came to her that she could so easily drive him away. She'd bent towards him, near to tears that she must try to heal the injury she'd caused.

'I'm talking like a fool. I don't know why I went to the police. I wish I hadn't now, but I couldn't think straight. It's because I didn't know what to do.'

'I can understand that,' he'd said simply. 'It must be terrible for yer. I'm glad yer came to me. An' I'm glad of what we did. I'm glad. But don't do anythink stupid. 'Ave a good think about what yer've told me. I can't tell yer what ter do. I don't think I'm the right person after what's gone on between us terday. But I know what you're saying. I think I'd feel the same. In fact I did when me wife did the dirty on me. So I do know.'

He'd pulled her gently down on the seat, his arm going about her. 'Just one thing, best ter steer clear of the police. You might regret it. What I mean is it could be there on yer mind all yer life, what yer did, and yer don't want that. As for what you intend ter do about divorce, whatever yer decide, Gel, remember I'm 'ere if yer need me and I'll stand by yer, no matter what. I love yer. I'll 'elp yer in every way I can. But please think before yer do anythink crazy, that's all.'

He leaned towards her to kiss her before letting her go. 'I'll wait 'ere till you've gone,' he'd said and she had nodded wordlessly, got out of the van, and too distraught to look back, had hurried on into the underground station, forgetting taxis.

Now home, she recalled that not once had he said, 'I want to marry you.'

Did he want her only for what he could get and to hell with the responsibility of marriage? That wasn't his character. Perhaps what they'd done today would be the first and last time, an accident he'd rather not repeat. But surely a man in love as he said he was would want it repeated. If only he'd spoken of marriage. But to marry again, first she must end her present marriage. That in a way was like breaking off a limb, for until a few days ago she had thought of herself and Tony as a loving and contented couple.

Real contentment for her, of course, would have been having a child. But she seemed incapable of conceiving since losing Caroline, or was it more that Tony wasn't particularly interested in a family, cramping his society style maybe?

Sitting in the living room, Geraldine remembered the many excuses made not to make love: too tired, had to go out soon and no time, the coming in late and never waking her, the nights when he never came home at all, and he too busy working during the day to indulge in even a short time off to be frivolous and indulge in a spot of making love.

Contentment in her marriage had also been its advantages: material things, society friends, good times – all this would go if she left him. But what did they matter if all she could do was pine for him aware that he no longer cared for her? Yet the love she'd known prior to discovering his infidelity must still count for something no matter how she hated him, that love dying on its feet at this very moment. This strange desire to cling on, to win him back, knowing she'd never now want him back, was more a sort of primitive instinct for self-preservation.

And then there was Alan. But Alan hadn't mentioned marriage.

In a dilemma, Geraldine sat brooding. She was still sitting there, still in her hat and coat two hours later, the afternoon sun sinking fast, when Tony's voice floated up from the shop below talking to Mr Bell.

Instantly she stiffened. He would be up here at any moment. Swiftly she ripped off the hat and coat, went and hooked them on the hall stand and hurried to the bathroom to wash her face and apply powder to hide all sign of tears. When he entered the flat, she was sitting waiting for him, this time determined to have it out with him.

'And where've you been?'

He looked blank. It was an unfair question, he coming home at a reasonable hour for any man working during the day. He'd been away from the shop for most of the day, but so had she been out. Where, he had no idea.

At first he'd cringed with anxiety. It wasn't a pleasant thing, your wife finding out you've been unfaithful, but he was so in love with Di that not even Geraldine would stand in the way of that. Soon would start the rows, the accusations, the cry of divorce – he'd expected that. He suspected this evening would see its commencement. Geraldine had been bottling it all up these last couple of days and now he sensed it was about to burst, this unreasonable demand, 'Where have you been?' as if he had been out all night. Well, damn her, he wasn't ready to be cowed by a raging wife.

Casually he took off his trilby and top coat. 'Where d'you think I've been?' He made his voice a casual drawl.

'I don't know where you've been. That's what I'm asking.'

'I do have work to do,' he answered, flinging the coat and hat on a nearby chair – blowed if he was going to hang it up, she loving to have the place so spic and span. 'There are people I need to go and see during a working day.'

'Like *her*!'

'Like business people,' he corrected.

'Like those *business* people you hang around with,' came the irate reply. 'Crooks, thieves whose dirty work you do for them, them bringing the stuff they've lifted for you to do your part.'

This put his back up. 'Let me remind you that you don't do too bad out of it either, do you? The only time you complain about what I'm doing is when it's not going all your way.'

'Does that include you going off to some other woman?'

'I told you before, it's only people making up lies about me. They enjoy spreading dirty rumours.'

'And you can call them your friends?' she sneered, but then resumed her glaring at him again. 'Don't give me that lark. You practically admitted it yourself.'

He allowed a laugh. 'And when did I admit that?'

'When I told you what I knew and you asked me what I was going to do about it.'

'I was annoyed, being accused out of hand.' He gave a sigh. 'So I thought if that's what you want to believe then go ahead and believe it.'

'Oh, no,' she came back at him. 'You can't wriggle out of it like that.'

Feigning nonchalance though he didn't feel it, he

flipped open a silver box beside him for a cigarette. 'And you prefer to take notice of gossip.'

'I believe what I was told.'

She'd begun to bellow, alarming him. He'd have chosen all this to be more civilised, at the most she pleading for him to drop Di Manners. Instead she was standing squarely facing him, dry-eyed, a raging virago.

'Cynthia actually thought I knew all about it, like everyone else does. She said she thought I was being so brave. Brave! I could almost see her biting her tongue when she realised I knew nothing and that she'd let the cat out of the bag. That's how much of mere gossip it is. So don't try giving me that, Tony. I know. What's more, you know I know. You asked me what I was going to do about it. What did you think I was going to do, sit meekly by and let you get away with it? That's the last thing I intend to do.' Her yells had risen higher. 'I *know* where you've been today so don't give me none of your crap about business meetings. You've been with her!'

He hadn't. Today he had been doing business, maybe not legitimate, but business even so. Sam Treater had telephoned him, had said to come over right away, something he needed to talk to him about urgently. It could only mean some important job.

There'd been a certain amount of tension in the voice and he'd put it down to the size of the job soon to be carried out. A real big haul, he was told when he got there. The Big One. He was to be ready for a lot of stuff coming through, taking days, maybe weeks for him to reduce it to more manageable ingots. Others would take it from there, people he didn't know, people who would pass it through banks here and abroad until everything was reduced to innocent paper money and everyone finally got his cut.

'This is a job in a million, in fact it's actually worth millions, if not more. We'll all be able to retire on it, live respectable lives in great comfort. More comfort than you've ever dreamed of. Your cut too will be substantial, as I expect you've guessed by now. You do very valuable work for us. You're someone we can rely on, someone we can trust. That saves a lot of worry at the end of it. That's why I'm telling you all this now, Tone, old son.'

He'd nodded sombrely, aware that those words, *we'll all*, meant those he was in league with, and had promised to keep his mouth shut about what he'd just been told. If he didn't he'd be in for it. Anyway, he'd never dream of shopping anyone. What, and land himself in the stewpot as well? No fear.

In fact he'd come home excited, looking forward to starting on the job, carefully placing the bright precious haul piece by piece, whatever shape and design it was, into his smelter, the heat on his face. He couldn't wait to see it come pouring out in a smooth, liquid, golden stream like some living thing into the moulds to become the required smaller ingots, as he sweated with toil and greed, for he could feel the greed inside him even now.

And what a marvellous feeling it was, one Geraldine was now trying to destroy for him, interested only in herself. No wonder he'd turned long ago to Di Manners with her selfless care for him, her beautiful body, her lovely face, her amazing blue eyes, her ability to make him burn all over for her. He just wanted to be rid of

Geraldine and spend the rest of his life in Diana's arms.

She was still going on, flinging herself about the room now, her hands gesticulating, screaming something about getting back at him for what he'd done, that she'd never divorce him, he could stew, and more than that, she had been to the police about what he did for money, his crooked alliance with a whole gang of thieves and criminals.

That was when his brain stopped thinking about gold and Diana and the future.

Reaching out, he grabbed Geraldine viciously by one arm as she swept past him in her tantrum. 'What did you say?'

She managed to stop ranting to stare at him. 'What?'

'I said, what did you say? That you've been to the police about me?'

He saw her pale, the red anger melt. Her mouth had remained wide open, her words caught in her throat. He saw the mouth shut to a tight line. Then in a steady, defiant voice, she said, 'Yes, that's right, Tony. I went to the police about you. I told them what you did. I gave them your name.'

Before he could stop, fury leapt from him like Satan himself, his free arm sweeping back its full length to return in a fierce arc, the flat of his hand smashing across her cheek with such force that it knocked her from his grasp and onto the floor.

For a second he thought he was about to kick the prone, shocked form, but instead, with fear filling every tiny extremity of him, he dashed out of the flat, coatless, hatless, out into the street and flung himself into his motor. Sam had to be warned.

It took an hour or two of driving around, trying to think straight, to get his mind together, his nerves shattered. Should he alert Sam or Ernie to what Geraldine said she had done?

What if he said nothing? The police might have totally dismissed the gabbling of some stupid woman, and racing off to alert Sam would only be disastrous, those who trusted him realising their trust was in danger of being betrayed by his stupid wife. The wives of these men would never dream of doing such a thing. They knew on which side their bread was buttered, were loyal to their husbands who were thoughtful of their happiness and tender fathers to their children. What they did outside the home was no concern of the wives who loved them and if they bothered to consider it at all, saw what they did as their work, much as any other man's. Geraldine wasn't like them. There were times when she worried and fretted about what he did, and that wasn't healthy. If Sam knew what she was like underneath that society exterior of hers, he'd be dropped like a hot potato, or worse. Tony shuddered at what that worse could spell.

But what if the police did follow up what Geraldine had reported. What if it got back to the others and he got blamed for it. What if the police made investigations, waited for them to do a job, even this big one coming up, and because he had failed to alert anyone to that possibility, they were caught? Those that weren't would come looking for him. Then God knows what would happen. Jail for him, or even worse.

Sam would have to be alerted. He'd taken him into his confidence, only hours before had asked him over, had invited him in and offered him a drink, had sat talking to him in the chummiest of terms about the value of the job taking place within the next day or two, and that he would be included in a generous cut, *enough to retire on.* Yes, Sam had been straight with him, and he had to be straight with Sam. He must be told. But the thought set Tony's nerves jangling again, blurring his vision and making his driving erratic.

It was gone eight o'clock when he finally entered Sam's extensive driveway. Lights were on in the hall but nowhere else, although he didn't take much account as panic again began to mount, every bit as bad as that at his own home. By the time he got out of the car he was shaking with anger at Geraldine and in terror of breaking this fearful news. Sam could kill him, quite literally. His hand shook as it pressed the bell, his finger seeming to be stuck there, incapable of releasing it until suddenly the door opened to reveal a young woman, her plain face flustered by the continuous ringing. She drew back from the contorted face of the caller, her own face filled with fear.

'Mr and Mrs Treater's out,' she managed to his staccato enquiry.

'Where's he gone?' came the manic demand.

The woman's voice shook. 'I don't know, sir. They went off to dinner somewhere. I give eye to the children. They didn't say where. Sorry, sir.'

Before Tony could ask any more questions she had shut the door, eager only to repel this madman, leaving him to stare at the ornately carved door.

Around ten o'clock she tremulously answered the door to yet another caller, a large man with grim, heavy features who also looked rather frightening, and to whom she repeated what she'd already told the first. The man's face became even grimmer as he gave his name, asking her to say he'd called, but then changed his mind and told her to say nothing, that he'd come back tomorrow morning.

By that time she'd have gone home anyway with no need to see either of these strange men and certainly with no wish to.

# Chapter Twenty-seven

Getting herself slowly up from the floor, there had been a sense of utter disbelief more than shock at finding herself reeling away like that, helpless to stop herself falling. There was a feeling of wretchedness too.

Tony had never raised a hand to her until now. In all her moments of pique, of outburst over this or that, he had never resorted to any physical reaction. A raised voice was as far as he had ever gone. One could say that for him: he had always been mild-mannered, could become a little overexuberant at times, jumping in without thinking, but no more than that, not even if drunk. It was usually her who had the tantrums.

Geraldine lowered herself into an armchair, her face still numbed from that mighty smack. Soon the numbness would go and the ache would begin, not a smarting but an ache, she knew it, for it had not been a mere slap, the flat of the hand had landed like a hammer blow.

He must have been thoroughly terrified to do what he did and to bring the blow down with such force. She should never have taunted him that far, or said anything

401

about going to the police. In his place she'd have lashed out too, finding herself in peril. Not that she forgave him a thing, not the blow and certainly not his infidelity.

It was daylight when she awoke to the ring of the downstairs doorbell of the private entrance, realising she had been asleep in the armchair all night, stiff from lying in one position. The clock on the mantelshelf registered five past eight – too early yet to open up the shop and no one she knew would be calling at this hour. The postman perhaps, with a parcel, but parcels delivered to the shop came later. Perhaps it was Tony, having forgotten his door key in his headlong rush from the flat. But he must have had the key to his car on the same chain. Where had he rushed off to? To her to seek her bed and a sympathetic ear? No need for a car when buses, trams and trains still ran that time of night and he in desperate need of what Di Manners could give him. The thought of them coupling began to turn her stomach. She could see them making love as though they were doing it here in front of her.

The doorbell sounded again, bringing her back to the present and sharpening her befuddled mind. Her cheek throbbed only a little now, and when she looked in the mirror in passing, to run fingers through her short hair so as not to look too dishevelled to whoever was standing there, she could see that any red imprint of his hand had faded enough not to be noticed.

Again the doorbell rang insistent now, being pressed several times in quick succession as though in frustration at being kept waiting, making her quicken her descent downstairs with a sudden sense of urgency. Names went through her mind faster than she could reach to open the door.

Mum, Dad, Wally, there to say something dreadful had happened at home? Fenella – she'd seen Fenella just before Easter – had something happened there? Maybe not. Maybe only Tony coming back to apologise. If that were so, he'd be doing it to empty air. She wanted none of his apologies.

In the breakfast room Sam Treater was reading *The Times* over his boiled egg; Lily was eating a piece of toast, the butter spread sparingly as she was watching her already slim figure. The dress she'd worn last night for dinner with friends had become just a tiniest bit tight across the hips, although she had only worn it the once before and, made to fit, it had been fine then.

'I'll have to cut out potatoes and cereal as well,' she told Sam, having already complained of her problem.

He lowered his paper to glance at her over the top. His scrutiny was appreciative, taking in the small breasts, suited to the current fashion, the flat stomach, both visible behind the open edges of her silk wrap.

'You look fine. I've never gone much for skinny women, not enough to get me hands around. I like to feel something in me hands. So watch it, me love, or I'll be looking for someone else.'

He gave a short bellow of a laugh and returned to his newspaper, she pushing away the last of her tiny bit of toast regardless of his flattery, to inform him that she was off to get dressed and kiss the girls goodbye.

Their two children attended private school, and having already finished their breakfast were upstairs getting into their uniforms; Sam's chauffeur would be taking them.

Alone now, Sam was pouring himself another cup of

coffee when the maid came to say there was a man at the door. 'He says his name's Fred Jordan but he wouldn't say what he wanted, only that he wanted to see you.'

Sam's eyes lit up expectantly. He put down the coffee jug and got up, wiping his thick lips on a napkin and dropping it onto the white tablecloth.

'That's all right, Maud, I'll see him in the lounge.'

That he was still in his dressing gown wouldn't matter for Jordan wasn't an important caller in that respect. He was an ordinary police constable but he might very well have something valuable to impart. There were several bent coppers who were in contact with him, each of them he made sure were well paid for their information. When Sam reached the lounge, the man, now in plain clothes, was already standing awkwardly in the centre of the room.

Treater greeted him heartily, 'You're a bit early. We've only just had breakfast. Been on duty all night then?' When the man shook his head, he asked him, 'Had any breakfast?' Again Jordan shook his head.

'Want some?'

There came another shake of the head. There were none of the cordial smiles he usually presented, cordial and ingratiating and greedy, knowing full well that any information he passed on would be well rewarded.

Treater frowned. 'Well, have a seat.' He had all the time in the world, a man of leisure who could live well off his wits, who need never dirty his hands, letting others do that, he the brains – he and Billy Schulter.

'How's the wife and kiddie?' he began, opening up a large silver cigar box as Jordan dutifully sat and, offering him one, took one for himself as the man politely refused.

Snipping off its end, Treater, still standing to prove his authority, took his time lighting it from the table lighter. He gazed down at the man, his broad face lit by a friendly smile. 'I don't seem to have seen much of you lately. I even got to asking myself, has he forgotten us?'

Jordan squirmed at the implication. 'Bin a bit busy down at the station, Mr Treater. No time to breathe. But not much going on that'd interest your sort of work. Be of any worth to you, importance I mean.'

'That's all right, old man. Plenty of time to make us feel wanted again. So what've you come about that's so important this early in the morning?'

There was still no answering grin. The man licked his lips nervously. When he spoke, his tone was hesitant. 'I don't think the information I've got for you is something that'll make you any too 'appy, Mr Treater. It ain't my doing. I just thought you ought to be told about it.'

Treater regarded him closely. Jordan's mouth was one thin, straight line, the eyes in the square, heavy face, dark and full of foreboding.

'What is it? What's up? Come on, you'll be well paid no matter what it is. Nothing's gone wrong, has it? Have you had a tip-off or something?'

It was this man who had first tipped them off about the consignment of bullion and had been well paid for it. His contact, someone in the company looking for a bit of extra money in these hard times, had also been well paid for his inside information, coupled with the threat that if he didn't keep his mouth shut, the money wouldn't be the only reward he'd get.

Things had gone on from there that no longer concerned either man. They had no idea where the heist

would be made after the van left for its destination.
Treater saw it all in his mind's eye, a lonely bit of road
late at night in a few days' time, a certain dark spot,
little or no traffic that time of night, their own van waiting,
blocking the road, forcing the approaching vehicle to
stop, half a dozen men leaping from the bushes to
surround it, hopefully the terrified driver and guard
complying to the order to open up the back or get beaten
up. A handgun waved in their faces would help to do
the trick. A smoke bomb through the grill would bring
the guard in the back stumbling out. All three tied up
and harmless, the van brought to the side of the road,
the other backed up to it, the bullion transferred, and
away. Perfect. But Treater, seeing this man's long face,
felt apprehension creep over him. God, not now! Not at
this late stage with everything so well in place.

'So what is it?' he demanded and saw Jordan reach
into his breast pocket and draw out a sheet of paper, a
police form, holding it out.

'Didn't want to use the telephone. Can't trust them
things. Could be overheard, y'know.'

'Exactly,' said Treater. 'So what's this?'

'Something reported to us yesterday. Luckily it was
me took down the details. It's self-explanatory. That's
why I needed to come here with it.'

It took Treater seconds to realise the content. His face
reddened then turned ashy. 'Oh, Christ – Jesus Christ.'

Treater's heart was bumping like a clown on a trampo-
line as he glared down at Jordan, his face now thunderous
enough to make the man's eyelids twitch. 'You bloody
fool! Why the fucking hell didn't you bring this to me
straight away?'

Jordan was fighting to steady his flickering eyelids, talking fast. 'I couldn't. I was on duty. Can't just hop off duty like that. Raise suspicion.' His voice had become an unbroken gabble. 'Time I got away, got 'ere, you and your missus was gone out – to dinner the woman what answered said. I didn't know what to do. I hung on till this morning. That's why I'm so early. Thought you should know quick as possible, in case—'

'In case, bloody nothing!' roared Treater. 'You should've telephoned.'

'Others might of overheard me.'

'From a bloody telephone booth.'

'Not easy to've talked. Telephone exchange might of overheard.'

'You could've said it in such a way they wouldn't have caught on, you flaming idiot. But no, you had to wait until this morning, taking your bloody time about it. D'you know what you've done? If you'd done your stuff, I'd have not let out as much as I did to that effing stool pigeon Hanford. Because of your damned bungling you've landed me in the shit, you know that? Now what d'we do?'

'I don't know—'

'Shut up!' Jordan found himself towered over. 'You steaming, useless idiot! Get out of here.'

Seeing no reward this time and preferring not to hang around for it, lest it be something he'd rather not have, Jordan made to rise but was immediately pushed back down, the large face closing within inches of his, any escape trapped by two sturdy, dressing-gown-clad forearms supported by the chair arms on each side of him. The face, as much as he could see of it, was one huge snarl. 'And you say one word of this – just one word – to anyone, you'll find yourself without a tongue to say anything to anyone ever again. You understand?'

Jordan allowed himself a nervous nod only to nearly jump his own height as 'DO YOU BLOODY UNDERSTAND?' was again bellowed one inch from his nose. Frantically he nodded, the threatened tongue cleaving aridly to the roof of his mouth.

'SAY IT! Say "I understand, Mr Treater."'

'I understand, Mr Treater.'

Sam withdrew his face. 'Now get out.'

The man ran like a scared rabbit, but no more scared than Sam Treater felt at this moment. It took hardly two seconds before he realised that he might be getting rid of a valuable source of information. Not easy to find a good one and Jordan, stupid as he'd been this time, was reliable. To cut off the nose to spite the face was the action of a fool.

Dashing to the bureau, Treater whipped out a wad of large white notes, counted out five fivers, thrust the rest back into the drawer, hurried through the hall and flung open the front door just as Jordan was in the act of getting astride the motorcycle he'd come on.

'Just a sec!' bawled Treater and his fear for a second managed to melt into a grin as Jordan nearly fell off his vehicle seeing him stalking towards him. 'Here.' He had to grab the trembling hand to thrust the notes into it. 'Remember what I said. Keep your trap shut.'

This was as much a sweetener as anything else. The man would do as he was told, that he knew.

'Yes, Mr Treater, sir,' came the shaky reply. Glimpsing more than a single fiver being pressed into his palm, five to be exact, twenty-five nicker, he who seldom touched the richness of so many notes together unless for a favour given, a grin spread from ear to ear in gratitude and in relief that he hadn't been about to be annihilated on the spot.

'Thank you, Mr Treater. Thank you very much, sir.'

A copper's wages were forty bob a week if that, so twenty-five quid for giving a bit of information was a fortune, and being not such good news, amazing.

'Don't spend it all at once,' Treater cautioned, ignoring the glistening greed in the man's eyes. 'Or put it all into a bank or post-office savings. Someone might get suspicious. Right?'

'Right.'

The man's palm had been greased. He'd say nothing, knowing which side his bread was buttered, but Sam was already on his way back indoors, still far from happy, his chest heaving with apprehension, his mind working.

Billy Schulter's arrival at his house was so quick after the phone call that Sam could easily have believed Billy to have sprouted wings.

'I can't believe he'd do a thing like that,' said Billy on being told what had happened. 'Why?'

'He's got scared, that's why. Bastard's looking to shop us all.'

'But why?' demanded Billy again, spreading his hands. 'If it's reward money he's looking for, he stands to get more from us for doing a job than anything he'd get from the police. Besides, it don't make sense when he knows he'd be implicating himself as well.'

'Not necessarily. All he needed to say was he got wind of a heist, and then beat it.'

'But it was her who went to the police, not him.'

'Using her. Not got the guts to do it himself. And if he's so bloody innocent, why didn't he come and warn us what she did? It proves he had a hand in it.'

'Maybe he don't even know,' William Schulter mused, nibbling at his lip. 'She could've gone behind his back. You can't condemn the bloke before you really know.'

'It don't matter. Someone's grassed, and that's all I'm interested in.'

Billy picked up the incomplete police report. 'It just says here that a Mrs Hanford reported her husband as a receiver of stolen goods, that's all.'

'He knows us, and that's enough. He's been told his part in this job and he can shop us all. And he sat there yesterday afternoon smiling and grinning like a bloody vicar, and all the time he knew what he'd done, the bastard!'

Billy was still scanning the report. 'The time here says it was reported at three in the afternoon. According to you, Hanford was here around that time.'

'He could've gone there before coming here.'

'And been here in under ten minutes? Christ, he'd have had to drive at over seventy miles an hour and no one can do that, don't matter how big a car it is. It has to be her who's scared, not him. And I still believe he's got no notion of what she's done. I think we're going to have to pay her a visit, see how much she does know about us. Right now! What d'you think?'

Tony had been in a quandary after leaving Sam's house without seeing him. What if he blamed him for all this? And all because of Geraldine.

He shouldn't have gone off at her like that. He should have stopped to think, get the whole thing from her, how much she'd told the police. He'd been stupid telling her anything about this job in the first place but he had been so excited about the money he would get and what they'd do with it. That was of course before she'd been told about Di Manners. That bloody bitch Cynthia!

He'd turned his motor in the direction of Di's home to lay this trouble at her feet. She would understand, give advice, soothe, where Geraldine would only have ranted and raged and called him a fool.

As he expected, Di had received him with concern and sympathy. Making love helped take away some of his fear but lying in bed beside her, unable to sleep at three in the morning, it had all come back. He should have given that maid or whatever she was at least some indication that his call had been a matter of urgency concerning *certain things*. Sam would have got the message instantly. He'd have been alerted, would have got on the phone to him straight away and something would have been done about it. He should have gone home to await that call instead of racing off here but he hadn't exactly been in charge of his wits.

'I should go back there early tomorrow morning,' he murmured and heard Di give a contented sigh.

'Yes, perhaps you should, darling.'

She turned over and wrapped a slim, bare arm about his naked chest. 'It wasn't your fault, my darling. You couldn't have known what your wife was going to do, so how could you have stopped her?'

Tony took the arm and raised it to his lips, kissing the warm flesh. 'What worries me most is that they might

411

say I'm not trustworthy and find someone else to melt down the stuff.'

He'd confided a good deal of it to her when he'd first known about it, talking of the money he would get out of it and what he would buy her.

Now, of course, things had changed between him and Geraldine and it would be with Di that he would go abroad on the money and live like a lord. After all, his cut of the two million Sam had spoken about wouldn't be peanuts. Without him smelting down the haul they wouldn't be able to move it. Not easy to shift stuff like that in its original state.

'I could kill her,' he went on, thinking about Geraldine. 'She could ruin everything.'

Di gently freed her hand from the pressure of his lips and it began to slowly travel down his torso and his stomach with a light touch that set him tingling. 'They wouldn't dare drop you, my love. You know too much. No, they'll be annoyed, my sweet, no doubt about that, but they know which side their bread is buttered.'

She stopped fondling him and sat up abruptly. 'You know what I think? If your wife had really spilled the beans to the police yesterday afternoon, don't you think they'd have swooped by the time you got there? They wouldn't have let any moss grow under their feet over something like that, now would they?'

He had to admit she was right. Perhaps not much harm had been done after all. But he would still go there first thing tomorrow. Di had begun to caress him again, taking away all thoughts but those of her as he felt himself rise and fill, and for the second time that night had Di take him to the realms of paradise, twice in a single night, something Geraldine had never been able to do.

Next morning around six-thirty he left Chelsea and made straight for Sam's home near Vauxhall Bridge. A maid answered, left him standing there for a moment then came back to say that Mrs Treater had said Mr Treater and his colleague Mr Schulter had left early without saying where they were going. All Tony could do was turn his motor car in the direction of his home and have things out with Geraldine.

He needed to clear the air, needed to put his cards on the table. What she'd done had been the last straw in their marriage. He was through with her. She was dangerous. The more he thought about her going to the police the more scared he became as he drove through West London.

He couldn't wait to be out of this business, be safe for the rest of his life. Once this job was done, and he was sure he'd still be required to do it, he and Di would take a long holiday out of the country. He'd have plenty of money by then. The business could take care of itself. Geraldine could manage that, she often had when he wasn't there, and she'd have Bell to help her. Later he'd settle a good allowance on her. He wouldn't want to see her go short once the divorce was settled. He wasn't that vindictive even if she was.

Thank Christ she didn't know where he kept his smelter. Only those he worked with knew. The bullion would be taken there by van late at night, unseen in the total darkness of the Rainham marshes. It would take ages, of course, to melt down that much and he'd have to sleep there.

But after that he'd go home to Di, lie low until he got his cut, a substantial one Treater had promised, enough to retire on. Then with the money he and Di could live in luxury somewhere abroad.

The excitement of that thought all but rubbed out the fear. Perhaps, like Di had said, it wasn't as bad as it seemed. Would the police really have taken notice of a woman apparently talking rubbish about her husband being a fence? Not unless they felt bloody-minded enough to follow it up. And she might have realised that she too could find herself implicated and tell them it was all silly imagination. They had nothing to go on, did they?

Once home he would tax Geraldine to see just how much she had told the police. It surely couldn't have been that much because what she knew had only been what he'd told her and only that he was doing a big job for someone and stood to reap a good payout. Then he would telephone Treater or one of the others if he still wasn't home and do a bit of careful explaining, apologising, a bit of wriggling. He wouldn't be in their good books but it hadn't been him who'd contacted the law. Maybe no harm had been done at all, he managed to convince himself just under a mile from home.

Feeling better and able to breathe more easily, he slowed to a stop outside a tobacconists not far from Hyde Park Corner to saunter in for a packet of Players, looking to delay the time when he must confront a possibly still irate Geraldine.

# Chapter Twenty-eight

Geraldine practically stumbled from the taxi as it stopped outside Alan's yard. She'd hardly been able to manage to give the address, her voice had shaken so much. She must have looked like some mad woman, face working, eyes staring from their sockets, her hair, short though it was, uncombed and her clothes dishevelled as she stumbled along Grove Road looking for a taxi and when one finally came along, frantically waving for it to stop.

She had never been so frightened in all her life. She had concluded that the ringing on the door had been Tony and had gone down determined to give him his marching orders for daring to lift his fist to her. Well, hand really. But it had felt like a fist. All right, he'd been beside himself at her going to the police like that and she couldn't blame him, but to hit her was inexcusable.

The ready words of vilification as she yanked open the door had died on her lips, Sam Treater's disarming smile confronting her. With him was William Schulter. Sam had asked if Tony was around and when she'd said he was not, in no uncertain terms, anger still there, he'd

smiled even sweeter and asked if they could come in
and wait. Caught on the rebound she had snapped that
she had no idea if he'd even be back and couldn't care
less if he never did. Treater had said sympathetically,
'Like that is it? Had a row then?' And when she'd replied
that she supposed it could be called that, he'd said, 'Well,
never mind. We'll come in for a moment anyway. It may
be we'll only need to speak to you.'

When she had asked what about, he'd slowly reached
out and gently but firmly pushed her to one side, he and
Schulter entering before she could think to stop them,
taken aback by Treater's almighty presumptuousness.

She'd followed up the stairs, growing more and more
angry at their rude arrogance, had even demanded who
they thought they were. Neither took any notice of her
until they were in her lounge, gazing about the place as
if they owned it and as she followed them in had turned
to face her, Treater's heavy face by then bereft of any
smile. His words still pierced her brain.

'I'll tell you who we think we are. We're your
husband's colleagues who've entertained him, put him
where he is, welcomed you into our midst – our wives
have been good friends to you, we've given you good
times, the best of everything. And now we find we aren't
worth a second of loyalty.'

When she'd asked what they were talking about,
Treater had replied in a tone that had frightened the living
daylights out of her. 'We're talking about you, my dear,
going to the police about what your husband does for a
living. No consideration for us, that we might be for the
drop because of you. You may not care for what he or
we do for a living, but both of you are happy to share

in the spoils, aren't you? Not one word of gratitude, but when things look too rough, it's off to the police with a tongue as loose as a prostitute's pussy. And there's us putting all our trust in you both – yes, you're as much involved as him – and thinking of all the good turns we've done you both in having him working for us and getting good returns for it.'

He'd begun poking a finger at her, the finger connecting with her shoulder, jerking her backwards with each sentence. She'd glanced round for escape to find that the silent Schulter had got between her and the door. She remembered crying out, 'What d'you want?' but still the toneless tirade went on. The digging finger became a fist punching at her shoulder until she was crying out in protest.

Backed up against Schulter, she had felt the flat of Treater's hand connect with the side of her head, not her face, no marks left to show, and continued to slap against the top of her head, knocking it from one side to the other. All the time the voice had grated that they knew she'd been to the police, were very put out by it, and when they got hold of Tony he'd get worse than this; that if he thought they would use him now he had another think coming – the deal off, as was the whole job, thanks to her, so where was her husband, when would she expect him home? And don't lie!

The smacking had got worse, Schulter beginning to dig her in the back with his knuckles, not enough to do damage but painful. Squirming and trying to fight back, she heard herself being referred to as a silly girl who had behaved like a child, and needed a lesson like all naughty children. The next second she found herself pushed back and lying over Schulter's knees, face down as he lowered himself onto a nearby chair. Like the child they said she was, she felt her skirt being pulled up over her waist. But she wasn't a child and as the blue silk knickers were displayed to these male eyes, her brain screamed at the thought of rape. Instead, struggling like a mad thing at the prospect, she had felt a smarting slap connecting with her bottom. Slap after stinging slap had landed, the silk of little protection, the sick dread of that first thought gave way to the humiliation of this present treatment.

The flesh numbed, she'd suddenly been dropped unceremoniously to the floor. They'd strode out without another word, satisfied that she'd been given a lesson. Tony would receive harsher treatment and it was her fault. She had really messed things up for them both yet she couldn't feel fearful for him. He'd caused all this in the first place, she told herself. How was a wife expected to feel and react, wronged as she'd been, kept in the dark?

Humiliation and the fright she'd received overrode all sense of guilt as she stumbled from the flat, her nether parts stinging as though they had been whipped. Her head still throbbed from the battering of those flat-handed blows. All she'd wanted was to find help, though what sort she had no idea. She'd had the presence of mind to snatch at her coat and handbag, though she was into Piccadilly before realising she was hatless, where no woman going about her business in this part of the world would dream of ever being seen out of doors without one, people passing her in that busy road glancing askance at her.

Seeing a taxi she'd waved it down, almost fell into it and had given Alan's work address. If he weren't there, where would she go? She couldn't go to her own people, not like this. She sat in the taxi shaking uncontrollably inside from delayed shock, lips trembling, eyes brimming with tears of humiliation and from the horror of what had happened. Outside Alan's business she felt overwhelming relief to see the gate standing open and men moving about in the yard beyond. He had to be there.

The peak-capped cabby stated his fare as she fumbled for the money, only to find her purse had been left behind. The handbag she had grabbed was one used for evenings, held hardly anything – a handkerchief, a silver cigarette case, a lipstick, a comb and a powder compact. No need for money, Tony paid for everything when they were out together.

'Can you wait?' she gasped. 'I'll get some money from inside.'

With the cabby yelling, 'Hey! Wait a minute, 'ere, 'old on!' she raced off through the gates, vaguely aware of the driver scrambling out of his cab to pursue her, his voice going on faintly behind her. 'I mighta known your lark when I picked yer up! But y'ain't getting' away wiv it though, lass.'

She almost fell into Alan's office, praying he'd be there. He was, looking up in astonishment from what he was doing.

'What in God's name—'

'Alan! Have you got any money. I need ter pay the cab.'

The man had arrived at the door, more fleet-footed

than she was. ''Ere, what's the lark . . . ?' He stopped, seeing Alan, then went on, 'This lady ain't—'

'How much?' queried Alan, cutting him short.

'Three bob. Come all the way from the West End she 'as. A bloomin' long way, that is, an' I ain't—'

'Here. And somethink for your trouble.'

Seeing the extra shilling falling brightly into his quickly outstretched hand, his angry face changed to a grin. He touched his cap. 'Sorry, mate. Didn't mean ter be awkward like, but . . . Well, cheers, an' all the best.' And he was gone.

Geraldine, watching the small scene, could only bend her head as Alan let out a laugh and came to put a hand under her chin ready to chide her. Her expression killed the laugh stone dead.

'Gel, what in 'eaven's name's the matter?'

In reply she burst into tears, flinging herself forward into his arms, making him bend to catch her to him. Crouching before her he held her away to gaze into her face as best he could with her wanting only to hide it against the dusty overalls he wore. Relenting, he let her rest her face against him, smoothing her hair and rocking her gently until at last the sobbing subsided. She felt a movement as he raised a hand at one time to wave away someone who came into the hut, the man hastily drawing back and leaving.

Slowly she was able to calm down, lifting her face away from his chest to look wordlessly up at him. He was surveying her face, was frowning at the sight of the small, gathering bruise on her cheek bone. Despite Tony using the flat of his hand it had been a hard slap and had left its mark after all.

'Who did that to you?' came the demand. She lifted a hand to it, a sort of reflex action of attempting to hide it. 'Come on, Gel, who did that?'

This time she found her voice and it came out in a torrent of words. 'I told Tony I went to the police. He lashed out at me. He'd have never done that if he hadn't been frightened. He's never laid a hand on me before. I should never have gone. I wasn't thinking straight. I was so incensed that he'd been carrying on with someone else behind my back. I felt betrayed. I thought he loved me.'

She was jabbering on faster and faster, her voice threatening to break into sobbing again. Alan lifted a gentle hand to her lips to stop the flow of words.

'When was this?' he asked, noticeably holding back anger.

'Last night. Then he stalked out. I haven't seen him since.'

'What were yer doing all night on yer own? Why didn't yer come to me?'

'I was too shocked to do anything, even to move. I ended up falling asleep in an armchair.'

'And got yerself in a state all over again this morning.'

'No, there's more.' The need to tell him everything and feel safe again was why she was here. It was an effort to control the wavering of her voice. Nor did she care to watch her accent any more. 'I was woke up this morning by someone ringing the doorbell. I thought it was Tony come back. I was so angry by then that I rushed down to tell 'im to bugger off – I didn't want to see 'im ever again. But it wasn't him. It was two men he deals with. One called Sam Treater and one called

421

William Schulter. They barged their way in and then began threatening me.'

In halting tones she forced herself to recount what had occurred. It felt as if she was going through it all again. It was telling on her but each time she faltered, she was urged on. Alan's expression was as dark as a thundercloud and almost as frightening. It felt as though she was as much helpless in his hands as she had been in those of her callers that morning and it came to her suddenly that her own will was being taken from her, taken from her first by the vileness of those intruders and now by the love of a man looking only to protect her, but either way that she was being reduced to a weak and babbling female. Her reaction was immediate, her voice sharp.

'I don't want to say any more. I think I've said all I need to say.'

Alan seemed to come out of some sort of coma, shaking himself like a wet dog. 'Good God!' was all he said, and looking at her with something like incredibility at what she'd been telling him, said again, 'Good God!'

What else he might have said, maybe his resorting to cursing and ranting, didn't happen. It seemed that by a physical effort he was controlling all that was seething inside him. When he spoke his voice shook for only a moment or two, then steadied.

'What I think we'll do is take yer to yer mum's—'

She drew away. 'I don't want to go there. I don't want 'em to see me like this.'

'I'll be with you, love. I won't leave yer until yer've settled. Yer mum is the person yer really want at this minute.'

He didn't know her mum. 'I only want you, Alan.'

'Well, you've got me. I'm coming with yer. And I won't leave yer.'

It was said with such simplicity, coupled with a light kiss on her lips, so instantly comforting, that she bowed her head and let him take her to his van, he threading her arm through his in a firm grip against his side as he called across to his somewhat bemused foreman to carry on while he was out.

'Now, who's that this time in the morning?' asked Hilda Glover to the empty air as a knock came at her street door.

It was coming up to nine-thirty. Everyone gone to work ages ago, she was sitting over a nice, well-earned cup of tea and a biscuit after having got up early, done sandwiches, made toast all round for breakfasts, called up time and time again for Evie to get herself up, lazy little cow, her father gone well before daylight, his present job at the West India Docks doing well, decent money coming in once more after a bout of short time.

Fred too never needed calling twice, so enthusiastic about his job with the *News Chronicle* paper, reckoning on going places. Had a steady girlfriend now, Alice, nice little girl, she was. Him obviously very much in love, Hilda just hoped all this soppiness of his wouldn't get between him and his job and dampen all that enthusiasm. But if he was that serious he'd need to save for the future. It did look serious because he'd been going with her for nearly seven months, taking her here, taking her there, the two of them cycling off for miles into the country – Epping Forest, Ongar, even all those miles to

Southend – and where they got the stamina from beat her. Before that he'd had a new girl every few weeks or so.

With the breakfast things washed up and put away, this time was for her before going off shopping, and she meant to relax, for the last half-hour or so trying to avoid gazing around the kitchen and seeing something she ought to be doing instead of sitting here idle-like.

After shopping she'd call in at Mavis's, taking in a bit of grub for their midday snack. She never went there empty-handed. Mavis's Tom was in work but only just and money was tight with three kiddies to look after, Simon now five, Barbara four, Edie now two, and now Mavis was carrying again. The only thing Tom seemed good at was giving a woman babies. It'd be nice if he was as keen at keeping a job as he was at his bits of diddly-diddly in bed. Still, he didn't drink away what he did earn, like some men, she had to say that for him, and he wasn't a violent man with his family either – in fact, too easy sometimes. Mavis always nagged on at him being blessed useless, except of course when it came to the other, then it seemed he was God's gift judging by the times she'd fallen pregnant. Four kids in six years after this fourth one came in four months time. Now there were newfangled means of controlling births, you'd think she'd learn. Though, of course, such methods did cost.

'In my day,' she addressed the kitchen between sips of tea, 'in my day you 'ad ter learn 'ow ter keep yer man at bay, say yer was at that time of the month even if yer weren't, if yer could get away with it. Yer learnt ter give any excuse what come to 'and, yer know, and learn quick or yer'd be always 'aving babies. No books on birth control then. 'Ad ter 'ave yer wits about yer an' that was all. 'Course, some never did. That's why—'

The double knock on her street door put a stop to her soliloquy to ask, 'Now, who's that this time in the morning?'

She wasn't expecting anyone. Someone peddling a load of rubbish no doubt – well, she'd soon see them off. She hadn't money to throw around on brushes and dustcloths. What she had was there to keep her family.

Yanking open the door to send them on their way, her words, 'Not terday, thanks,' died on her lips seeing Alan Presley and Geraldine standing there, his motor van drawn up in the kerb. Neither of them looked all that happy. In fact her daughter looked positively out of sorts, clinging to Alan's arm as though she might fall if she let go.

'Sorry to call so early in the morning, Mrs Glover,' Alan began. 'Your Geraldine ain't none too dusty. She's 'ad a bit of a fright. Can we come in?'

'Well of course yer can,' were the first words out of her mouth. 'Take 'er inter the back room. There ain't no one in but me.'


Seated in her father's wooden armchair, the only comfortable one in that room, Geraldine kept silent as Alan began to reiterate all she had told him. There was much more but she felt she could not bring herself to give tongue to it, the terror she'd felt, the way they had treated her, the fear of what she'd thought her intruders might do to her, the humiliation of being spanked, her silk combinations being on show to those men. These were things she could never tell anyone.

Maggie Ford

'So you see, Mrs Glover,' Alan concluded, 'I thought she ought to come to you, 'er mum. Gels need their mums at times like this, don't they?'

'Yes, they do,' came the reply, and Geraldine was conscious of her mother looking across at her. In response she lifted her eyes to meet those older hazel ones, expecting to see them hard and unforgiving. Instead she saw only concern and suddenly her eyes brimmed with tears.

# Chapter Twenty-nine

Leaving Geraldine with her mum, Alan let himself out – his quest, that swine Hanford, his purpose, to put him straight on a few things.

Neither of them had noticed him much after he'd told Mrs Glover all he knew of what Geraldine had been through that morning. He'd refrained from mentioning her husband's infidelity having read the look of pleading in her eyes as he began to touch on the subject of Tony and had immediately switched to something else. The relief and gratitude that replaced the trepidation in those lovely, wide, hazel eyes of hers went straight to his heart. He wanted so much to spend the rest of his life with her, see her happy again. He knew he could make her happy, though the money he made would never come up to that which her husband made. Then again, his money was honestly come by, Anthony Hanford's never had been, so it seemed. Honest money carried no fear with it, and from what he'd gleaned from Geraldine, she'd been in constant if not heightened fear of his illegal dealings being discovered and he being sent to jail.

All this and more went through his head as he got into his ramshackle van and turned it in the direction of the West End. If he could prevent it, Geraldine ought never again to set foot in that flat of hers, to be forever reminded of all the unhappiness it held: the loss of her baby which he suspected she had never really got over; discovering her husband's affair with another woman and how it must have felt; now those crooks barging into her home, roughing her up, frightening the living daylights out of a helpless woman. Never mind the good times she'd had in the company of her society friends. She'd be better off out of it and he intended to see that she would be. It was the only way forward for her really.

It wouldn't be easy dissuading her from going back there, knowing her. She was a survivor, refused to let anything put her down, would hate herself in allowing it to. He could already hear her excuses – the business had to be kept going, bills had to be paid, the part-time shop assistant would need his wages, and so on.

Could he convince her how dangerous it would be to go back there? He wanted her safe from harm. And another thing, he needed to talk her out of this notion of revenge on her husband. Not pursuing her first impulse to go to the police and shop him – she'd been well frightened off that idea – but this other thing she'd spoken about, this refusal to divorce him in mistaken hope of making him suffer. What about her, cutting off her nose to spite her face? And what about himself? She remaining married to Tony Hanford left him with no chance.

He gnawed at his lip as he drove. He was in love with her, had always been in love with her. Could it be that despite all that had happened she still loved Hanford, still clung to the secret hope of winning him back, and he was merely deluding himself? Surely he couldn't have misinterpreted that day they'd made love. Or maybe he had. She'd never once spoken of loving him, not even during their climax. Maybe she had allowed it to happen out of frustration, a need to be loved and comforted, he happening to be handy. Yet he couldn't believe that of her. But if she did go through with divorce would she ever want to marry again, once bitten twice shy so to speak?

Not only that, but how could he offer marriage to someone who'd had everything? Oddly enough it had always been this thought that had driven him on to make something of himself, otherwise he would probably have remained a builder and odd-job man.

None of this could he confide to anyone. He had no close friend – he'd striven too hard to make good to go out and make friends. Taking his parents into his confidence was also out of the question – they'd tell him not to be so silly chasing after a married woman, and indeed he would feel silly. There was only one person he could think of to whom he could talk without being made to feel a fool and that was Geraldine's own mother, strangely enough. He'd always felt comfortable with Mrs Glover. Surely she would listen, even offer help.

His head full of fanciful hopes helped dull some of the anger against her husband, until finding himself in Bond Street outside Hanford's shop, not having truly concentrated on driving there, it came flooding back.

The place was closed. Probably a day off for the

assistant, and with Geraldine running terrified from the place of violence the shop would have been the last thing on her mind. It hadn't occurred to him that Hanford might not be there and for a few moments he sat in the van pondering what to do, the other traffic passing him by unnoticed, slow in the busy street. He'd been a fool, as always, rushing off half cocked. The only thing to do was to turn round and go back the way he'd come. At least he could try the bell on the door beside the closed shop. Someone might give him an idea where the owner was.

Bewildered, Tony stared at the disordered lounge. He'd called to Geraldine as he came upstairs but there had been no answer. He'd not been surprised at her not being here, in fact felt relief, not having to defend himself against the tirade he was expecting. It had taken courage to come back to apologise for hitting her like that. It was against his nature to hit a woman, but she'd so frightened him, anyone would have lashed out under those circumstances.

Angry and hurt though she must have been, it was unlike her to walk out leaving behind a mess, a hard chair left in the centre of the room, two cushions on the floor, slippers left beside the armchair where she normally put them away tidily in the bedroom before leaving to go out. She must have been enraged indeed.

She would be even more enraged to know that the real reason behind apologies was to talk her into accepting that their marriage was over, that he could never come back and the only solution was for them to part company. He was willing to do the decent thing, give her grounds for divorce, no blame attached to her whatsoever, even have his solicitor draw up a contract for the business to be split down the middle, her half of all profits sent to her.

He'd offer Bell a full-time job, the man would jump at it in these times of huge unemployment although things were beginning to improve. As for Geraldine, he couldn't very well throw her out of her home. He'd let her stay in the flat until she found somewhere else, which he hoped would be quick – the last thing he'd want after the divorce would be to bump into her if he had to come here on business. He'd pay whatever she wanted for another place and you couldn't say fairer than that. But he'd dreaded this getting down to brass tacks, and now that she wasn't even there, in a way he felt almost cheated after having rehearsed it all.

He was about to go into the kitchen when the bell downstairs rang. Instantly all his nerves gave a jump. She was back and just as he was getting himself together.

Well, best to get it over and done with. Then he would go and see if Sam Treater was back home, and having squared things with him would go on to Di's place. Then he could take up his new life.

A man stood at the door and for a moment Tony felt his heart leap into his mouth. Someone from Sam Treater? He'd got wind of Geraldine going to the police. Bad news travels fast. He should have insisted on hanging around until Sam returned home, explained it from his own angle. Instead someone had got there before him. Sam had inside contacts all over the place, including some even in the police force. He wouldn't be where he was if he hadn't.

'Yes?' he asked nervously.

The man was tall, good-looking, a workman by his clothes. Outside stood a ramshackle green van, this man's most likely. He didn't look like a hit man or any sort of villain, and he was open-faced although with a somewhat angry look. 'Can I help you?'

'Anthony Hanford?' came the question and again Tony quaked inwardly despite the brave face he was presenting.

'And who might you be?'

'My name's Presley. I want a word with you.' So it was something sinister. Sam had got word. 'You might remember we've met before.'

The caller continued, 'I've just come from your wife. She came ter find me this mornin'. She was in a proper state. I was a friend of hers a long time ago before she married you. Before that she was going out with me, but that's neiver 'ere nor there. What I'm 'ere for is that she 'ad a nasty experience this morning, and it's all due ter you. I don't suppose you realise that, so I'm 'ere to explain. I'd like ter come in if that's all right with you. We don't want ter go on yapping on your doorstep of this posh area, do we?'

Despite what the man said, it wasn't wise letting a virtual stranger in. He might be here under the pretext of having a message from Geraldine. He had no wish to be beaten up in the privacy of his own home and this man looked quite muscular – not exactly a bruiser, but he could have a knife hidden somewhere in those overalls. Even so, a certain trust was beginning to make itself felt, the openness of the gaze most likely. Making up his mind, Tony stepped back, allowing the man entry but making sure to follow him up the stairs rather than leading the way.

'First door on your left,' he directed, and once in the lounge, the door left conveniently ajar, he asked, 'Want a drink?'

'No thanks. I need to get this off me chest as quick as possible and be off.'

Tony kept his face towards his caller. 'So what is it you have to say that you couldn't say downstairs?'

'Right.' Presley's face had hardened, sending out warning signals. 'First of all, I know about 'er going to the police. She's told me all about you, yer see, what yer do on the side.'

Tony felt his face go cold and stiff, made to speak, to defend himself, but Presley hadn't finished.

'Yer needn't be scared. I ain't goin' ter do anythink about it. I ain't that keen in getting' involved in your mucky pastimes. She did tell me yer did a bit of work for a gang of crooks, although she didn't mention names if that's what's worrying yer. But I don't want ter know about that either. What concerns me is—'

'What concerns you?' echoed Tony, seeing a glimmer of something he hadn't known about. 'Why the hell should anything about her concern you?'

'Because I'm a friend of 'ers. Been a friend of 'ers for years.'

'I bet you have!' But his sneer was ignored.

'I'm 'ere about two things, if yer care ter listen. First is about what you've bin getting up to behind 'er back. She loved you. I once 'oped she'd love me, but she settled for you and as far as I'm concerned she made a bad choice. I'd never of done to 'er what you've done, picking up with some other woman, leaving 'er in ignorance about what you was up to all this time. Yes, she told me.'

'I bet she did.' Tony was feeling brave now. This man was no threat from Sam Treater and his friends after all. 'And I bet you and she took full advantage of it. I can guess the kind of sympathy you gave her.'

For a moment the connotation seemed to stun Presley. He gulped, but then his lips tightened. 'You never gave a second thought to 'ow she'd feel, her 'usband 'aving it off with some other woman. That's you well-off blokes all over, no thought fer anyone but yerselves.'

It was a silly argument. Tony was beginning to feel the superior one of them, felt he could now talk down to this man.

'So what do you intend to do about it? It seems what you've been telling me is a case of sauce for the goose is sauce for the gander. No doubt she got from you what she refused me. Can you wonder I looked to someone else, being the only time she and I made love was when she hoped it would get her a baby? That's all she's ever thought about for years. Making love for her is just a means to an end. There's more to it than just begetting a kid, and kids cramp one's style, so maybe she thinks you can do better for her. Pity your money won't match what she's used to.'

He stopped more from lack of breath after his tirade than loss of any more to say. He could have said screeds, except that Presley was glaring at him and looked about to lash out at him. But then Presley stepped back. His previously squared shoulders appeared to relax and droop, and just as Tony was about to push his luck even further, he was cut dead by a firm, commanding tone.

'What you do is no concern of mine, but when it comes ter your crooked mates arriving 'ere to terrorise the livin' daylights out of her, threatening ter knock 'er about, shoving 'er around the room like she was a rag doll, humiliating 'er by laying 'er across their laps and smacking her bottom till it was red an' then warning 'er of worse ter come if she ever talked to the police again, that's when it starts to concern me.'

This was the reason for the untidy room, but Tony was too taken aback by what his caller was saying to dwell on tidiness. He glared at the man. 'Liar!'

'Your wife's words,' came the reply. 'And judging by the state of her I believed her.'

'They wouldn't do a thing like that. Why would they do a thing like that?'

'They obviously know about her going to the police.'

'How?'

Presley shrugged, but it wasn't a shrug of someone who couldn't care less – coupled with a pair of raised eyebrows, to Tony it was more a question aimed directly at himself. Automatically he answered to that. 'Someone got wind of it and informed on her to them.'

He was beginning to feel frightened. It crept over him like fog creeping up from a river. It even felt cold. If they'd done to Geraldine what she said they had, then what would they do to him? He had to go and explain things to them. He should have made more certain of doing that in the first place instead of complacently driving away to Diana for solace when he'd found Sam not in. He should have hung around until Sam Treater had come home. He had thought no one would know what Geraldine had done and therefore it might not matter. But he'd thought wrong.

He glared at Presley. 'I want you to leave. I have to go out. You can tell her if she wants a divorce, I won't fight it and I won't see her left without, she can have whatever she wants.'

'She wants you.'

Tony couldn't help the guffaw that tore itself out of him in a great hail of breath, though more from nerves than amusement.

'No she don't,' he snarled, calming. 'She wants the money, the easy life it brings. Why d'you think she's turned a blind eye to my work all these years, eh? Because it kept her in luxury and she's greedy for that and little else despite what she's been up to with you. And she condemns me. How long's it been going on then?'

He was talking only to calm jangling nerves, the fear of Sam Treater's crowd, what they'd do when he went to face them and tell them to keep their hands off his wife, try to convince them that her going to the police wasn't his doing, that he was innocent and wanted to make restitution for what she'd done, that she hadn't got as far as naming names, so they were safe. He had to appease them. What if they refused to use him in this big job coming up in a few days' time? All that promised money. All the plans he had for it. He and Di needed that money. It'd be their future, for God's sake.

Ignoring Presley's protest that nothing had been going on, he'd hardly paused for breath even while his mind flowed in that other, too awful to contemplate direction.

'I'm not jealous of her – I don't care what she does.

436

She can make love to the local dustman for all I care, so long as she agrees to a divorce. I've got someone who can really give me what I want without always moaning. All I want is to be free. You can tell her I won't see her going without.'

'Yer just said that,' Presley reminded, his tone sharp.

Had he? He couldn't remember what he'd said. Had he mentioned any names? 'Well, whatever. Now you'll have to leave. I have to go out.' He'd said that too, ages ago, it seemed.

He was ushering the man to the door, arms stretched out from his sides in a gesture of beseeching more than commanding and for a moment it looked as though Presley intended to stand his ground, gazing at him with an expression of contempt. Then the expression relaxed, the shoulders gave a small shrug of defeat. Elation hit Tony like a fresh wind as the man finally turned to go.

Following him down the stairs to make sure of his leaving, Tony added as he opened the door. 'Tell her I don't hold any grudge—'

'What?' Presley turned abruptly to him.

'I mean,' Tony fumbled, 'I hope there won't be any animosity in this, no nastiness with the divorce.'

'Oo says there's going ter be a divorce?' came the retort. 'She says she'll never divorce you, that yer can sing for it, yer can rot before she lets you off the hook. Them's 'er words, not mine. You and me both, we're in queer streets there. You won't be able ter marry yer fancy piece and I won't be able to marry Gerry. As fer grudges, I think she's the one with a grudge, don't you?' He paused while Tony stared at him open-mouthed. 'Oh, and there's one more thing . . .'

Before Tony could even think to leap aside, the fist came towards him with the speed of a striking cobra, catching him square on the mouth, sending him careering backwards to finish up on his back on the stairs. Through a mist of lights he saw the door close quietly behind his assailant, leaving him alone in a low glimmer from the frosted-glass window above it.

Sam Treater was at home. With him, having been summoned at short notice after Tony had unloaded himself of Geraldine's burden of guilt, were those who called themselves friends, though to Tony's rueful eyes they appeared far from friends, every face turned on him, grim and unwavering. He squirmed even as he presented them with an ingratiating smile.

'I should have told you sooner, but you weren't in, Sam. I know I should have waited for you but I had no idea when you'd be home.'

'So you breezed off to your girlfriend's and stayed there enjoying yourself instead, that it?'

'I couldn't go home after what she did. But I got it out of her,' he lied, 'that she only mentioned me, no one else.'

'And you didn't think that would matter, that the cops are too fucking dumb to put two and two together and come up with the rest of us.'

It was Tony's hope to brazen it out, though already he could see the money he'd get from this job slipping rapidly away from him. He had to win their confidence. That money meant everything to him, more than he'd ever seen or would again in his lifetime.

'How did you come to know she went to them?' he asked.

The reply came back like a whiplash. 'Don't you think we've got our sources of information? D'you think we're that dumb?'

'No. I just thought—'

'You do too much thinking for your own good, Tony, you know that? I've always said you did.'

'Then why did you trust me yesterday, telling me all about what was going on. You've never done that before. And I was here at the time she was talking to the police. That proves it wasn't me, Sam.'

None of the others had said a word, but their stances spoke volumes. He tried not to show how much he was quaking. Please, he prayed, don't let them cut me out of the deal now, not at this late stage. What was he going to tell Di? Would she drop him like a hot cake seeing no high living ahead of her any more, but he having to continue working as a small-time jeweller for the rest of his life. Jobs like these came only once in a lifetime. Sam had said to him in the most amicable terms while they waited for the others to arrive that this job was worth nearly two million, handled the right way. It had taken his breath away, but he'd been jubilant at being forgiven so easily. That was until the others had arrived. Now he wasn't feeling at all jubilant.

'You can still trust me, Sam. I've finished with Geraldine. She's left. She won't be back. She can't do anything to us.'

'Us?' He ignored the question.

'I've too much at stake to do you lot down. So much depends on this.'

'You can say that again, old man. But she knows us all.

439

Who's to say she won't go to the cops again with more names when the fancy takes?'

'She won't. She was frightened off by them, and by you and Billy.'

Being invited into Treater's house, he'd begun by half warning him to lay off Geraldine. Treater had even apologised, said it had happened in the heat of the moment, they got carried away, and wouldn't happen again.

What he said must have worked, for Sam relaxed back in his chair, at the same time as the other four – Billy, Ernie, Fruity Hicks and Jimmy with his snake-like glare – appeared to stand back without really moving. It was encouraging and Tony allowed himself a smile to encompass them all.

'You can trust me, Sam, all of you.'

'Of course, old man,' said Treater evenly. 'No question about it, and to put you in the picture, Tony, old man, we're all going somewhere, you included, so that you'll be able to realise just how much we can trust you. That okay by you?'

He rose out of his chair as Tony nodded eagerly, and with them all following, led the way to where his handsome Rolls-Royce stood in the drive.

# Chapter Thirty

It was June. Since that day Alan had rushed off to find Tony just after Easter, there had been no word of her husband. Alan must truly have put the wind up him. He hadn't said much about it when he'd come back, she still shaken from her rough treatment, except that he'd seen him on his way. Geraldine felt so proud of him. Tony would never have had the gumption to fight back. Maybe he hadn't even gone to give those animals a piece of his mind for what they'd done to her; had more likely crept on his belly to them, seeing the money he'd be making from the job they had planned fly out of the window if he did. She had nothing but contempt for him now.

In a way Geraldine was glad that he'd made himself scarce. She wanted no more to do with him after the way he'd ruined her marriage. In other ways there was a faint anxiety as to where he might be, annoyed with herself for even wondering if he was all right. And anger too, yes, mostly anger, that he'd not even bothered to contact her – no doubt enjoying life too much miles away with the woman he'd left her for, to even care how she was.

She would have thought that by now, three months on, he would have at least written about her considering a divorce. But perhaps he wasn't so bothered now he had all he wanted. As to where he was, she had no idea. A few enquiries might have helped but she wanted only to stay as far away as possible from those who knew him and who'd humiliated her.

Soon after Tony's disappearance the papers had splashed news of a big robbery of around two million pounds' worth of gold bullion from a van on a lonely stretch of road; the police had no clue as to the culprits. Geraldine wondered if it was the one in which Tony would have been playing his part.

'How long would it take to smelt down that much gold?' she'd asked Alan at the time.

'Lord knows,' he'd answered. 'Quite a bit I imagine. Why?'

'Tony operated a smelter. He never told me where, but he used to blab about things to me, how he made his money, what work he was on, that sort of thing. He never could keep a still tongue. What if the police knew where he operated and who he worked for at times?'

They'd been walking together, hand in hand, in Victoria Park around dusk just before closing time and Alan hadn't continued the conversation but drew her to him and had kissed her instead. The kiss had been warm and tender and she forgot to think about Tony.

But it wasn't simple to forget him. He kept returning to her mind, especially since the robbery – had he made the thousands he'd hoped for, melting down all that gold?

Were he and Di Manners enjoying his ill-gotten gains while she was left looking after the jewellery shop, wanting only to be rid of it but unable to while it was still in their joint ownership and she at a loss to know where he was? She hated the flat, hated going back there with its echoes of what she'd gone through. She could have ceased to pay rent, the premises reclaimed, but it wasn't her place to do that with the possibility of Tony returning at any time. Of course, there was always one way.

'I could so easily go to them with what he's told me,' she said to Alan when two months later the police still hadn't caught the villains. 'Even if it is only scanty, it might lead somewhere. He could be sent to jail for a long time. I could get rid of the business then.'

She was at Alan's where she spent a lot of time these days, sometimes not going back to her parents' home until next morning. They had to be aware of what they were up to, something decent people frowned on, but Mum was apparently turning a blind eye to it so it was as well to say nothing.

There still existed something of a rift between them, their conversations stilted, Mum still cold and distant. Maybe it was becoming more pronounced with age; as they say, a person's nature gets more pronounced with old age. Mum wasn't that old but she was getting there. Gran had died the previous year – she was testy and frigid, and Mum took after her. Yet she was warm enough to everyone else. It was odd. True, she'd shown plainly that she'd never liked Tony, and she'd always behaved as if the sun shone out of Alan's backside. So why couldn't Mum start to unbend towards her now Tony was gone? It was as if she had it in her mind never to forgive her for going off and apparently snubbing everyone, being too big for her boots, no matter what she was trying to do now to make amends.

Dad too said little, taking his cue from her mother regarding her staying with Alan all night. In a way it wasn't like living at home as once it had been, she more a guest and wondering if there would ever come a time when this invisible barrier would be dropped and she would become one of the family once more. She'd even dropped her so-called *posh* talk in their company but it was a waste of time.

There was a look of alarm on Alan's face. 'Please, Gel, don't get yerself involved with the police.'

Having just got into bed beside her, he lifted himself up on one arm to gaze at her. 'Yer'll be biting off more'n yer can chew. They'll tie you up with them crooks straight away once yer tell 'em yer know about your husband.'

That was true. 'I only wondered what would happen if I did,' she laughed, but he remained serious.

'Don't be tempted, love. It could spoil everythink just as you and me are sorting out our lives tergether. We are, aren't we?' he went on in an uncertain tone. 'Yer don't still want ter get back at him, do yer?'

No, she didn't, not now.

'Because if yer did, anyone could take it that yer still feel somethink for him, enough ter want ter get back at him.'

She turned her head to look at him. 'You mustn't think things like that, darling. It's just that I can't help remembering how I felt when I found out about him and Di Manners, carrying on behind my back. It's not easy for any woman to forget things like that. They feel cast off, rather than betrayed, sort of unlovely, unwanted. It's a horrible feeling. But with you I feel wanted and necessary, and I do love you, Alan. If he came to me right now on his knees pleading to be taken back and offering me the whole world, I'd turn my back on him and all his promises. It's over, Alan.'

'Then why won't you start divorce proceedings?'

She had expected him to sink down beside her, contented with her explanation and her admission of loving him. Instead he was challenging her, demanding she prove her love. Why did she have to prove her love? Wasn't the fact that she was in his bed, had been in his bed several times since coming back here, proof enough? In sudden anger she said as much and saw his face become grim.

'I don't want you to prove nothink, Gel. I'm not asking you ter forget him. I know what you've been through because I've been through it meself, remember? I know what it's like to be done down. But while yer delaying things, we can't get married.'

Geraldine sat upright. This was the first time he'd spoken of marriage.

'Are you asking me to marry you?' she blurted.

'I don't 'ave to ask, do I?' He was looking at her in amazement. 'I took it yer'd expect ter marry me once you're free of 'im. Trouble is, I keep getting the feeling that yer'll miss all the things he gave yer. All them nice clothes, all them 'olidays you 'ad – goin' off ter France and that Egypt thing you went on . . .' Yes, it was on that *Egypt thing* that Tony's affair with Di Manners had begun. 'And all them fine friends you 'ad—'

'I wouldn't swap what you have for any of it,' she broke in. 'It's you I want.'

She heard him sigh as he sank down beside her, and pulling the cord of the light over the bed, he plunged the room into darkness. She felt his arm steal under her head, drawing her towards him and during that long kiss, his free hand explored her, sending shivers of pleasure and desire through her until they were making love with a fierce passion she couldn't recall ever experiencing with Tony.

Unless it was that time had dimmed it. Towards the end they'd hardly made love at all, and even before it all went wrong he'd not been as attentive as he might, and she'd know why though never admitted it to herself – in case it produced a child, cramping his style and his fun of high living. She was well out of it, she told herself as she and Alan fell apart exhausted, then realised that even as she lay there fulfilled, her mind had been full of Tony and how bad he still made her feel. Alan was right, Tony was still coming between them no matter what they did. She had to get him out of her mind but that was easier said than done. One thing, she wouldn't speak his name to Alan ever again, not even to recall what he had put her through or even to wonder at his continued silence.

After three months of it the old need for revenge was indeed fading, but now and again came in passing an embedded fancy to catch a glimpse of him, see him nowhere near as happy as she, the grass he'd thought so much greener with Diana Manners turning brown. The mere fact that such thoughts crossed her mind told her that she would never truly get Tony out of her mind, that divorce wasn't the answer.

Did Alan feel the same about his former marriage after all his years divorced from his wife? Did he once in a while hanker to see if she fared well or not in her second marriage, whether she still had him or had been left? She would never ask. For her, life was different now, as different as chalk from cheese, and she did love him.

One thing Geraldine did feel sorry about – it hurt to see Alan doing his best to match up to giving her what she'd once had, wanting to take her to West End shops to buy new clothes.

'I've enough clothes to last me years,' she'd tell him, trying to be light-hearted about it.

He would reply, 'They'll go out of fashion soon enough,' and she'd have her work cut out trying to dissuade him.

He'd take her to West End cinemas to see the latest films, or book theatre seats, though hardest of all to bear was seeing him needing to compromise by seats in the upper circle rather than the dress circle. With his business thriving he was far from hard up, but he saw himself as never coming up to the standards he was sure she'd once known, not realising for all she tried to tell him, that with it had gone many unhappy times, uncertain times, of concern and underlying fears. Money could never compensate for that. Yet no matter how many times she tried to tell him, he remained unconvinced. All she wanted now was him, yet she could see his doubts.

Maybe it was that she had money of her own and didn't need his. Hers was quite a sizeable bank account, she had to grant Tony that for all he'd done to her he'd always made sure of that, even more so after meeting Di Manners – perhaps then it was conscience money which she hadn't even realised until lately.

There was the shop too, still doing well. She'd taken Mr Bell on full-time. He had struggled on part-time money, too scared to give that up and probably go on the dole, and had been overjoyed at his luck. With him in the shop she had no need to be there, hating the place, merely paying his wages and settling bills.

When she and Tony had first gone in he'd arranged with the bank for her to sign cheques and deal with things. But with the business still in his name she couldn't close it down. It was now becoming a millstone around her neck.

Nor did she set foot in the flat unless forced to. Unable to bear the place with its memories of what had happened there, she'd shudder each time, making sure Alan was there with her. It was all so unfair, Tony living it up with Di Manners, maybe abroad, South of France, New York, Rio de Janeiro, while she must keep the business going.

'If yer divorced 'im,' Alan told her when she complained, 'yer could get rid of the whole shebang. Yer could 'ave 'im on two things, adultery and desertion – he wouldn't have a leg to stand on in court.'

Maybe she would. Maybe she would apply to the court and see what would happen, but it would be a lengthy business with Tony not present.

'It needs thinking about,' she told Alan and saw his face light up with relief at this first really positive reply she had given him so far.

By now the bills were rolling in, many of which she still hadn't settled, her nerves too wound up by Tony's disappearance to bother with them; they had mounted up to a considerable pile. Demands had begun to arrive, alarming her at first. Tony had always been prompt with bills. Then it occurred to her that by ignoring them his creditors would get more demanding, more irate, and finally begin to threaten court action, talking of making him bankrupt. And why not? It was nothing more than he deserved, his business bankrupted, bought out, the flat along with it. She hated that flat with its memories. It would be one way of getting back at him.

Of course with his cut of the robbery – generous he'd called it – it would be just a pinprick, but it would rile him and she'd feel better in her own small way. They could lay claim to his private and business bank accounts, everything he owned if it got that far, if they could find him! And why not? He'd left her to deal with everything, paying Mr Bell's wages from her own bank account, keeping going a shop she hated. She wouldn't suffer. She was his wife. No one would throw her on the streets. And she had her own bit of money.

With no idea where he was, never contacting her, she felt justified. In fact the idea seemed so good that she began to run up debt in his name, stocking the shop on credit with no intention of paying, and new furniture for the flat, on credit of course, on the assumption that Tony's credit was good, even payments on the lease were allowed to accrue.

If finally she should be turned out of the home she hated anyway, there was always Mum and Dad to go to. Surely they wouldn't turn her away. Or she could rent a place somewhere, but her money would soon be gone and it would mean working again. She didn't want that.

She said nothing to Alan, he'd call it dishonest, but

bankruptcy would fall on Tony's shoulders not hers. If she left without a bean, Alan would be happier that she'd no longer be independent of him.

Meantime there were other little things, bought on the business again on credit – new furniture for Mum and Dad which they accepted but with not all that good grace though she hadn't expected it, they who'd never taken off anyone in their lives.

'I ain't on the poverty line,' Dad said. 'I can pay me own way.'

'It's just a gift, Dad.'

'Gifts like that,' echoed Mum, 'ain't what yer call little. Don't seem right. It makes us look like we're spongers. An' we ain't.'

'Oh, fer goodness sake!' she told them, exasperated by their attitude. 'I'm not giving you me life blood. It's not my money anyway, it's Tony's and he ain't here, is he?'

If it didn't quite break the ice that still existed, it at least cracked it a little and she was heartened.

When she bought them a wireless set, a top-class one not needing earphones but which had an aerial and a large, shiny brass horn so that any number of people could listen, she had half expected them to sniff at it. Instead they gathered around it that first night with young Fred, Evie, Mavis and her family, Wally and his, with a couple of neighbours thrown in, like ants around honey, everyone avidly scanning the *Radio Times*, published these past two years now. For the first time it did Geraldine's heart good not to see her present dismissed with a shrug or maybe rejected out of hand, Mum saying as though in an aside, 'Yer shouldn't of done it, Gel,' which in itself was music to the ears of one become used to being snubbed.

Mavis too accepted her gifts, though Mavis always had even if as always she had to make some comment.

'Must be doin' well for yerself since yer 'usband walked out on yer,' to which Geraldine preferred to hold her tongue, knowing her sister of old.

Evie of course was ecstatic with all she was given – some nice dresses, a bottle of good perfume, a bit of jewellery.

Fred managed to say that he could afford things himself now that he was doing so well, but thanked her anyway for the leather wallet and gold cufflinks.

Wally as always accepted her gifts with good grace, even extracting the reason for all this generosity, despite her intention to say nothing, swearing himself to secrecy even from his wife who accepted with grateful amazement the two fashionable dresses her sister-in-law presented her with.

'Though where I'm going to wear them, I've no idea. We don't go out much, and not ter fancy places, what with the kiddies an' all.' Little Vera was three now, and the other little one, Johnny, had been born last year. 'We don't 'ave 'olidays except ter take the kiddies on the train ter the country for a day.'

Distributing little gifts to other relatives brought comments similar to those from Mavis, to which she smiled and said nothing. None of it made her all that happy as it would have had she given them with a good heart, but it was what was needed. It was a means to an end – small revenge but a sweet one.

'Oh, God!' At her cry, Alan looked up from the worksheets he was going over. They'd been together all night and were now having Sunday breakfast before she went back to Mum's where she was normally expected to stay.

No doubt she would return there to the usual studied silence and sideways looks from her, the deliberate withholding of any comment even though Mum liked Alan immensely. It was because of this that Geraldine insisted she didn't stay overnight with Alan too often. It was bad enough his neighbours chancing to glimpse her creeping off early from his house, worse to be seen coming back first thing of a Sunday morning to Mum's, they immediately making something of it. There were nosy neighbours everywhere, only too eager to see the worst of others especially if they thought *something was going on*. Not that it made much difference if it was carried to Mum's ears, she already knowing about it, except that Mum would feel embarrassed and belittled knowing it was the talk of the neighbourhood, and that was different.

Geraldine, still in her dressing gown, had been reading the Sunday paper, just delivered, while Alan, still in his as he sifted through his worksheets for Monday, had been sipping his tea. He put down the cup to gaze questioningly across the breakfast table at her.

'What is it, Gel?'

She looked up. 'This. Oh, Alan.' Folding the newspaper into a more manageable size with the piece she'd seen easier to read, she held it out to him. 'It says, "First aerial murder, London jeweller thrown from aeroplane." Tony's a London jeweller.'

Her fingers were to her lips in horror as, still gazing at her, he took it and read it quickly. When he looked up, he was smiling.

'Oh, love, it's a different name. Look.' He held it out for her to see. 'Yer should of read on, love.'

She felt herself almost collapse in relief, quickly needing to explain herself as she saw the look on Alan's face.

'Oh, darling, don't look like that,' she burst out. 'It's just that . . . I don't want anything more to do with him, you must know that by now, but I wouldn't want to see that sort of thing happen to him.'

She forced herself to calm down, speak more evenly, yet inside she was a mass of anxiety that she needed to share with Alan.

'I don't love him any more. It's you I want. But reading that gave me such a shock and brought it all home to me – that I was the one who told the police about him. What if it got to other people's ears, those crooks he works with? I'm sure they'd be capable of something like that, and it'd be my fault.'

Tony got up and came to her, crouching in front of her. 'Don't think like that, Gel. It wouldn't be your fault at all. He was the one what got 'imself in deep with 'em. Besides, they might be crooks but they wouldn't go to them lengths, throwing people out of planes. They're small-time.'

'Until they got away with millions of pounds' worth of bullion,' she reminded him. 'And the police still ain't caught them. What if they have connected what I did with Tony? They could've done all sorts of things to him. They could've done away with him. And to think they called themselves our friends, their wives always so friendly, yet look how they came after me. Alan, I'm scared. What if they have gone and . . .'

She felt herself being gathered into his arms, his voice crooning in her ear. 'Listen, Gel. Yer've got ter put them sort of things out of yer mind. It's all over between you and him, you and them sort of people. You're with me now, and I ain't goin' ter see anythink bad 'appen to yer.'

'I know,' she murmured, but his voice continued.

'Yer've got to forget that life you 'ad. And don't worry about 'im either. Chances are he's living it up with all that money he made. And there's you, 'alf yer time taken up worrying about that damned shop. Divorce 'im, Gel, an' get rid of it. I've got enough to keep you on. I've got a good business and it's growing. Please, Gerry, start doing somethink about it, eh?'

She was doing something, making Tony bankrupt, doing him down in some small way, in some small measure denting his ego.

'Listen, Gerry,' he was going on. At her insistence he'd begun calling her Gerry when he remembered. 'Listen, I can look after yer. Maybe not give yer all the things he gave yer.'

'I don't want them,' she cut in. 'They carried too much baggage with them.' But he was racing on.

'But I can give yer more than he ever did. I can give yer loyalty and a contented life. Gerry, love, go an' see a solicitor. You could 'ave 'im for adultery and yer wouldn't 'ave to fight the case. You're the one what was wronged.'

Slowly she nodded. It would be painful, maybe drawn out, but she'd be helped on her way that he would also discover himself owing huge sums of money to the creditors she had never paid, threatened with bankruptcy.

By the time the divorce came to court, he might even find his once precious business taken from him, he hopefully by then having got through those ill-gotten thousands she believed he must have flown the country with and have nothing left – knowing his joy of big spending and living it up, that would most likely be the case. He'd have nothing. What a wonderful feeling it gave her.

# Chapter Thirty-one

They'd come home to her parents' place this August Saturday evening after going to a matinee of Noël Coward's new play *Hay Fever*, Alan doing his utmost to compensate for what he saw as the good times she'd left behind. The other thing was that she no longer stayed with him on Saturday nights.

'Yer don't want people talking' about yer,' Mum had finally said. 'If yer want ter spend all yer time with him, then marry 'im.'

'Mum, I'm still married to Tony,' she pointed out. Mum hadn't even blinked.

'Then get yerself unmarried!' was all she'd said.

It was still hard taking that final step and seeing a solicitor. Alan was becoming frustrated, certain she didn't want him as much as she professed and Dad had warned that if she did decide to go through with it and it was found that she too had been spending her time in some other bloke's house – he shied away from using the phrase *sleeping with him* – then she could end up the loser. It made sense and since then she and Alan had decided she should sleep at her own home, sharing Evie's bed for want of room here, but it was hard.

Her own home was now with her parents, the better of two evils she told herself. She loathed going to the flat. There was never any sign of Tony having been there and it had developed a cold, unlived-in atmosphere that made her shudder every time she set foot in it. When she finally managed to bankrupt Tony, the flat would go as well. No base for him to come back to, though would that trouble him? She kept forgetting he must be rolling in money now and had no need of a rented flat – probably had enough to buy himself a mansion.

On the way home Alan bought the afternoon edition of the *Daily Mail* and fish and chips all round, and now they were sitting with Mum and Dad round Mum's table. Both Evie and Fred were out, Evie with her current boyfriend and Fred with the girl he'd been going with these past eleven months and now talking of an engagement. 'A bit young fer that,' Mum had observed, but she liked Carrie. Geraldine was glad that was the name she went by, it being short for Carol or Caroline, that name spoken a painful reminder of the child she had lost, still acute after all these years. Another child would have made all the difference but Tony had thought otherwise. If only for that, she'd want to do him down.

Both Alan and Dad were engrossed in their newspapers and Mum was eating her portion of fish and chips with little to say to her, as usual, so she sat thinking of the show and those times when she'd have been taken to a high-class restaurant instead of being bought fish and chips after a matinee – as a matter of fact, they would never have gone to a matinee but an evening show, sitting in the dress circle, during the interval meeting friends in the bar and sipping champagne. Maybe she and Tony would have been invited to meet the great Noël Coward himself, depending on how close a friend they were to those in the bar already invited. She thought of how disappointed she'd have been to be left out, how angry. Now it left her angry to think how she'd once slavered after such titbits of favours from those fancy friends, not one of them true.

She smiled at the humble room about her. Despite Mum, this was a far better, contented life, one that never demanded lick-spit after anyone. Tony's shop was going downhill fast. Poor Mr Bell was worried, but she had to look after her own interests. She'd give him a good reference and the dole queues were nowhere near as long as they'd been, the country getting back on its feet to some extent. Dad was in work most of the time now, Wally was doing well, and at her request Alan had given Mavis's Tom a job at his yard so long as he kept his nose to the grindstone this time, and Lord knows Mavis needed a steady income with her tribe to feed.

She was thinking how good it would be to see the business Tony had worked to build up fall apart, good to see the flat go as well, when Alan interrupted her reverie. 'Want the paper?'

As she took it from him, glad of something else to occupy her mind, there came a knock at the door. 'I'll get it,' Mum said. 'Yer Aunt Ada an' Uncle George said they might pop in later. Ain't seen them fer ages.'

Geraldine watched her hurry out into the passage. It had been cleared of family paraphernalia long ago: Wally and Mavis were married with their own places, she too having left, though she was back now; only Evie and Fred's bikes were propped tight against the wall, one behind the other, allowing enough room even in the narrow space to get to the street door these days.

The *Daily Mail* Alan had passed to her ignored, she picked at her fish as she listened intrigued to the whispering going on out there while Alan and Dad finished the last of their fish and chips, Dad still engrossed in his paper as he ate. Who was that whispering? If it had been her aunt and uncle, Mum would have brought them straight in. She was about to get up and go to see when Mum reappeared. Her face had lost its colour; her usual disapproving expression when things weren't right looked even more disapproving.

'Someone 'ere ter see yer,' she said to Geraldine, the tenseness of her tone causing Alan and her father to looked up expectantly. But Geraldine was looking beyond her mother to the man standing right behind her.

In the dim light of the passage the face above its dark clothes appeared to be disembodied. Only as he stepped into the brighter light of the room could Geraldine see it was a uniform. He held his helmet under his arm out of respect for being in someone's house.

'This is me daughter, Geraldine,' Mum said as the man, with natural inquisitiveness instilled in him by his job, glanced briefly around the room. His gaze came to settle on her as Geraldine made to rise.

'No, please sit down, Mrs Hanford.' The police constable's tone was kind though a certain ring of authority could be heard behind the kindness. 'You are Mrs Geraldine Hanford?'

She sat as bidden and nodded her affirmation. Her first

thoughts were that Tony must have been apprehended, that he must have implicated her in his confession, and a quiet fury began to boil up inside her at his treachery. Not content with leaving her for another woman, he was now intent on bringing her down with him, the bloody toad!

The constable's tone remained gentle. In fact she heard him take a deep, almost sad breath before continuing. 'The wife of Mr Anthony Felton Hanford?'

The last time she had heard Tony's second name spoken had been at their wedding. It sounded strange now. Again she nodded, dismally this time. The constable moved forward a little into the room in a way that almost looked as though he were ready to offer aid.

'It's my unpleasant duty,' he began in a lowered voice, 'to tell you that a man's body has been found in the Thames, washed up on the mud by the receding tide, and we have reason to believe it might be your husband, Mrs Hanford.'

'Oh, no!' The cry tore itself from her even as the constable went on.

'The man had been in the water for some time, I'm afraid, and the only identification we have is the name of the tailor on the suit, and a—'

'What makes you think it's my husband?' Geraldine burst through his words, all other thoughts pushed aside.

'We found what was left of a leather pocket book in the breast pocket, with the name Anthony Felton Hanford impressed in gold in one corner.'

Yes, she remembered buying it for him two years ago. She didn't know he still had it, and the knowledge brought a pang of that old love she'd once known. The constable was still speaking, rapidly, as though eager to have this business over with.

'The name on the pocket book led us to Hanford's, the jewellers in Bond Street. The assistant told us Mr Hanford had been missing for some while and that you were living at this address. I'm very sorry, Mrs Hanford. I understand how you must be feeling but we need you to formally identify the clothing and pocket book, and maybe the body.'

Alan had moved to her side, was holding her steady as Geraldine felt her knees growing weak and must have looked as though she were about to collapse. She was more grateful for his support than he realised.

'It may not be your husband, Mrs Hanford,' the constable was saying. 'But we have to be certain. I know what we're asking isn't pleasant for you, but we have to be certain. It is very important. It could be that of someone who had stolen the pocket book and some time later fallen into the river and drowned. May I ask if you know the name of your husband's tailor?'

As if in a dream, Geraldine supplied the name. The constable nodded solemnly. 'It could still be that whoever was fished out took the coat as well. We have to consider every possibility. Of course, it's not easy to establish whether this was an accident, a suicide or even a murder. We will have to make investigations . . .'

'Murder?' She clung to Alan. 'You can't . . .'

'Mrs Hanford.' The policeman had moved closer, yet his voice seemed to be coming from some way off. 'All we need from you now is to identify the belongings. Then we can go on from there.'

His voice seemed to be drifting away from her.

461

Alan was holding her tightly and Dad had come to stand close beside her. She could hear him speaking but could make no sense of it. No doubt he was taking in what the constable was saying about where they were to go to make the identification, but nothing was penetrating her brain except the word murder.

An accident was possible, but why should Tony need to be anywhere near the Thames? Suicide had to be ruled out – with all that money, surely not, unless his part in the robbery had been denied him and he'd come away with nothing. But it wasn't enough to make him commit suicide. He'd had what was at the time a thriving business. Maybe Di Manners had finished with him. She couldn't imagine that either. Murder then? Those villains who'd called themselves his friends? She going to the police?

'Alan, I can't do it.' It was more guilt now than fear of seeing a dead body.

'I'm afraid you have to, Mrs Hanford.' Gone the sympathy, in its place officialdom. But she held back.

'Alan . . .'

'I'll be with yer, love.' He was holding her so tightly it was difficult to breathe. 'I won't let yer do anythink yer don't want to.'

Between her father and Alan, Geraldine stood by the slab with its coarse cloth forming a mound over what lay beneath. The clothes and pocket book had been his. She still hadn't quite collected her wits, stood now like a lump of clay, her mind and body feeling numb as though neither belonged to her. She winced as she heard her father ask how long did they think the man had been in the water, and the reply, a couple of months at least.

She heard herself being asked if her husband had any distinguishing marks on his body and remembered the wide scar on his thigh, a war wound he'd said. That seemed to be good enough, and she heard herself being told that this was her husband.

Unable even to feel relieved that she hadn't been required to view the body, all she wanted now was to leave here and go home. Without a word, hardly bowing her head to the commiserations from those men conducting this business, she let herself be led from the building and helped into Alan's van, she and Dad squeezed on the seat next to him.

There was a lot to be done: funeral arrangements; papers to be signed; Tony's parents had been told, naturally. Geraldine wrote to them, giving them the date of the funeral, the time and place. It wasn't easy writing. She'd had as little to do with them as had Tony and owed them nothing, but she worded the letter as kindly as she could.

They wrote back by return, their reply cold as she had half expected it to be, though at least she had thought they'd have thawed a little towards her in their combined hour of grief. But no, it was formal, stating they were sorry and also their sorrow at Tony cutting himself off as he had on marrying her. As if they blamed her entirely. They'd attend the funeral, would have preferred to arrange it themselves but of course she was his widow. The letter had tailed off there, that in itself sounding like an accusation, the brief letter being signed merely with his father's quite unreadable signature.

Fenella was far more genuine. Geraldine couldn't bring herself just to write or even phone her. So the very same afternoon of being told herself of Tony's death, she went to see her. Alan had offered to go along with her but she insisted on going alone. Tony concerned only herself and his sister. It had been hard enough telling her without someone who was a stranger to her looking on. She'd been the first one Geraldine had told about Tony's affair.

Her advice had been to give like for like, let him see what he was losing. 'Might even make him jealous enough to come back to you,' she'd offered. It hadn't been the brightest of advice but the best she'd been able to give, but just having her take her side was in itself a help.

When Geraldine finally told her about Alan, she her most loyal confidante, Fenella had cuddled her with something like triumph and said, 'Good for you, darling, you took my advice, how wonderful! That'll show him, the crazy man. I know he's my brother but he can be quite stupid. Now he'll maybe see you're not to be done down and come back, tail between his legs.'

Of course he hadn't, but she wondered if he might have done if this thing hadn't happened.

As Fenella had been the one Geraldine had turned to from the very start, in some way making up for his cold-hearted parents, Geraldine now felt she must support her, Tony's only sister. It was hard going there in person: the trauma of telling her, the awfulness of seeing Fenella's expression of shocked disbelief, then grief, the two of them holding each other, each in their separate kind of sorrow and misgivings, the self-condemnation that a death always brings, sorrowing after the things left undone and those things done that shouldn't have, each nursing their own trivial personal guilts, neither voicing them to the other.

On the day of the funeral Fenella and her husband arrived at the house early, bringing neighbours out to gawk as Geraldine saw her and her husband alight from their large, cream-coloured Renault – not exactly a funereal colour, Geraldine had to admit, but with a smirk for Fenella, ever the flamboyant one. She showed no distaste for Mum and Dad's ordinary home and cuddled Mum to her as though she were a true relative, as she did Alan on being introduced to him, whispering in his ear, Alan told her later, 'Look after her, Alan, my dear, she deserves some happiness.'

She merely shook hands with Dad, but the handshake was warm and genuinely friendly.

Cuddling Geraldine to her, she gushed, 'Darling, such an awful time for you, even though . . . well, you know. But he was my brother and it's such a terrible thing to have happened. I've been so down in the mouth ever since you told me, and I keep crying.'

Later she said, 'I've spoke to Mother and she and Father will be at the cemetery, and afterwards will go straight back home. They said that they thought it would be too much for them to come back to the house. After all, they lost Tony's brother in the war and now they've lost their other son.'

One would have thought they'd have made more of their other son when he was alive, being as he was the only one left, thought Geraldine as she agreed it would be too traumatic for them to prolong their day of mourning. She was glad she did not have to face them, and indeed found herself totally ignored as they established themselves on one side of the aisle and then on the other side of the grave. Mrs Hanford did give her a wan smile and bent her head briefly before following her husband to his Rolls-Royce parked in the cemetery roadway.

Geraldine returned the smile but looked away immediately. She had married their son but she was nothing to these people. She would be even less now if that were possible, gratefully forgotten.

It was November and still Tony's affairs hadn't been settled. Without a will, intestacy took far longer than if there'd been one. On top of that were all the debts of the business to be settled. If anything came to her as his widow, Geraldine knew it would be precious little and she had only herself to blame.

'How could I have been such a fool?' She stared glumly at Alan's back as he gazed from his living-room window to the houses opposite through a November drizzle. 'But it was the only way I could get back at him.'

He'd weathered her anger with herself this Sunday afternoon rather well, she thought. He must be weary of hearing it from her, yet she couldn't stop herself. There were days when she felt quite normal, others when guilt would rip through her, she blaming herself for Tony's death and, a much more self-seeking regret, the way she had worked towards that wish to see him bankrupt. His death had put a stop to that but not before a great deal of harm had been done. Now, on top of all else she was in a quandary about what to do with the rapidly sinking business, and for the last half-hour had been leaping from the one to the other in this verbal soul-searching.

'After what he did, of course I'd want to get back at him. It was only natural. But it's what I did going to the police that upsets me.'

Alan turned slowly, but his expression was mild. 'Yer can't go on blaming yerself, Gerry. Yer've got ter stop it.'

'But I do blame myself. I should never have gone to the police like I did. If it hadn't been for me, he might've been alive today.'

'Yer can't be sure of that.' Alan strode over to her and took her by the shoulders forcing her to look at him. She now saw exasperation on his face. There was only so much even a mild-mannered man could take.

'Gel, yer've been goin' over this lark time and time again, on an' off ever since yer 'usband went. Sooner or later yer've got ter get over it or yer'll put yerself in an early grave in the end.'

Easy to say, but he wasn't her. 'I don't think I'll ever be able to get over it, ever forgive myself. In a way I've got what I deserve, haven't I, by doing what I did about his business and having that come back on me. I've made a rod for my own back there, haven't I? It's almost as if he's got his revenge on me.'

'Don't be silly.'

'Well, it's true. If I hadn't led him into such debt I wouldn't have a failing business around my neck now. I inherit everything he had, including his business rapidly going down the pan because of me. I've got my deserts.'

His hands on her shoulders tightened in an effort to stop her ranting. 'Look, I can understand that business worrying the life out of yer, but yer've got ter stop blamin' yerself for the other thing. He could of slipped and fallen in.'

'How?' she challenged. 'People don't just fall into the Thames by accident.' How many times had she said this? 'You can't unless it's from a boat. Bridges have parapets and railings. Places like the Embankment have parapets and railings. Unless you stand on one and that's only to commit suicide. I don't believe he would have done that. No, Alan, it was them thugs. They found out what I did and got rid of him before he blabbed as well, I'm sure of it.' Nothing would ever change her mind about that.

She knew what she was doing was frightening Alan, he seeing their wedding never happening. Sometimes she frightened even herself. She so wanted to marry him. Two months ago he had proposed, she'd responded with an immediate yes, at the time able to put her past behind her. But like all shadows it persisted in creeping up behind her, catching her up and running ahead to loom back at her. Now she was in danger of pushing him from her. But it was so hard to stop what kept going through her head. Oddly enough she had no nightmares, just this daytime remorse that she ought to be controlling by now.

Alan was talking to her as he'd never spoken before. Easing her down onto the settee, he put an arm around her shoulders and held her close. His tone was low and even. 'No matter how much yer blame yerself, yer can't do nothink about it, yer know that?' She nodded, and he went on in the same even, gentle tone. 'Now, we're goin' ter get married, yes?' Again she nodded. 'But what sort of marriage are yer condemning me to? I want us ter be 'appy and how can we if you're going ter dig up the past for the rest of our lives? Think about that, Gel, yer not only making yerself miserable, yer making me too, and if yer love me, why do yer want ter do that?' She shook her head. 'Right then, I ain't sayin' no more. You 'ave ter make up yer own mind. Remember, Gel, I love yer. But I ain't prepared ter be made miserable fer the rest of me life. It's up ter you.'

Letting go of her, he got up and went to stand at the window again to stare out into what was developing into a downpour of rain, misting the houses opposite.

Seeing his strong back, his broad shoulders, it was as if everything was clicking into place, her jangled thoughts calming. If those so-called friends of Tony's had done away with him it would have been before giving him a chance to smelt down that gold. He wouldn't have got a share of the gains. He wouldn't have gone off with Di Manners either. With no reason for her to know what had happened to him, Di Manners might be thinking at this very minute that he'd forsaken her, just as he'd forsaken his wife.

At that thought all guilt, all sorrow, all self-pity departed as though a skin had been sloughed. She even felt her lips twist into a satisfied grimace.

But what about Tony's business? Nothing to smile about there. So eager to see him bankrupted by a horde of creditors, she was now saddled with a business in deep trouble. All Tony's money had been tied up in that and would now come back on her. Would she end up totally penniless?

Alan turned as she voiced her concern in some panic, and retraced his steps to her.

'Then we'd best start getting our house in order, hadn't we?' he said quietly, almost a note of relief in his voice. He sounded almost glad that she would be broke. It was at that moment she knew she'd never again refer to Tony in the light of revenge or mention the manner of his death. She would rely on Alan to sort out her creditors and be grateful. They would take everything, the shop, the contents, every stick of furniture in the flat. She felt no regret. It would be starting with a clean sheet, like being baptised again.

It was well after Christmas, in fact two weeks into 1926, that they finally heard from the authorities dealing with Tony's affairs. Geraldine was at home with Mum and Dad that Saturday at breakfast when it came, Dad's work in the docks always uncertain, having nothing until Monday. Glancing up from reading what had been sent, she met their anxious stares with a grin that was faintly wry. 'Not a bean. All gone to pay debts. Nothing left. A few personal bits, that's all.'

She did have what was left in her own bank account, plenty of lovely clothes still, a bit of her own jewellery, and of course memories, some nice, some she would rather not have. The shop and its stock had gone to pay crediters. The flat too, and all the furniture she'd bought to help sink Tony into even deeper debt.

She'd worked so hard towards that, and all the time he had been at the bottom of the Thames, washed up on the bank by an outgoing tide only when that capricious river decided it had had enough of him.

She couldn't help it, she let out a slightly insane giggle. 'Guess what, Mum, after all the lovely things I had, all the holidays and all those society friends, I'm back where I started.'

Mum didn't laugh. Busy setting the breakfast table, she shot a look at Dad as a small explosive sound of contempt hissed between his teeth so that he shut up instantly, then she turned back to her daughter, her tone as ever sharp and to the point.

'Not exactly. Yer've got your Alan now. Yes, 'e's *your* Alan,' she went on as Geraldine made a half-negative gesture. 'He's asked yer ter marry 'im an' you've told 'im yer would, ain't yer? Well then,' she continued as there came a half nod, 'yer ain't quite back where yer started. He's got a decent business. Yer won't exactly be broke. Not yer 'igh an' mighty life yer thought was the be-all-and-end-all of everythink, but comfortable enough.'

Geraldine bit her lip in a surge of uncertainty. Was this the time to tell Mum what she'd known for the past six weeks? Alan should be the one to be told before anyone else. It concerned him the most and would be a shock enough without being told second-hand. Mum would be shocked too, she with her old-fashioned principles, but she could keep it to herself no longer.

'Mum, I've somethink to tell yer.' Already she had reverted to her old way of speaking, no longer any need to watch every word she spoke. Yet a faint trace of that laboured effort to adopt an accent that had never been hers still lingered. 'I'm going to have a baby.' There, she'd said it. But Mum gave no sign of surprise, somewhat angering her. Things hadn't changed.

'I thought there was a look about yer. A woman looks diff'rent when she's carryin' a baby. How far are yer?'

'Only about six weeks.'

'Then yer'd best get married a bit sharp or the neighbours'll start ter gossip.'

Just like Mum to worry about neighbours, not about her but what people might think. 'I can take care of myself,' she returned huffily. Mum shook her head.

'Ain't made a good job of it so far, 'ave yer?' She turned sharply on Geraldine's father as he started to speak. 'This is woman's talk, Jack. You go an' look at yer pigeons for a bit.' It didn't seem to concern her that it was freezing outside in the yard and even trying to snow, but her husband, with a heavy sigh, moved to obey. She turned to Geraldine as he disappeared.

'Alan said you two was planning on a July weddin'. Well, I think you ought ter bring it forward ter March at the very latest. You tell 'im I said so. Then no one'll be bothered.'

She was interrupted by Dad coming back in. 'I told you . . .' began Mum, but stopped as Alan was observed following close behind, having come around the back, no doubt popping in between jobs to see Geraldine. Both men were all smiles.

'I've just told 'im about yer, Gel,' Dad burst out. 'An' look at 'im, 'e's as pleased as punch, even if you two ain't married yet.'

Despite a sudden rush of irritation at her father which was also reflected on his wife's face, Geraldine couldn't be annoyed seeing the joy wreathing itself around Alan's huge grin. Even so, she wasn't pleased with her father.

'Dad, it was my place to tell him!'

It was almost funny, the way Dad's face fell, but Alan had her in his arms. 'I think we're goin' to 'ave ter get married a bit earlier than expected,' he said.

That in itself made her happy, Mum done out of giving the order. The old rift was still there, wasn't it? That was until the woman came over, almost forcibly parting the two, and to Geraldine's surprise, ready with an angry retort thinking her mother about to interfere, put her arms about her in the first cuddle that in many an age had genuine emotion.

Seconds later Mum had broken away as though embarrassed by her uncharacteristic show of affection.

'If I don't get this breakfast ready, we'll be eatin' dinner! And you, Jack . . .' she turned to him. 'If yer don't put that top back on that tomato sauce bottle after yer've used it, I ain't goin' ter buy any more.'

She turned to Geraldine. 'Honest, he always forgets ter put the lid back on prop'ly and last week when I shook it ter use it, we 'ad red sauce all over me clean tablecloth. But that's men for yer. Never think, do they?'

Geraldine stared at her, amazed at being confided in in this way. This was how it had been before she had married and had gone off, thinking of herself as made.

Suddenly she was home. Come March, she and Alan would marry, a simple, rather hasty wedding, nothing elaborate. But more than anything else, she carried his baby, she who'd thought herself unable to have any more children after losing her first one and had assumed herself damaged.

This time there would be no such slip-ups. This time Mum would be on hand to tend her and it seemed Mum knew it as she came to stand even closer. She would look after her, make sure she came to no harm, make sure this baby, Alan's baby, would be born whole and healthy and strong.

As Alan began to laugh at what Mum had said, Geraldine took her cue and turned on him in mock severity. 'And if you do that, I'll do the same as Mum and stop buying any.'

Mum's hand laid itself on her arm. 'That's right, you tell 'im,' she said in a quiet tone.